"Keith Doyle, there's something about this hillside, something I feel is wrong here."

"It's okay!" Keith assured Holl. "Nothing's happened to me yet. Hey, the hill feels strange under my feet." He stamped on it, felt the reverberations through his feet. "Almost hollow, like a drum. Come on in, the magic's fine!"

"Out, you widdy! The place is surrounded by Restricted notices. Someone doesn't want you tramping around on it."

"Hey, one second. Look at these, Holl," Keith said, pushing aside the foxglove and kneeling down to inspect another bunch of plants. "They're white, and sort of shaped like bells."

"Come away, Keith Doyle," Holl ordered, more urgently. The effort of shouting made him feel faint, and he sat down in the long straw. He felt cold chills, though the sun was shining directly down on them. "There's something powerful in there," Holl whispered, trying to project his voice. A buzzing started in his ears, and grew louder and louder until he could hear nothing else. He knew Keith was shouting at him, but he saw only the young man's mouth move. He couldn't understand the words at all.

Keith reached Holl just as the other started to slump over onto the grass...

Also by Jody Lynn Nye

MYTHOLOGY 101

MYTHOLOGY ABROAD

JODY LYNN NYE

A Time Warner Company

WARNER BOOKS EDITION

Cover design by Don Puckey
Cover illustration by Don Maitz

Warner Books, Inc.
666 Fifth Avenue
New York, NY 10103

A Time Warner Company

Printed in the United States of America

First Printing: February, 1991

10 9 8 7 6 5 4 3 2 1

To Diane & Peter,
Wayne & Anne,
and Brian & Donna,

Who understand to what lengths one might go
in the cause of love.

MYTHOLOGY ABROAD

Chapter 1

"Now, now, my wee darlings, get along. This isn't for you, as well you know." Mrs. Mackenzie gently shooed her yowling cats out of her path as she pushed open the kitchen door. Sniffing the sweet, heady scent of milk in the bowl she held, the four cats followed her out into the garden, their erect tails hopeful.

"Enough of your din. You'll have your tea in a moment, my lovelies," Mrs. Mackenzie chided them, laughing. "This is for those who haven't got a mum to give them meals and treats." With her free arm, she held back a low branch of a stunted apple tree and scooted by between the tree and the garden wall. The blossoms had just begun withering away, and tiny green knobs swelled behind them. Mrs. Mackenzie started to count them, and smiled. Even in the wild Atlantic winds that crossed over and over the Isle of Lewis, her garden prospered well enough, as did the small hayfield, fenced in to guard it from the sheep. For this she gave thanks in her church on Sundays, but since she had lived here all her life, she knew better than to ignore the other powers of the land, and offered them thanks as well.

At the end of the garden path sat a square stone with a bowl-like depression in the top. The stone had sat there for heaven knew how many centuries and generations. Its rough, yellowed sides were covered with moss, and its corners had been shaved round by the wind. It was thought to be cut from the same stone which formed the forest of man-made monoliths on the hilltop above their farm, but was probably far older. She stopped in front of it and waited until the liquid in her bowl had stilled. The cats rubbed against her ankles and set up a fresh wail. Paying them no attention, Mrs. Mackenzie poured the bowl of milk into the hollow. "There. The first milk of the first milking from our Flora."

The moment she touched the stone, the cats lost all interest in her or the milk, and wandered back up the path. The chief cat, and only female, started a game of tag with the youngest male, and the other two joined in, racing up and down between the plantings of young carrots and strawberries. Mrs. Mackenzie followed them toward the house, calling at them impatiently to go inside for their tea.

• Chapter 2 •

"Do you want to sit by the window or on the aisle?" Keith Doyle asked Holl as they struggled toward their row on the 747 aircraft. The flight attendants smiled at the thin, redheaded youth and the blond, applecheeked child in the baseball cap following him, and directed them across the body of the big jet and down another aisle. Keith ducked around a well-dressed man who was removing his coat in the business section. "At least they said the flight isn't too full. If no one claims the middle seat of our row we can stretch out. Can you believe how small these things are? How do tall people sit in them?"

A wide-eyed Holl stared distrustfully at the paneled plastic walls as he trod, zombie-like, behind Keith. All around him, Big Folk, strangers, stowed their possessions in highset boxes and sat down with expressions of expectation in endless rows of identically colored chairs with metal armrests. Holl shuddered, feeling immediately claustrophobic. Though the other passengers ignored him now, eight hours of boredom might draw their attention to the sole representative of the Little Folk on the plane, and he'd be trapped. Keith called his people elves, which just went to prove how little even the Big Ones who understood them best knew them. The two hours they had had in the terminal before the flight's scheduled departure was too much time for him to sit and consider the dangers of the trip. Statistics he had read over the last few weeks on accidents involving commercial jet aircraft flashed alarming red numbers inside his head. Perhaps it was not a good idea to have been raised in a library. He had access to too many alarming facts. "Keith Doyle, I no longer think this is a good idea. Can I go back?"

Keith looked back at the mob of passengers following them along the narrow passage from the jetway, and sighed. "I think it's too late. We've gone through passport control and x-ray. You'll just have to hang on the best you can, and keep your mind occupied. Try and sleep, or something."

"This feeble little box will carry us safely four thousand miles?" Under the brim of the Cubs cap he wore to disguise his tall, pointed ears, the young elf's eyes were big and round with fear.

"The aisle," Keith decided firmly. "Wait for me to get in. Here we are." Their row number appeared to the left of the overhead bin and Keith shot his carry-on bag into the compartment. He took Holl's small bag and tossed it up next to his, then squeezed into the window seat. "Hey, we're not over the wing. Great! We'll be able to see everything!"

"Don't ask me to look," Holl said, settling down into the aisle seat. It squeaked alarmingly, and the smooth armrests were cold. "Sticks and stones, these chairs are uncomfortable!"

"There are pillows up there," Keith offered, then he caught Holl's outraged expression. He measured the distance with his eyes, and pulled himself to a standing position. "Never mind. I'll get them."

"Talk about your artificial environments," Holl said disgustedly. "Did you take a look in their lavatories?"

Keith was relieved that his friend had recovered enough to complain. The takeoff had been a trauma he didn't expect. Keith, however, enjoyed the pressure when the jet was racing down the runway, building momentum, and the breathless feeling of weightlessness he got just as it left the ground. It was fun, the way that the drop-off over the crest of a rollercoaster track was fun. He'd forgotten just for that second that Holl had never been on a plane before, let alone a rollercoaster. He was as innocent of modern transportation as the ten- or twelve-year-old Big Person he seemed to be. No one from Holl's village had ever traveled anywhere on anything except on their feet. In a brief glance toward the seat on his left, Keith saw Holl's face go chalky white; his eyes were squeezed shut and he was gripping the armrests with his fists.

"Hey, it's over," Keith nudged him gently. "We're airborne."

"My stomach's still down there somewhere," Holl replied apologetically, opening his eyes. "And you talk about my people's magic. This thing oughtn't to be able to fly!"

"Well, we're defying gravity at about 500 miles per hour, and we're heading for the clouds. Wait, don't look. I'll keep the window shut. Do you want to get up and look around?"

"Need I?" Holl asked, nervously.

"No, but others are getting out of their seats and stretching. Why don't you take a quick look around? We've got lots of time before we get to Scotland. Hours, in fact." Keith grinned. "You ought to see what you're traveling in. Consider it research. You can tell the others all about it."

It was true that few of his folk would ever have the opportunity to do what he was doing: flying in an aircraft across the Atlantic Ocean, Holl considered. His friends and family would demand details of his adventure, and if he didn't have them, they would be disappointed. Watching other passengers negotiate the aisles without care, Holl flicked open the catch on his safety belt, defying his own fear. "All right. I will, then."

As Keith kept a surreptitious eye on him, the young elf paced out the length of the aisle and doubled back through the galley to the other aisle. He had a look into the cockpit, where the pilot and crew smiled at him, seeing only another youngster curious about the workings of the jet. Holl even took a peek into the upper level of the aircraft, into the first class lounge, before the steward on duty up there chased him down again.

"No one else seems worried," Holl reported, returning to his seat just as a flight attendant rolled a beverage cart into their aisle.

"They're not. They do this all the time. It's almost safer than walking," Keith promised him, and looked up at the attendant's question. "What'll you have? Everything's free but the liquor, and I can't give you that anyhow. You're underage, my dear nephew."

The attendant gave them plastic cups of soda and two impermeable packets of sugared peanuts. Keith turned the knob in front of him to let the table down for his drink. Holl was pleased by the design of the fold-down tables, and examined the suspension mechanism closely.

"First flight?" the stewardess asked Keith, glancing at Holl.

"Yes, ma'am. He's twelve." They exchanged smiles. "Hey, Holl, your drink."

The elf received his refreshments and put them on his tray table. After a few attempts to tear open the plastic package of peanuts, he reached surreptitiously for his whittling knife and poked a hole in the celluloid. He caught Keith gawking at him.

"How did you get that through the security check?" Keith demanded, staring at the long, gleaming blade as his friend tucked it away in its sheath. "The buzzers should have gone crazy with a long hunk of steel like that passing through them."

"They didn't notice, that's all," Holl replied, offhandedly. "And it isn't made of steel. You know what too much steel does to us. It's titanium. I made it from scrap lifted from the science labs, and difficult it was to do, I will tell you. I wasn't leaving home without it. You never know what you'll need. Money can't buy it all."

"I don't know," Keith said dubiously. "I still think it should have set off the metal detectors. You must have done something magic to them." He waited for Holl to clarify, but the Little Person wasn't talking. Another thought struck Keith. "Speaking of not being able to buy it all, how'd you get the money to come with me?"

Holl made an offhand gesture. "From sweepstakes and the like. At first, we had to figure out which ones actually had drawings after the entries were sent in instead of choosing them in advance."

Keith sputtered. "You can't use magic to win contests! That's cheating!"

Holl was nonplussed. "We didn't use magic to win. You should see the things professional contesters do to their envelopes to get them chosen. Ours were innocent by comparison. We just wanted to ensure that our envelopes made it to the final draw. We had every chance to lose after that point, one among thousands in a turning drum. But when we had enough money for our needs, we stopped. Lee Eisley said the barn roof needed repair, and we can't make tar paper for ourselves. We won a good bit, but only out of need."

"In my name, I suppose." Holl nodded. Keith groaned. "Pray the accounting companies never check the system for magical intervention. I hope you have enough left over for me to pay the income tax on the winnings."

"The Master said so." The village headman, who also taught one of Midwestern University's more interesting and exclusive study groups, was known only by his title. Keith respected the Master's encyclopedic knowledge, but was just a little put off by his formidable personality.

He shrugged. "If the Master says it's okay, I guess it is, the way you guys research things. I oughta let you just take over my life. You make more money in my name than I do. But where did you get a passport?" Keith continued in a low voice, glancing over his shoulder between the seats to make sure no one was listening. "Without a birth certificate, without any identification?"

"Don't ask how and I'll tell you no lies," was all Holl would say. Keith shrugged and sipped his drink. He watched the sky through the window next to the seat in front of him. Through breaks in the clouds, he could see the green checker-board pattern of farms and roads. Holl quaffed soda and ate the peanuts methodically, one at a time, staring straight forward at the bulkhead.

"Okay, I've waited to ask," Keith said at last, "but I guess you're not going to tell me. Why are you coming with me?"

Holl raised his hands, palms up. "You're a trend-setter again, Keith Doyle. When they heard you were making your way to Scotland and Ireland, there was much discussion of whether one of us should accompany you."

"I'm just going on an archaeology educational tour for credit. I don't see what use that would be to you."

"But afterward? When you visit Ireland to look for your distant relatives? The old ones have decided that it's important we make contact with the ones that were left behind—if there are any still alive, and where we left them. We're tired of being isolated. If there are Folk left to find, in this day of easy global communication, there's no need for them to remain isolated any longer."

"Yeah, I've heard this thesis somewhere before," Keith said drily. "I think it was mine. But Holl, you were born in Midwestern University. You're what, forty-one? Your folks left home longer ago than that. You don't know where to go to find them, do you?"

"I can find them," Holl stated, "with your help."

"'Bring 'Em Back Alive' Doyle, that's me. But wouldn't it have been easier to send one of the old folks back to look? There must be plenty of them who remember how to get there. What about the Master? Why you?"

"I volunteered to go," Holl said firmly, as if that should settle the matter.

"Uh-huh." Keith could tell Holl was hedging by the way his invisible whiskers twitched, and searched his friend's face for clues. The very idea of hunting for more Little People in the wilds of Ireland intrigued him, but there had to be more to it than that. "Okay... but your Irish relatives have never seen you before. They may not trust a strange face, even if you have the pointy ears to prove kinship. Why not someone who remembers them? Anyone still alive from when your people left home? People who know the homestead on sight? Can you help me find it?"

"Well, I might." But Holl sounded unsure.

Keith picked up on his tone immediately. "Okay, if you're as lost as I am, there must be another reason." Holl started to speak several times, but stopped short before uttering a word. Keith waited.

"My reasons are my own," the elf said, and fell obstinately silent.

"C'mon, Holl. I'm your friend," Keith wheedled. "You're not like me. You don't blunder in and get lucky. You plan. There's got to be a better reason than 'it's important.'"

The buzz of the steward's cart grumbled toward them, breaking the concentrated mood. The attendant leaned over to collect their cups. Holl instantly stuck the earpieces of his headphones into the entertainment system and stared straight ahead, ignoring Keith. Keith sighed and settled back into his seat with a book. Presently, meal service passed through the cabin and the attendant placed trays in front of them.

"You'll like the food." After taking a bite of the entrée, Holl pulled the earpiece away from his head and nudged Keith. "It tastes exactly the same as what you get at school."

* * *

While they ate, Keith talked. He could see that his friend was still anxious, but he was negotiating the jet's aisles without lurching, and he handled the air turbulence over Nova Scotia without comment or color changes. So what was bugging him? He looked haggard, more tired than he had ever seen him. Something wrong in the village? Or something more personal? "I'm really looking forward to exploring Scotland, aren't you?" Keith blabbed. "I'm especially anxious to see the standing stones at Callanish. It's supposed to be Scotland's answer to Stonehenge—you know, really magical."

No response. "The Hebrides are so far distant from everything, that they haven't been spoiled by development yet. I've got lots of books with me about the area and the local legends. You might be interested in some of them." Keith smiled winningly at his friend and waited.

Holl, made more comfortable by food and the fact that night had fallen, obscuring the view from 37,000 feet up over open water, shook his head wryly. If he couldn't trust Keith Doyle, whom could he trust? Besides, he needed the boy's help. "You've worn me out, widdy. I'll confess. I've been through a trauma the likes of which I never want to repeat in my lifetime. It's well that you've provided an opportunity for me to remove myself from the situation for a while. I just asked the Master for permission to marry his daughter, and you can imagine what that was like."

"Holy cow!" exclaimed Keith, sympathetically regarding Holl. "You've still got all your hide, though. I take it he said yes? Congratulations! When's the wedding?"

"Maura still has yet to be asked, foolish one. But that's not all we discussed, hence my departure with you to discover our original home." Holl sighed. More and more in the recent past, he and the Master had butted heads over issues, and Holl had come in second each time. Experience and logic won over youthful energy and good intentions over and over again. "There's the welfare of the other Folk to be considered. Did you know there hasn't been a wedding since we came to Midwestern, more than four decades gone?"

"Really? Wow! So you'll be the first. Great. When are you going to ask her? Can I come to the wedding?"

"*If*. If I can. There's something I need to find before I do."

"In Ireland? What? The Ring of Kerry? A four-leaf clover?" Keith laughed.

Holl glowered. "Your interminable questions, Keith Doyle! I almost wish I'd not told you. We've always had the custom that a wedding couple wear white bellflowers. No one has married since we came to Midwestern. We'll be the first in a string of decades. It sounds squashy and sentimental when I think about it, but there you are—no white bellflowers survive among our plants. My mother's sister was in charge of propagating all the seeds our folk would need, but that one slipped by, whether dying off infertile or simply being left behind in the old place, she can't say, it's been that long. Many of the kernels and seeds she's preserved have never been grown, since the bottom of the library building is no fit place for them, and there's been no need for the flower in all this time, so it wasn't missed."

"That vital to the process, eh?" Keith asked.

"We've never done without it. They're imbued with a charm of joining, among a host of other useful natural properties, good for healing wounds or curing the tongue-tied."

"Yes," Keith nodded solemnly. "I can see where you'd want to be holding one of those before you propose."

Holl ignored the jibe. "Of course, this is all before my time. I've not witnessed a wedding myself. But I have a feeling that many of my generation have only been waiting to pick white bellflowers to ask their loved ones to marry."

"And the Master made it one of the conditions of his approval, didn't he?" Keith asked shrewdly, and was rewarded by an expression of respect on his companion's face. "Well, you did say it was for the welfare of everyone else, too. What do they look like? There's a lot of different kinds of bell-shaped flowers in the world. Lily-of-the-valley, bluebells, foxglove, you name it."

"I'll know them when I see them," Holl said, uneasily. "They probably are similar to any of the other *campanulaceae*."

"So where do you find them?"

"I don't know, exactly, but the Master felt I should look in the old places from where our folk come. They might be in fairy rings, well-guarded earth mounds in hidden places, and the like."

"I suppose you know it's illegal to carry plants back into the U.S. without a license?" Keith asked. Holl nodded. "Well, I suppose that magic flowers wouldn't count. Now that we've cleared that out of the way, let's open the atlas and find our most likely prospects."

Holl and Keith discussed the subject well into the night, until the in-flight movie was announced. At the stewardess's request, the lights were shut off and the window shades pulled down. Through his rented headphones, Holl listened to the tinny soundtrack, and relaxed back into his nest of pillows. It wasn't half bad, really, watching a film this way. There were no extraneous noises to distract one from the program, barring the constant atonal whistle from the air system. He glanced over to ask Keith Doyle a question, and saw that the boy had fallen asleep, head back and jaw open, in his corner of the row. Holl grinned at him paternally. The lad had been so intent on making sure he, Holl, was comfortable that he wore himself out. Gently, Holl eased the headset off Keith's ears and hooked it on the cloth pocket of the seat in front of him.

The Big Folk took their technology so much for granted, they didn't realize how much of a miracle it would seem to someone else, Holl thought. If it wasn't magic to fly through the thin, high air, in relative comfort with hot food and entertainment, then it was a near cousin, and it took not a whit of energy out of one's own aura to be a part of these marvels. Holl could feel the threatening presence of too much metal under and around him, though it was unlikely to break through the protective cloth and plastic coats in which the Big Folk clad it to attack him.

It did indeed make him nervous to be surrounded by so many strange Big Folk. He realized how sheltered he had been all his life, coming into contact only with the few who could be trusted. He had to keep reminding himself that no one knew him, and that none would observe that for which they weren't looking. Trying to put that thought from him, he reminded himself he was on a mission of great importance. Strange as it may sound, he couldn't be in better hands than those of Keith Doyle. If something came too close to him, Keith would draw away attention and make a joke out of it. There was surprising safety in humor. Holl took off the baseball cap and ruffled his hair with his fingers with a sigh of relief. No need to put it back on until the lights came up again. Now was his chance to do something about the uncomfortable seat. He unbuckled his belt and scooted forward off the pad. A searching tendril of knowledge he put into the cushions suggested that there was just enough fiber to be comfortable, but it had been flattened down by who knew how many bottoms before his. He forced them to repel from one another, springing out against their covering, puffing the cushions up from within. The charge abated swiftly, for the fibers were poor conductors, and Holl was able to settle back in the seat without feeling the bars and rods poking at him any more.

The film's plot was predictable, one of the nine plots repeated over and over throughout five thousand years of literature and ninety of filmmaking, so Holl's attention wandered. Looking around at his fellow passengers to ensure he was disturbing no one, he reached across Keith, slid up the shade and looked out of the window at the night.

He had heard of all sorts of terrible accidents in planes, owing to bad maintenance or fatigued metal. Holl preferred to live long enough to see the far lands on the other side of the ocean, and return home again. There was so much that was precious to him, only the thought that he would return allowed him to wrench himself away. Feeling outward gently with a cohesion spell, he touched the braces and bulkheads of the giant airliner, seeking weak spots and untightened bolts. The jet's complexity of construction amazed him. Not surprisingly, the massed metal repelled his touch, but reassuringly sent back impressions that it was solid and whole, needing none of his magic to finish its journey in safety. Holl relaxed, satisfied. This jet was well built and correctly maintained. As a craftsman, he approved such work.

The stars were remarkably clear up here. The disturbing sight of the far-distant ground was covered by a soft carpet of white clouds, ghostly fleece under the moon. Holl spotted constellations and counted stars until he fell asleep with his face toward the moon.

• Chapter 3 •

"Good morning!" The sheer power of the loudspeaker over their heads belied the flight attendant's friendly greeting. "We will be landing in just about an hour. We'll be serving breakfast and distributing landing cards now. Please have them with you when you pass through Customs."

Holl woke up like a shot at the first blast of sound. "They dole out sleep in grudging amounts, don't they?" he asked grumpily, planting his cap on top of his disordered hair. Keith had been curled up like a grasshopper with his thin knees against his chest until the flight attendant's voice shocked him awake. Both legs shot out and banged into the seat in front of him, earning a sleepy grunt from its occupant. "Sorry," Keith murmured. He focused his reddened eyes on his friend and ran his hands through tousled hair.

"Good morning," Holl said politely.

"I guess they don't want us to get too comfortable." Keith noticed the glare of the sun coming over his shoulder. "Sounds like we crashed straight into tomorrow. Oops. I must have nudged the shade open while I was asleep. Sorry." He glanced down at the shimmering gray sea far below them, visible through thinning, white clouds.

"Don't bother," Holl said, catching his hand. "I don't mind any more. It doesn't look real up this high. There, I see coastline, clear as I can see you. Where is it? Can we open up your maps?"

Breakfast was a basket containing a cold, sweet pastry, fruit cocktail, and a sealed cup of orange juice; it was accompanied by a white document identified by the flight attendant as a landing card, which all non-United Kingdom residents needed to fill out. Holl tasted a single bite of the pastry and rejected it, as he read the card.

"Newsprint mixed with sugar, and topped with more," he complained. The fruit was edible, but the orange juice proved to be as difficult to open as the peanuts. "They must have an endless supply of that plastic."

"Don't worry," said Keith. "I have emergency rations in my bag. Cookies, candy bars, and sandwiches. Do you want peanut butter and jelly, or ham, tomato, and mustard?"

"I apologize, Keith Doyle, for all the bleating," Holl said, shamefacedly accepting a sandwich. "Grousing about such trifles as food, when I've just flown three thousand miles and more. A wonder, and I'm not even properly grateful. Your pardon."

"I promise, I would never have assumed you were scared out of your skull," Keith replied, very solemnly, but his eyes twinkled. "If I didn't know better, I would have put it down to blind panic."

Holl laughed. "That's the truth of it. I don't react well in crisis, do I?"

"Lack of experience. You're much better on your home ground," Keith reasoned. "Why not let yourself go, and take the adventure as it comes? The food wasn't poisoned or anything, just not that good. I prefer home cooking myself." Keith, who prided himself that he could eat anything, had finished both their pastries and a sandwich, and was rolling down the wrapper on a candy bar. "It's a whole new experience for me, too, traveling to another country. At least this one speaks the same language I do."

A flight attendant appeared beside them to take away their trays. "Well, how are we this morning?" she asked, brightly. Her swept-back brown hair looked freshly coiffed, and her makeup had been newly applied.

"Better," Keith smiled up at her, wondering how she looked so good when he felt so lousy. Maybe the flight attendants' seats were more comfortable.

"Good! The captain would like your little brother to have his wings, for completing his first flight across the Atlantic." The woman handed Holl a small card to which was pinned a pot-metal representation of pilot's insignia. "Thank you for flying with us, young man. We hope you've enjoyed yourself." Holl stared at the card, then up at the woman with disbelief in his eyes.

"Say thank you," Keith urged him, with an elbow in the ribs.

"Thank you," Holl gritted out. "I suppose I deserve a medal for living through this," he said under his breath, as the flight attendant walked away.

"Don't hate it too much," Keith cautioned him. "We have to do it all over again on the way home."

Within the hour, the plane touched down, and the passengers disembarked into Glasgow Airport. In the midst of the milling crowd, Keith and Holl followed the signs for Customs. The longest line in the Customs hall proved to be for U.S. and Canadian citizens. It was close in the room. The heat was not as much a problem as the humidity, which made breathing a task in the stagnant air, especially for travelers short of sleep. They shuffled back and forth in the serpentine queue, which was bounded by colored ropes and bronze posts. "I feel like I'm on Mulholland Drive in the middle of an L.A. summer."

"No air conditioning," Holl observed. "When it's there, you complain of it. When you don't have it, you miss it."

"Passports?" said the man behind the narrow desk, with little to no inflection in his voice. Obediently, Keith and Holl handed over their dark blue booklets and white landing cards. "Business or playsure?" The final "r" rolled off his tongue in a rumbling burr.

His was the first real Scottish accent they had heard, and Keith's ears perked up. "Uh, we're here to join a university class," he explained, hoping the man would say something else.

The deeply etched mouth lifted slightly in one corner, and the dark blue eyes twinkled. "Taychnically, that'd be playsure, do you no' agree; still it might be a bit o' a job?" Keith absorbed the tones avidly, and nodded. The man stamped their passports with a square and a line of print and waved them on to the baggage hall.

"Whew! Did you hear him? Great!"

"Fascinating," Holl agreed. "He sounds like and not like Curran, the chief of my clan. Are we that close to Ireland?"

"We're separated from it only by a narrow sea and a sense of direction. Remember King James VI and all. Hey, come on. Our bags won't be on the baggage carousel yet. I want to call home."

There was a money-exchange inside the baggage hall which took Keith's traveler's checks and gave him a handful of very colorful paper money and coins of several sizes and shapes.

"Uh-oh. I hope the phone doesn't just take . . . what is this?" he wondered, examining a small, silver coin with seven sides. "Twenty pence."

Holl looked through the collection of cash with fascination. "They're all different, and graduated in size by value, I see. Would you mind lending me a bit of that for the duration of the journey, Keith Doyle?"

"Sure—whoa! Didn't you bring any money with you?" Keith asked, aghast. He experienced a moment of panic, calculating his meager supply of liquid cash, and dividing by two. It wasn't a comforting total. "Who the heck travels without spending money?"

"And how should I know, when I've never been ten miles from my home in my life?" Holl defended himself, and produced his wallet, which he thrust at Keith. "You should have warned me, Keith Doyle. I didn't know I'd need traveler's checks, for all the ads I've read. I thought one would be as good as the other for the exchange."

Keith glanced at the money in the leather folder and sighed with relief. "Holl, they will take U.S. $100 bills, I promise."

"I don't need the blue money to make an exchange?" Holl asked meekly.

"Nope. They're both good, the rate's just a little lower for cash. I might even ask you for a loan later on. I don't have anywhere near 700 bucks on me. I'll wait for you."

Returning from the exchange desk with a handful of fascinating British money, Holl found Keith reading the instructions on long cards surrounding the pay telephone.

"Piece of cake," the young man called, as the elf caught his eye. "It takes all the coins." Keith fed in the change, then dialed. "It's ringing . . . Hi, Dad. Yeah, we're here. The flight was fine. I'm on a pay phone, and it's ticking off the money pretty fast. I'll call again in two days. Give my love to Mom. Sure, I'll send postcards! 'Bye!" He punched a square, blue button under the hook marked "Follow-On Call," and dialed again. "Whew! The sign says that's what you're supposed to do to keep from losing your change. Dad says hi, and hopes you're okay. Diane? Good morning!"

"Keith?" Diane muttered sleepily into the receiver. "Hi. I'm not up yet. Can you call later?"

"Whaddaya mean you're not out of bed yet?" the cheerful voice demanded. "It must be four in the morning!"

Her eyes flew open. "Are you guys okay? How's Scotland?" Diane asked anxiously. Unable to restrain a yawn, she covered the receiver with the other hand, and gaped at the clock. She peered out of her apartment window at a gray false-dawn, and groaned.

"Haven't seen it yet. We're still waiting for our suitcases. Say, can you let them know on the farm that Holl is okay?"

Diane clicked her tongue in exasperation. "Don't you have

their phone number? Call them yourself. They'd be thrilled to hear from you. Can I go back to sleep now?''

"By my guest,'' Keith said magnanimously. "Call you again later in the week?''

"Later in the week *and* the day. Bring me a souvenir. A pot of gold would be nice. Love you.''

"Yeah, love you, too,'' Keith echoed, fondly. He winked at Holl, pushed the blue button again, and dialed another number. He waited for it to begin clicking through to the American exchange, then handed the surprised elf the receiver. "Here. Phone home.''

"They thought it was a young miracle, hearing my voice travel four thousand miles,'' Holl told him afterward, impressed by the feat. "They're all well, though Dola has the sore throat again.''

"Probably still. You've only been gone a couple of days,'' Keith chided him lightly. "Not much usually happens in that short a time. Sorry I ran out of coins, there.''

Holl waved a dismissive hand. "Ah, they'll never know the difference. Having never received a call of this distance, I don't think they know how one should end.''

"Did you talk to everyone?'' Keith grinned, picturing a crowd of fascinated elves huddled around the phone, perking up their ears.

"Nearly,'' Holl returned the impish smile. "Those I missed this time will demand their turn when I call again.''

They got their bags and followed the crowd past the baggage carousels to the two wide doorways marked Red Channel and Green Channel. As they had nothing to declare, Keith and Holl obediently joined the queue going through Green, which wasn't moving at all. They stood yawning behind a family wheeling a huge number of bags, and waited for the way to clear.

"They must have just returned from going around the world,'' Keith muttered behind his hand to Holl. He shifted his weight from one foot to the other.

Holl was becoming impatient. "Wait a moment.'' He left his bag beside Keith and ran forward to the edge of the Green Channel. A woman in a fur coat was gesticulating with an official in shirtsleeves. Both were surrounded by customs men opening a host of matching luggage. The woman's face was bright red. One by one, the customs men set bottles of liquor on the metal tables. There seemed to be dozens in each bag.

He marched back to Keith, and explained what he had seen. "The whole channel is constricted by customs agents helping to move her bags aside. Come with me."

Seizing Keith's arm, he steered them around the queue and into the Red Channel.

"What are you doing?" Keith demanded in an undertone. "We can't go that way. They'll search us."

"They won't even look at us," Holl promised. "I'm putting an aversion between us and them."

It was true. The agents in the Red Channel seemed to look everywhere but at the two youths walking between them. They passed unnoticed by everyone, and abruptly found themselves amidst a huge, busy crowd in the waiting room of the airport. Everyone else seemed to know where they were going. A number of the people waiting for passengers had small white signs of cardboard in their hands. Keith peered at them all as he went by, looking for the Educatour representative.

"Now where to?" Holl asked, feeling lost and helpless among all the Big Folk.

"I don't know," Keith answered, casting around.

A tall, thin, elderly lady with silver hair tied back in a knot scurried up to them. In one hand she held a clipboard; in the other, a cardboard sign reading "Educatours." She peered at Keith through thick, round glasses which magnified eyes of flower blue. "Doyle? Are you Keith Doyle?"

"Yes, ma'am," he answered politely, hoisting the strap off his shoulder and setting his bag down on his foot.

She thrust the sign among the papers on the clipboard, took Keith's right hand and pumped it enthusiastically. "I'm Miss Anderson. How do you do? And is this Holland?"

"Holl," the elf said, extending his hand to her. She gripped it, and Holl winced in astonishment.

"How do you do, Holl? I'm the Educatour director for this tour. Nice to have you with us. The weather's not as fine as we could have hoped, but it may improve as the day progresses. I often find that it's foul before noon, and fair afterward." Keith was fascinated by the perfection of her diction.

"Perhaps it has the same trouble I do getting out of bed in the morning," Keith joked.

The blue eyes gleamed behind the glass circles. "Hm! It

wouldn't surprise me at all. If you tend to be a slugabed, you'll have to scotch your tendencies over the next six weeks. We get an early start every day. This way. Our motor coach is waiting in front of the terminal building. You look tired. Let me take that. I must meet one more flight, and then we may leave for Glasgow proper.'' She hoisted Keith's large bag over one shoulder without the least suggestion of effort and strode ahead. The electronic-eye doors parted before her.

''Boy, if that's an example of the old ladies of Scotland, I don't want to get in any fights with the wee lads,'' Keith muttered under his breath to Holl as they scurried behind with their carry-ons.

''She's likely an example of why they're so polite,'' Holl suggested. ''All bones and wires. She must have ten times their energy.''

''Michaels here, sir. We caught sight of Danny O'Day on his way through immigration.'' The mustachioed man in the nondescript tweed suit spoke into a telephone at the front of the airport. He sent a suspicious glance around, watching out for illicit listeners, but no one seemed interested in a middle-aged man who looked like a retired mathematics professor lately returned from a fishing holiday. ''Aye, it had to be him. Face like the very map of Ireland, and a midget with him pretending to be a kid, on a plane from the States. Oh, yes, big bill-cap and all. Cool as you please. They came through the Red Channel, if you like. Yes, incredible. No, no one on the floor saw them. I got word from the operator minding the security cameras. The bloke got all excited when he watched those two trot unmolested through the channel, and made me a phone call. Left here with a tour group led by an old bag. Wondering what he's smuggling in this time. Whatever it is would have to be light. They have no sizeable luggage. The airline said there's nothing in 'em but clothes and books. A lot of books.''

''No idea, Michaels,'' said the chief of operations. ''Might be disks or microfilms of classified information hidden away, like the last time, but it's just as likely to be diamonds. We're fortunate you spotted him. The gen was that he'd be entering from the U.S. either here or in Manchester.''

''Shall I have him stopped?''

There was a pause on the other end of the telephone line. Michaels eyed a woman who was waiting impatiently for him to finish, then turned his back on her. "No," the chief answered, reluctantly. "They'll laugh themselves sick at Scotland Yard at our expense if we stop him, and he's here empty to make a pickup instead of a delivery. Keep an eye on him, will you? Report anything he does that looks suspicious."

"I will, sir." Michaels pushed the Follow-On Call button, and punched 100, requesting Directory Inquiries to tell him what it could about a company called Educatours.

Miss Anderson shepherded them into the waiting motor coach, painted a natty silver and blue with "Educatours" blazoned in white across the sides and front of the vehicle. "Keith Doyle and Holl Doyle," she said formally, indicating the other passengers with a sweep of her hand, "meet your classmates for the next six weeks."

The group assembled on the coach was a mixed one. A cluster of college-age male students huddled together at the back of the bus. They stared blankly through a haze of acrid cigarette smoke at Keith when he was introduced to them. Max, Martin, Charles, Edwin, Matthew, and Tom came from the same college at Edinburgh University. Alistair was one of Miss Anderson's own pupils at Glasgow University. In spite of their casual insouciance, they were dressed in button-down shirts with identical ties. Keith was glad he hadn't given in to the temptation of comfort and worn a T-shirt. Two middle-aged women, Mrs. Green and Mrs. Turner, whom Keith guessed to be teachers, sat together in the second seat behind and to the left of the driver. They gave him polite, shy smiles, but positively beamed at Holl. Miss Anderson dashed off and returned with a petite Indian girl dressed in a sari.

"There. With Narit's arrival, we have our full complement." Miss Anderson plumped herself into the seat in front of the pair of teachers. "Open the windows, extinguish cigarettes, thank *you*! It's too nice a day not to take the air."

Keith and Holl took a seat on the left side halfway back, between the Scottish students and the English teachers. Even though he had seen the driver seated on the right when he got on, Keith still did a double take when the bus pulled out to the right, with apparently no one driving it. They left the one-way system in front of the airport, and pulled onto the motorway.

"Now, now!" Miss Anderson clapped her hands at Keith.

He had just settled back with his head on his rolled-up jacket. "No naps yet. We've too much to do!"

"I can hardly stay awake," Keith pleaded.

"Nonsense!" cried Miss Anderson. "Today is your first day of class!" There was a chorus of groans from the back of the coach. "Now, pay attention, and I will begin. The area of the island of Great Britain known as the Highlands had a surprisingly rich Neolithic culture, which was during the period between 4400 and 2400 B.C. In the ensuing millenia, the population in many of these centers has declined. As a result, a number of the Stone Age and following Bronze Age sites have remained relatively undisturbed, because until air transport and surveillance became a reality, they were unknown. It was the custom for most of these ancient peoples to bury substantial goods with the dead, and from these grave goods, we are able to deduce as much about the way they lived as we can from the remains of the people themselves.

"The first site we will explore is just southwest of here, where Bronze Age settlements were common. Alas, this area has been heavily settled through the ages since the beginning, so we are hard-pressed to discover undisturbed sites near here. In this case, we're immediately in front of the bulldozers. There will be construction on the site in ten months' time unless something of significant cultural or historical importance is unearthed, so time is precious. The teams do not expect such a find, so they are working quickly to document the site while they still can."

"Do they hope that they'll find something that will save the site?" Keith sat up, remembering Gillington Library on the Midwestern campus and how he had worked to prevent its demolition.

Miss Anderson shook her head. "Indeed, no, not really. That would only delay the inevitable a short time. In this case, we're merely record takers, making notes of what was where, and when, for future historians. We can't hope to preserve all the sites where our ancestors lived—we'd soon run out of places to live! Most of what we find will be reburied *in situ*. The second and third digs, both in the ancient province of Alban, now known as Inverness-shire and the Islands, are much better—neither is immediately subject to development."

She went on with her lecture, which was peppered with antique references and two-dollar words. Keith strained to comprehend and remember what she was saying, but realized, hopelessly, that the words were bouncing off his jetlagged ears. Holl had dozed off miles back. Maybe one of his fellow classmates could fill them in later.

The coach turned off the main street and passed by an arched, stone gate. Keith glimpsed relief carvings on the archway and a square banked by solid walls of buildings surrounding a grass sward, inside of the same soot-darkened stone as the arch. He was awed by the antiquity of the University buildings, compared with those of Midwestern University. What they offered here was Education, with a capital E, tried but untroubled by the passing ages. He was enormously impressed, and couldn't wait to explore.

"That is the MacLeod Building," Miss Anderson pointed out. "We'll have seminars in the Small Lecture Room once a week, where those of you taking this tour for credit will present weekly essays, which I'll explain later. The University is not in session during the summer, so we've got the place pretty much to ourselves. You'll all be staying in rooms in the Western Residence Hall just along this road for the next two weeks. Meals are in the refectory. Your names are on the doors of your dormitories."

The party clambered out of the coach before a gray, granite building with no windows on the ground floor. Checking Miss Anderson's chart, Keith and Holl found they were sharing a suite with Martin and Matthew on the second floor, which meant that they had to climb two flights of stairs to get there. "We're on the ground floor, now," the teacher explained, for the benefit of the two Americans, as they pulled into the car park next to the building. "First is just above us."

"Miss Anderson," Keith began apologetically. "Can I get a review sheet, or something of the lecture you gave on the bus? I don't think I absorbed very much of it."

"Never mind, lad," the teacher smiled brightly. "I was talking simply to keep you awake on the coach, though it won't hurt if you retained some of it. We'll be reviewing the same information tomorrow morning before we go out. Wear old clothes; we'll be getting a bit mucky."

Keith enkindled instant admiration for the wiry instructor. "Yes, ma'am!" He pulled a smart salute. Holl groaned.

With a smile, she shooed them away. "Get on with you before your roommates scoff the best beds!"

▪ Chapter 4 ▪

The accommodations were comfortable enough. Holl and Keith shared a tiny bedroom that bore a striking resemblance to Keith's dormitory room at Midwestern. "Even the dressers are in the same place," Keith pointed out with amusement. "I bet they stamp them out of a mold in Hong Kong."

"Keith Doyle," Holl spoke up suddenly from behind him. "I've been meaning to ask—those rows upon rows of houses in Illinois and those we saw on the way from Glasgow Airport? Are there really molds large enough to make houses?"

Keith, turning around to face Holl, tried to stifle a grin, but was unable to do anything about the twinkle in his eye. "They don't stock much in the way of architecture texts in Gillington Library, do they?"

"No . . ." Holl admitted thoughtfully, turning red. "They've a subscription to *Architecture Quarterly*, but that deals mostly with unique structures. Not the mass-produced sorts we saw."

"It's just an expression," Keith assured him, going back to unpacking his suitcase, "although they sometimes make them out of prefabricated sections. It would save a lot of time if they could cast a whole block's worth of houses at once."

Holl's jaw dropped. "Do you mean those identical, cheap-looking boxes are constructed one by one? On purpose? There are frauds passing themselves off as craftsmen, then."

A rap sounded at the door, cutting off further exclamations of outrage. Holl sat down on the bed with his cap pulled down over his forehead, and yanked a half-whittled stick and his knife out of his jacket pocket.

"It's open," Keith called over his shoulder.

Matthew and Martin leaned in. "Are you settled now?" Matthew asked. He was about Keith's height and build, but his face was sharper in outline. His hair was black and smooth, but his pale skin seemed curiously thin, showing pink through it over the cheekbones.

"Just about," Keith said, shutting a drawer full of T-shirts.

"If you do' mind it, we can show you about the town. Maybe nip into the pub for a quick one. It's well on into lunchtime, though they'll serve meals until two," Martin grinned, exposing crooked, white teeth. His hair was taffy-colored, similar to Holl's, cut short in the back, but long enough in front to droop over his eyes. "We know where to find the best cider in Glasgow."

"Cider? Sounds good. I'm thirsty," Keith said.

"It gets dry on those jets," Holl added, sliding the cap's bill further back on his head with the point of his knife.

"Um, he's your nephew?" Matthew asked the American youth, aiming a shoulder at Holl. The lilting cadence made it a question, though he had none of the broad accents of the customs officer or his roommate. "We've got legal age limits in the pub. How old is he?"

"Twelve," said Keith.

"Fourteen," said Holl at the same time. With a long-suffering look at Keith, he handed over his passport. The date of birth bore him out. Keith looked at it curiously, but said nothing.

"You certain he's a relative?" Martin joked.

"Well, I suppose he could have aged while I wasn't looking," Keith defended himself lamely. "It seems such a long time since he was born."

"Small for your age, my lad. Still, that's old enough to get in, though not to drink cider," Matthew affirmed cheerfully. "There's squashes and other things for you. Come on, then."

"What made you come to Glasgow for the summer?" Matthew asked, when they plumped into a booth in the Black Bull pub in Byres Road, just outside the grounds of the university. The tour had taken them over an hour—they had been on and off the cylindrical orange trains of the Underground transportation system three or four times at different points around the city. Glasgow was a city of four-hundred-year-old golden sandstone and gray granite buildings standing alongside new glass-and-chromium-tube constructions, far more than one could see in a day. Keith was ready for a snack and a drink by the time they returned.

"Curiosity, I guess," he admitted. "My best excuse is that I get college credit for this tour, while getting to know another country."

"The same for me," Holl put in. "I've never been away from home before."

"Well, we don't have the endless money you Americans do, so we have to get our education at home," Martin said darkly. "No jollicking off for us."

"Hey, I work for my tuition," Keith retorted. "My family isn't rich. You've been watching too much American television."

"What's your job?" Matthew asked, hurrying to make peace and defuse the argument.

Keith, always eager to talk about the success of Hollow Tree Industries, began to explain. "I sell handmade woodcrafts to gift shops, made by some friends of mine. Holl, here . . ." his voice dropped when he realized what he might have been about to say. "Holl here has seen some of the items. Shortbread molds, toys, boxes, jewelry like necklaces, and so on. They're pretty nice, very good workmanship. I get a commission on the sales so my craftsmen don't have to go out and find buyers themselves." Holl nodded approval, and Keith beamed.

"That can't be easy," Matthew acknowledged. "I work in a bakery near my home half days, starting early in the morning. I'm on holiday for the next month. Two weeks' pay I'm losing at the end of this course, but like you, it's credit toward graduation."

"You get four weeks vacation a year?" Keith gawked. "Wow. We only get two weeks."

"Have you ever had cider?" Martin inquired, getting up to put in their order at the bar. Hanging signs under the inverted bottles behind the counter advertised Tennant's Ale and Strongbow.

"Oh, sure. There's lots of orchards near where I live," Keith said. "You can get fresh cider every fall." The two Scots exchanged glances, and Martin chuckled.

"I'll get the first round. We can order from the bar menu for lunch while we drink it."

"This is a St. Clements for you, lad," Martin said, returning with a small, round tray full of glasses. "Fizzy lemonade and orange, nothing toxic."

Holl took the light, orange drink, and sipped cautiously. He nodded happily and ran his tongue across his lips to catch the thin foam. "That's refreshing. Thank you."

"I got you a mild cider, Doyle," Martin continued, innocently passing him a large glass of a cloudy, burnt-gold fluid.

Grinning at Holl's watchful gaze, Keith drank. The other boys sat back nonchalantly, only their eyes alert and mischievous, waiting "That's good!"

Martin did a double-take. "You knew it was alcoholic, did you?"

"I *do* live near orchards, I told you." Keith lifted the glass happily, and studied the color against the light. "This is the smoothest applejack I've ever tasted."

"Well, watch it," Matthew warned him mildly, holding no grudge for being cheated of his fun. "You may think you know your capacity, but don't trust cider. It sneaks up on you. You get apple-juice palsy well before you know you've had a drop too much."

"No problem," Keith assured him. "Next round's on me."

Holl took an interested sniff of the cider. Pity about the drinking laws, but he didn't want to cause a fuss and draw attention to himself. Still, he felt the need for a calming drink after the trauma of plane travel. When the second round of St. Clement's came to the table, he concentrated quietly on his glass, enhancing the sugars until they fermented into alcohol. He took an investigative sip. Not as good as one of Marm's brews, but passable. The others, deep in their conversations, took no notice of him.

They talked about their homes, comparing the differences between their early lives, and exclaiming over the many similarities. Keith found his two roommates to be outgoing and curious, and thankfully, less reticent than he'd been warned. He didn't press them for details, and found that once the boys relaxed, they told him about themselves without urging.

"You're not like we thought Americans would be," Matthew admitted, candidly. "I was sure you'd be posing us for pictures in front of every stone building and bobby. You know." He pantomimed frantic snapping with an invisible camera.

"I probably would have, but I haven't got any film left," Keith confessed, putting on an abashed expression, and the others laughed.

"You're a friendly lot, you Yanks," Martin said. "If you'd been English, we'd probably not have talked to you."

"Too shirty and superior," agreed Matthew playfully, hoisting his nose in the air with a forefinger.

"With a name like Doyle, there's not much chance of that, is there? I don't want to be offensive, but you sound almost English to me," Keith continued, apologetically. "You don't have a burr in your voice. You talk like the BBC announcers. Cultured."

"We've gone to English day schools and colleges," Martin explained. "I come from a wee place near Edinburgh." He pronounced it "edin-burra," and Keith marked it for future use. "My dad's in finance, and if I want to follow him, I can't keep my old regional, even if I wanted to."

"Speak fer yerself," Matthew said, dropping into a thick burr. "Hey, Keith, hae you ey'r heard o' Billy Connolly?"

They chose their meals from a long list of entrées, each of which came with chips—french fried potatoes—and peas. Keith looked down the menu for fish and chips, but to his surprise, it wasn't listed. "Have plaice, if you want good fish," Matthew said, answering his tentative question. "It'll be fresh, at least. Fresher than the cod."

Baskets of greasy chicken and chips and peas, fish and chips and peas, and, to Keith's amusement, lasagna with chips and peas, were set before them. They washed down their lunch with more cider. The other youths seemed in no hurry to leave, and the bartender ignored them as long as they were relatively quiet.

"Everyone comes into the pub. If you don't know anybody in a town, you can wander into a pub for society. There's not much else for young people without a lot of money to do in Glasgow, unless you want to skate at St. Enoch's Center," Martin explained.

Holl chuckled, sharing the joke with Keith in an undertone. "I'll certainly pull his leg hard when we get home. Saint Enoch."

"We're in the local pub at home almost every evening. You'd like it, since you care for old places," Matthew said. "The building is a restored inn, over 350 years old. You ought to come home with us some time at the weekend for a visit."

"You bet! Thanks," Keith exclaimed.

"But leave your camera behind," Martin warned. "It's not bloody Trafalgar Square."

"Whatever you say," Keith assented, pulling his forelock.

The Black Bull was a companionable place. Keith felt very much at home, surrounded by dark, brown wooden paneling and beveled mirrors. No yuppie plants in the windows; this place was functional, not just for show. The only thing he couldn't identify were designs cut out of circles of brass hanging on leather strips over the stone fireplace and from the ceiling beams. The colorful machines in the corner with whirling wheels and strips of lights that read "10p" had to be the local equivalent of arcade games. Matthew and Martin began to discuss Rugby football, which sounded more brutal even than American football. They explained the British game to Keith, who listened closely, and offered comparisons.

"What's this apple-juice palsy like?" Keith put in, setting down an empty pint glass. He was starting to feel a little lightheaded, but put it down to jet lag. According to his watch, it was just after noon at home, but it felt as though he'd been awake for days. Holl reclined limply under his cap in the corner of the booth, offering a word or two when one of the others spoke directly to him.

"Ach, you know," Martin gestured, trying to conjure an image out of the air with his hands. "You go weak at the knees, and you see things like little pink lizards. Snakes and bugs, too. And then you feel like your head wants to come off."

"Lizards?" Keith exclaimed, squinted impishly at the table. "Pink ones?"

"Aye." The boys' cultured voices were sliding into homier dialects as their blood-to-alcohol ratio went down. "Thot's right."

As Holl watched in horror, a fingerlong pink lizard rose out of one of the spilled puddles of cider on the table and scooted toward Martin. It made a run of about a foot before it reached a dry place on the table and popped. Martin jumped, and Keith grinned.

"Did you see that, Matt?" the youth demanded, clutching his friend's arm and pointing. "Lizards!"

"Nae. Just a bit of reflection from the street," the other reassured him, distinctly. "Maybe from a lorry. I saw a little flash of pink in the slop. This table wants wiping. What a clumsy lot we are." He rose unsteadily and went to the bar to borrow a towel.

"You're probably hallucinating," Keith added. "This cider is insidious stuff, isn't it?"

Holl wasn't fooled by Keith's innocent expression, and eyed him as the other lad blotted up the spills. Enoch, the Master's son, had been trading driving lessons in Keith's car for magic instruction over the last few months. Evidently, the Big Person was getting good at simple tricks like cohesiveness and shaping. Holl was surprised and dismayed by his proficiency. Maybe there was something after all, in the boy's insistence that he was related to the Little Folk. But the red-haired student was losing all his inhibitions as he got more drunk. In a moment, he'd do something stupid, and expose them. Holl had no wish to wind up a museum exhibit in a foreign country thousands of miles from home, doing charms and tricks for a lot of scientists. The "extraterrestrial" movie Keith had brought once for the Folk to see had opened their eyes amazingly. Holl had had nightmares for weeks.

"I've got to get some sleep, or I'll be sick," he spoke up suddenly, as the others were discussing another round of drinks. "My head's pounding, and *I* haven't had any cider."

"He can't be sick here. You'd better take him back to the Hall," Matthew told Keith, worriedly.

The American youth looked at Holl almost as if he'd never seen him before and shook his head to clear it. "Right. C'mon, Holl. I wouldn't mind an hour's nap either." He slid out from behind the table and attempted to stand. His knees buckled, and Holl sprang to catch him as he clawed at the dark, wooden walls of the booth for support.

"There go your knees," Martin crowed. "Apple-juice palsy it is."

"Up you go, uncle," Holl gritted, supporting Keith's weight on his shoulder. "You've had too much for one day."

"How do you feel?" Matthew asked Keith the next morning on the way down to the refectory for breakfast.

"I'll never do that again," Keith vowed. His face was pasty, with green showing just below the skin. "What a hangover. I think I was sick on the way back, but I don't remember. My knees didn't follow me back to the dorm until about 3 A.M. I saw the sun rise then. It was blinding."

"You might have a little less until you get used to it," Matthew suggested kindly, without a suggestion of "I told you so."

"Maybe. Maybe I'll just go teetotal for a while," Keith said, meekly. Holl had lectured him fiercely on the walk back to the dormitory on the responsible use of talent, and he felt contrite for his indiscretion. Secretly, he was pleased to have created such a realistic illusion, but after last night, he vowed to practice only in private. He felt thoroughly ashamed. After all, he had spent nearly a year making certain that no one would discover the Little Folks' home and helping them move to a new place on Hollow Tree Farm, isolated from Big Folk. He had nearly blown it all in one night.

"If you can't hold your liquor better than that," the elf had hissed at him, "then I'll have to put a block on you so you can't use charms at all. I don't want strangers to look too closely at me when queer things happen."

Keith could only agree. He carried his plate to the table and sat down gingerly next to Holl. His head hurt when he moved too quickly, and the sound of forks ringing against plates reverberated between his ears like the clapper in a bell. Holl didn't say a word to him when he sat down. Keith poured himself a cup of dark, brown liquid from the metal pot on the table and let the steam bathe his face, relaxing a knot or two behind his forehead. He shot a glance to his left, but Holl, focused on his breakfast, paid no attention to him.

"Try the tea. It's strong, but it's pretty good," he said to Holl. No answer.

"Are you still mad?" he asked quietly, as he sawed a piece of bacon with his knife. It was louder to him than a hacksaw going through wood and he winced. The taste was like boiled and salted leather, but he felt he deserved no better. A glossy fried egg shone up at him like a plastic display dummy. He shuddered at it, and reached for a piece of toast from an upright rack on the table. It was cold. He scraped butter on it to the tune of Brazil nuts cracking in his ears.

Holl sighed and set down his fork. "No. Do you feel as poorly as you look?"

Keith grimaced. "Worse, I think. They were absolutely right. It feels like your head will come off. There's got to be more than apples in that stuff. This never happened at home."

His friend clucked his tongue and shook his head. "Here, then." Holl spread his fingers and planted his hand against Keith's cranium. "Breathe in and out, and forget about me."

Keith closed his eyes gratefully. Instantly, the agony began to slip away from the inside of his head, like wax melting out of an inverted glass. In a few moments, he drew a deep breath. "Oh, that's great," he crooned, rocking his head from side to side and enjoying the sensation of relief. "That's terrific. My headache's completely gone. I wish you could market that. You'd make a mint."

Holl watched him with a wry smile curling up one side of his mouth. "I can't market it. But I'll give your headache back in full force if you do such a silly thing ever again."

"I won't. I promise," Keith said fervently.

As she had assured Keith, Miss Anderson repeated her lecture of the day before, and dismissed the class before noon. "We'll be taking the coach out to the dig site later, to meet the team of archaeologists, and begin work. You may not understand what you're doing unless you've read the text, but please remember to follow their every instruction. We are there to make an accurate record of the past, and any errors, any deviation from the correct steps, could have long-range ramifications. Go have lunch, and meet me in the quad at half-past one."

Like all the rest of the smaller information-gathering branches, the Secret Intelligence Service was second or third priority in getting their questions answered or their projects funded. A lot more attention was paid to the electronic wizards and their toys, but where would they be without the hard work and footslogging of the SIS, Michaels wanted to know. With difficulty, he had managed to get assignment of a small car and set out along the M8 in pursuit of the Educatours vehicle. In the most ordinary way possible, the coach had deposited its passengers, O'Day and his accomplice among them, in the heart of Glasgow. With the way the old buildings echoed, it was no problem to hear everything that went on in them. Michaels learned that the "boy" was carrying a formidable knife concealed in a pants pocket. O'Day was not notably a violent man. Perhaps his small associate was the one he ought to watch in a close-up fight. Personnel checks on the others in the tour would have to be made a priority. Unlikely as it seemed, one of them could be O'Day's contact.

Chapter 5

The coach transported them along the M8 motorway leading to the southwest. The boys were all dressed in corduroy or twill, except Keith and Holl, who were wearing jeans. To the surprise of the others. Narit had appeared wearing jeans, too, and her long hair was braided into a tail that hung down her back.

"Where's the sari?" Keith had asked. "We half expected you to be formal."

Narit had laughed prettily, a quiet, tinkly sound. "I wear the traditional dress only to please my grandmother when I visit her. I much prefer English fashions. They don't get caught in doors."

The seating in the coach had worked out much the same way as the day before. Keith, armed with his camera and a new roll of film, had a seat to himself, and took pictures of the landscape through the thick, plexiglass plate windows.

"Look, there's nothing special out there. Just houses," Matthew, behind him, pointed out.

"They're different from American houses," Keith said happily. "Look! A milestone!" He crouched over his viewfinder, fumbling with the focusing ring on the lens.

"Please yourself," Matthew grumbled, sinking back into his seat. "It's your film you're wasting. *Milestones*."

Holl sat on the opposite side of the coach from Keith, also watching the scenery. They had quickly passed out of the city limits and into reassuringly rural countryside. None of the land was like the ironing-board flat plains of the American midwest, so it was interesting to the eye. When he had excitedly named the characteristics of the hills and valleys they were passing to Keith Doyle, that one had teased him, accusing him of learning them out of a book. It was a fact—he had. So far in his short life, the geographic features he was seeing had been flat pictures to him. He was storing up all his impressions of the wide world, to bring back to the other Folk. So far, this part was big and wild and empty. Keith was correct about the houses, too. They had an air that held them apart from American construction, what little he'd seen of it. But they were hauntingly similar, in a generations-removed way, to the houses of the under-library village in which his Folk had lived. He wondered if Keith had seen the likeness. What connection was there between his folk and the people who lived here? What would his clan say about the resemblance? The younger ones would likely speculate, while the old ones, who might actually know, would very probably say nothing at all. It was frustrating how they kept the younger generations in the dark. But with evidence, he could start a controversy that might bring out useful revelations.

"Say, Keith Doyle," Holl called across the aisle. "There's an interesting house coming up here on the side of the road. Take its portrait, will you?"

The hot summer sunshine slanted down across Keith's shoulders and burned the tips of his ears while he worked on his patch of earth. The grass on the broad hilltop had been cleared in a section about twenty feet long by six feet wide. The exposed area was divided into sections three feet by three feet by pegs to which string had been tied. When the group arrived, each student or worker was issued a pan, a loosely woven sieve, a trowel, and a pair of brushes. Under the supervision of Dr. Crutchley, the Professor of Ancient Studies from London University, they were expected to scrutinize the earth for artifacts, brushing away particles of earth from the marked patch to uncover each layer. The brushings were to be dropped into the sieve and broken up gently to see if there was anything hidden in them. If an artifact appeared, the site was measured and a note was made of where it lay. At least, that was what Keith understood them to want. He had been working for hours on his section, and had found nothing worth measuring or noting. He carefully brushed away the surface of the dirt with the larger, stiff brush, and scooped it into his pan, sifting through it for particles of metal or pottery. At times he would see a spot of another color and work feverishly to uncover it, but it would never turn out to be more than a pebble.

"Not even a toenail clipping," Keith grumbled to Matthew, whose patch was across from his. "I never realized that scientists came up with their impressions of history based on such thin evidence. It's like finding photographs, when you were expecting a movie. There's so much in those exhibits in museums, I supposed there would be more to see in a site. I think this part must have been the garden. Are they sure this *was* part of the site? The building boundaries are way over there." He gestured with his trowel toward the tables where Crutchley's assistants were sorting potsherds and animal bones. Behind them, inside a square, pavilion tent, more of the professor's team, nearly invisible in the shadows, moved back and forth with flat trays, filled with the results of other days' successful searching.

"Don't give up," Matthew said, absently. "They wouldn't still be here if they thought the site was milked dry."

"Well, this is where Professor Keith Doyle says that they *didn't* have either the cooking or sleeping quarters," he said emphatically, gesturing at his patch with the trowel. "Or anything else of importance, except maybe a footprint from the family pet dinosaur."

Matthew grinned without looking up at him, then his expression changed. He began brushing furiously with the stiff brush at a spot in the earth before him, his cheeks pink. "Hoy, help a body here, eh?"

"Do you have something?"

"Here I thought it was one of the everpresent pebbles, but this one's not shifting," Matthew explained, his voice increasingly more excited. "It's red-brown in color. Do you see it?"

Keith dived over to help. "Yeah. Brush away from it. Clear the earth level. Hey, it's round."

"What's there?" Holl asked, from partway up the row of workspaces.

"Don't know yet, but it looks like Matt struck gold," Keith said, his eyes shining. What disappointment he had been harboring evaporated in the excitement of an actual find. No matter that it was in someone else's section, it was an archaeological artifact, and he was watching it—no, helping it—be uncovered. He grinned widely as the edges began to emerge. "It's a covered pot of some kind. And it's intact."

The dig staff saw the crowd gathering at the end of the site and hurried over to see what was going on. Miss Sanders, Professor Crutchley's assistant, a middle-aged woman with light ruddy-brown hair, leaned over Keith's shoulder to watch as the pot emerged.

"Carefully now. It could be very fragile. Stop using the brushes now, and use your fingers instead. Clear away the earth from its sides with your fingers. There might be small handles, and you could break them."

"Yes, ma'am," both youths breathed, working more slowly.

"Stop, Keith Doyle," Holl's voice came softly in Keith's left ear. "I can feel cracks in the fabric. It's only hardened clay. Stop now and move outward. You'll have to pick it up from below."

Keith glanced up at Holl, and pulled away from the edges of the brown jar's rim. "Matt, let's move out and break up the dirt. It might widen out further down. We don't want it to smash just as we're getting something at last." He dragged his fingertips along the ground until the pressure of Holl's hand on his shoulder told him to stop. Matthew, shooting him a curious glance, followed suit, and started breaking up the soil.

"Good, good," the assistant encouraged them. "Now, *lift* . . ."

A collective sigh of joy gusted from the crowd. Between their fingertips, Matthew and Keith held a glazed, clay jar with a small, round lid crusted in place by more dirt. Its shape was slightly reminiscent of an amphora, except that the foot was flat, and instead of the earlike handles, it had only pinched-looking tabs under the curled rim. At Miss Sander's instruction, they set it down in an empty pan on someone's outspread handkerchief. The assistant dropped to her knees beside Keith and whisked at the jar with a soft brush until the lid came free and rattled in place.

"Well done, you!" Miss Sanders exclaimed. "Someone get the camera."

Another assistant hurried up. The jar was photographed in the pan. A ruler was laid and chalk powder dribbled around the location in which it was found, and the assistant took another exposure. Dr. Crutchley beamed down on his workers proudly as if he'd thrown the pot himself. He was a man in his late fifties, with perfect wings of white in his dark brown hair. Wiry eyebrows stood out between those dramatic temples, just barely not touching above a beaklike nose.

"A perfect example of corded ware, Miss Sanders. I never did expect this site to be another Jorvik, but it is encouraging to find fine specimens of this nature. Very gratifying. It's an

Irish-style vessel, isn't it, except that there are well-preserved traces of paste ornamentation, and the firing—hmm!—is much finer than you would expect. And a lid . . . not a seal or a stopper. Most unusual."

"There's something broken off inside," Keith said. "I felt it sloshing around when we picked it up."

The professor gently lifted the lid, and set it down on the cloth. With two fingers, he extracted from the jar a long string of globular, translucent golden beads. "Amber! An amber trading string." The aged, blackened cord began to deteriorate as he lifted it, and he scooped his other hand underneath to catch the beads before they fell. "A small fortune in tally beads. Well, a good omen as a first find, I'd say."

"Someone's cache, sir?" Miss Sanders inquired, picking up the pan containing the jar and lid.

"Impossible to say until we've examined the entire site. "It might have been interred with a shallow burial, not uncommon for wealth as grave goods . . ." The two scientists drifted away to the table, offering speculations to one another, and exclaiming over the artifacts. The second assistant followed respectfully with the camera. Matthew and Keith watched them go with open mouths.

"They've forgotten all about us," Matthew said, a little indignantly. "We passed a miracle, and they've forgotten we exist!"

"Oh, carry on, you lot!" Miss Sanders called over her shoulder.

"There," Keith grinned at him. "That's better."

Enthusiasm rekindled, Keith doubled his efforts at searching, breaking up even the tiniest pieces of earth in his sieve and shaking them through. Miss Sanders had hinted of a shallow burial. There might be a skeleton here some place. Most likely, it would be cremated fragments in a funerary urn, which was relatively small and easy to overlook if you weren't digging smack over it. The others were coming up with small artifacts, or fragments of larger items. With respectful hands, Holl was turning over a green, flaking piece of metal that could have been a bronze axehead. The two ladies and Edwin were standing back so the assistant could sprinkle chalk along the outline of a long bundle that lay exposed across their three sections. Keith's patch still showed no signs of yielding up anything interesting.

He went on digging, undaunted by failure. Since his patch was adjacent to Matthew's, it was possible that there was something hidden there, another clue to the solution of the puzzle of the Bronze Age settlement that had once been there. With a mighty heave, Keith tossed the earth from his sorting pan over his shoulder and bent down, trowel in hand, to start filling it up again.

"What are you doing, lad?" a voice roared from behind him. "More care! more care!" Arrested, Keith tilted his head back until he was looking straight up into the red face of Dr. Crutchley, face red above the collar of his white short-sleeved shirt over which he was wearing a sleeveless knitted waistcoat. Over which someone had inconsiderately sprinkled a truckload of dirt. Keith swallowed guiltily.

He sprang to his feet and began to brush off the protesting professor. "Uh-oh. I'm so sorry, sir. I wasn't watching where that was going."

"Take it more slowly in future," Dr. Crutchley ordered, batting irritatedly at the front of his waistcoat, which sent clouds of gray dust floating into the air. "I came over to compliment you lads on the skill you showed at bringing out that pottery piece, but it may have been a fluke! You could be missing something working at a pace like that, or worse yet, destroying it in your haste. More care is needed. Or perhaps it would be better if you stopped what you were doing and helped to catalog our finds instead?" He pointed the stem of his pipe toward the table. Keith followed his thrust and shook his head vigorously.

"Oh, no. I'd rather help out finding things, sir. Normally I'm good at digging things up."

Crutchley flicked particles of dust off one arm with a decisive finger. "Yes, though more like a surgeon exposing tissues, boy, and less like a dog burying a bone."

"Yes, sir. Sorry, sir."

"I admire your initiative, but keep the energy for endurance, not speed. Carry on." The professor walked away, reaching into his back pocket for a tobacco pouch and plunging the bowl of his pipe into it.

"Ooh, that was a rough ticking off," Edwin said under his breath.

"Hah," said Keith, going back to digging, but much more

slowly. His face was invisible to the others, but his ears were red. "That was nothing. I've been chewed out by experts."

As the sun began to throw longer shadows over the dig, the team called a halt to the work. Some contrast was useful, as it threw the edges of hidden objects into relief, but if the angle was too great, pebbles began to look like potsherds. Gratefully, Keith and the others creaked to their feet and exercised stiff legs and backs. Miss Sanders and the male assistant made tea inside the square tent, and distributed it to the workers in stained, chunky, pottery mugs.

"From the look of these," Mrs. Green quipped, "ceramics skills haven't changed much in forty centuries."

"Man hasn't changed significantly over the ages," Dr. Crutchley replied, settling down in a canvas director's chair with a sigh. "In my opinion, only his tools have advanced in sophistication. Well, that was a good day's work. I thank you all, especially our newcomers. Now we like to sit down and have a chat over what we've done today. What you Americans would call the 'recap.' " Keith grinned at Holl, and the others chuckled.

"Before you came," Miss Sanders began, "my lot were turning over the rubbish tip. Once we had an idea of the perimeter of the settlement, we started nosing about downwind. There it was, just about twenty paces behind one of the structures. Fairly extensive."

"You can't still smell any of it, can you?" Mrs. Turner asked in alarm, wrinkling her nose.

"Not at all," the archaeologist answered, impishly. "Kitchen refuse becomes quite sanitized after four thousand years. We've come up with the bones of many herd animals, and an enormous quantity of remains of fish and shellfish. We take that to mean that the settlement was prosperous, since they weren't reliant upon a strict diet of fish. Herd animals would be more rare in a poor environment."

"Doesn't the amber necklace prove that they were wealthy?" Matthew asked. He took a proprietary pride in his find, and no one seemed to object.

"Amber," Dr. Crutchley began, in a lecturing air, "was both an irreducible tally and in itself valuable. Our ancestors weren't utter barbarians. They were attracted by the beauty of the substance. By its placement, and by the types of artifacts, we are coming to the conclusion that this was a trading village. Now, without any other evidence to support it, what do you think the pot was doing out there at the bottom of the settlement?''

Encouraged by the professor, the students offered their own conclusions. The professional archaeologists took their theories seriously, discussing the pros and cons of each suggestion. Keith found the give and take stimulating, and volunteered his own theory.

''Maybe that amber string was somebody's ace in the hole. You know, cookie jar money; and he wanted to keep his advantage hidden.''

The others laughed. Dr. Crutchley let the corners of his mouth curl up.

''Very interesting, Keith,'' he said. He seemed to harbor no ill will for Keith having showered him with dirt, and even confessed that not only had it happened to him before, but he'd done it to others himself.

''Am I right?'' asked Keith, eagerly.

''Probably not, son,'' said the archaeologist, grinding ash out of the pipe bowl and tamping fresh tobacco into it with his thumb. Keith's face fell. Dr. Crutchley went on. ''But you make me think that you're heading in the right direction. I am reminded of a book in my library—I must send for it from London—that mentions a similar artifact. You may not have the right answers, but you function nicely as a catalyst for others to make them think. Do remember, there's no theory so silly that it hasn't been proposed in quite serious scientific papers by my learned colleagues.'' He lit the pipe and drew on it, watching the others humorously through the thicket of his eyebrows. ''What *I* would like to find, though it is nearly impossible with the dearth of evidence, was what early man thought about.'' He looked around at his circle of listeners. ''What inspired him? What brought him here? Whom or what did he blame when it rained? Luckily, the Celts and Saxons were inclined to tell stories to us, their extreme descendants, through the decoration and ornamentation of household goods, what they ate, what things they held dear and,'' with a wave toward Keith, ''what they kept hidden. Yes, I will have to send for that book.''

''I've made a note of it, professor,'' Miss Sanders said, flourishing her pen.

From the crest of the hill where they sat, the students could see the shining ribbon of the river leading down to the sea. The hills around them were similar to that one: scattered scrub along the sides and clearings of windbrushed grass atop the flat bluffs. Most of the land was marked off as restricted sites, cordoned off at road level by twisted wire fences and red printed signs warning away trespassers. Theirs was the only one of the peaks which was unmarked and unfenced.

"This is not a terribly important site, but it is a nice one," Crutchley continued. "Good, defensible location, but still reachable. As the population grew upriver, the shipping trade routes dealt with cities so much further inland. Wool and iron rejuvenated this area in the Middle Ages, so this site became obsolete. Lucky for us, since we can now investigate a stopped moment in time."

The tea cups were gathered up and washed in a tub behind the tent. Keith and the others picked their way down the hillside to wait for the Educatours coach. Everyone else was chattering excitedly about the day's work. He sat next to Holl in the tall grass, playing with a straw between his fingers, gazing at nothing, and thinking about Dr. Crutchley's lecture. To understand a site, you had to make up a story using what was there, artifacts, layout, weather patterns; and hope that nothing you excavated later made the story invalid. The work was backbreaking, but it was fun. He was fond of making up theories. If he was a better catalyst than a scientist, then he'd better come up with some good suggestions. To stimulate the others' minds, of course.

"Doesn't really tell you who they belong to, does it?" Keith asked. Holl, distracted from his thoughts about flowers and ancestors, followed his eyes, and read the Restricted signs swinging on the barbed wire across the road.

"Perhaps the owners want privacy," Holl reasoned, peering up between the thick bushes and waist-high grass on one obscured hillside. "What could they possibly be building out here among all these private sites?"

"What?" Keith asked, not really paying attention. "Who?"

"Don't you remember the reason they're hurrying with this excavation? 'Right in front of the bulldozer' was the way Miss Anderson put it. Someone's building something among all these unfriendly neighbors."

Keith walked backward and squinted under the flat of his hand toward the crest of the hill across the road. "I don't know. No buildings. Not even a tent. No one *lives* there, anyway.

Maybe it's a nature preserve of some kind. There's a path leading up the hill. I'm going to have a look." He started for the fence.

"A preserve, preserved one hill at a time? What has that to do with bulldozers? In any case, you shouldn't touch, Keith Doyle," Holl warned him. "I don't know what they'll do to you if you're caught meddling over here. Think of me stranded here by myself in a strange place before you decide to get yourself tossed in jail."

Keith grinned. "I guess you're right. Hello, Mom?" he pantomimed a telephone receiver, "can you send me 500 pounds bail?"

"You'll have to bail out later. Get up. The coach is coming."

• Chapter 6 •

The dig was the exclusive topic of conversation in the coach all the way back to Glasgow. Miss Anderson circulated up and down the aisle among the tour group, chatting and asking questions. She gave Matthew hearty congratulations on his find, and discussed funerary customs with him. After a hasty dinner which no one really tasted, Keith and Holl joined the other young men for a celebratory pub crawl around Glasgow. Miss Anderson, the two schoolteachers, and Narit stayed behind to talk quietly among themselves.

"And I vote for a good pudding, too," Alistair suggested, as they emerged on the street.

"Dessert?" Keith translated. "Sounds great to me."

"I should get to sleep," Holl began, thinking of the wildflowers he had seen growing on the hilltops around the dig site. He intended to sneak away the next day while the others were eating their lunch, and examine some of the plants up close. That would take a long night's recharge, and jet lag was still troubling him.

"No, come with us," Keith urged, enthusiastically. Reluctantly, Holl nodded as the others added their encouragement. "We won't be out all night. Just a snack. How about the rest of you?''

There was a chorus of approval, and Alistair nodded decisively. ''I know a place nearby with fine sweets and a cellar second to none.'' He steered them out of the university complex and around the corner into an alley. An unobtrusive doorway let into a quiet but crowded establishment, with the curious name of the Ubiquitous Chip. The host looked them over cautiously, judging them to be sober enough not to make trouble, and escorted them to a long table.

The restaurant, uncomfortably like an American fern bar in decor, proved to have a genius making desserts in the kitchen. Keith licked his spoon thoughtfully and wondered if he should order a second selection. He decided against it, and amused himself throwing leftover crumbs to the enormous goldfish in the fountain that ran along one side of the main room.

On top of homemade ice cream, mousses, and tortes, the others poured down wine and liqueurs, and discussed the events of the day with great interest. Matthew was acclaimed a hero for his great find, and decided on his own reasons for the interment of the covered jar. He was in a mood to take no prisoners, which the others took as a personal challenge.

''Well, what do you know about it anyway?'' Martin asked, challengingly, ''All you've ever dug up before is your Mum's tulip bulbs.''

Keith and Holl plowed straight into the thick of a loud and passionate argument about whether or not the professor was right in his theories. Holl was able to stop worrying for a short time about the importance of his private mission. This was like some of the stimulating discussions the Master's class engaged in—everyone had their own theories.

Keith tipped Holl a wink. The languid, sullen pose assumed by most of the boys turned out to be nothing more than that. Something important had actually happened, progress had been made, and they were a part of it. Their daily lives had been unmarked by change or excitement. They were bored, and pretended they didn't care. Hard work did bring out the best in some people. No one who felt like taking it easy would have joined a tour like this to begin with.

As the wait staff began to clear the surrounding tables, Edwin rose to his feet. ''Let's go. We can talk in the pubs until closing time.''

"Where should we go?" Matthew asked. The others started to argue for their favorites.

"How about the King's Head?" Martin suggested.

"Why not the Black Bull? It's only across the road."

"What about the Curlers?"

Keith snickered at the names. "What's that, a combination pub and hairdresser's?"

Charles pushed him toward the door. He was a big youth with heroic looks: a sharply planed jaw, curly brown hair, and mild blue eyes which wore a glint of amusement. "No, you silly git, curling is a sport. You take a big, round, flat stone, and slide it across a frozen lake, sweeping the ice before it as you go . . ."

"No, they've only got Tennant's lager," Max said, interrupting them. "Come on, I'll choose the first one. We'll go down to City Centre and stop in at the Skye Boatman, then make the rounds from there." On a chorus of approval, the party turned toward the stop for the Strathclyde Underground. Holl sighed as he saw his hours of sleep melting away like the candles the boys were burning at both ends. Well, there were more days of the trip left ahead of him.

"Nine for the orange caterpillars," Edwin shouted, letting his voice echo in the brick-walled station. They trotted down the stairs toward the trains. A man in a rumpled suit detached himself from a group at the ticket machines and followed them unobtrusively into the bowels of the station.

The Skye Boatman was crowded and jolly, mashing its patrons into two small, smoky, L-shaped rooms surrounding the bar. The party had to shout at one another just to be heard over the clamor of the 'fruit machines,' a cross between slot machines and arcade games, and the canned music. Though it was early in the week, the pub was full of men and women laughing over glasses of cider or a brown-red brew which the other students told Keith was bitter ale. Keith tasted a mouthful and ordered some for himself. He was much more cautious this time with his liquor. Where the others finished one pint and ordered another, he nursed a single pint of bitter throughout the evening then switched to a St. Clement's with Holl when they moved on to the next pub.

"That's no way to drink," Alistair chided him, when he ordered his fifth orange-and-lemonade. "One minchy pint, and you're calling a halt? Ooh, you Americans are made of weak fabric."

"I'm working up my tolerance a little at a time," Keith replied, goodnaturedly, refusing to be drawn into a contest. For all the kidding they gave him, Matthew had confided that they didn't drink a lot every night. This evening was by way of being a celebration. A good thing, too. The dark ale was rich and heavy, not bitter at all, but Keith could tell by the light feeling in the top of his head that the alcohol content was a lot higher than beer back home. "There is no way I'm going to relive this morning's headache. That was one hell of a hang-over." And a close shave with disaster, he reflected, catching Holl's eye. The young elf seemed relieved by Keith's prudence, and was considerably more relaxed, even among the everchanging mob of strange Big Folk. The others had long ago forgotten his ostensible youth, and had accepted him along with Keith as one of them.

At eleven o'clock, the publican of the Black Bull rang a bell and called, "Time, gentlemen, time. Your wives are waiting for ye!"

Seeing that no one was taking the initiative, Keith got to his feet. "Come on, guys. Someone is going to have to direct me back to the Underground station."

"I can feel me right leg, but I think me left one's gone to sleep," Edwin said, looking surprised as he tried to lever himself out of the booth.

"Don't you hate when that happens?" Keith asked, helping him up. "That means it's going to be awake all night."

With Holl's aid, Keith managed to steer the others back to the train and home to Hillhead Station. There were few passengers on the late train. Only one man rode all the way to their stop with them, and trudged up the stairs in their wake. The light drizzle that met them as they emerged from the station was bracing, and woke everyone up enough to stagger the rest of the way to the residence hall.

"Whew!" Keith blew a lock of hair out of his eyes with an upward gust as he sagged onto his bed. "And I thought American college students were party animals."

"You'd hardly connect the serious archaeologists of the afternoon with the drunken louts we just put to bed," Holl agreed. He yawned. "It's late, and we've had an eventful day. I could sleep for weeks."

"Could still be some of the jet lag, too," Keith reasoned,

pulling off his sneakers. "Look at that. My feet are swollen. By the end of this trip, I'm going to be wearing clown shoes."

"And I'm going to be wearing your discards." Holl rubbed his own toes. "Blisters. This is my first pair of hard-soled shoes, and it may well be my last if they don't soften soon. I may survive well enough, as we're doing all our work from our knees."

"Are you enjoying yourself?" Keith asked, anxiously. "I know this kind of trip wasn't exactly your choice, since you signed on at the last minute to go with me."

Holl waved an impatient hand. "I *am* interested. Realize how little practical experience any of us young ones have with the outside world. I'm as keen as your fellow tourists to see what else we can find up there. It's nice to know that there's a past that stretches back beyond the date of my birth, one for which there's tangible, if unreadable proof."

"Hmph. Won't the old folks tell you what life was like before you came to Midwestern?"

"Not much. You can tell it isn't something they want to talk about. And the younger ones just tell of extended travel and wandering. They're home and secure and happy now, so the past doesn't exist. That's shortsighted, in my opinion." Disgusted, Holl dropped his shoes on the floor, and lay down, hands behind his head. "I find it frustrating, as do the rest of us born at Midwestern. Don't you find it an interesting place we're digging up? You can see why the settlers chose to live there. They get the full sun every day, but they're not exposed to the high winds. Small game would be plentiful, as would be fish. The fields are sunny. The place is defensible, but not unreachable."

"Do you suppose that they had any dealings with your ancestors?" Keith asked hopefully. "I mean, I noticed that you could tell that the pot we were uncovering was cracked, without touching it. Did you see something? Was it made by one of your Folk?"

Holl chuckled. "Ah, no. It was just a craftsman's instincts. I could feel the weakness in the material. It was nearly crying out its infirmity. It had no essence of magic or charm to it. But it was well made, and all of four thousand years old. I admire that."

"Is there anything in the site which has got the essence of magic?" Keith pressed. "I mean, what do you think? Would these people have had any contact with yours?"

"I don't know," Holl mused. "The site is not inimical to it. And there's almost no iron among the remains, and it's ages too early for steel. All their metals are bronze or softer, which you might have noticed doesn't hurt me. That would make it more comfortable for contact... but this is all speculation, Keith Doyle."

"That's what I'm best at, speculation and guesses. Besides, the professionals are guessing too; that's what Dr. Crutchley said. The more evidence we get, the more accurate the picture they can put together."

"Well, I don't know what to look for. I've barely seen the habitations occupied by Big Folk *this* century, let alone one forty times as old." The Little One sighed. "There's no sign of anything belonging to my people. In a way, it makes me feel lost and alone. It's true that we tend not to leave many marks of our passing, out of self protection, but I wish that they would have. That site is dry and cold and empty, so far as I can tell. Not a lot for me to go on, in my particular search. You're the expert bogey hunter; what do you think?"

"Well..." Keith mused. "You know, the Little People are hardly likely to have set up shop right next to the Big Folk's town. You, I mean *they* would be unnatural creatures." A sly smile. "They didn't have the benefit of a library full of... texts, like we do. If they had, they would have been blamed for all disasters, whether or not they were responsible. You guys would be easy scapegoats, if for no better reason than size. You know, they might have lived further inland, in the woods, or in one of those little valleys we passed surrounded by scrub...?"

"Dells," Holl supplied.

"Right. You can hardly see a hundred yards in any direction. The locals wouldn't bother to punch through that, not with meadows and bluffs already cleared for them by nature."

Holl cheered up. "It doesn't mean they mightn't have been nearby. We can have a look, if there's time."

"Yeah!" the red-haired youth agreed. "According to my legend books, this is the kind of place where wood elves and certain kinds of brownies can be found. They seemed to live just about forever, getting older and more crochety, or wiser, take your pick. If there's anyone still here, we can ask them about what life was like 4000 years back, and give Dr. Crutchley something he can use to spike his competition."

"If they don't give us the spike first. I have a feeling

that after four thousand years, they won't likely be too talkative."

The rest of the week went on like the beginning of the first day. To Keith's relief and joy, he was moved off his patch to a new one at Matthew's left, clearing the grass downslope from the site of the lidded pot's discovery and beginning an excavation there. "We must find that urn, intact, if possible," Dr. Crutchley pleaded. "If the small jar was undamaged, the chances are good that other artifacts nearby will be in a similarly well-preserved condition. I am sure this was a burial, not a cache, and this grass appears to be undisturbed. My textbooks suggest that these amber beads were not personal ornamentation, but the bookkeeping strings of a wealthy trader. I believe some similar pieces are on display in the British Museum."

The group was impressed. Closer personalization of the people they were investigating evoked a deeper involvement on the part of the team. Keith vowed to find the trader's burial site, or die trying.

On Wednesday, Miss Anderson made an announcement on the way to the dig. "Anyone who is taking this tour for credit should be prepared to give me his or her weekly essay on Friday. Verbal is acceptable, through handwritten or typed would be welcome. There are typewriters we may use in the Archaeology Department office. I'll schedule individual appointments this evening." She smiled around at them, her eyes twinkling behind her thick glasses. "That will give you a day to decide whether or not you wish to go to the extra trouble."

"Why not?" Keith said. "It's one fewer course in basket-weaving I've got to take to finish off my college credits."

• Chapter 7 •

Keith bought a handful of postcards and wrote enthusiastic messages to his friends and family as the coach carried them toward the dig early on the second Monday. One for his roommate, Patrick Morgan, one for his parents, one for his resident advisor, Rick, and one for Diane, over which he lingered lovingly, crowding all the detail he could in the small message square. He had saved a special card for Ludmilla Hempert, the old woman with whom he shared the Little Folks' secret. It was a hot, sunny morning, with just a striping of clouds arching overhead. Slung across his back was a straw coolie hat he had found in one of the souvenir shops the week before and had worn every day since burning his ears and neck. The others laughed at him for worrying about a little sun, and turned down his offer of hats for each of them. None of them wore hats, sunscreen, or even sunglasses.

"No sense worrying about what doesn't stay long, or hadn't you noticed?" Edwin asked, deprecatingly. "This isn't the tropics, laddie."

"Americans worry too much about natural things," Charles added.

"Skin cancer is natural?" Keith asked pointedly.

"Oh, come off it. In this soft light? You must be made of wax," Edwin laughed.

"Look at Miss Anderson," Keith defended himself. "She's got a hat on."

"I rarely stay through the afternoon," the teacher said, mildly, adjusting the confection of straw and flowers on her head, "but I concur with Keith. I feel that hot heads make for hasty judgment. But don't take me as an example. I'm prone to sunstroke."

The coach turned off the road and pulled up behind a queue of unfamiliar cars parked at the foot of the hill along the narrow lane. The driver looked quizzically over his shoulder at Miss Anderson. "No place to pull up," he announced.

Miss Anderson studied the line of cars and bobbed her pointed chin vigorously several times. "They must have the press or guests here today," she said. "Reverse out, and take the small road to the left. You can let us off there. I saw another path on the leeward side of the bluff."

"Yes, ma'am," the driver said, nudging up the side of his cap with a forefinger as a sort of salute.

Her students groaned audibly as they saw the path Miss Anderson meant them to climb. It was a muddy, slick trench, almost perpendicular to the road.

"Now, now, you're all younger than I am. You've got the energy to make it up there. Go on, and I'll be up after you in a wee while," the teacher urged them cheerfully.

"Holy Mother, we'll need a ladder," Matthew complained, standing and gazing upward. Narit, who never complained, pushed past him and started to climb the hill, clutching the long grass as handholds. The boys looked at one another, half amused, half outraged, watching her long plait of hair swaying above them.

"I'm not going to let a mere girl clinch the title," Martin said, starting after her. "Hoy, it's not so bad. Come on, lads!"

"The sheep can get up there, and they weigh more than you," Edwin called.

"Smarter, too," Max chimed in, and glanced at the others. "Well, what about you slackers?"

"Yar boo sucks," Matthew answered, goodnaturedly. "Coming, Keith?"

"Right behind you," the American said. "Hey, Holl, do you want to go up ahead of me? That way I can catch you if you slip."

The elf snorted. "More likely it will be so you don't fall on me from above with your big, clumsy body. I'll be fine. After you," he gestured toward the slope, with a slight bow. Keith saluted wryly and jumped for the first foothold, grabbing sheaves of grass with both hands. Holl followed him, less energetically.

"Hey, this is a view we haven't had before," Keith said, stopping on a relatively level part and looking around. The others had disappeared over the crest of the bluff, and their voices faded into distant echoes like the cries of gulls. "More fences. I swear that this is the only piece of ground for ten miles that isn't roped off." Holl, toiling up behind him, grunted his acknowledgement, but didn't look up. Out of the corner of his eye, Keith caught sight of a depression in the grass on the hillside across the road, which had been invisible from the road behind stands of underbrush. He squinted at it from under his hand. It was the shadow thrown by a small hillock. The inverted bowl-shaped mound was almost perfectly round, and it was surrounded by woodland plants that didn't encroach on the smooth grass thereupon. Something in his memory went *ting*! "Hey, look over there, Holl. It's a fairy ring."

"What?" Holl struggled up to stand next to Keith. "Go on with you."

"Well, it's got all the right characteristics. It's a low, rounded grassy mound, surrounded by little purple flowers and mushrooms." He wrinkled his nose, wishing he could see more detail under the shadows of the low trees on the other side. "And I think there's something on the top. Some kind of flower with bell-shaped cups on tall stalks."

"What? What color are they?" Holl demanded, brimming with hope. Could the object of his quest be so close? Right under his nose?

"I'm not sure. But I've got to have a look." Keith skipped down the track, past an inquisitive sheep or two, and ducked under the wire fence on the other side. His long legs took the slope in easy strides.

"Wait for me!" Holl half-slid, half-ran after him.

As soon as he crossed the road, he felt a wave of malignity smack into him, as if he had hit a wall. Ignoring it, he pulled up the loose wire strand and hurried to catch up with Keith. There was something about the hill he didn't like, something sinister. It was the same sort of suffocating wash he had experienced on the jet. Perhaps Keith's fairy ring had its own defenses, a guardian of some kind.

"It's pink!" Keith's voice came from above. "Does pink count, or do your flowers have to be white?"

"White's all I know of," Holl called up to him. "Wait, and I'll come up and see." He reached out to grab a handhold among the plants, and came away with a handful of tiny, red, stinging blisters. "Ow!" A fierce guardian, if these inimical plants were anything to judge by. Hoping he could keep his balance, he wormed his way through the undergrowth.

Keith circled around the low mound, his invisible whiskers erect with excitement. He knew that most things ancient humankind thought of as fairy rings were actually the outward growth from successive generations of some kinds of plants, like mushrooms, but this couldn't be in that category. The hillock was too perfect to be completely natural. Six inches above the ground, there was a barrier encircling it, consisting of a single wire attached at intervals to small, wooden posts, and smaller signs that read "Restricted." The flowers in the dead center of the mound stood defiantly tall amidst the low grass. That grass was strange in itself; the natural growth on the rest of the hillside would be almost knee high except that it lay flat on the ground. Holl appeared through the underbrush.

"Here, look!" Keith called. "Come on over and tell me what you think!"

Holding his stung hand gingerly, Holl came over and peered at the tall flower stalks. As he approached the mound, the feeling of ill-will was stronger, almost overwhelming. His face fell as he got his first good look at Keith's quarry. "It's pink foxglove," he said. "I've seen it before. It wouldn't be of any use at all. That is to say, it has some medicinal uses, but it isn't magical."

"Are you sure?" Keith asked, disappointed. "Well, I'm not going to write the whole experience off as a waste. I've never seen a fairy mound before. How about a closer look?"

"No, thank you!" Holl said, warily. "Keith Doyle, there's something about this hillside, something I feel is wrong here."

"You're just nervous," Keith chided him. He peered up at the inviting green grass, hoped that there weren't dire consequences for intruding. With a quick apology to whatever powers had designed it, he stepped gingerly over the perimeter and up onto the green.

Holl's mouth formed an O of horror. "What are you doing, you silly fellow?"

"It's okay!" Keith assured him. "Nothing's happened to me yet. Hey, the hill feels strange under my feet." He stamped on it, felt the reverberations through his feet. "Almost hollow, like a drum. Come on in, the magic's fine!"

"Out, you widdy! The place is surrounded by 'Restricted' notices. Someone doesn't want you tramping around on it."

Struck by a curious thought, Keith looked up. "Yeah! Do you suppose that means the British government believes in magic? Why else would they rope off a hill? What do they know that they're not telling?"

"Perhaps the grass you're stamping out of existence is an endangered plant," Holl pointed out acidly. "Come down from there."

"Hey, one second. Look at these, Holl," Keith said, pushing aside the foxglove and kneeling down to inspect another bunch of plants. "They're white, and sort of shaped like bells."

"Come away, Keith Doyle," Holl ordered, more urgently. The effort of shouting made him feel faint, and he sat down in the long straw. He felt cold chills, though the sun was shining directly down on them.

"Holl, what's the matter?" Keith asked, leaping down from the mound. The little man didn't answer. His chin sagged onto his chest, and he shuddered. "Holl?"

"There's something powerful in there," Holl whispered, trying to project his voice. A buzzing started in his ears, and grew louder and louder until he could hear nothing else. He knew Keith was shouting at him, but he saw only the young man's mouth move. He couldn't understand the words at all.

Keith reached Holl just as the other started to slump over onto the grass. His skin was red and hot, as if he had been sunburned, but they had hardly been out under the sky long enough to get warm. Keith felt for a heartbeat, and found it: rapid, shallow, and unsteady. What kind of attack was this? Had something evil under the hill reached out at the more sensitive one of the two when Keith broached its barriers? "Holl, can you hear me?" The elf made a sort of choking noise. Keith pried the jaw open with a thumb, and looked down the throat. His breathing didn't appear to be blocked by anything physical. "I have got to get you to a doctor." He settled Holl gently into the long grass with the coolie hat over his face to keep the sun off. "You wait here. I promise I'll be right back."

He ran down the hill and around the bend, looking for the tour bus. It was long gone from its temporary parking place. Desperation dragged him scrambling up the hill to the dig site. He stumbled over his feet at the top of the rise, and practically fell over the project coordinator's table, which lay at the end of the site. "Ah, there you are, Keith," Dr. Crutchley said cheerfully, from the edge of the cut turf where the boys were digging. He waved to the young man to join him. "I wondered what had become of my most energetic worker."

"When do Miss Anderson and the tour bus come back?" Keith asked breathlessly. The rest of the team stared at him.

"Why, not for several hours, at least, son. Haven't you just arrived? We have a lot of work to do."

"Holl, my nephew, he just passed out. I have to get him to a doctor!"

"What's wrong?" Miss Sanders rose from the table, and laid a concerned hand on Keith's arm.

Keith started, wild-eyed. "He's gasping, and his skin is all red. I don't know what caused it.'' He willed himself to calm down. The others hurried over to him.

''Did he swallow something? Is his throat obstructed? Time is crucial if someone is choking!''

''He just said he felt funny, and passed out,'' Keith explained, helplessly, surrounded by the crowd. He felt he had to move, to do something quickly, or burst. He was responsible for Holl. Holl trusted him.

Matthew came up, offering Keith a small rectangular box, and yanked up a slim wire at the top. ''Here, use my portable phone. Dial 999 for the rescue squad. They'll send someone.''

Miss Sanders waved the phone away. ''It would take too long for them to find us. I have a car. We'll take him to the National Health Service clinic. It isn't too far. I'll drive you. You bring him to the side of the road, and I'll pick you up.''

''Thanks, Miss Sanders, I appreciate it,'' Keith wheezed, and dashed back to where he had left Holl lying. The others dropped their pans and followed him.

Keith hurried up to Holl. There was no change. Holl was still in a near-somnolent state, responding only with fluttering eyelids to Keith's voice. The American stuffed the fallen baseball cap in his pocket and picked the young elf up. To his surprise, his friend was very light. ''Well, I guess personality doesn't weigh anything,'' he joked out loud, but his insides were twisting in panic. There seemed to be nothing he could do for Holl. What would he say to the Elf Master, to Maura, if something happened to Holl while in his care? Then reality intruded. The others were right behind him. There was no way for him to hide Holl's most characteristic features. He dropped to his knees, and turned his back on the advancing crowd, laying the elf on the grass, and raising his head gently. ''Holl, can you hear me?'' he pleaded in a rushed undertone. ''I'm going to ask you for the biggest favor ever. I promise, I'd never ask this if it wasn't vital. I mean, a matter of life and death. Please, make your ears look round.'' Holl didn't respond. ''Darn it, do it!'' Keith insisted. ''You've got to hide those points. Otherwise they'll know what you are and we'll never get out of here. You don't want that to happen. If you won't do it for me, think of Maura.''

The Little Folk's breath caught once, and Keith held his breath. Before his eyes, the ears changed, shortening, shrinking, the tips receding into the pinnae as if they were withering.

Keith touched one, curiously. It felt exactly as it looked. Keith felt a little bit of a shock go through him. That was all it took to remove the Little Folks' specialness. Without the ears, Holl was a kid. A short, blondhaired kid. Mentally, Keith kicked himself, having fallen into that trap once before, with embarrassing results, and had promised it wouldn't happen again. It hadn't, but boy, how deceiving looks could be! Keith hoisted the disguised Holl off the grass and bundled him into the back of Miss Sanders's small Fiat Uno as the others crowded around him, clucking their concern.

The doctors at the National Health clinic were firm and kind. "An attack of some kind? Does he have any allergies?" a white-coated man asked, writing down facts on a history sheet. Holl's discarded cap and Keith's coolie hat lay on a table behind them.

"I don't know," Keith answered, helplessly. "He eats everything."

"How old is he?" The doctor checked the sheet Keith had just filled in. "Fourteen. Hm, small for his age, isn't he? Looks about the same age as my nephew, eleven or twelve." The doctor took Holl's chin in his hand and moved it from side to side.

"Well, it's not really unusual," Keith said, hurriedly, wondering if Holl had a weird blood type or some other indicator showing that he wasn't exactly human. "Not in his family. I mean, his side of our family. My sister's in-laws. They tend to be short. What's all that swelling, doctor?" He pointed to the reddening on Holl's cheek.

"That looks rather nasty, but it's only nettle rash. As for the burning, I'll want to keep him here for observation a few days." The doctor clucked. "Look, you're all over nettles yourself, lad. Your skin must be burning you. You're brave to ignore your own hurts to look after the boy. Sit down, and let the nurse put a deadening cream on it."

Obediently, Keith sat down, and let them fuss over him. He was too bound up in guilt to notice any stinging, but it started to itch immediately as soon as the doctor mentioned it. He felt guilty for not having gotten off the mound when Holl told him to. Holl was probably right, that whatever possessed that mound got upset about trespassers. He might have been responsible for the attack Holl had suffered. But how could he tell the doctor about a speculation like that? He scratched at the inflammation, which only made it feel worse.

Keith felt as if he had betrayed a trust. He had never known one of the Little Folk to be ill before. He sat and stared at Holl, head lolling to one side on the examining table, and willed him with all his heart to get well. He knew Holl had never wanted to leave Hollow Tree Farm. Traveling shook him. He even disliked car trips. He was an old homebody, but he had volunteered to make the trip, insisted on it, because he trusted Keith to look after him. It was like the blind leading the blind, really, because neither of them was all that worldly. Enoch was the one who was interested in going out and seeing the world. Keith kept wondering what had hit them on the hillside. Could it be a spell that someone put on the hill before, as Puck of Pook's Hill said, all of the *sidhe* left England? Or was it something more mundane and sinister?

"You can go now, Mr. Doyle. You can visit your nephew later, when we've had a chance to observe him. We have the telephone number, and we will call you when we know anything." The nurse escorted him firmly to the door and into the reception room. Keith tried vainly to keep Holl in sight until she closed the examining room door on him.

• Chapter 8 •

"O'Day was spotted cavorting on top of that government installation, sir, just like he knew it was there. So much for all that pretty camouflage, with the horticulture and all. The hidden cameras are on totally silent swivels. They snapped his photo, and the johnnies in security were on to us in a flash. They've got copies of all our advisories. And then the kid had some kind of attack. Instead of intercepting them, I followed them to the Health Service. I've been keeping a close lookout ever since, in case he tried anything suspicious. He might be here to bribe one of our men to find out what's under there." Michaels squirmed uncomfortably in the office chair. The seats in the Chief's office were not meant to encourage long stays. The room was nondescript and cluttered, but probably chocked to the rafters with listening and recording equipment behind the walls. "Not that I know myself. We're on the same side, or so I thought," Michaels said resentfully. "O'Day seems so normal, sir, and genuinely concerned about the kid."

"Even spies have relatives, Michaels," the Chief reminded him. "That's how the Rooskies keep their operatives' loyalty. Have you any hard information on them?"

"Aye, sir. He's travelling on an American passport under the name of Keith Doyle," Michaels reported. "I've got the numbers out of the medical history the clinic took. It's a clean one, fairly new, with a few trips on it, legitimate, to Canada. The 'boy' is going as a Doyle, too. By the report from the medico, the lad was genuinely ill. Except for some nettle rash on his hand and face, he can't figure out quite what was wrong with him. Is there a loose nuclear source at that site, chief? He had what looked to me like mild radiation sickness: red, burned skin and fever, lightheadedness."

"The sources say no," the Chief said, puzzled. "Nothing up there but good old electricity. I'll have it checked out. The boffins up there are so hush-hush on what they're doing. I'm sure they don't know themselves. I think perhaps our smugglers might be doing us a service after all, pointing that out for us. And then, again, it could just be summer allergies. I've got a bit of sniffles from that damned pollen myself."

"What is going on up there, Chief? It must be pretty choice, if the right hand, that's us, doesn't know what the left's up to."

"I haven't the least idea," his senior said, peevishly. "The last time they had a site that was so hands off, it was under contract to one of the American cola companies. These Doyles of yours may be doing nothing but a spot of industrial spying, which is no business of ours."

"They do seem like a pair of personable chaps."

"So were Mungojerrie and Rumpelteazer," the Chief pointed out, sternly. "A couple of charming thieves. Well, now we've got them on a genuine charge of criminal trespass, if we need to swear out a warrant for a quick pickup. Stay close and keep an eye on them. They've obviously been in no hurry up 'til now. They may be preparing to make their move. And when they do . . ."

Michaels rose, decisively. It was more comfortable to stand. "I'll lower the net on them smartly, sir. Count on it."

* * *

Holl, languishing in a bed in the corner of a hospital ward, stared at the white walls and the blank, curtained windows. He had never felt so lonely in his life. There were others in the beds around the room of the ward, Big children, all his own size or larger, but clearly younger than he and frightened, and none of them with a thought for anyone else. He had to admit that he was frightened, too. He couldn't recall clearly what had happened to bring him here. He had already examined his ear-tips, and discovered that they were round, instead of pointed as they were normally. At first he thought it was Keith Doyle's doing, but a hazy memory reminded him he had done it himself at the Big One's urging.

His skin under the white cotton robe was tender. His arms were slightly puffy, as they had been once when he had gotten sun poisoning. That was before Catra, the archivist, had issued an advisory about sunscreens and vitamin B5. Then he remembered the burning and choking feeling he had suffered on the hillside. The absence of pain was a chilling void.

"Good morning, Holl," caroled a woman in a stiff-starched white dress. "Have a good sleep?" Her warm voice had a burr in it, which was the friendliest thing he had found in this strange place so far.

"Yes, ma'am," he said, looking up at her. "How long have I been here?"

She took his wrist in a businesslike grip and consulted the watch on her other arm. "You were admitted in the afternoon the day before yesterday. You've slept the clock 'round, and half again. I'm surprised the usual tumultuous clamour of this ward didn't rouse you at dawn. Pulse normal, but you've still got a nasty burn. You'll be staying with us at least one more day, for observation."

"Two days? Does K . . . does my uncle know I'm here?" Holl asked, pushing himself upright. The nurse took the pillows from behind him, plumped and replaced them, settling him back against the head of the bed.

"Good Lord, yes. He's probably out in the corridor now. We've had to chase him out at the end of visiting hours already. I'll send him in just as soon as you have had breakfast."

As soon as the cart containing the dirty trays was wheeled out through the swinging doors, Keith slipped into the ward. He had an armful of books, which he shifted to one elbow to wave. "Hi! How are you feeling?" he asked in a low voice, as he sat down on a chair beside the hospital bed. He settled his burden on the floor underneath his seat.

"Fine, I think. Well enough, though I can't remember anything that happened after I climbed up the hill. Must I stay here?" he asked plaintively.

"You're still pretty red. Do you know what happened to you?" Keith asked, studying his face closely.

"No."

"Then I think you ought to stay, just in case." Keith explained the events of Holl's collapse, and ended by saying, "I would rather you were where they can treat a convulsion instead of worrying if you're going to have an attack in the middle of nowhere. When they say you're all right, then you can get out of here. It shouldn't be more than another day."

"I don't like the hospitality of strangers," Holl said darkly. "Most especially strange Big Folk."

Keith sighed. "I know, but they're professional medical specialists. I'm just your ordinary cub scout who had CPR training once in swim class. Come on, humor me. How would I explain to the Master if I came back with you on a stretcher? He'd probably make me sit in a corner and write five-page essays on health care for the rest of my life."

Holl threw up his hands. "Very well, I submit. I'll stay until they release me. But with a protest."

"Fine. They have vaccines for that sort of thing. I brought you a few things to make your incarceration more interesting." From under his chair, Keith retrieved a small hardcover book, which he gave to Holl. "This book will eventually be a Doyle family heirloom. My cousin gave it to me when I was six and home with chicken pox. My mother put it in my suitcase at the last minute as a sort of traveling talisman. I think you should keep it with you while you're here."

"How to Go About Laying An Egg?" There was a cartoon drawing of a white chicken on the paper dustjacket.

"Full of good advice," Keith insisted, airily. "Very Zen."

Holl looked from it into Keith's twinkling eyes and fell back on his pillows laughing. "I like your family, Keith Doyle. They all seem to be a little mad, but in a good way."

Next, Keith handed him a yellow paper envelope. "Here. More surprises. I brought you the pictures I took at the farm, during the going-away party your folk gave me. I mean, us.

Look, here's Maura. And there's the Master in the corner with his wife."

"See him glare," Holl noted with amusement. "He didn't care for that."

"Told me to go away and play," Keith averred with satisfaction. "Well, he wouldn't pose, so how else was I going to get a picture? There's Enoch and Marcy, and here's Dola, pretending to be a movie star. She's going to be a knockout when she grows up. What is she, ten?"

"Just about," Holl said, taking the photograph from Keith and adding it to the stack.

"Here's your baby sister. The next picture was nothing but a big blob because she put her hand in the lens. Almost gave me a black eye."

Holl laughed, but then the laughter constricted into gasping breaths. Keith, still seeming jolly on the outside to hide the worry on the inside, sprang up to press the bell for the nurse. Holl forestalled him with a wave.

"No, leave her be. I'll be all right. I'm just out of energy. So strange. There was some truly mighty force on that hillside, but whether it was natural or not I can't tell." He sat upright again, and with Keith's assistance replaced the pillows propping him up. "Do you know, I haven't been this ill since I was a tot. That was in the days when the steam tunnels were still exposed near our home. We had to be so quiet all of the time. My mother sat by me, soothing and silencing." He gave Keith a wordless look full of woe.

Keith smiled sympathetically, and moved from the chair to the edge of the narrow bed. "You want your mom. I know how you feel."

Shamefaced, Holl nodded. "I guess I'm harkening back to my childhood. I've only just realized that I can't sense any of my Folk this far away. I *know* they're there, so I understand the link's still good, but I can't differentiate between them, if you see what I mean. There's a tiny dot on the horizon, and I know it's them. I didn't mind it while I was well, but being feverish leaves me gloomy and sorry for myself."

Grinning, Keith passed his hands in the air a few times like a conjuror and produced a small, narrow, black box from his jacket pocket. "The pictures and books weren't all I brought. Would it help if you could talk to them?"

Holl eyed it warily. "What's that?"

"Matthew's portable phone. He said you could keep it here until you're sprung. I think you was framed," Keith went on, in his bargain-basement imitation of Humphrey Bogart. "But we'll have you outta here and playing the violin again in no time. Dial zero one zero, then one, then your area code and number." He handed the small phone to Holl. Holl dialed.

There was an audible click from the receiver, and the distant sound of ringing, then another click. A shrill voice, audible even to Keith, demanded "What is it?"

"Keva," Holl explained, his hand over the mouthpiece. "She's never learned just to say 'hello,' as the etiquette manual suggests." Keith grinned. Keva was a law unto herself regarding manners, or anything else. Holl uncovered the receiver. "Keva, this is Holl speaking. Can you ask our mother if she'll come to the phone?"

There was a long wait, then Keith could hear the overtones of a more gentle voice. Holl's mother, Calla, was a tiny woman, small even for the Little Folk, with a very young face under a wave of soft, silver hair. Keith guessed that she was a bare eighteen or twenty years older than her outspoken daughter. That was unusual enough. Normally, the Folk only thought of getting married in their fifties and sixties. Some never did. Babies came much later on. At forty-one, Holl was pushing it a little even to be thinking of engagement.

"Mother? Yes. I know, I'm far away, and the link is weak. You sound as clear as if you're standing here. A miracle, these small machines." Holl dropped from English into the Little Folk language, a tongue Keith was becoming used to hearing, though he couldn't understand it.

It was boring to listen to a conversation in a foreign language. Keith tried to make sense out of the tone, instead. At first, Holl seemed to be merely exchanging news with his mother. After a while, though, the subject changed, and Holl's voice became angry, then thick. Something his mother was telling him bothered him very much, nearly choking him. Keith felt he was intruding on something private, and got up to leave, but Holl waved him to stay. After a while, the conversation must have turned to more cheerful topics, which he was willing to share with Keith.

Holl translated a phrase from time to time, moving the receiver aside. "The she-cat has had kittens, Mother says. There are six of them. The well has been cleared out at last, and is flowing so generously it threatens to burst the old pipes. Deliveries are keeping apace of orders, and Ms. Voordman has sent word through Diane that if you are really in Scotland, you must send her a postcard."

"That sounds like an order," Keith joked, snapping off a salute.

More words were exchanged in the Little Folks' language. "Dola wouldn't look askance at a small present, but is too well brought up to ask," Holl told him, with a wry grin.

"Now, that's a hint," Keith acknowledged, "but it carries the same weight as an order."

"I'll tell her. And many photographs of the strange places we visit would be welcome." More talk. Holl's voice fell to soft, nearly inaudible tones. Keith felt uncomfortable, but didn't leave because Holl wanted him to stay.

To break the tension, Keith opened a book of his own, *Popular Tales of the West Highlands,* and read for a while, trying to block out the conversation. He became engrossed in J.F. Campbell's description of the *bodach* of Jura and other tales of magic. Those sounded friendly. He wished he could find one of those to interview. Interesting also how the stories coincided so neatly with other books he had read.

Thoughtfully, Holl took the phone away from his ear and pushed the off button. Keith closed his book on one finger. Holl looked depressed, but he mustered a grateful smile.

"Thank you," he said. "That helped. There's . . . a lot going on at home. Express my gratitude to Matthew, and let me know what it costs for the call."

Keith quickly judged that Holl didn't want to talk about his news until he had had time to digest it, and cast about swiftly for another topic of conversation. "So, when you get out of here, should we go and find whatever it was I offended and apologize to them?"

"I wouldn't if I were you," Holl warned him, momentarily distracted by Keith's endless interest in his hobby, though his eyes kept their troubled look. "Most of the hidden ones want to stay hidden, without your great feet tramping all over their privacy."

"Well, we were always brought up to think that Americans abroad should act as good will ambassadors wherever they went. Don't you want to be the ambassador for your people wherever you go?"

"No," Holl answered, keeping the banter going, but without much spirit. "Especially not in your company; they'd probably declare eternal war on my folk once they'd met you."

Keith waved away the suggestion that his presence could cause an interspecies feud. "They'd get used to me. I've never asked, you know, but do *you* believe in sprites and fairies and things like that, Holl? I mean, what I'm looking for could be fantasy to your folk, as much as it is to mine."

"I don't know. I've never made a study of it. But I'm here. And since the legend writers group my Folk in with them, I suppose there might be others out there. You're counting on it, aren't you?"

Keith considered the question. "I'm looking for whatever is out there, but naturally, I'd prefer them to be my kind of Little People, who consort with dragons and do magic." He pointed out a passage on one of the pages. "This J.F. Campbell compares legends of the Fair Folk with actual people he met in Lapland. The way he describes them, they could walk under his outstretched arm with their tall hats on without bending over, but never touch him." Keith measured his friend with an eye. "Just about the right size. Do you think you're descended from Laplanders, Holl?"

Holl snorted. "I don't know where my people are from, if not from the old place we're trying to find. So far as I know they've always been there. All my father would say was that it was terrible when they left it, without much helpful detail. We didn't spring out of the ground, so I expect we came from somewhere. You'll need to ask one of the old ones. Why?"

There was a long pause. Keith's eyes twinkled. "I read this feature article about a man in Lapland who everybody thinks is Santa Claus," he offered, impishly. He grinned at the expression on Holl's face, who realized he'd been led into a trap. "Even the adults who meet him think so."

"Aargh! Be off with you before I have a relapse!" Holl seized his pillow and yanked it over his face. Keith shut his book, and stood up to go.

"Oh, by the way," he said casually, "I found the body. It was in a funeral urn, about five feet down the pike from where Matthew dug up the lidded pot. He's dead all right. It was moider. No doubt about it. Moider. Case closed, shweetheart." Running his finger along the brim of an imaginary fedora, Keith winked at Holl and swaggered out the swinging door.

Holl pushed the pillow back into place behind his head, and settled back with a sigh. "Thank you, Keith Doyle," he said softly. "You're a host and a cure in yourself. I have a lot to think about now."

The guard at the quadrangle gate had become used to seeing Michaels walking in and out of the University grounds. Perhaps the guard thought the old boy in the tweed suit was a visiting doctor. The way the National Health chopped and changed, he could have brought in a host of agents and never been questioned.

Surveillance on the portable phone link the blond lad had been using revealed one interesting fact: the boy's first language was not English. The lingo boffins hadn't pinned down the root language yet, but it sounded halfway between Icelandic and Balkan. Were other powers involved in O'Day's latest pickup? Michaels hoped the answers lay in Inverness, the tour's next stop.

• Chapter 9 •

"This is a great place," Keith exclaimed, all but hanging out the coach window to get a good look at Inverness, and take a picture for the record. Where Glasgow was gray granite and yellow sandstone, Inverness was red sandstone and black iron. He had shot three rolls of film of new scenery in the last two hours alone. "That's weird. This castle looks almost brand new. It's almost exactly the same color as cream-of-tomato soup."

"I'm sure that's precisely how they put it in the travel brochures," Martin quipped sarcastically, from two seats behind Keith. "'Our national treasures and how they compare with canned goods.'"

Inverness was hilly, set along the deeply cut bed of the river. With passersby wearing shirtsleeves and light dresses, it was hard to believe that the city lay 200 miles further north than

Glasgow. The storefronts were trim and clean, and painted hoardings disguised construction sites. Flowerpots made a colorful contrast to the wrought iron lightpoles from which they depended. From pegs in the walls around some of the shops, lengths of tweed and woven shawls flapped gently in the breeze like plaid pennants. Above the buildings in every direction, distant mountains—the snow topping their peaks a shock in July—arched broad, green backs to the sun and clear blue sky.

Holl leaned against the window across the aisle, and soaked up the new sights. He was feeling much better, and after a few days of forced inactivity, was ready to do some exploring. The others had been solicitous of him, cheering him up with stories of the dig. Matthew had been especially kind. He waved away the idea that Holl should pay him back for the telephone call home. "It was necessary medicine," he assured Holl, "and we'd never stint you that."

The camaraderie of the little group, the unquestioning acceptance of Big Folk toward complete strangers touched Holl. Beside his own village, the Big students in the Master's course at Midwestern had been his only real outside contact. The ancient Conservative faction within the village held that the seeming friendliness of Big Folk was a sham. He was pleased to be bringing back to them proof that that was not so.

What did not delight him was the memory of the mysterious attack he had suffered on the hillside. If this was what happened to trespassers on charmed soil, he planned to keep Keith off any fairy mounds in the future. Thank heavens that nothing like this existed in Illinois. On the other hand, at home he would have had the experience of one of the old ones to hand, and there probably would never have been such a trap sprung from which he would need rescuing.

Though he was at pains to conceal it from Keith, he was troubled, and had been ever since he had called home. There was gossip going around the farm about Maura and Gerol, another male a few years older than Holl. They were spending a lot of time together, and the attraction seemed to be both obvious and mutual. She hadn't said anything to Calla to the effect that her 'understanding' with Holl was off, but that was the way many of their clan read it. Holl was very hurt. He had taken on this quest so he would have the right to ask her to marry him when he returned, following all the traditional forms. Apparently, she had taken his departure as a rejection.

The impulse returned again and again that he should go home immediately, abandon the search for the white bellflowers. But did he give up his quest, thereby abrogating his right to be headman of the village one day? That was never an ambition he had intended for himself. It was merely what others had always expected of him. They were counting on him. If he went home now, there would be others who would lack the bellflowers for their weddings, and he felt somewhat guilty about that, but he didn't want to be outmatched by a rival when he couldn't be there to defend his suit. The Conservatives would attack him as a culture-killing Progressive, sucking up to Big ways, but he wondered if he cared about that if he lost Maura. Still, the Elf Master had made it a condition of his proposal to find the flowers before he could marry Maura. Holl wished he had taken her aside and told her his intentions before he had left, but that wasn't the way the Little Folk did things. Until her parents said he had their permission, he had to hold his tongue.

There wasn't so much bad about the Big Folks' life. Would he wed instead after their fashion, making up their own ceremonies when it suited them and when convention couldn't apply. They seemed to get along fine. And yet, had Maura rejected the old ways? Was she choosing her own mate over her long-time suitor in defiance of tradition? He wished he could talk to Keith about his worries, but he wanted to think it through further first. It was important not to let the situation at home drag down his spirits.

"We are now passing over the River Ness," Miss Anderson put in, as the coach drove over an iron bridge. The others squinted to see through sunshine that was brilliantly reflected off the flowing water. Small, black-headed gulls swooped around the coach.

"Have they ever decided what it is that so many people report seeing in the Loch?" Holl inquired, and wondered why everyone else laughed.

"Do you mean Nessie?" Miss Anderson asked brightly. "No, there are ten times as many theories as there are reported sightings. You'll have a chance to look for yourselves. You're on your own for today, ladies and gentlemen. Dr. Stroud would prefer that we start with him Tuesday. He wants only his team on site this afternoon. I believe they are at a delicate stage of the proceedings. I am sure you wouldn't want to interfere."

There was a chorus of amiable protest. "We're more like day

trippers to the profs," Edwin said, speaking for them all. "If they're doing something serious, we won't get in the way."

"Somewhat inelegantly put," Mrs. Green added, smiling over her shoulder at the tall, young man, "but essentially what I would have said."

"Those of you taking this for credit are not excused from your essays, though," the tour director warned. "But allow me to suggest a topic you might explore. Picture yourself as far forward in the future as we are now to our Bronze age subjects. What would you be likely to find left of Inverness in the 60th century?

"I think you will find Inverness worth your exploration. I have a schedule of day tours available, if anyone would care to inspect it, and there are more to be had from the Tourist Information Center. We'll be staying in a guest house this time, instead of a residence hall. Evening meals will be provided for you as well as breakfast. If you want to make your own arrangements for supper, please let the owner know early in the day."

It was downhill from their lodgings to the city center, via a long flight of narrow stone steps and a broader, sharply turning staircase. From the head of the twisting steps, they found they were on a level with the red stone castle, which gave them a good view to the east. Most of the section of Inverness in which they were staying appeared to be laid out along a similar plan to provide access to the higher neighborhoods. Down on High Street, Keith caught sight of endless stairs reaching up and back into the shadows between buildings.

As in Glasgow, the traffic was fast, with taxis taking death-dealing turns around corners under the noses of wary pedestrians. Except for the perils of traffic, Inverness was easy to get around in. Keith found it cheerful and clean. The group stopped for lunch in a small, family-style restaurant by the side of the River Ness, just out of the shadow of the main bridge spanning it. The Hearty Trencherman boasted a sign showing a plump, happy diner beaming over a huge plate and brandishing a knife and fork.

Matthew made a face at the sign. "Ooh, I hate campy adverts."

"Let's call it the Trench, for short," Martin suggested, as they pushed inside. "Look at the high banks of the river, surrounding us. We're in the bottom of a pit."

"Well, if you look at it that way, anything good you get here'll be a nice surprise," Keith reasoned. He sat down and accepted a menu from the female server standing beside their table. "Hi, beautiful. What's good here, besides the service?"

The waitress tossed a light-brown ponytail and dimpled prettily. "Nearly anything," she said. "The salmon's off, but all the rest is ready."

Keith waggled his eyebrows at her outrageously, collecting a blush. "So'm I."

"Keith Doyle!" Holl exclaimed, shocked. "What would Diane say?"

"Diane?" Keith, surprised, turned innocent, hazel eyes on him. "What's this got to do with her? We're just having a conversation. It doesn't mean anything." He promptly went back to flirting, and Holl turned a hot red in embarrassment. The waitress seemed to take the whole business in stride, all the time noting down orders.

The menu was predictable, including the ubiquitous "and peas," but the food was well-prepared. The young men leaned back from their empty plates with satisfaction, waiting for the bill. Keith peered out of the plate glass window at the river.

"This would be a good place to watch the sun set."

"Aye," said Matthew. "But we're just into Midsummer, and far enough north that the sun nearly never sets."

"I know," said Charles, "we'll go and have a sit down in the nearest local, and when the publican cries closing time at eleven, we'll know it's sunset."

The others agreed it was a good plan. They paid the bill and walked out into the sunlight. At the first sign of a likely pub, most of the young men turned in. "Aren't you coming in with us?" Max asked Keith, holding open the door.

"Nope," Keith replied, grinning. "We're going to take a tour down to the Loch and look for the monster."

"Oh. Happy fishing," Edwin said sarcastically.

"See you later," Keith promised. "I'll look for you guys here around sunset."

Directed by Miss Anderson to look for the signs with the small, script "i," Keith located the Tourist Information Center on a street perpendicular to the main thoroughfare not far from the Trench. The TICs provided numerous services for travelers, including directions, event schedules, lodging arrangements, maps, and an assembly point for tours.

"The next one sets out in twenty minutes," the woman in the glass-fronted booth told Keith. "You can pay for your tickets now or on the coach."

With time to kill, Keith studied the wall map of the city, while Holl perused displays of handcrafted knick-knacks for sale in the front of the center. Keith compared the scale from the city to Loch Ness, the long, narrow stretch of water angling southwest from the river which bisected Inverness. It was a curious shape, long and narrow like a spear.

"Keith Doyle?" Holl's voice interrupted his reverie. "Can you come here for a minute?"

Holl gestured him quietly to a small display case which contained ceramic pieces. Behind a tiny card which said "Nessie" were ranged a half dozen separate pieces: a head, four semicircular loops with ridges over the back, and a tiny squib of a pointed tail, which made it appear as if the monster was swimming with half its length submerged in the table. "Is that what it looks like?"

"That's what most of the people who have seen her say," Keith said. "They don't have any concrete proof, of course. Some of the pictures they've got suggest that descendents of plesiosaurs are living in the Loch." Holl's eyes went wide. "The legends also say she might be a selkie, which is a sort of magical, seagoing horse. Does that look like a horse to you, or even a plesiosaur?"

"Don't you go talking down aur Nessie," the clerk chided them playfully from the other side of the shop. "We're fond of her in these parts."

Keith clapped his spread fingertips to his chest. "Me? I believe in her," he assured the clerk, earnestly. "I know of stranger things in real life. But it's not like she's ever appeared on the evening news."

"There are those who believe and those who doubt," the clerk said offhandedly. "But you'll prove it to yourself at the Official Loch Ness Monster Exhibition. Queue up for the coach just outside the door."

The offical monster exhibition was in Drumnadrochit, several miles southwest of Inverness. The guide doing the presentation offered them walls filled with blurred photographs and written eyewitness accounts as proof of the monster's existence. The multimedia program was more interesting, and dropped delicious hints that investigating scientists were on the edge of making an announcement as to Nessie's species and location. They showed the audience films taken by spotters, who had accidentally caught sight of the mysterious denizen of the Loch. After glancing at the displays, which held far less scientific theory than they had hoped, Keith and Holl made their way through the turnstile to the book and gift shop.

"Now here's something that looks like home," Holl said, spreading his arms out to the walls of books.

Outside the Exhibition hall was a pond, in which a twenty-foot concrete dinosaur model was posed swimming. "It's a plesiosaur, all right," Holl agreed. "But is that really what's in the Loch?"

"No one really knows," Keith said, thoughtfully. "But I might come back some day and try to find out."

The tour's next stop was the ruin of Urquhart Castle, a fabulous ruin on the west side of the Loch. Keith slapped a new roll of film into his camera, and crawled all over the stones taking pictures. Holl followed him more sedately, stopping to inspect the layout and read the small signs describing what used to lie in each part of the castle.

"Keith, let me take one picture of you," Holl suggested, when he stopped to reload. "That way, you'll have at least one piece of proof you were here along with your camera, instead of it having a nice vacation on its own."

"Great idea," Keith said. "Let's go back up the road so you can get most of the castle into the frame with me." Together, they trotted over the rise and up toward the road.

They gazed appreciatively around them at the scenery outside of the castle grounds. In the thick grass on the roadside, small blossoms of pink and yellow grew abundantly. Urquhart Castle was downhill from the road, so they had to walk some distance from the grounds to where they could see it again.

"I have to have you take a picture so it looks like I'm holding the castle on the palm of my hand, or my father'll be disappointed," Keith explained. "It's an old family tradition."

"Ah," Holl acknowledged, amused. "How about seeming to pick it up between your thumb and forefinger? It's already a ruin. You can do it no more damage."

"Ha, ha," Keith said. He posed, and Holl snapped the picture.

"How are you feeling now? It's only been about three days

since you got out of bed again. I haven't given up on trying to find your flowers for you," Keith said, solicitously.

"I'm well enough," Holl replied. "I'd prefer that you didn't go charging up fairy mounds and the like again."

"Well, if I see one, I'll go up it myself, with you out at a safe distance," Keith insisted, "in case there's something mean that just doesn't like other magical folk. I guess I'm immune to whatever hit you in the first site, so you point, and I'll fetch. Okay?"

"Okay. So where's your monster?" Holl asked, teasingly, gesturing with a sweep of his arm. "Now that we have seen the amazingly overpainted model, we know what to look for."

"I've got the bait right here," Keith said, pulling half a cheese sandwich out of his pocket and unwrapping it. "Just you wait. She loves cheese. Here, Nessie, Nessie, Nessie," he called, hurling a corner of it out over the loch. A seagull came out of midair and snagged the scrap of food. "Whoops. Took my bait. I'll have to try again."

Holl grinned sheepishly. "Oh, you can't be serious, Keith Doyle."

"Never more than half," Keith assured him, unquenchably, breaking off a piece of the sandwich and giving it to Holl. "But wouldn't they be amazed if it worked?"

"You'll never die of hypertension, that's certain," Holl said. "Your frivolity is quite an act. You give an amazing imitation of grasshopper, Keith Doyle, but I have always suspected you of being mostly ant."

They threw crumbs into the loch for a while, in no hurry to go back to the castle and rejoin the tour.

"I wish I could drive a car over here," Keith said wistfully, watching the spare traffic race past the lay-by in which they were standing. "If we're going to have a lot of time to kill, I want to get out and see some more of the countryside. It's beautiful here."

"It is," Holl agreed, taking a deep breath of the fragrant air. "I wish I could show some of the others more of the world. They wouldn't be so fearful of going out into it once in a while."

Keith made a noise that sounded sympathetic and derisive at the same time. "It could be ninety-nine percent wonderful, and they'd hate it because of one percent of things that would be off kilter."

"You've shown more than one percent of going wrong, and they still accept you," Holl pointed out.

"By the way, I hope you notice I've been good, not trying out you-know-what in front of other people," Keith said defensively.

"And for which I'm grateful. Such behavior deserves reward, is that your thought?" Holl asked shrewdly. "Never mind. It's all right with me. Since Enoch isn't here to continue your education, I'll give you the next lesson, I've wanted a quiet moment to listen for home. You may as well learn something about that."

"What do you mean?" Keith asked eagerly, sitting down on a low boulder at the edge of the road and pulling his knees up. He glanced around. Behind him, it was almost a sheer drop to the Loch. He scooted forward, keeping as much of the rock between him and the precipice as he could. Holl sat on a rock next to him.

"Concentrate and sit quietly, and think in the direction that the Folk are," Holl instructed him, closing his own eyes. "Send your knowledge toward them. See them."

"With your third eye?" Keith inquired, screwing his eyes shut.

"No, you innocent," Holl said, rapping him on the head with his knuckles. "With your heart. Think of the ones dearest to you to make the best link."

"Well, you're my best friend and the one I know best. Hmm. I don't think I can use the Master as a focus. I think he'd disapprove."

"I'm sure you're right," Holl agreed. "How about Maura? You know her well."

Keith thought for a second, looking uneasy. He cracked one eye and peered at his friend. "Maybe not. I wouldn't be able to concentrate on her with you here."

"Eh?"

"Well, it's like horning in on your date," he explained lamely. "I may flirt, but I don't poach."

Holl snorted. "You're amazing, Keith Doyle. I wish everyone had your scruples. How about Dola? She's fond of you."

"Okay. I'll give it a try." Keith concentrated, letting his body relax. He knew that thousands of miles to the southwest, sort of along the axis of the Great Glen, across the ocean in America, lay the village. He thought for a moment that he could see an infinitesimal golden spark on the horizon that felt right, in the correct direction. "I think I've got—what did you call it, a link? But there's something like radio interference in the way. I'm not sensing anybody particular. Of course, I haven't got tons of magical energy to use."

"All you need is practice, widdy, not tons." Holl closed his eyes again and let his muscles go slack. After a few minutes, he sighed. "You're right," he said, disappointed. "We're so far away I can't touch them properly. There's too much of the world between us. Something's in the way."

"Ireland," said Keith wisely. "Ireland's that way, too." They sat for a moment, quietly concentrating. Holl's forehead was drawn down and troubled.

After a long silence, Keith spoke up. "That sounded significant, the part about scruples," he put in gently. "That reminded me: when you were talking to your mother, you sounded angry. I didn't know what was up."

Holl clicked his tongue. "It was rude of us to speak in a different dialect in front of you."

"Oh, don't worry about that. I felt like a jerk eavesdropping on you anyway. Something I can help with?" When Holl hesitated, he insisted. "Go on, you can confide in me. All discussions become privileged information here at Uncle Keith's Lonelyhearts Club, Fishmarket and Filling Station." He presented earnest, hazel eyes for Holl's inspection.

Holl turned his head away, and looked out over the loch. "Keith Doyle, do you feel right, going out drinking every night with the others?"

"Well, when in Rome, do as the Romans do. You notice I'm not trying to match them drink for drink, after all. It's the way they socialize over here. The pub really is a great invention. I wonder why nobody has ever tried to import them to the U.S." Keith made a mental note to find out more about pubs.

"What about flirting with the waitresses?" Holl pressed.

"Oh, ho, is that what's bothering you?" Keith demanded. "It's nothing serious. If it bothered her, I wouldn't do it, but I'm just being friendly. Why?"

"She might have an intended of her own," Holl said significantly.

"If she didn't want me to joke around with her, I assume she'd tell me to flake off," Keith said, confidently. "Just because I'm a customer doesn't give me any special rights to move in on her."

"Oh. So you'd expect her to send you on your way, if she had someone of her own."

"Usually." Keith threw another crumb into the loch and waited. Holl was silent for a while, then sighed.

"It would seem that I have a rival," Holl said at last. "No sooner did I leave the farm than the village is full of talk about Maura spending all her time walking or sitting with Gerol. You know him?"

Keith pictured a strongly built, broad-shouldered elf with a moustache and a sweep of black hair across his forehead who specialized in heavy construction. "Yeah. Nice guy. Reminds me of a picture of Ernest Hemingway. He's Bracey's brother, isn't he?"

"That's right. I thought he was a friend of ours, but now, what can I think? What can I think of Maura? We had an understanding, or so I believed."

"Have you talked to Maura?" Keith pressed.

"No. It isn't something which I can talk about on the telephone, only face to face. I'm not even supposed to bring up the subject of marriage without the Master's approval. I should go home. Shouldn't I?" Holl looked up helplessly into Keith's face.

"I can't make that decision for you," Keith said, sympathetically but firmly. "I'm on your side, you know. If you want to go home, I'll even drive you to the airport, but you have got to be the one to tell me what you want to do." There was a long pause. "Well?"

"Well," Holl stared mournfully at the waters of the Loch. "I'll stay for now," he said, unsure of his own resolve. "But why isn't she sending him on his way?" Holl burst out.

"Maybe she's lonely," Keith said. "Did you take her aside and tell her why you were going away?"

"No. If I failed, I didn't want too many hopes raised and dashed."

"Did you ask her not to date anyone while you were gone?"

"No. I would never have thought I had to," Holl said, sadly. "It's been an understanding between us, all our lives."

"In my vast and far-reaching experience," Keith said in a ponderous voice that made Holl smile even in his misery, "assumption is the mother of all disappointments. I've heard it phrased differently, but that one'll do for now." That made Holl look even more depressed. "Look, if you've had an understanding all these years, why should she throw it over now? You love her, right?"

"Right," Holl said.

"She loves you, right?"

"Well, I've always thought so."

"Right?"

"Right," Holl acknowledged, listlessly.

"So what's the problem? You can't do anything from here. Except trust her."

"I'll stay," Holl said, more certainly.

"Good," Keith cheered. He heard voices, and leaned over the edge of the bank. A couple of men were sitting on the footpath below them, fishing in the loch. Their creels sat beside them, as did a nearly empty bottle of Scotch and a couple of lunchboxes.

"Hey, Holl, how'd you like to help me with magic practice?"

Holl looked out across the vast expanse of water, and returned a questioning gaze to Keith. "What, a finding? A calling?"

"Nope," Keith replied, with glee. He parted the tall grass with a quiet hand, and showed Holl the two men quietly fishing. "A forming. On the surface of the water. I don't have enough *oomph* to do it myself."

"It wouldn't last long," Holl warned, skeptically, but his own eyes were twinkling. He was getting caught up in the idea in spite of himself. "It's flowing fairly fast."

"That's okay," Keith assured him. "It doesn't have to last."

"You're a bad influence, my boy."

"Aw, let down your hair a little," Keith returned, innocently. "You're just doing your part for Scottish tourism."

"Ah, there's no harm in it, I suppose." Holl thrust his arm forward. "Lay your arm next to mine, and lend me your strength. Concentrate. There, that's the way. You're not half bad at it, for a beginner." With his other hand outstretched toward the water, Holl drew on the air a half loop, a whole loop, and another, and another, and finished off with a sharp little gesture like an apostrophe.

"Beautiful," said Keith, admiringly, staring at the loch below. "I want to be just like you when I grow up."

"You're never going to grow up, Keith Doyle," Holl retorted, but he chuckled, too. "It is good, isn't it?"

"Look!" cried a voice below them, highly excited. "There's *Nessie*!"

Michaels reported to his chief over the telephone that afternoon from Drumnadrochit. "I can't help it if you don't believe me, sir. You'll be seeing the report on the evening news. I wasn't the only one who spotted her. That's right, Nessie. I was observing O'Day and his accomplice. There it was, large as life on the waters of the loch, and neither of them were paying the least attention to it. Very strange, sir. What's that?" Michaels sighed. "Aye, sir. I assure you, I saw it, as plain as I can see . . . well, this telephone here. What was it? It was a sea serpent, or as close as makes no difference to me. There has to be a logical explanation for it. But it's curious, sir. I can't understand why they weren't excited by it. It's as if they never saw it. They're up to something, sir, and it must be something *big*."

• Chapter 10 •

Tuesday morning dawned with further instructions from Dr. Stroud not to come to the dig site. So did Wednesday. At the end of the week, the group was allowed to attend for a couple of days. They assembled for the coach to pick them up, radiating excitement and relief.

The settlement under investigation lay to the southeast of Inverness. In terms of distance, the location wasn't far from the city, but it was slow going on the roads, which swooped unexpectedly into ravines, and took hairpin turns which the bus could barely negotiate. Amid broken slabs of rock, deep streams of brown water flowed noisily beside to the narrow roadway. It looked pretty, but provided no maneuvering room for the ungainly vehicle. There were only inches of clearance for the coach's tires.

"One slip, and we're fishbait," Keith stated, peering out the window. He was acting as lookout. A low swinging gate appeared ahead across the road. "Your turn, Max."

Low gates like that were common in the area, dividing property in the rural area to allow sheep grazing on both sides of the road. Max swung himself out of the coach, and ran down to open the gate. The coach eased through it. Max relocked the fence, and dashed ahead to climb back on. "That's the last one! Here we are at last," said Miss Anderson, sitting up poker straight to see better. The coach ambled into a pleasant valley with a gentle, almost imperceptible rise toward the distant hills. The group's anticipation was almost palpable as the coach rolled to a stop at the roadside behind a line of automobiles parked on the verge. They piled happily out of the coach. Charles and Edwin both ran to open the field gate for the party.

The sound, or lack of it, nearly stopped them altogether in surprise as they approached the work area. Compared with Dr. Crutchley's small band, the large team working here was a mob, but a quiet one. Thirty or forty men and boys were scattered in the fenced field, absorbed in their tasks, hardly speaking to one another. Some were in shirtsleeves, but most were barechested and pink to the waist with exertion. Only low conversation blended with the sounds of excavation and the clink of stones hitting sorting pans.

"Welcome," a man called, coming up to greet them. He was in his early thirties, bull-chested with fair coloring. Keith had seen a hundred men just like him in Inverness. He shook hands with everyone in the party. "I'm Thomas Belgrave, the professor's assistant. I'm happy to see you. Let me give you a quick tour around before we begin. We've had some good fortune here, and we're rather proud of it." He led the way to a pavilion tent.

Matthew's eyes gleamed hungrily as the group was given a tour of the team's gleanings thus far. Among its findings were sealed jars which once contained grain. One of the lids had been replaced with clear plastic film so that the contents could be seen without exposing the team to bacteria or other organic parasites that might be living in the rotted remains of cereal.

"There was a helicopter reconaissance of the site before we ever put shovel to turf. The village millstone was practically the first thing we tripped over," the assistant confided. "From the air, one could see a dimple in the earth over its resting place. It had come to rest on something soft, like chaff or straw, which deteriorated over time. We more or less expected the typical village outline, animal bones, broken crockery, but never this much, abandoned *in situ*. No one had any idea that such an extensive remnant of this settlement still existed near here. The jars must have been abandoned when the settlement burned. They were in a pit inside the largest hut. We still haven't guessed why the people didn't return for their possessions after the fire went out.'' He pointed out scorchmarks on the stones and clay items, and brought them to where vestiges of the original circular hut walls remained, standing in narrow knee-deep trenches cut around them in the earth by the archaeological team. The assistant lifted the sheet of plastic covering one as a medical examiner might pull back the sheet on a dead body.

''Dr. Stroud suspects that it was a new colonization, hardly settled yet, as there are none of the characteristic stone buildings of the age, not even a barrier wall. The ditch and bank were only partly formed. Thus vulnerable, they were victims of an enemy attack.'' The man paused, and grinned longsufferingly. ''As always, he wants more data.''

''How sad that it was all destroyed,'' said Mrs. Green, squatting on her heels to peer down at the walls. The group tried to picture the village as it might have been, wooden walls thatched with brush.

Household items had been found in plenty, and lay on a table in the pavilion, tagged and numbered. There were also a number of what the guide described as children's toys, though to the newcomers, they looked like no more than broken bits of junk. A few pieces of jewelry and other small items had been unearthed practically as good as new. The Educatour students were impressed. It was indeed a rich find, and the assistant displayed an excusable degree of smugness.

''What a lot of flint you have here,'' Miss Anderson said, turning over a stone hand axe. ''Wouldn't its presence suggest to you a late Neolithic settlement rather than early Bronze Age?'' she asked. ''Surely this is part of the Inner Moray Firth culture.''

For answer, the young man shrugged his shoulders significantly and jerked his head over toward the team leader.

''You might argue also that the presence of vaissils for storing wheat place this in the latter grouping,'' Belgrave said, apologetically, his diction occasionally falling into broad Highland Scots. "He says it's airly to tell yet." The teacher raised her eyebrows, but said nothing.

Most of the group were given the task of sieving pans of earth already removed by Dr. Stroud's regular team. Huge amounts of it lay in heaps beside each of the excavations, since the floor of the settlement was a few feet under the modern surface. Four of the others, Keith among them, were assigned to help clear the earth inside the boundaries of one of the large huts using brush and trowel. The assistant admonished them not to bump the trenches guarding the exposed walls, and to call for help immediately if they uncovered anything. It got to be monotonous, since Edwin was nearly on top of an "axe factory store," a collection of knapped stone and flint, that lay almost waist deep within the earth along one wall of his hut. In time, the assistant assigned to the group grew used to them, and was able to keep from hovering while they worked.

Dr. Stroud never spoke directly to any of the tour group. He made side comments to his associates in their presence that he didn't care if they overheard, about moneyed dilettantes wasting everyone's time. He was especially upset that Holl, a child, should have been foisted off on him. The group worked hard, but it never seemed to dent the contempt he showed for them. Matthew and Keith, who were particularly serious about learning more, felt personally affronted by the professor's attitude.

He turned up everywhere to criticize, spoiling morale further each time. Without a third hand to steady his burden, Max, who was working near Keith, had to move his heavy pan of scraped earth very slowly to the edge of his patch and over the stub of wall to the sorting pile. The brush, kept in the crook of his thumb, squirted suddenly out of his grasp. Swearing, Max flailed for it, and accidentally let go of the pan, which slipped awkwardly to the ground, spilling soil everywhere. He looked up to see the professor glaring down upon him.

"Inexperienced muggins," he sneered to one of his team that happened to be passing by. The assistant looked startled, and Stroud cocked his head toward Max. "Bloody paying guests."

Max reddened. Leaving his tools propped against the pan of spilled dirt, he sauntered to the roped-off area at the edge of the dig site which served as No-Man's-Land for the smokers in the group. Very deliberately, he shook a filterless cigarette from a pack in his shirt pocket and lit up. He didn't return to the hut for the rest of the day.

The atmosphere on the coach was far different than it had been in the morning. Several of the boys were ready for an argument, and everyone was out of temper. By then Max had run out of cigarettes, and was rebuffed in his efforts to borrow one from his friends. The refusals made him cross all over again. Blankfaced, Narit kept her eyes on her lap all the way back to the guest house. Keith had noticed there were no women on the site except for the three from the tour group. He guessed that the professor had made some disparaging comment in Narit's hearing that hurt her feelings, and felt sorry for her. Stroud probably didn't like women. Mrs. Green and Mrs. Turner also seemed unusually quiet. Miss Anderson said nothing, but watched them and waited for reactions.

"He's a bully and a louse," Keith said, at last, breaking the silence. "The only reason we're taking his crap is because we thought we could learn something from him. Also, he probably thinks it's a crime we see what he does for a living as fun. It's only another week, and then we never have to see him again. I'm not going to let him drive me away."

"Bloody cereal isn't all that's rotten there," Matthew grumbled, but he concurred with Keith.

Grudgingly, everyone agreed to try and hold their tempers, and peace was maintained over the weekend. Keith and the others saw more of Inverness, but spent most of their free time in the pubs carefully *not* talking about archaeology.

The next weekday, the coach came off the main road into the lane nearest the site and rolled to a stop. Before any of the tour could alight, Dr. Stroud detached himself from his team and strode through the gate toward the coach, waving his arms and shouting.

Miss Anderson swung out of the door and went to meet him. They had an argument in pantomime, since the thick window glass of the coach prevented anyone inside from hearing what the two were saying. Pink-cheeked, the teacher returned to the coach and gave instructions to the driver in a low voice. Her lips pressed together, Miss Anderson sat down.

"I'm sorry," she said, tightly. "I have tried, but he pointed out that our contract cannot guarantee us access to the sites. He feels that the presence of non-professionals could jeopardize the safety of artifacts, or accidentally muddle clues. I'm sorry."

"Well, what's wrong with the silly bugger?" Matthew shouted. "Don't these old codgers talk wi' one another? We did a sterling job in Glasgow."

"Aye, we did. Did we make a single mistake on Thursday or Friday?" Edwin growled. "We did not."

"Perhaps one of us did," Mrs. Green suggested mildly, glancing sympathetically at Narit.

"No!" "It's not us, it's him!" Unable to contain their frustration any longer, the others started a shouting match among themselves. There was a consensus that they couldn't blame Miss Anderson or the tour company for their exclusion, but that she ought to be able to do something.

"I think Stroud's a snob and an ass," Martin stated, folding his arms sullenly. "I'm not sure I'd go back even if he let us."

Miss Anderson let them shout themselves out, and resumed in a quieter voice. "I remember a group I was leading to South Cadbury where we were similarly driven off. The team leader feared that the 'crazed Arthurians' among us would inadvertently destroy precious and delicate artifacts. In the end, of course, there was little to see but the placement of the walls, buildings and wells. We were fobbed off elsewhere.

"I'm sorry to say that it's a game of chance. Educatours gives an honorarium to the archaeological teams for letting us visit and participate, but it isn't much. In some cases, not enough to stir any consciences when we're denied what was agreed to under contract. Sometimes they give it back if they change their minds."

"Has Dr. Stroud given the money back?" Matthew asked, narrowing one eye. "You deserve a refund from him."

"We'll most likely get it all back in the end," Miss Anderson said, deprecatingly. "I believe that Dr. Stroud has a powerful corporate sponsor, so he doesn't need our few pence."

"Oh, I see," Max said acidly. "Well, why doesn't he just label every fossil with his little corporate logo. That's what I want to ask. That way we'll know what we're dealing with."

"The company has started to negotiate a refund, but that's nothing for you to fret about. But hold on," she requested, extending her hands to them. "I promise that the Isle of Lewis will be nothing like this. In the meantime, Educatours has considered this eventuality, and is putting the coach at your disposal for local touring. Tomorrow," she said, looking around at them brightly, "we'll have a day out at the Official Loch

Ness Monster Exhibition and the ruins of Urquhart Castle. I'm sure you'll enjoy that."

Keith and Holl looked at each other, and exchanged resigned grins.

• Chapter 11 •

"Another bloody boring day in Inverness," Charles grunted, a few days later, throwing himself into a booth in the local pub they frequented. "I'm ready to go home. If I have to sit for one more day on the steps of Inverness Castle until the sun goes down, I'll just jump off the bank into the river. At least that'll give me a different view."

The weather had continued to be bright and warm, which only exacerbated the boys' annoyance that they couldn't be out at the dig site.

"If it had been gloomy, we'd have a reason to stay off. But you know if he said to come it'd rain every day," Martin pointed out.

"You're probably right," Keith said gloomily. He propped his chin up on his hands and glanced at Holl. The spirit of tolerance among the tour group was fast dissipating. It was a good thing the week was coming to an end.

"I knew I could find you here," said a low-pitched female voice. They looked up to see Narit standing beside their booth. "May I join you?"

"Of course," Matthew said, standing up to let her slide in along the bench.

"We thought you liked to spend the evenings with the other ladies," Alistair added, abashed.

She tossed her head, and her long pigtail whiplashed. "It is all right when we are busy," Narit answered, patiently, "but when there is nothing to do all they talk about is ailments and grandchildren. I have neither. I don't care to stay in and watch the 'East Enders' so I came looking for you. Do you mind?"

"Far from it," said Keith, gallantly. "We thought you wanted to stay in and talk girl talk."

"Sometimes. I wish there were other girls my age on this tour, because then I would have somewhere I belonged when this happens."

"I know what you mean," Holl put in. The search for the object of Holl's quest had been fruitless so far. Keith had pushed himself extra miles if they even spotted a glimpse of white in the undergrowth at the side of the road and pedaled back to report, saving Holl the effort. He was grateful, but it would take more than gratitude to solve the knotty problem he was wrestling with. The internal argument still roiled within him. He knew that if he found the white flowers tomorrow, he'd be on the jet home to Maura that afternoon, Ireland or no Ireland.

He had also been unable to make contact with his folk except by use of the telephone. It wasn't easy to conceal from Keith how unhappy it made him being isolated from his family and friends, but it wasn't fair to worry him with a new concern. "You *didn't* do anything wrong at the dig, did you?"

"No!" Narit protested. "I sorted the small pieces exactly the way his assistant told me to, and I entered the notations very neatly, precisely as they were written on the sheets. When I looked up, he was there, glaring at me. I had no idea what he thought."

"No one's blaming you," Keith said soothingly. "I think he hates women. You notice there weren't any others on the team. We've all come to the conclusion that Stroud's an a— . . . uh, idiot."

"Aye." There was a chorus of agreement. Max grinned at Keith. He knew that the American had substituted a last-minute euphemism out of consideration for Narit. Holl watched the glance, and added his own smile. These young people had formed a common front against an enemy, and were supporting one another. He enjoyed socializing like this. It was so easy for Big Folk to get to know strangers, to make friends with them. Some of their ways were worth exporting to the Little Folk. If he made headman one day, he'd incorporate some of their notions into daily life—slowly, of course. But that also meant completing his quest. He didn't know what to do.

"You've not been at the Bored Meetings these last couple of

afternoons,'' Charles accused Keith. ''We were counting on a full membership on the castle steps.''

''Oh, well,'' Keith said. That afternoon, they had been out as far as they could range on rented bicycles, looking for Holl's bellflowers. He was frustrated, hot, and his legs ached. He hated to guess how Holl felt. ''Holl and I have been out having a look around. The Highlands have a lot of mystical associations, and I'm interested in that sort of thing. You might call me a . . . research mythologist.''

''Come again?''

''I track down the source of legends. I'm really interested in how those old stories got started. I mean besides Nessie,'' he said, forestalling Charles from making the obvious association. ''There's thousands of fascinating tales in your history. This place is great for legends.''

''What, like Robin Hood, or King Arthur?'' Alistair asked.

''No, more like magical things,'' Keith corrected him, warming to his favorite topic. ''Dragons, elves, unicorns, banshees, you know. There's legends about things of magic in every early culture. You wonder where they all came from.''

''I don't,'' Martin protested.

''So you go about like Sir Arthur Conan Doyle, eh? Looking for fairies and so on?'' Matthew asked, an eyebrow arched cynically skyward.

''Only partly. He believed in those things with all his heart. I do, too, but I've got to convince my head as well.''

''Ah,'' Martin nodded sagely. He and Matthew exchanged winks. ''Well then. We might have something to show you later, eh?''

''Do you believe in the unseen, Keith?'' Narit asked in her soft, lilting voice. She seldom spoke up in the group, so Keith turned his whole attention to her. ''My family believe in karma. I practice with the Tarot cards, myself. I find they have great meaning for me. The symbols here are not familiar in my people's history, but they have their equivalents. May I read the cards for you?'' She reached for her handbag. From it she drew a silk-wrapped bundle as long as her hand and half as wide.

''Well, uh, why not?'' Keith accepted, a little unsure. ''Thanks. I'd really appreciate it. How do you do it?''

''I shuffle the cards,'' she began, taking the silk off and smoothing the edge of the deck with her fingers. The backs were a plain bi-colored design, but the faces were exotic and colorful. Keith peeked at them as Narit shuffled. She separated the cards into two piles and sifted them together again and again with skillful motions. "Cut."

Keith gathered a third of the deck between thumb and forefinger and handed it to her. Narit took the remainder and placed it on top of the smaller section. "The last card of the section you chose is your significator, the card which represents you." The card she pulled showed a young man with a hobo's bundle over one shoulder and a dog romping behind him up a craggy path. "The Fool."

The others laughed. "Good choice, Keith," Charles crowed.

"He represents potential, substance rather than form." She dealt the cards into a cross, and to its right, an extra column of four starting at the bottom up. "that's interesting. You have several of the Major Arcana in your reading. This means that much of your situation is not of your own devising, that you're being led by circumstances rather than creating them. Many things which you think you encounter by chance are karmically arranged. But that is not necessarily a bad thing. It means there is much power in your life. It is far from ordinary."

Keith glanced surreptitiously at Holl, whose eyebrows were in his hairline. The others hooted. "I guess. What does the rest mean?"

Delicately, she turned over the cards one at a time. "Here in your potential future is the Star. Whether that means help will come to you, or that you will provide help for others is yet open to question. Ah!" Narit's voice took on a note of concern as she flipped the card at the right arm of the cross. It showed a crowned turret being struck by lightning. Keith's eyebrows lifted. "The Tower. There will be the abrupt end of a path, and a new beginning. It can mean death, but you needn't take it as that. Your final outcome is the Three of Cups, which shows fulfillment and celebration, so it is doubtful the Tower predicts a death in this case."

"Well, what does Death mean?" Keith asked, poking a finger at another card, which depicted a cloaked skeleton wielding a sickle, the second card from the bottom of the column of four.

"Change," Narit said promptly. "Many times for the good. Death is not a threat if you consider the pitfalls of everlasting life."

"I'd want to live forever," Charles put in. "Who wouldn't?"

"Only if you couldn't get replacement parts," Keith replied, mildly, enumerating them. "Teeth, hair, eyes, knees . . ."

"D'you really believe in this stuff?" Martin exploded scornfully, amused by the serious acceptance Keith offered Narit.

"Karma works in your life whether you believe in it or not," Narit said coolly. "Do you want to know your own future?"

"Not me!"

"I would," Holl piped up.

"Think of a question, if you have one." Narit gathered the cards and shuffled them deftly. Holl reached out to cut the deck in half, and found his fingers only wanted a few cards. There was something to these cards. They weren't charmed themselves, but felt rather more like a conduit of power. He leaned forward curiously.

"The Hermit. You seek, as Diogenes did," Narit said, her voice seeming to Holl to come from far away. "He is alone in all ways, in his mind, his heart. This is a very old card for a child."

Holl ignored the inference. "What do the others mean?"

Narit turned them all face up before speaking again. She pointed to the last, a card with the face of a jolly, fat man. "The Nine of Cups is also known as the wish card. You will have all that you require at the end. But there are many obstacles through which you must pass before getting your wish. It is by no means certain. The cards do not guarantee what you see. They are merely guidelines. You have several rod cards in this reading, trials of the spirit, and you are crossed by the Chariot, which is someone or something which has mastery over you. But you will be aided in the end by the Star. Help from a friend."

Overwhelmed, Holl could say little more than "Thank you." He retired back in his corner with his St. Clement's to think.

"That sounded a lot of mumbo jumbo," Matthew said, but his face was uncertain. Narit glanced at him reprovingly, and mixed the cards once more.

"Go ahead, cut," she ordered. "I think I can do one more tonight."

Tentatively, Matthew reached out to the long deck, picked up half and set it firmly on the table next to the other half. Narit picked up both halves, and began to deal them. "You are the Page of Swords. In the past you have been the Knight of Pentacles, interested in the material world and somewhat advanced there, but here at present, you're the Hermit, looking for something else," Narit said, pointing at one card after another. "Crossing you is the King of Pentacles."

"What's that mean?" Matthew asked, interested in spite of himself.

"A master of Earth, a teacher, a father, a man of authority with regard to the physical world, also the material or financial. Ah, here, where you appear once again, is the Knight of Swords. The seeker of Air."

"Oh, that's the truth," Martin said cynically. "Hot air, it is, too." Matthew's elbow took him in the midriff. "Oof!"

"Air is intellectual attainment," Narit continued, as if Martin hadn't spoken. She had a quiet authority when she handled the cards, and the boys were impressed. "Here is Death, who may be changing your life. If you win through your struggles," the forefinger picked out a sword card and a pentacle card showing a man hugging sacks of gold, "you will come to the Four of Rods, which is contentment of the spirit." She met his eyes and studied him closely. "You have decisions to make soon."

Matthew glanced at her with new respect. "Thank you," he said sincerely as she bent her head to gather up the cards. He fell silent, and studied the far wall. In a moment, he realized the others were staring at him.

He drained his glass, noisily. "I'll get the next round, shall I?" he asked the table. "Narit, what'll you have?"

"Well, that's it. I'm clappit out," Charles said, at about ten o'clock. He felt around in his pocket for money and came up with only twelve pence. "Until I find the till machine, that's it for me."

"I'm skint, too," Martin said. Hopefully, they both turned to Keith.

"Hey, don't look at me," that youth said, flinging up his hands. "I'm broke for tonight, too."

"Ach, you rich Americans," Edwin said scornfully, looking up from the glass of beer he was nursing. It was down to an inch or so of dark, amber fluid. "You know you're rolling in it. You could cough up a little for one more pint."

"Look, this rich American had to buy a plane ticket here," Keith protested. "You guys only had to buy three-pound train tickets from Edinburgh."

Matthew cocked his head wryly. "Not even that. Martin's father motored us down here."

"See?" Keith said, defensively. "Look, I'm sorry, but what money I've got has got to last me another three weeks. I haven't even bought my girlfriend a present yet. Not that I have any idea what she'd like. She's hard to buy for. But she'll kill me if I come home emptyhanded."

"Yer a stingy old goldpockets," Edwin slurred, leaning toward Keith threateningly.

"It takes one to know one," Keith shot back, angling toward the other. "Isn't it supposed to be Scotsmen who can squeeze a penny until it screams?"

"You—you *capitalist*," Edwin spat, raising his fist. Keith braced himself.

"Hey!" Shocked, Alistair rose and put an arm between them. "None of this, now. Sit down. Perhaps we've all had a drop too much."

Keith felt a tug on his sleeve. "Keith Doyle," Holl whispered. "To quote your Robin Williams, doesn't the name General Custer mean anything to you?"

The red-haired youth opened his mouth to protest, and was overwhelmed by a wave of shame. "I'm drunk. No doubt about it. I'm only this tactless when I'm blasted." He put out a hand to Edwin. "I'm sorry, Ed. See, Narit was right. I am the fool. That was a stupid remark, considering I'm surrounded by thousands of people who would be totally right to mash my head through the pavement for spouting stupid stereotypes. I am a dunce. But honest, I've really got to stretch my budget."

Edwin buried his head in his hands. "I'm plain mortified with myself." He reached up tentatively to Keith. "Truce."

"Nope," Keith insisted, collecting a round of astonished gazes. "Peace." He took Edwin's hand and they shook. The others pounded the two of them on the backs.

"And to celebrate," Holl spoke up over the hubbub, "I'll stand you all to black coffee. Then a good, brisk walk back to the guest house will clear everyone's head."

"Oh, but we've got something to show Keith, first," Matthew said, eagerly pulling the American down the street. Holl trailed behind, puzzled.

"Yeah. Since you're a specialist, you might be interested in this," Martin added. "Come on."

"Not me," said Edwin. "I'm for bed. My head's about to explode."

"We've got to walk Narit back. It's about dark," Alistair explained.

"Suit yourself," Matthew called, guiding Keith around a corner.

Keith tried to free his arm from the other's tight grasp. "Hey, guys, where are we going?" They crossed the main bridge over the Ness and hurried down the street on the west side.

"We saw the very thing you're interested in," Martin assured him, after a few blocks. "Right in there." He stopped out of the street light in front of a gate. The sign beside it said "Bught Park."

When they departed the pub in such a hurry, none of them noticed the shadow which followed them to the bridge and over it to the Ness Road. Michaels hunched his shoulders into his light coat and tried to look as if he was minding his own business without losing sight of the three young men and the boy nearly half a block ahead of him. The Educatours people had been happy to give him the itinerary for their Scotland summer expedition. A pity no one had kept him apprised of the fact the man in charge of the Inverness dig was an obstructive bastard. Michaels had put miles on the Bureau car he'd borrowed morning after unconscionably early morning, until he realized that O'Day and the others weren't going out there at all.

The directional microphone he had clipped inside his coat wasn't powerful enough to pick up what the boys were saying, only that they were talking. He'd have to be closer than sixty feet to get clear transmission. It was almost the oldest equipment of its kind available. The local office refused to devote much of its stretched resources to the pursuit of an international smuggler who might or might not be making a pickup in their demesne. Even a boom mike was out of the question for him. Privately, he cursed the field operatives of the American service, who got all the powerful miniaturized toys they wanted, in tie clips and eyeglass frames, with recorders or transmitters in, just for the asking.

He wormed his way into the park as the young men settled themselves into concealment about twenty yards from the park gate. There was nothing he could do to hear better. Was the pickup tonight? He'd have to search the young bloke's room later, after he'd gone to sleep. Michaels fervently hoped O'Day had had enough to drink to gag him soundly. Sleeping gas was another thing the James Bonds of the American service could get, practically delivered by the pint bottle on their doorsteps every morning like milk. If he bagged O'Day, they'd allot a good deal more money to the department, and about time, too. Uncomfortably, he eased himself behind a clump of bushes and aimed his microphone.

Later, he would tell the Chief that this stakeout had all been a great waste of time. "There was no acceptance or delivery, sir," Michaels assured him, wearily. "They might have been setting something up, but it sounded like code to me. Nothing I've ever heard before. I couldn't get much of it on that bloody Stone Age mike, but they all seemed to understand one another. It was a great big joke between them. We still don't know what the hell's up."

"Did you see that?" Matthew hissed into Keith's ear, pulling his arm and pointing down the field toward a clump of tall flowers and a pond which reflected the city lights in its depths.

"See what?" Keith demanded, trying to follow Matthew's gaze in the dark. He parted the bushes, spitting out leaves and twigs that brushed his face. His invisible whiskers didn't protect him from the waving shrubbery.

"There goes another one!" Martin poked him in the side. "And another. Oh, you'd better look quicker than that!"

"Wait," Matthew said, his voice dropping to a conspiratorial whisper. "Now wait for it, here comes one. Yes! Look there, Keith!"

"Where?" Keith wailed, desperately. "What? What are we looking for?"

Matthew stopped and gawked at Keith. He rolled to one side to regard him with mock amazement. "Do you mean to tell me quite seriously and with no deception whatever," his voice started to crack as a broad grin forced its way past his teeth and plastered itself across his face, "that a great big investigator like you has never heard about there being fairies at the bottom of the garden?" He collapsed to the ground, giggling. Martin threw himself onto the ground and howled hysterically, flapping limply at Matthew's legs with one hand.

"Ha, ha," Keith retorted sarcastically, glowing beet red in the dark. He glared at Holl, who was doubled up, too. "And what are *you* laughing at?"

The little man wiped his eyes on the back of his hand and swallowed his hilarity enough to speak. "You have to admit, Keith Doyle, you left yourself open to it. Conan Doyle couldn't have made his own trap and fallen into it any neater than you did yourself. Led straight up the garden path by the hand, in fact, just like he was in the great fairy hoax."

Caught off guard, Keith rubbed his lip, beginning to get the joke. He grinned and threw up his arms. "All right! All right, I've been had. Royally. What can I say? I guess it just goes with the name."

• Chapter 12 •

Miss Anderson's word was good: Educatours kept them occupied. She guided the tour group out on short trips throughout the Inverness region every day until Sunday morning, when the coach was loaded for its final destination, on the Isle of Lewis, northwest of the coast of Scotland.

If the Scottish landscape had been dramatic before, it become breathtaking now. North of Inverness, the land rolled away from the road in curving valleys and fields, and changed gradually to sweeping glens and expanses of forest cradled between mountain ridges shaded in distant blue, dark green, and gold. The road followed river valleys cut deep into the heart of the land or broad and shining like strips of silver painted on the green earth. Few habitations lay beyond Inverness, but the highlands were far from lonesome. Instead, they radiated an ancient, eternal patience that was soothing and awesome.

" 'My heart's in the Highlands, my heart is not here,' " murmured Holl, gazing wonderingly out of the coach window and drinking in the feeling that beauty was a palpable thing. " 'My heart's in the highlands, a-chasing the deer.' "

"Isn't that William Saroyan?" Keith asked, squinting through his viewfinder at a photogenic ridge.

Holl's mood was broken, and he felt suddenly as if he had

lost something precious. " 'My Heart's in the Highlands' is by Robert Burns," he said, longsufferingly. "Don't you read any poetry that's not on the syllabus, you cultural infant?"

"That's what we keep a Maven like you around for," Keith pointed out unquenchably, ratcheting the film noisily forward in his camera. "Isn't it great up here? I love it. I could stay up here forever just staring at the scenery. The mountains and clouds are sort of unreal, like someone's paintings. Look, stuffed animals."

To the right of the road, a herd was grazing calmly. Except for pairs of wickedly pointed long horns bobbing close to the ground, the broad, short animals were undifferentiated mounds of ochre hair. One lifted up its nose at the passing coach and revealed huge, mild, brown eyes under the yellow thatch.

"They're cows!"

"Highland cattle," Miss Anderson corrected Keith.

"I thought they might be woolly mammoths without trunks. I should yell 'moo' out the window at them," Keith pondered, playfully. "My dad always does. They're cute, but I bet they could stomp their weight in cattle rustlers."

"You're perfectly safe if you come upon a herd," Miss Anderson said, conversationally, beaming at them one by one. "The bull is peaceful except when one of his cows is threatened. If you come upon a bull alone, keep moving."

"Move?" asked Martin, astonished. "I'd fly! How long until we get to the ferry port, Miss Anderson?"

"Another hour or so to Ullapool," the teacher replied, checking her wristwatch. "Should we have a song to pass the time? Who would like to start?"

"How about the intrepid fairy hunter here?" Martin asked, mischievously, glancing sideways at Keith. The American student turned red, remembering the garden episode. Once his hobby had been revealed, they seemed to recall and repeat every detail of the things he'd said offhandedly throughout the trip. He wished the novelty would wear off already. The ladies and the coach driver had already heard the story and dismissed it, but the boys continued to remind Keith mercilessly whenever it occurred to them. "Bring-'em-back-alive Frank Puck here must know something."

"Such a hobby for a grown man," Matthew appealed to Holl. "Have you ever heard such foolishness?"

"No," he replied, calmly. "And the widdy's always going on about it. It's an obsession with him."

Keith turned to Holl, an acid retort half formed on his tongue. Then with a shock, he noticed that Holl's cap was off, and the short, blond hair was neatly brushed. The elf's ears were still rounded like a human's. In fact, he realized they had been ever since Holl got out of the hospital. What was going on with him? He couldn't draw attention to the aberration now. He would have to wait and tackle Holl privately. "Okay," he said, weakly, feeling betrayed, "I can take a joke. Um, does anyone know 'Take Me Out to the Ball Game'?"

The ferry was scheduled to depart at 5:00 A.M. from the port of Ullapool. In the morning half-light, under a homogenous sky of light gray stratus clouds, the party sat aboard the coach, waiting their turn on the pier to drive into the hold of the ferry. The ship bobbed gently at the pier's end, a massive inverted wedge of black and white.

Once on board, the passengers left their vehicles and ascended to the upper decks for the three-and-a-half-hour passage. Shivering with fatigue from their short night and early rising, Keith and the others scrambled down from the coach in the narrow space left between two small cars and a dust-covered minivan on which someone had scrawled with a fingertip "Also available in *clean*." Following a silent herd of fellow passengers, the group found a small lounge at the rear of the ship's restaurant, and settled down on the leather-covered couches with hot drinks to try and wake up. Other passengers slipped through the glass-walled lounge and into the cafeteria beyond it like bats: silent, avoiding the chairs and laden tables with weary expertise.

"The Outer Hebrides have yielded up the oldest samples of rock in the British Isles. Some of them have been dated at 2,800 million years," Miss Anderson stated, as the ferry's engines thrummed to life beneath them, awaiting departure time.

"Or two point eight billion years in American," Keith calculated, yawning, and wrapped his hands around his cup of tea. A British billion was one million million. "Old."

"Not as old as I feel," Matthew said, peering into the depths of his coffee as if he expected the steam rising from it to revive him. The two English ladies sat nearby, huddled over folded arms and blinking owlishly at the others. "You remember the chap we unearthed on top of the hill in Renfrewshire?'' he asked Keith, who nodded. ''My grandson.''

The others chuckled. A huge grinding noise interrupted them, and the ferry lurched suddenly to the right. The land visible out of the broad windows lining the lounge began to move, and the noise moderated to a hum. They were under way.

Tired though they were, the group was already in better spirits than they had been in Inverness. Keith taught them and the rest of the passengers in the lounge how to play Buzz-Fizz. ''It's a counting game. Buzz is five, and seven is fizz. You keep going until you make a mistake, and the next person takes over where you left off. Don't forget about multiples. I'll start. One, two, three, four, buzz, six, fizz, eight, nine, buzz-buzz, eleven, twelve, thirteen, fizz-fizz, fifteen . . . .''

''You mean buzz-buzz-buzz,'' Edwin triumphantly corrected him. Keith grinned sheepishly and made an ''over-to-you'' gesture in the large youth's direction. Edwin started, counting carefully, with his eyes on the ceiling and a broad smile on his lips as he tried to remember what was a multiple of what. When he got tangled up amidst the z's, Max took a turn. They played until no one could shout out the right buzzes and fizzes for a high number over the laughter from the rest of the crowd.

''Thank you, dear,'' Mrs. Green complimented Keith, as he brought her a fresh pot of tea when the game broke up. ''You're good at traveling with a group.''

''I'm one of five kids. My father taught us these games as a matter of self-defense on long trips. Otherwise, we would've driven him crazy asking 'are we there yet?' ''

''My two sons liked to ask us that,'' Mrs. Green acknowledged with the corners of her mouth turned up. ''Somehow we managed to stave off the question until we actually were *there*. And Holl is your elder sister's son?''

Keith gulped, trying to remember what he'd told whom. Mrs. Green was stirring sugar into her cup, head bent over her task. She didn't seem to notice any hesitation. ''Right. You can see the family resemblance.''

''Yes, I can. It's very strong, especially in the jaw and ears. Your foreheads and noses are very different, though.''

''That's heredity, I guess,'' Keith said, lightly, wondering what the older woman would say if he speculated on how far back in history the resemblance would have to reach. He stood up. "Excuse me, please. Hey, Holl, let's go up on deck and watch the scenery."

"A fine idea." The Little One extracted himself from a group having a discussion around one of the small cocktail tables. He gathered up a sketch he had been making, and followed Keith. "I'll be happy to get out of this big metal room. How do you stand it?"

They made their way up the stairs, and together forced open a door on the uppermost deck of the ferry. The wind was still whistling up a gale, but the dull, leaden gray of the sky was brightening steadily as they sailed westward. Keith could feel his invisible whiskers whipping sharply against his cheeks. He concentrated on making them lie flat, then gave up. The coast had dwindled to a dark, irregular line nestled on the horizon far to the east, indistinguishable from the dark sea and the waves of clouds overhead.

"Look how murky the water is," Holl shouted, pointing over the rail. "It must be icy cold."

"Well, I wouldn't want to get out and swim," Keith admitted. He decided to bite the bullet, and find out the answer to the ear question as long as they were alone. "Hey, Holl . . ." he began, but cut off his sentence as a gaggle of tourists came out of the stairwell and passed within earshot. The elf looked at him questioningly, but he waved a dismissive hand. "Never mind. I'll remember later what I wanted to say."

Holl nodded. "There's nothing in sight to the west. The Isle of Lewis must be more than seventeen miles away. That's the distance you are able to see at sea level before the curvature of the Earth drops the edge out of eyeshot. I've never been anywhere I could test the hypothesis."

"Are you doing okay?" Keith asked. "I mean, I know you've never been on a boat before, and lots of people do get seasick."

"I thank you for your concern, but I don't feel a thing out of the ordinary," Holl replied, leaning comfortably on the rail and squinting at the horizon, careful to keep his sleeves between the metal and his skin. "I'm having a very good time, as well. From what the old ones told me, I thought sailing would be terrifying. I don't find it so. It's no worse than riding in a car on bumpy roads."

"Smoother," Keith said, after a moment. "I've got to get

new shocks.'' He thrust a hand out across the sea, and waved a finger. ''Hey, look at that. Land ho!''

''Seventeen miles, and a small bit more, of course, allowing for the extra elevation of the ship,'' Holl said, satisfied, surveying the low ripple of land. ''My ears are freezing in this wind.''

''Mine, too,'' Keith agreed, wondering if that was an opening for a discussion. No, the elf's face showed only curiosity and excitement as he stared out over the water at the island. Keith shrugged, and folded his elbows on the rail to watch Lewis growing nearer. He yawned. ''I wonder if anyone there beside us is awake at this hour.''

Michaels sat at the rear of the lounge with his coat buttoned up to the chin and watched the two smugglers go above deck. O'Day must suspect that he was under surveillance. Why else would he go to the far end of nowhere with the tour group? Unless the Isle of Lewis was *it*, the pickup site where his contact was waiting. It seemed like a mucking great lot of trouble to waste four weeks—four weeks!—hoiking about Scotland to establish his bona fides as a tourist. The research boys suggested that there was a major scientific discovery for sale. If he kept his eyes open, he should be able to bag O'Day just as the information changed hands.

After Glasgow and Inverness, Stornoway was a small town. Before Keith and the others on the coach had had more than a quick glance at the city, they were out of it, and following a narrow road into the countryside. A thin curtain of trees parted suddenly, revealing a rough, torn landscape. Outside of the capital city and the tree farms, the Isle of Lewis seemed to be little more than rock and peat with grass and heather growing on it. At first glance, it looked almost like a war zone. Miss Anderson described the fantastic splinters of friable rock to her open-mouthed group as Lewisian gneiss, unique to this part of the world. Rocks turned up all over the dark-hued ground as if careless giants, rummaging through geologic drawers, had found what they wanted at the bottom, then departed without cleaning up after themselves.

Thousands of sheep, some sheared and recognizable, and the unsheared looking like shaggy hassocks with tiny pipestem legs sticking out from underneath, grazed calmly on the backs of the hills. Halfgrown lambs galloped crazily up and down, venturing out from the ewes long enough to get a look at the world, and hurrying back every time something surprised them. Their placid elders cropped the greenery or stared off into the distance with nobly thoughtful expressions.

Rounded valleys between the hills were filled partway with water, as if the island was porous to the sea. Every so often, the coach would pass a small farmhouse or news-agent shop, but between them was the endless sea of peat under an almost peat-colored sky.

"My God," said Matthew, despairingly, looking out the window at the scenery. "It's a desert island. I haven't seen a single pub for the last twenty miles!"

Keith shrugged. "It's just like middle Illinois in winter," he said. "No pubs. You'd just pick up a sixpack if there's no place to go."

"There, I knew the colonies were backward," Matthew crowed. "Bottled beer! But what do they do for fun here?"

"We'll be in Stornoway for supper every night," Miss Anderson pointed out imperturbably. "There are plenty of public houses and shops there. We're here to learn, not carouse."

"I'd rather carouse," Martin muttered defiantly under his breath. "Have you ever seen such desolation?"

The wild ruggedness of the island did take some getting used to. After driving through Illinois wheatfields, Keith was accustomed to long stretches of nothingness, but the dramatically sharp rise and fall of the dark land was new to him. As they drove west, the wind whipped up more fiercely, soughing among the fences and shrubs, and causing the hanging fleece on the sheeps' backs to sway like wash on a line.

"This is Callanish," Miss Anderson announced, as the coach suddenly came upon a double row of small houses and farms. "To save a long, long drive every morning from Stornoway, everyone has been assigned to bed-and-breakfast establishments right here." The coach slowed down sharply as they rounded a high curve. Suddenly, on their left was a low building with a peaked roof, looking as if it had weathered millenia. Ahead of them was a tiger-trap of pointed, weatherworn monoliths.

"And there," Miss Anderson continued, pointing unnecessarily, "are the standing stones, which date to 2000 B.C. The arms of the cross point toward the compass directions, though all but one of them are out of true. In the center of the inner ring is a round, chambered tomb.''

As they drew closer, the undifferentiated cluster spread into two thin arms of stones. Another double axis of tall stones pointed from the curve in the road toward a hill topped with more blocks. Several stones were missing from the pattern, but the effect was still impressive. Keith snapped away happily at the monument with his camera.

Two at a time, the group was dropped at the doors of farm houses boasting small ''B&B'' signs in their front windows or nailed to the fences facing the road. For their housing among the spare population on the island, Keith and Holl were instructed to get out at the door of a small, trim house with a large, hedged garden looking down over the western sea. Miss Anderson pushed between them, and knocked briskly on the door.

A slender, black-haired woman answered. ''Mrs. Mackenzie,'' Miss Anderson said. ''These are your two young guests, Keith and Holl Doyle. When you've settled, meet us at the tea shop at the top of the hill,'' the teacher instructed them.

''Yes, Miss Anderson,'' they said in unison. She smiled. The boys watched her climb back aboard the bus, and shouldered their bags.

''Ah, come in, come in,'' Mrs. Mackenzie urged, shooing them like chickens. ''Close the door. The wind is strong today. There's a fierce, cold bite to it.''

''Yeah,'' Keith said, pushing the door to with some effort. ''And I thought this was July.''

''Well, come in and warm up,'' Mrs. Mackenzie invited them. ''Do you want some tea?''

''Uh, no, thanks,'' Keith smiled, feeling his cheeks thawing already, once they were out of the wind. ''This is a nice place.''

''Thank you. We like it here,'' the slim woman said, ushering them through a doorway. ''Make yourselves at home.''

An electric fire was glowing in the hearth of her sitting room. As they entered, four plump, tan cushions on the very edge of the woven, oval hearth rug moved, and arose into tall, smooth silhouettes, shoulderless like wine bottles and crowned with triangular, sable ears.

''Hi, kitties,'' Keith said, dropping to his knees beside them.

The Siamese cats regarded him with cool, summing, blue eyes. All of them blinked once. "They're beautiful." He reached out to stroke one on the end, and the cat in the middle of the rug emitted an inviting, throaty groan.

"You may as well fuss Her Majesty first," Mrs. Mackenzie warned him, indulgently. "She's in charge here."

"Sure," Keith said, scratching the cat behind her ears. She was slightly smaller than the other three, and her mask and paws were darker. Keith moved a finger around to scratch under the angle of the cat's jaw. She purred, lowering her head to give his hand a wet, fishy-smelling kiss with her upper lip.

Holl approached the cats more cautiously. "They're like Lladro statues," he said, touching one with gingerly care. It leaned into his hand and slitted its eyes. Encouraged, he rubbed his knuckle softly around the pointed cup of its ear. His caress was answered by a huge rumble, surprising in such a slim beast. "Friendly."

"Aye, well, he knows what you are," the landlady said. "So do I."

Aghast, Holl stopped playing with the cat and looked up at her. "He does?" The cat bumped impatiently at his hand, demanding more petting.

"Aye," Mrs. Mackenzie repeated, with satisfaction. "You're cat people. They always know. Cats are wise. Will you come this way now, and we'll see you settled?"

While Holl mentally counted his pulse and commanded it to slow down again, Keith grinned and picked up all their bags. Their hostess led them into a long hallway and pushed open the levered handle on one of the doors.

The room had been decorated in yellow and white, with sheer drapes over a wide window which faced the sea. The beds were deep twins covered with thick, yellow-and-white flowered quilts. "This will be your room. Lav's up the way. Breakfast is served between 7:30 and 9:00 in the morning. Will that suit you?"

"Sure," said Keith, exchanging approving glances with Holl. They dropped their bags in the corner, and took turns in the bathroom washing off the grime of travel. Then, gathering their strength, they pushed out once more into the frigid wind.

At the top of the hill, Michaels waited in his rented car. At last, his two quarries emerged from the farm house at the bottom of the hill and started toward him. His thermos of coffee was chilling down quickly in the unseasonable cold. He wished he could go into the tea shop, only a few feet from the car, to warm up, but there was a fifty-fifty chance that his subjects were going in there, too. It wouldn't do to get close enough for them to identify him later.

Chapter 13

If anything, the wind had become worse while they were inside the house. There was no movement amidst the clouds to tell from which direction the wind was coming, or any glimpse of the blue sky they had seen on the sail toward the island. They hiked up the hill against a downward gale.

"There's ice in this wind, Keith Doyle," Holl gritted, pulling his collar up around his face to just under his eyes. "The tide must be turning, or it would be blowing inland, following us."

"I feel like Nanook of the North—no, I wish I *was* Nanook," Keith grumbled pulling the hem of his light jacket as close to his thin frame as he could to keep out the gusts. "*He* had a warm fur coat."

The low, dark silhouette of the Callanish Tea Shop was in plain sight on the right side of the road they were climbing. Keith focused on its curious, peaked roof like a rock formation to mark the end of a long hike. About twenty feet further up the steep path, the road leveled out somewhat, and Keith stood erect for the first time.

Before him, the stones of Callanish marched across the fenced-in field of grass. He was so fascinated by the formation that for a few moments, he forgot how cold he was. There was a clear and deliberate purpose in the way the stones had been laid out. He was curious who was so important in the ancient days that they buried him in the round cairn Keith knew to be in the middle of all that stone. It had to be the product of maybe thousands of hours of work, and hundreds of workers' sweat. There was a feeling of power in the air, perhaps emanating from the stones themselves. Maybe the deceased was the priest of whatever this temple signified, or the chieftain responsible for its construction. Well, it wasn't the Great Pyramid, but Keith was impressed. The Egyptians didn't have to deal with ice storms in July when they built the Valley of Kings.

A few figures in colorful clothing were wandering among the dentine monoliths, stopping to touch the stones as they passed. Another small knot of people were sitting in a circle on the grass between the stones, talking earnestly, ignoring the wind blowing around them. Keith shivered, and wondered how they managed that. He had only been out a few minutes, but his ears and nose were already whipped into red icicles.

Huddled along the side of the Tea Shop was a cluster of grimy tents. More men and women, wearing odd combinations of garments, such as long skirts and surplus army jackets with shawls flung over, or loose cotton trousers with leather coats and wool hats, sat or lay full length near a fire set on stones in the midst of the grassy common. They glanced up disinterestedly at Keith and Holl as they passed.

The door was on the far side of the croft. Keith and Holl fled another gust of cold wind and all but tumbled inside through the narrow doorway.

The room within was low and modestly lit, but it seemed bright after the lowering sky outside. The thick walls held enough heat to thaw their faces and hands almost immediately. Keith let the surroundings register to his returning senses. On the left, the long chamber was lined with tables and benches of golden wood, which looked invitingly warm. His friends were seated at one of these, cradling tea cups between their hands. They waved to Keith and Holl to join them. Immediately before them was a glass-topped counter, over which a girl was squinting at them.

"Close the door, then," she ordered. She had dark hair and lashes, sharply contrasting with her pale skin, and eyes which tilted up slightly at the corners.

"Is it usually like this in summer?" Keith asked over his shoulder, as he pushed the door shut.

"Sometimes," she admitted.

Keith rubbed his cheeks and felt his nose. It was still there, though numb. "Wow, what's it like in winter?"

"More of the same, but livelier," the girl said, smiling. Keith glanced to the right, and discovered that the rest of the Tea Shop was a small dry goods and souvenir store. A tall shelf unit filled with bolts of fabric stood next to the door, and beyond that was a rack of sweaters and coats.

"Coats! Great. Maybe I'd better buy a warm jacket," he said, impulsively. "That is, if you're sure it won't get nice tomorrow."

"It might, and it might not. I can't promise."

"Hmm, I thought so." Keith grinned. "Well, I'll never make it home alive in this thing. How about you, Holl?"

But the young elf was already inspecting the rack of garments with interest. Keith shot a smile to the girl, and started pushing the hangers along one at a time. All the coats and jackets were made of the same kind of woven fabric. It felt coarse and smooth at the same time under his hand. A label fluttered from the neck of one hanger. Keith straightened it out to read it. "Harris Tweed," it said.

The fabrics were surprisingly complex. The rough wool, which looked solid-colored from a distance, had dozens of colors blended into each piece. In a fabric which seemed made up only of shades of red, tiny hints of gold and blue like hidden jewels winked out at him between single black threads, invisible unless he stared at it closely. One bolt rolled up on the rack near the door had as part of its pattern vertical stripes of grey which were made up of twisted fibers of pink, black, and green.

There was a little pamphlet about the history of Harris tweed on the wall. He read it, then picked up a few of the coats to try on for size. Holl was silent in fascination, letting out only an admiring hiss as he browsed. "The coats are made by hand by a few local people," the girl's voice came from behind them. "The weavers are all locals, too."

"You mean there are people weaving this stuff at home?" Keith asked, surprised, turning to face the young lady.

"Um-hm, and selling it, too. Stop anywhere you see a sign that says 'Harris tweed.' The genuine fabrics are stamped with the orb-and-cross Association insignia by an inspector. But I'll warn you," she shook a finger in Keith's face, "you'd better like what you buy, because you'll be wearing it forever."

"Wow." Discarding garments of red and black, or peat brown, Keith chose a jacket of a blue and green tweed that sparkled with red, black, and gold, and paid the young woman over the counter. "I feel warmer already," he assured her.

"Hey, Doyle, come on!" Charles called. "You're the last ones."

"Thanks again," Keith said, and headed toward his friends.

"I'll bring you some tea," the young woman told him.

"What's that for?" Edwin asked, as Keith sat down with his new purchase across his lap.

"Staving off death by hypothermia."

"What for? It'll be nice again in a few days, and you'll have spent all your beer money."

"I'm not betting my chances of getting pneumonia against two weeks of drinking. I only brought a windbreaker with me." There was a gasp of laughter, and Miss Anderson corrected him, without a hair out of place.

"I think we call the same thing a windcheater, Keith. Your term has a rather indelicate meaning for us." Her voice was stern, but her eyes twinkled. Keith tilted his head apologetically.

"I'm going to write a book comparing the logic of British slang with American," he insisted, with a sheepish grin. We're only pushing the wind aside. You're cheating it. Hey, Holl, come and sit down! You can shop later."

Reluctantly, Holl pulled himself away from the shelves of tweed fabric. "They'd love that at home," he told Keith, meaningfully. "Especially if it lasts forever."

Keith waved a generous hand. "Bring some back. Bring lots. We're going to have plenty of time to look around at the other weavers' shops over the next two weeks. I'm going to wear this one on the dig. The lady said that it's windproof."

"You're going to look a prize Charley in a tweed jacket and a coolie hat," Martin assured Keith.

"Yeah, but at least I'll be unique. You're going to look like everyone else on this island," Keith jeered playfully.

Over tea and cake, Miss Anderson outlined their activities for the next two weeks. "The team works down in the valley, but none of us will be going down there today. They left word with the tea shop's proprietress for me." Over the groans of the group, Miss Anderson raised her voice and coaxed them back into silence, "Now, now, I promise this won't be like Inverness. You'll like Professor Parker. He's a friendly man."

The boys remained unconvinced. Matthew and Martin exchanged sour glances and ate cake with grim ferocity. Keith thought of Dr. Stroud and wondered how he would tolerate two more weeks of unappreciated slavery.

The door opened to admit a small, roundfaced man with a scarf holding his tweed hat onto his head. "Miss Anderson," he crowed from the threshold, unwinding the lengths of wool with his large hands. "Penelope Anderson! How lovely to see you. You look most attractive in blue, did I ever tell you?"

Clearly pleased, Miss Anderson's face compressed into a warm smile. "Professor Parker. Now here's a nice surprise. This is your new workforce." She fluttered a delicate hand toward the group, who stopped what they were doing and sat up at attention.

The man's long face glowed with good humor, and he came toward them with his arms outstretched. "I apologize for being late. I rather underestimated the time it would take to drive here in the rain. I am so pleased to see all of you, you have no idea." He descended the two steps down into the croft, and the level of his eyes fell nearly below that of the party seated at the table. Keith realized with amazement that Professor Parker was a dwarf. He looked at Holl, who was staring wide-eyed. "It's a completely ordinary variation in the gene pool," Keith hissed. "Don't stare."

Holl forced himself to blink and look away. "My apologies on a breach of good manners," he muttered. "For a minute there, I thought it was one of my folk."

"No kidding," Keith agreed. "It was like seeing the Master come into the room, wasn't it?"

"He's even smaller than we are," Holl replied, astonished, as the man approached them. Keith poked an elbow into his friend's ribs.

"Shh. Later. He's talking."

The professor clambered up and settled himself on the bench beside Miss Anderson, and addressed the group very seriously. "You must understand how important we feel this site is."

"Here it comes," said Matthew audibly. He was unperturbed by the archaeologist's appearance, and was obviously wondering when Parker would lower the boom on them. Any good-natured trust he had had at the beginning of the tour had been evaporated by Dr. Stroud. It wasn't fair to Parker, but Keith couldn't really blame Matthew.

Parker enveloped all of them in his wide-flung arms. "We're counting on you to give us your best. I always feel that some of the greatest enthusiasts join these Educatours outings. You're all welcome. I hope we can get to know one another better."

That was so far from what Matthew expected the professor to say that he gaped openly at Parker. Miss Anderson looked pointedly at Matthew. She put a forefinger under her chin and pushed her own jaw upward. Matthew understood the pantomime and closed his mouth. "I did promise a different experience from the one in Inverness," the teacher said, mildly.

"Hurray," cheered Edwin. Max twisted his lips into a satisfied grin and leaned back against the wall of the croft, arms folded behind his head.

"Would there be some cake left for me, I hope?" Parker asked, as the dark-haired girl appeared to clear away the plates. She smiled down at him and nodded toward the covered plates near the till. "Thank you," he said, as a dish and cup were swiftly placed before him. "As the area is somewhat isolated, we have arranged with the kind and indispensable ladies of the tea shop to provide lunch for my team every day." Parker aimed the point of his fork toward them. "Of course, now that includes all of you. As the weather is so inclement, the rest of my people are spending today in Stornoway. The site is down at the bottom of the hill, across the road, and there's no protection from the wind. You'll have noticed that there are almost no trees on the Isle of Lewis, no windbreaks. It isn't sensible to allow the wind to damage the very pieces we're trying to unearth whole, is it? The others are doing a little shopping. You'll meet them tomorrow. Allow me to describe just what it is we're doing here."

With the help of a small chart he unfolded from his coat pocket, Professor Parker outlined the project, and detailed how much had already been done. With jabs of his fork, he indicated what he hoped to have accomplished every few days. "But you have to understand that the peat makes it very hard work. Between the time the Leodhas Cairns were built and the present day, the Isle of Lewis has undergone several climactic and topographical changes. There was thick forest here, once, and when that died, the heather began to cover everything. I'm counting on all of you to have patience. You've had a month's experience already at hard labor, so you know what is needed here." The others chuckled. They had already forgotten the professor's stature, and were genuinely listening to what he had to say.

Holl watched him closely. This Big Person's size made Holl feel a sudden kinship for him. He felt that he shouldn't be permitting such a superficial similarity to make a difference, but it did. He smiled whenever Parker met his eyes, which the professor did frequently with all the members of the group, drawing them in and making them feel accepted.

This one's a born leader, Holl thought. *I wonder if I will make the same good showing when my turn comes to lead.*

The next morning when they came out of the Mackenzie house, the sun was already high in a clear, bright blue sky.

Keith stretched, and listened to the vertebrae in his back click into place. "I'm stiff. The cats got into the room last night and sat on me in a different place every time I turned over."

Holl grunted, stumping down the hill beside him. "You're a magnet for lower life forms, Keith Doyle. They feel a kinship with you."

"Ha, ha," Keith said, refusing to acknowledge a putdown. It was a bright morning, and there were songbirds trilling in the distance. It was unbelievably pastoral. He felt relaxed and energetic at the same time. He couldn't wait to get down to the site and start work.

The day was not as warm as one in Inverness, but it felt springlike. The sun was trying to burn its way through the thick layer of cumulus clouds that interrupted its beams from time to time, but it was there. Everything looked and felt so sharp it crackled. At the bottom of the hill, the sea had been hewn out of silver-gray flint, and polished into waves. The noise of waves crashing seemed detached from it. In the field next door, the sheep sang them a morning chorus in baritone and alto voices, drowning out the birds.

"Morning, ladies," Keith called, feeling expansive after a big, hot breakfast. "These are all shorn," he observed to Holl.

"You were wearing their winter coats on your back yesterday," Holl pointed out. "I'm sure they're relieved now, but they'd have been glad of it a day ago."

"I know, can you believe the change?" Keith said, looking around him at the hills, and taking in the beauty of the land. He stretched out his arms and felt the heat of the sun through his thin sleeves. "Yesterday it was next door to a blizzard, and today it's summer again. I thought only the midwest did this much of a quick change act. Of course, Lewis might have been at it longer. This place feels *old*."

"Aye, it does," Holl acknowledged, concentrating. "Old bones, and little to keep the skin from sloughing away in the wind."

"I feel that there's something deeper to this place than it looks. Don't you feel it? Maybe there's magic here," Keith suggested hopefully.

Holl shook his head. "I don't sense much of it, myself."

"Well, what about that circle of stones up there? We walked through it yesterday. That's supposed to be a temple or something."

"As nice an office building as I've ever been in," Holl said flatly, ignoring the bait Keith had laid before him. "But I do like this island. It isn't a bad place at all."

"Nope. I like it, too. All browns, greens, and dark blues. It's kind of a macho landscape," Keith added, trying to sum up the sensation. "It's beautiful without being full of little roses and daisies. You know, I think we're going to have to forget about your bellflowers for the time being. There's hardly anything growing around here except for heather and yellow gorse."

"I know it," Holl said mournfully. His hair fluttered in the wind, and he pushed it out of his eyes with an impatient hand. Keith noticed that the ears were still in their Big Person form. He decided to brave the question.

He cleared his throat, and tried to sound casual. "Say, Holl, why haven't you changed your ears back?"

The elf started, and then shrugged, his shoulders sagging low. "Oh, I intended to. As soon as I got out of the hospital, I was going to change them back. Our ears are badges of pride to us, as you know. I realized that you had urged me to alter them to save my life, but I'd sooner evade detection by wit."

"Yeah, but you were in no condition to use wit. It was the best thing I could think of with you lying there unconscious. So why are they still round? Going native?" Keith asked, forcing his voice to be light.

Holl was silent for a long time. The words stung him, because that's just what Curran and the other Conservatives would say to him back home. "Well, it's easier this way to get along," Holl said uneasily, but he was as little satisfied with the answer as Keith.

"You're getting along fine. The other guys like you just as you are."

"They don't know what I am. They accept me well enough," Holl acknowledged, grudgingly, "so long as they think I'm one of them, and a child at that. Only now, I can take off my hat in company. Imagine what they would say if I went bareheaded among them in my normal state."

"I can't imagine you doing that," Keith said, truthfully. "But the guys are used to your hat, too."

"It's artificial in this culture. It was easier in downstate Illinois, where many men wear their caps in diners and stores. Here, I stand out too much. It's considered an affectation for my head to remain covered all the time."

"Oh," said Keith, sadly. "Well, *I* like you the way you were, bullheaded tradition and all. I admired the way you survive by sneaking around but never pretending to be different. I'm sorry you've lost pride in yourself, denying your elfhood."

"Elfhood! Your terms, Keith Doyle . . . well, I haven't!" Holl protested hotly, kicking stones down the hill. "It's just . . . easier to be this way."

"Forever?" Keith asked, softly. Holl gave him a sad look which made him wish he had kept his mouth shut. The mixture of unhappy emotions that had surfaced in Holl's face for that brief moment surprised him. Keith would have offered an apology, but they had nearly reached the site, and other people were now within earshot. There was nothing Keith could do to take back his words. The discussion was over.

• Chapter 14 •

"Good morning," Dr. Parker hailed them. "I cannot get used to having the sun up so early. How strange to have it light nearly the clock round! It makes me feel as if I should be up and doing at what usually proves to be an ungodly hour. As you can see, we're a small group, so we greet your arrival with pleasure, as we will miss you when your time is up. By then, we're expecting a group of students from the University of Wales, but that's, let's see, nearly three weeks away. Ah, but let me introduce you to your co-workers. Mind the gate there. The latch sticks."

A waist-high wooden fence of pickets and wire had been driven into the tall grass, encircling the site and dipping down the shallow slope to where the land fell off abruptly into the sea. The half-revealed mound of small, smooth boulders they were investigating, which seemed set in a depression lower than the surrounding terrain, lay nearly on the shore of a small inlet west of the standing stones, which were visible above them on the high hilltop. Parker hurried forward to open the gate, nearly disappearing behind it, and admitted Keith and Holl with a wave. By its pale, unweathered color, Keith judged that the fence was recent.

"Why is this here?" Keith said. "It's not like you have to keep the crowds out."

"I don't mind the curious onlooker," Parker said, expansively, latching the gate behind them, "so long as it's human. I don't want to have to pay the local sheepherders for the loss of a nosy ewe. The sheep are everywhere on this island, if you hadn't noticed. You're the last two to arrive, I think." Parker screwed up his long face and did a mental count. "Yes. Please, come with me.

"Not much of the Neolithic culture remains on view here, except for cairns and round, chambered tombs, which is what we have on this site. The Leodhas Cairns have had rather an interesting history. They were built long before the peat covered Lewis, and were shown on topographical maps to be no more than irregularities in the gneiss. Can you imagine? They were already two thousand years old when the Romans came to this island." Keith and Holl waited while Parker clambered over a low projection under the grass. Keith started almost guiltily when he realized that he had just stepped over the same ridge without conscious effort. He and Holl slowed their pace until the small professor caught up. Parker didn't seem to notice any hesitation on their part or expect any special consideration, and continued his chat.

"You'll have noticed on the way here from town how very much construction is going on here on the Isle, haven't you?" He met their eyes again, in his friendly way, and waited for nods. "Ah. Well, demolition here above the western shores of Loch Roag caused subsidence in the neighboring fields. The sea was much lower when all these monuments were built. Air pockets and water pockets have been waiting for just such a momentous disturbance, and some of them burst. The outlines of long-buried stone structures were exposed in the peat, like furniture in an empty house under bedsheets. Suddenly, all this came into view."

Keith could easily see what Parker was talking about. The other two low mounds lay revealed some yards away from the one which the party was excavating. He had seen similar lumps of peat and grass in a dozen places between Stornoway and Callanish, and wondered just what it was that told the scientists they were different from all the other lumps. The marks of tearing and wrenching were just a little newer than most of the features of the Lewisian landscape.

"There's bound to be some damage to the structures underneath, since what these poor old fellows have just experienced is tantamount to an earthquake. That's one of the things we need to determine. We hope it won't be much. It'll be some years before we've uncovered all the secrets of this place, but it's rather exciting to be the first to open the box, if you see what I mean," Parker continued, engagingly. "Now, some underground caverns may have collapsed. The sea has been nibbling away at Lewis for ages, drowning farmland, and possibly other burial sites. Those small islands you see out there were once simply high ground. Hence our haste to uncover the secrets of the past in the low places. We don't want it to disappear before we've had a good look, eh? Nor you to disappear into the bowels of the earth. I caution you to pick your way warily, because we don't know if there is further instability under the site itself. There's strange stories told of the Western Islands, and of the Long Island in particular."

Keith felt his whiskers twitch in anticipation. He wondered if Dr. Parker knew any of those stories, and if he would tell them.

The group was divided among the professor's regular assistants. "Can any of you type?" Parker asked, hopefully. Of the ones who raised their hands, Holl and Mrs. Turner were chosen, and paired off with a blond-maned young man to organize the data and transfer measurements and notations into a personal computer right there on the site. Keith was relieved. He didn't feel he could work the whole day alongside Holl, unless they could settle their argument and undo the tension it had caused between them. There was more going on with his friend than mere unwanted cosmetic alteration. Holl was moody, and he seemed to walk around in a daze half the time. Maybe after a day of hard work Holl would have a chance to cool off, and *then* they could talk. Keith knew that he wasn't to blame for his friend's mood. The ear thing was just the tip, so to speak, of Holl's troubles. Holl was just going to have to call long distance and see what was really happening on the farm. Maybe one of the others, Marm or Tay, perhaps, would give him a true report.

Keith found that he and Narit were assigned to work with Dr. Stafford. Dr. Parker's second in command was a giant, with rough, blond hair and beard, and a deeply tanned, lined face, giving him the aspect of a lion walking upright. He had returned only a few weeks ago from an archaeological exploration in Africa. While they worked, the "Lion" described in a booming voice the investigations in which he had participated near a site known as Great Zimbabwe. "I'd have been there longer, but the governments down there tend to limit the amount of time that foreign scientists can stay each year. It means you've got to pass the baton on to someone who joins you partway into the dig, like in a relay race, to look for things you were still seeking when your time ran out. No continuity." Keith glanced occasionally over his shoulder at Matthew, who was listening to Stafford with a sort of hero worship written indelibly all over him like tattoos, while hoisting buckets of the heavy peat out of the pit. Dr. Stafford treated them all with a dry, humorous affection that Keith found appealing.

The Neolithic era was positively new minting as far as Stafford's usual speciality went, but he had come to the Hebrides to assist Dr. Parker, who had been his tutor thirty years ago. Now he was a tenured professor in the department which Parker chaired. Stafford clucked over Parker protectively when the small professor was trying to do too much.

"And he hasn't changed his ways at all in thirty years. He's still not taking care of himself," the Lion complained in his booming voice.

Keith liked Stafford instantly, and he started watching Parker, too, turning the director away from treading on loose rocks that would plummet him into the depths of a pit. Parker tended to work like a kitten, expending all his energies in great bursts of activity, then sitting down exhausted. The man was so involved in what he was doing that he seemed absentminded. It was mere appearance, though. Anyone who moved a stone or a shard of pottery or a bone without marking the site found Parker at his or her shoulder, fitting the piece back into the enveloping peat, signaling for the measuring rods and camera.

Parker attracted young scientists who were of a similarly intense but easygoing nature. The Educatours group found they were working very hard, but their questions were never treated as stupid or a waste of time by the team. The core group was small, a fact which worried Parker openly, when he reflected on how little time he had to examine this site.

As Keith worked on the open mound, and saw the outlines of the tombs begin to emerge more clearly in his eyes, he sympathized with Parker's longing to stay. Keith himself probably wouldn't be satisfied until he had explored all three structures. The wind played gently with them that day, sending tentative breezes among them instead of the forceful gales. As the sun rose higher, it got warmer, burning off the morning mist. The birds' morning song changed to conversational trill, and the sheep, sounding strangely distant, could be heard adding their music to the chorus.

"If there's any luck, we'll find an intact version of the chambered tomb which is up there," Parker told them, pointing up at the standing stones. "I'd give my eyeteeth for a few unspoiled artifacts as well. Peat is anaerobic, and does kindly by organic compounds, but with the sea so close, I've no idea what will be left."

Under the noon sun, the colors in the landscape were even more pronounced, greens and yellows drenched with light. When he paused for breath, Keith started picking out the colors that echoed the ones woven into his tweed jacket, in the things that he could see growing on the land.

"Are the dyes made from these things, like the peat for brown, and the heather for purple and green?" he asked the tea shop ladies at lunch. "I couldn't help but notice that what's out there ends up in there." He pointed to the shelves.

"You'd better ask the weavers that question," the dark-haired girl said, serving him a sandwich and a bowl of soup. "I know only that they design their own patterns, and mix the colors to suit themselves. You might ask old Mrs. MacLeod about it. I'm sure I don't know."

Holl paid little attention to the discussions going on behind his back. Ignoring his lunch, he fingered the lengths of cloth on the shelf again and again, trying to make up his mind what might best serve the needs of those in the village. "You've got to like something which is virtually indestructible, sews well, is remarkably warm, and has a natural waterproofing from the lanolin," he had explained to Keith over and over again in the bed-and-breakfast. "You don't see sheep with such a long wool staple in the Midwest as you do here. We're not yet self-sufficient enough to be making our own cloth, and it would still take years to achieve a quality like this."

Now Holl was using his interest as an excuse not to sit down and eat with Keith. "You've got tons of money with you," Keith pointed out, patiently, coming up and leaning over his friend's shoulder. "Why don't you just make up your mind and bring a lot of cloth back for your folk? They sell it by the yard here, and it isn't that expensive for the value."

"It's remarkable stuff," Holl said, almost to himself. He had fallen in love with the multicolored fabrics. He was inspecting each bolt, and making sketches of the various weaves with color notations.

"He's right," Keith commented to the tea shop's ladies. "This stuff is so good it's a wonder why you have any left on the shelf at all."

The young woman made a friendly grimace. "Ah, well, if we had more customers like you, we might sell out more frequently. But I think that *those* people scare away the tourists." Keith didn't need to ask who *those* people were. The unkempt band hanging around the tents behind the shop had put some of their group, Mrs. Green and Mrs. Turner particularly, on edge, though they never actually accosted any of the party. The ladies would only approach the croft with escorts. Keith had seen worse, but he didn't say so. The girl seemed genuinely distressed.

"Who are they?" Keith asked.

"Traveling folk, mostly. Gypsy folk, harmless. But they're a damned nuisance, and we wish they'd pull up their tents and move on."

"What are they waiting for?"

"They're worshipers of the Old Way. They've been here for the solstice, since the Wiltshire England police have blocked them out of Stonehenge for their destructive habits, and now they say they are waiting for the full moon. Their dirt and disrespectful attitudes chase away the shyer customers." The girl sighed. "Oh, some of them are probably genuine worshippers, but there're bad apples in every barrel. Look out for them."

"We will." Keith paid for their meals. He picked up Holl's sandwich and wrapped it in a paper napkin. On the way out of the building, he plumped the small package into Holl's hands. "Eat. You need strength to worry."

The elf regarded him with cynical amusement.

"Point taken, Keith Doyle."

Investigations on the others in the Educatours party came through from the Home Office, and were posted to Michaels on the island. Michaels perused them impatiently. None of the students or the adults had a criminal record, or in fact any notations of subversive behavior at all. None of them were likely to be his contact. They all seemed to be "above suspicion." O'Day had chosen his camouflage well.

There was another element present, one which Michaels suspected might prove to be the mysterious contact. The dirty lot of traveling folk who were camped out behind the tea shop were a possibility. But if he had been chasing Danny O'Day for a month for a mere shipment of drugs or stolen jewelry, the chief would go spare. No, Michaels's intuition told him there was more to O'Day's visit than ready valuables easily disposed of for cash.

The week began auspiciously, but the weather was not always as clement in the following days. Usually it was calmer in the mornings, though the moist dew clung to everything, making the peat cold and slippery. During the afternoons that were too windy or rainy for work, the boys spent the better part of the day sheltering in the tea shop before the coach took them to Stornoway for the evenings. There, they discussed the dig, with the same gusto they had evinced in Glasgow. Miss Anderson was pleased to see their good spirits had had a resurgence. Matthew and the others still complained being in the Western Islands was like exile, but it was good-natured griping. It wasn't really as if they had been entirely deprived of beer for a fortnight, what with all the pubs in Stornoway.

They were vitally interested in what was going on at the site.

Professor Parker was almost apologetic that almost no perishable grave goods were turning up. He had been hoping for some examples of craftworks to augment the funerary materials that were contained in the cairns. What they were finding was mostly fossilized bone and pottery. Keith knew that Matthew was disappointed. He had hoped to recreate his Glasgow experience, unearthing a successful find. Matthew was working hard to find something the professor would be pleased with.

"You have a true talent for this job," Holl told the young man, sincerely.

"Yeah, you sure do," Keith chorused.

Matthew's oddly thin skin blushed scarlet. "I'm enjoying it," he confessed.

Martin elbowed him. "Pretty soon the hols will be over, though."

Matthew nodded sadly. "I know it. I thought six weeks would be a long time, but it's not."

The tea shop served only tea and soft drinks, and it became crowded several times a day by the many coach tours that visited Callanish, so the group hung about there only when there was nowhere else to go. On the proprietress's part, the students were allowed to stay there only because they were well-groomed and clean, a contrast to the unwanted guests behind the shop, but it was made clear to them that they, too, remained under protest. Keith and the others tried not to wear out their welcome, but they could tell that the ladies would prefer it if the whole lot of them would clear off at once.

Holl's gloom had worn off by the end of the first day. In an effort to keep his friend from falling back into a gray mood, Keith asked Miss Anderson about setting up a tour of Lewis and Harris, the southern half of the Long Island, one that would include a lot of wool shops, but the teacher reluctantly had to refuse.

"The coach's brakes aren't in the best condition right now. We're doing pretty well in making it safely between Callanish and Stornoway every day—well, wait until you see the roads in the interior of the island before you protest that we could do it. They are steep and very narrow. I wouldn't advise trying an extended trip until the vehicle is fixed. The driver is awaiting a part to be sent to a garage here. Perhaps later, near the end of the tour."

"I tried," Keith reported back to Holl. "We'll have to wait for a while."

"Ah, well," the Little One said, resignedly. "Still, I appreciate you trying to cheer me up. It means a lot."

The U.S. passport office, in a pointed example of hands-across-the-water, had come through with the files which Michaels had requested. The chief's secretary read the details to Michaels over the phone. The agent stood in the only public telephone in the village. It was a new telephone and worked a treat, but the booth was unaccountably open to the elements six inches off the ground, like a lady holding her skirts up off the floor. It gave the wind a perfect chance to freeze his ankles while holding him virtually immobile.

"The passport issued to Keith E. Doyle is a fairly recent renewal, issued only weeks before he arrived in Britain." The chief's secretary read the information from the sheet over the phone to Michaels.

Michaels huffed into his moustache. The pay telephone from which he had placed his call was situated halfway between the Mackenzie farm and the dig site. From it, he could keep a reasonably constant eye on his quarries. "He mustn't have made up his mind on a pseudonym until the last minute."

"The one for Holland Doyle, aged fourteen . . ."

"Ha ha. If he's fourteen, I'm Winnie the Pooh."

"Yes, sir," the secretary continued. ". . . was issued even more recently, only a day or two before departure from the U.S. It seems there is a real Keith Doyle. We haven't been able to locate him, though. He's got two addresses, one in the north of the state of Illinois, and one in midstate. The FBI is sending an investigator to look into it."

"Could be a full-fledged plot, I mean the family's name is Irish, after all," Michaels pointed out significantly.

"We hope it's not that, sir."

"Aye, I hope not, too. Probably we'll find the boy is dossed down with a bird somewhere in between one place and the other."

"In the meantime, we want you to keep a close eye on those two."

"Well, I wish they'd go ahead and make a move. I haven't seen a trace of any stranger yet who might be O'Day's contact. The weather's a great bloody mess, and there's hardly a pub in the place. Praise God the coach takes them off to the town every night, where there's a little civilization. Regular old package tour, this is becoming. I feel like a gypsy."

"The chief asks that you keep him posted, sir."

"Thanks, love. I've already asked the local constabulary to lend me a hand if I have to lay gloves on our boys. More tomorrow."

• Chapter 15 •

"There'll be a full moon tonight," Keith said, early one morning when they were dressing for breakfast. He reached over the edge of the bed for his old pair of socks to toss them into his suitcase. They weren't there. "Holl, did you pick up my socks?"

"I'd sooner handle nuclear waste, and well you know it," Holl said, indignantly. "You must have stowed them somewhere yourself."

Keith glanced under the bed, then sifted through one side of his duffle for a clean pair. "Oh, well, I must have put them away last night without thinking. I'm about due to hit the laundromat again, unless Mrs. Mackenzie will let us use her washing machine. I was really beat yesterday. Dr. Parker is working us like robots, but you know, I'm enjoying myself, and learning a lot on top of everything. I'm going to have muscles in my brain as well as on my arms when I go home."

"At least that'll give your skull some makeweight," Holl said, tartly, but his heart wasn't in the banter. While working on transferring Parker's minutiae, he'd had plenty of time to think about his troubles. Holl had no idea whether his life as he left it would be ruined when he got home. Nothing could be done while he was here but worry, so worry he did. Whether he completed either half of his quest now was immaterial to him. He had considered over and over again phoning Maura at the farm as Keith Doyle suggested, and demanding to know what was going on. But if there was nothing to know, no truth to what his mother had said, then it would be a slap in the face of distrust to Maura, and shame to him. In the meantime, he had plenty of occupation for his hands.

"You know, I think this is probably what they mean by the midsummer full moon, Holl," Keith offered again, fastening his shoes.

"Midsummer Eve is the summer solstice, the twenty-first of June. Any buffoon knows that."

"No, but look: summer is June, July and August, right?" Keith argued. "This is July, so it's the middle of summer. That makes tonight midsummer. Right?"

"As a syllogist you're correct, but custom has dictated otherwise for centuries."

Keith made a face at him. "Yeah, I know, but it sounds like a good excuse. I want to go up to the stones under the full moon. If any of the fairy folk visit that circle, this would be the time of the month when they'd do it. You could come with me. . . ." Keith hinted temptingly.

"Hmph! Well, give my regards to Oberon and Titania if you see them. I'm going to stay and get a quiet night's sleep without you thrashing in the next bed."

At midnight, armed with a camera full of very fast film, and a notepad with pencil, Keith made his way out of the house. The moon was a burning, silver disk high in the twilight sky. It threw a sharp shadow behind every stone and pebble on the road, and made the shallow potholes appear bottomless pits. Keith trudged up the hill to the circle of standing stones, listening to his feet crunch on the pebbled road. It was very quiet, and only a soft breeze ruffled his hair. The sensation of still, sleeping power came to him again. He imagined it surrounding and lifting him up, until he could dive into the milky heart of the moon. He glanced back over his shoulder toward the dig site. It was dark, with the sea tossing up occasional white glints in the distance. Every light in the village was out. Though he could see every house and barn, there was no illumination in any of them, except for one white dot, like an eye, at the bottom of Mrs. Mackenzie's garden. Keith blinked at it. It was probably a birdbath, or something else which was reflective.

As he came over the breast of the hill, he saw the Callanish stones gleaming like candle flames under the moon, reflecting its silver light. It was hard to believe how few stones there actually were. In the sharp black and white it looked like there were thousands. Keith saw a sudden movement under the tallest monolith, heard a snatch of vocal tone like a shout, then a rhythmic booming. He pricked up his ears. Suddenly, white figures burst from the center circle and melted into the darkness between the other stones. Keith ran the rest of the distance to get a better look. Could this be the fay, rising from the center of the hill to its peak to dance in the ancient temple?

Then one of them tripped on a rock, and hopped around, uttering a curse. Keith blinked and shook his head. It was only the hippies who had been living in the parking lot for the last month. This was their long awaited full moon ceremony. They ran forward again, raising their arms and touching hands at the height. Their voices carried to him. They were chanting and dancing in a circle around the tallest stone. Once again Keith wondered at their ability to ignore the temperature—they were all stark naked.

Their ceremony appeared to be breaking up. Keith was relieved, since he had felt like an intruder watching. The sensation of mystic power hadn't passed yet. He waited until they were all back by their campsite before he crossed the gate and entered the monument at the south end.

He followed the broken avenue slowly, and stopped at the edge of the circle. With a mental apology to anything he might be disrupting, and a quiet prayer that it wouldn't be something as cranky as that fairy mound in Glasgow, he stepped forward.

Keith wandered around the circle, listening and waiting, the camera hanging by its strap from his shoulder. The sound of the sea and the low chatter of the worshipers reached him as a soft undercurrent to the silence. He waited at each compass point by the inner perimeter of the circle, looking around for any clue that there might be something else here. Something he hadn't seen or sensed yet. The west was barren. So was the north. He was doing a full rotation on his heels at the east, when a tall, dark figure, the moon behind it casting a ghostly outline, rose before him from the cairn. Keith gulped, and fumbled one handed for his camera. The other hand was steadying him on the monolith behind him. Abruptly the figure stretched out a hand and spoke, but not in staves of poetry or syllables of the wild magic.

"Ere, gi'es a hand, mate. I fell on my ruddy bum in here. Wot time is it?" So he wasn't faced with a prince of the underworld, or one of the returning dead. This was only a human being like himself, one of the hippies. Disappointed but vastly relieved, Keith waited for the hammering of his heart to stop.

He extended a hand, and helped the man out. One warm hand clasped his fingers, and the other grasped his wrist. Unlike his fellows, this traveler was clad in the usual daily mix of odd garments.

"Just after midnight," Keith said, squinting at his watch, as his new acquaintance beat the dust out of his clothes.

"Yank, are you? Hoy, I got an uncle in America." The lanky man caressed his temples with both hands. "Christ, I've been passed out for hours. Me head feels like it's been detonated. Where'd everyone go?"

Unwilling to trust his voice to perform without a squeak, Keith pointed toward the campsite, where the others, once again robed, were sitting around the fire. Now that their devotions were ended, they were breaking out cans of beer, and having one heck of a party.

"Ta," said the tall man, and stalked expertly between the stones to rejoin his friends. "Y'can come sit with us if you want. Plenty for everyone."

"No, thanks," Keith said, shaking his head. "I'm driving." The man lifted his hands palm up, and clapped Keith on the shoulder as he went by.

Dejected, the American left the circle and walked back to the house. Holl was right. There was nothing there. He let himself into the room and walked on tiptoe, trying to be quiet.

"Well, was there a dancing circle of magic elves under the moonlight?" a wry voice asked out of the darkness.

Keith felt for his bed and sat down on it. It gave under him with a wheeze and a thump. "I guess Shakespeare was wrong." Moodily, he pulled off his shoes and pushed them to one side with his foot. One by one, his socks went off in opposite directions.

"Did you see any fairies?"

"Nope. Just hippies."

"Hm. Not the same thing at all. Perhaps you should come next year in June, when it genuinely is midsummer," Holl suggested in a gentle tone. "The Fair Folk likely have rules, too."

Keith shrugged, disappointed. "I didn't feel a trace of

anything out of the ordinary up there, not in the circle. But I can't believe that there's nothing here to find, I mean not just on Midsummer Eve. It's such an amazing structure. This place feels so old, and magical, that I expect something. If it's here, though, I'll find it," he finished, with determination.

"I count on you for that," Holl said drowsily, and turned over to go back to sleep. "Good night, now."

The next morning, Keith arose feeling a little sleepy, and wondered if even the hippies had been a product of the moonlight and his own imagination. Yawning, he glanced at his watch, and blanched. "Hey, Holl, it's late! Breakfast is almost over."

"Eh?" The elf blinked at him, and sat up.

"Quarter to nine!" Keith seized his shaving kit and hurried out to the bathroom. When he returned, he started throwing on his clothes distractedly while Holl went out to take his turn under the shower. He came back, well-scrubbed, and feeling much more alert. The red-haired student was on his knees casting around under the bed.

"Have you seen my shoes?" Keith asked.

"I did. They're just outside the door, where you left them." Holl started dressing, much more calmly than his roommate.

Keith looked puzzled. "I didn't put them outside. I remember sitting on the bed to take them off. I think." He tilted his head, trying to bring back the events of the last evening. "Oh, well." He opened the door and dragged his shoes back into the room, and sat down on the bed to put them on.

"Holl," he said suddenly, in a strangled voice. "Now I'm sure that something is happening. Look!" He held up one of the shoes.

"It's clean. What about it?"

"No, but look. The heels are whole. And my socks are gone again. Boy, after the letdown I got up in the stone circle, it's hard to believe. I wonder if there isn't some kind of Wee Folk right here, who does little jobs around the house."

"Oh, come now!" Holl scoffed.

"They might take the socks as a fee," Keith continued thoughtfully, as if Holl hadn't spoken. "I didn't leave any money in the shoes. I mean, I didn't know that anyone would come by to fix them, so they took whatever else was around. They're nice socks, one hundred percent wool."

"Nonsense. What a lot of silly legends you do attribute to folk like mine," Holl said, exasperated. "Making supernatural repair men out of us. Shoemakers and housecleaners!"

"Okay," Keith demanded, rounding on him, "if the old story isn't true, how did you people get a reputation for fixing shoes and so on? You're master craftsmen, you might have wanted to do favors for some Big Folk, who, it turned out, knew a writer."

Holl was adamant. "Nothing to do with us. We're natural creatures. We've always kept to ourselves, live and let live."

Keith shook the shoe at him. "Well, what about this? You saw what they looked like yesterday. They were about to fall apart. Now the heels have grown back. Where there's smoke, there's fire," he reasoned.

"Yes, and where there are balloons, there's hot air," Holl retorted.

"Well, do you have any idea what to look for, to tell if there are other Little Folk in this place?"

"No, I have not. You're the one with all the experience with looking for bogeys. I've lived in one place all my life, and you've been everywhere else I've visited so far, and that's not much."

"Maybe Mrs. Mackenzie knows about her little helper. I'm going to ask her."

"She'll think you're as mad as I do."

Keith grinned. "You know, that's exactly what everyone used to say, and somehow I connected up with you guys, so I'm just going to keep on asking."

He put the question delicately to their hostess, expecting her to be disconcerted by the concept of magical folk, but instead, Keith was the one surprised. As soon as she ascertained what her American guest was asking, Mrs. Mackenzie burst into merry laughter. "Have I got a *what* roaming around my house? *I* polished your shoes, lad. They were in foul state after your night on the stanes, when you came in so late. My poor clean floor! I'd also bought a repair kit for my boy's boot heels, and there was enough left to patch yours. They were all to pieces, I saw. So, you were looking for the whippitie-stourie, were you?"

Keith seized his manual of Scots dialect from his back pocket and started to thumb through it. "A 'house brownie'? Um, I suppose something like that."

Mrs. Mackenzie kept on laughing, wiping tears from the corners of her eyes, until Keith had turned as red as his hair. "Nowt of it, lad. Look here." She led them through the dining room to the kitchen. Keith and Holl followed the sound of her chortling down the hall.

"I didna ken this oun,so I guessit t'be yours. It's too late to rescue."

From her nest next to the stove, the slim female Siamese blinked adoring blue eyes up at Keith. Under her sable paws, she held her prey, one of Keith's gray wool socks. Delicately, the cat dipped her head, and dragged a few fibers out of the sock, swallowed them, and did it again, like a child playing "he loves me, he loves me not."

"She's eating my sock," Keith said incredulously.

"Ach, she does that," complained the landlady, fondly. "Loves wool, she does. There's nothing we can do about it. It's scold her and scold her all the time, and nowt comes of it. It's a wonder she doesn't chase down the sheep for their fleece. She must have slippit in when I fetched out your boots. I'll clear out a drawer for you to keep them safe from now on."

Holl started laughing. Keith was outraged at the destruction of his clothes, but disappointed that there was no more to the mystery than a shoe-shining landlady and a sock-eating cat. "There you go, Keith Doyle. One more legend of the Fair Folk relegated to children's tales."

"Ah," Mrs. Mackenzie nodded. "If you wanted the true Fair Folk, you ought to look for them under the moonlight when the milk runs. That's what my gran used to tell me. Now, come and have breakfast. All this wild jumping at conclusions has no doubt left you ravening."

Chastened, Keith went back into the dining room, and took his place at the table. A homely clatter erupted from the kitchen. Soon, heralded by the appearance of the female cat, who was still holding part of Keith's sock in her mouth, Mrs. Mackenzie emerged with a tray. Keith matched stares with the cat, who took her prey out into the hall.

"There, that ought to fill you," the woman said, maternally, setting a full plate before him and ruffling his hair.

Keith took some toast out of the toast rack before it could cool, and buttered it. "Thanks. By the way, what's the holed stone out beyond the garden? There's traces of white in the bowl. I saw it sort of reflected in the moonlight from above on the way back from the circle, and I went down to look at it . . . Um, did I say something wrong?"

Mrs. Mackenzie had started like a rabbit. Before she answered, she looked right, left, and over her shoulder as if someone might be listening to her right there in her dining room. "It's old," she said at last. "Ancient as time. You reminded me, talking of the Hidden Things. My gran, who owned this farm, had the custom passed to her by her gran, and so to me, to pour the first milking there every full moon. I've done it for years."

"For prosperity, and so on?" Keith asked, surprisingly calm. She nodded. "To propitiate the *bodach*? And the cream of the well, too?"

"The what?" Holl asked, skeptically, looking from one to the other.

"Water drawn from a well on the first night of the new moon," Keith explained.

"That's right." Mrs. Mackenzie was embarrassed. "It's my ain silly superstitions, but I'm amazed that anyone understands how it is."

Keith put on his most persuasive and trustworthy face. "Come on, Mrs. Mackenzie. Tell me the rest. I study this kind of thing. I'm interested in it. I read a lot about legends and things. I promise we won't laugh. We take it very seriously. You can give us all the details."

She seemed a bit shamefaced, twisting a fold of her tweed skirt between her fingers, and wouldn't meet the boys' eyes. "Seems silly to tell you all," the landlady continued, "but I haven't stopped doing it for fear there's aught to it. It's there for the wee ones, to keep off the dark and help the farm along." Keith glanced triumphantly at Holl, who rolled his eyes impatiently at him. "They don't do jobs, but they do look after us. I put the milk by, and it's all gone in the morning. It might be cats, but I've never dared to stay and look."

"Does it have to be you who leaves the milk?" Keith asked.

"I don't ken it matters, so long as it's left," she replied, surprised. Keith pressed his advantage.

"It's the full moon tonight. Can I do it tonight? Please?"

Holl rose out of his seat and shook a finger in the young man's face. "Oh, no, Keith Doyle," he cautioned. "Don't you dare. Remember what the Master said. No meddling."

"It might be nothing at all, just some neighbor's cat, like Mrs. Mackenzie says," Keith informed him. "All I want to do is see what's out there, talk to whatever it is, and maybe take a few pictures."

"I wouldna mind," Mrs. Mackenzie added. "The creepity feelings of that stane make me nervous. If he's a mind to try, I've no objections."

"There, you see?" Keith finished, triumphantly. "And she thinks I'm brave."

Exasperated, Holl threw up his hands. "I'm against it, and so would any other creature of sense. My family tells stories of this kind of spirit to scare the children, not to encourage them to waylay it. You don't know if it's hornets or kittens making the buzzing, but you want to stick your hand into the nest. Please yourself."

" 'From ghosties and ghoulies and long leggity beasties/ And things that go bump in the night, Good Lord deliver us,' " Keith declaimed in a spooky voice. Mrs. Mackenzie nervously gathered up the tray and went back into the kitchen.

Holl pursed his lips. "You're mocking me. If you want to take your own silly risks, go ahead."

"How bad could it be? It might be nothing. I've followed up dead-end leads before. This is probably just one more." Keith quoted the research books he had been reading. "Remember the *bodach* of Jura. They're good guys. The little wise men of the oak trees, and so on. You'd want to meet someone like that, wouldn't you? This guy might be nothing more than a house brownie, like Mrs. Mackenzie says. Look, if I leave out their fee without trying to do them a kindness, I might be able to talk with them and get a few pictures without 'laying' it."

"Chasing it away," Holl translated, "if there was actually anything here. But this isn't Jura. The *bodach* of this land might be quite a bit different than the ones there. And Mrs. Mackenzie won't be pleased if you scare off her household protector."

"Well, she doesn't actually know if he does anything for them now, or if there's anyone who comes for the milk. This way, I'll settle the matter quietly for the lady, and prove its existence for her, and for you, too."

• Chapter 16 •

That night, as soon as the moon appeared, Keith promptly took himself outside, and made himself a comfortable nest in the grass next to the weathered stone at the end of the garden path. Mrs. Mackenzie came out with a bowl of milk balanced carefully on her hands. The cats followed her hopefully, but veered away as soon as she stopped next to the stone.

"It's from the first milking, that I'll guarantee," Mrs. Mackenzie said, looking a little nervous. "Everything should be proper."

"Thanks," Keith replied, blithely, pouring the milk into the depression on top of the stone and handing the bowl back to her. "It'll be all right. There's nothing to worry about. I've brought something extra, in case your visitor's upset that someone's here waiting for it." He produced a bottle of whiskey, propped it on top of the stone. His camera was loaded and waiting. There were new batteries in both the flash unit and the electric torch on his knee.

Mrs. Mackenzie was hesitant. "I'll leave ye to't, then, shall I?"

"Yup," Keith said happily. He felt confident. This was much better than the night before—his intuition told him so. "I'll be in later. Thanks again."

The landlady retreated along the path, followed by the cats. Keith was alone. It was only about eight o'clock. He figured he would have a long wait until the *bodach* thought everyone was in bed and came to claim its tribute. Keith had looked up the illustration of "whippitie-stourie" in one of his guides. It showed a small figure with a slim torso and tiny, long fingers. He was certain he could handle something like that. After discovering a whole village full of Little Folk who were a lot bigger than that, a brownie should be an ordinary night's work. *On the other hand, there* was *something supernatural about shivering in high July in the Northern Hemisphere in a tweed jacket and a woolly hat as if it was December,* Keith thought, as he hunkered down between two apple trees to wait.

"Sir, I think we've got something here," Michaels whispered excitedly into the pay telephone at the bottom of the hill. "I've been watching O'Day closely, and there's no doubt about it, he's up to something. He's been acting pretty strangely all day, hieing about with his camera. Can you get me clearance on whether there's a secure installation hereabout he might be preparing to photograph?"

On the other end of the line, the chief became very agitated. "I'll inquire of the Home Office in Edinburgh. Where's O'Day now?"

"I think he's waiting for a contact, sir. There's a bottle of whiskey on the stone he's sitting beside, and he looks settled in for a long night."

"Aha! This is probably it," the chief said. "Well done, Michaels. Take him. As soon as possible before our security is breached. Move in. You have our full support. And if nothing comes of it, we can say he was detained to help us with our enquiries."

"Yes, sir." Michaels hung up, and moved purposefully to his observation spot. At last, there was going to be an end to his vigil.

Holl denounced Keith's antics as a waste of time and declined to wait outside with him. Instead, he had gone into the sitting room and opened one of Keith's storybooks to pass the time. Two of the Siamese cats sat down on his legs, holding them in place with slim, dark paws and narrow chins. In a short time, Mrs. Mackenzie had appeared with a tea tray, laden with steaming pots, cups, and a plate of small cakes.

"I always have a wee bite when I'm up late. I don't think I could sleep! Whew! It's like the best ghost stories, isn't it, with him sitten out for the spirit's rising? You don't feel as your cousin does, then?" she asked, offering him tea. "You don't think there's a Presence out there?"

"No, I don't," Holl said firmly, stirring his cup with a minute spoon. "It's a lot of nonsense. He's going to spend a long, cold night. But at least you'll both be satisfied at the end of it."

"Aye," the landlady said. "Well, I don't believe it, but he does shape a convincing line of talk. I'm quite enjoying it." They sipped tea for a while in silence. Holl read his book, and Mrs. Mackenzie stared calmly at the electric fire. At last, she gathered up the tea things and rose.

"Any road, I'm going to me bed. I have early mornings."

"Good night," Holl said, and looked after her thoughtfully when the door closed. He folded the book over on his thumb.

So Keith Doyle looked as silly to his own kind as he did to Holls, playing about with stones and such. Why was Keith so willing to take foolish chances? Did he feel he had nothing to lose? Or did he consider himself so lucky that there was nothing he couldn't do? That was one of the differences between them. Well, it made one think. Keith Doyle seemed to see small adventures like this as part of his life, not an unwelcome intrusion or an overwhelming specter. If nothing happened, he didn't even feel he had wasted his time on the caper. "You can't learn from your mistakes if you never make any," he was fond of saying.

Holl felt that the parts of his own life were much too precious to risk. This trip was the largest departure from his normal routine that he had ever made—that he had ever thought of making—and look what it did to the rest of his comfortable existence.

Sticks and stones, I'm starting to think like Bilbo Baggins, Holl chided himself. Adventures which made one late for dinner! How hidebound I am, really. He decided all at once that it was silly to let Keith take such risks by himself. There was something about that garden place by the stone he disliked. He finally admitted to himself that he hadn't wanted to wait with his friend because it made him uncomfortable. And if it did, might there not be something to his feeling? Shaking off the cats, he went to wash his hands.

In the bathroom, he confronted his own reflection in the mirror. It angered him to see the simple, soft, rounded eartips pushing through his hair, where tall, elegant, sharply pointed ears ought to be. He was filled with a surge of rage.

"What an idiot I've been, hiding behind the semblance of one of the Big Folk. Enough of this masquerading!" Holl spat. "I'll be myself, with all the silly things I do, and whether or not they're right, I'll stand by my decisions." With an effort of will, he concentrated his energies on his ears. Like corn growing in time action photography, the simple round buds opened, and sprouted into tall, backswept points. Holl smiled at his reflection. "Better." He couldn't wait to tell Keith about his decision.

"If there's nothing to it, at least I'll keep him company. There'll be one supernatural being in the garden this way, at least in the eyes of Keith Doyle." And if it really was dangerous . . . He hurried out to join his friend. There was a lot to talk about. They had the whole night through to debate.

Content with his new resolve, he let himself out the kitchen door to the garden.

The moon was full above him, giving the garden a diffuse glow. The path split just outside the door, and took right angles around the rectangular lawn, past dark flower beds full of nodding bushes of blossom, translucent in the moonlight. From the far edge, it continued in a single line between a line of slim apple trees with hard, half-grown fruits clinging to the boughs. At the end of the path, Holl could see the whitewashed stone, and a dark form next to it with a gleaming, red crown. As he walked toward it, the figure became animated, raising thin limbs to its head. There was a brilliant flash of hot white light, then another, in quick succession. Then the shouting started. It wasn't Keith's voice doing the yelling.

His blood drained suddenly into his feet, making him feel faint. There was someone out there. He ran the final distance to the stone. Keith had stood up and was grappling with a figure slightly smaller than he. Holl dashed through the apple trees, beating the branches out of his way with an impatient arm. By the time he reached the stone, both figures were gone, and the garden was silent. Holl hadn't seen them go. He crossed the last few feet to the stone. The whiskey bottle was smashed on the paving stones, and the camera lay in the grass beside it.

"Keith! Keith Doyle!" Holl cried, casting around desperately. No answer. He had been taken away.

"Lad, lad, what is it?" Mrs. Mackenzie called, emerging from between the trees. She was in a long cotton nightdress, and was hastily wrapping an overcoat about herself. "Why are you shouting? Where's your cousin, hey?"

Holl turned wild eyes on her. "He's gone! I think he's been carried off!"

"What?" Mrs. Mackenzie looked at him curiously, scrutinizing the side of his head. His hair was well back from his ears, which were anything but hidden in the bright moonlight. Holl hastily blurred her vision, and guided her gaze to focus upon his eyes. She blinked, not sure she had seen anything out of the ordinary, and continued speaking normally, having hardly missed a beat. "Taken by the Wee Ones? Oh, no, lad. Look here." She led him to the edge of the garden. "See how the ground drops away right there? He fell down the hill, I'm certain. Ye can't see the bottom from where we're standing, what with the gorse being that thick. He'll be back up after he's gathered his wits." She pulled a protesting Holl away from the edge. "There's no sense you falling down after him. The ground is unchancy where they've been digging it up. You can lose a leg in the peat. Wait for him. See, there's his torch, here next to the stane. He's no light to lead him upward. Wait until morning, eh? If he's not back then, my husband'll help ye. Come on back inside. I'll give you a coop o'hot milk. That'll settle ye to sleep."

Numb with shock, Holl followed her to the house. His brain raced as he sat in the kitchen while the kindly woman bustled around him. Where could Keith be? Did he just fall down the hill? Surely he would have answered if he was able, if he hadn't been knocked unconscious. The strong sensation of power he had noticed by the stone during the day was amplified now.

"Now you drink that, and off ye go to bed. Your cousin will be in soon." She left him alone, and padded away down the corridor. Obediently, Holl drank the milk, which relaxed his tightly wound insides, and listened closely. The woman had shut her door and was already lying down in bed. In a moment, all was silent except for the gentle breathing of the others in the house.

"Oh, I've missed my ears," Holl said, clapping his hands over them. "Imagine having to live with the sorry level of near-deafness the Big Folk do." Feeling somewhat restored, Holl slipped toward the door, and eased it open. He heard an inquiring sound near his knees. It was the female cat.

"Now don't you hinder me, miss," Holl commanded her. "You're part of the reason he's in trouble." The cat sat down on her haunches with an "I don't know *what* you're talking about" expression, and began to wash her breast fur with nodding licks. Holl closed the door behind him and hurried down across the grass to the holed stone.

He couldn't shout for Keith Doyle again, not unless he wanted to raise the household. He and Keith hadn't yet met Mr. Mackenzie, but they had seen him once or twice from the back as he left the house early in the morning. He had an uncompromising way of walking. Holl got the impression that Mrs. Mackenzie's husband didn't approve of her telling silly folk tales to strangers.

More than anything else, Holl didn't want to be hindered in his search. If Keith had been swept away by a *thing*, Holl needed to be able to deal with it and not have to worry about Big Folk bystanders wandering into the line of fire. He unsheathed his whittling knife, and started poking around. Between the knife and his own abilities, he should be well able to take care of himself.

He had better night vision than the average among his Folk, and there was a full moon overhead, with only wisps of clouds across it. The sun was out of sight now, but the sky still wore a down-colored cloak that made it nearly as light as it had been at eight P.M. They were far enough north that there was no true night during the summer months. He tried listening for Keith, but he realized that he was too shaken to sense properly, so he would have to seek him in the mindblind, Big Folk way. Still, Holl had his hunter's training and all the book learning available to him from the stacks of Gillington Library.

The site of Keith's disappearance had little to tell him. The whitewashed stone bowl was dry. Somehow, the *bodach* had taken the traditional offering without actually touching the stone. The whiskey bottle lay smashed into glistening fragments on the pavement nearby. Holl hadn't noticed it before, but there was no smell of spilled liquor. The bottle, like the bowl, was dry. The tax seal on the neck hadn't been broken, but there wasn't a drop of liquor left on the grass or the ground. The *bodach* had taken Keith Doyle's gift, and Keith Doyle as well.

The ground had sealed up seamlessly above them, if this was where the two had vanished. This place had nothing more to tell him. Perhaps he could try Mrs. Mackenzie's suggestion, and examine the scree outside of the garden. He hoped that Keith might be there, nursing a sore leg or arm, but in his heart, Holl doubted it. He smelled magic. Not the simple tricks and bending of rules that his Big Friend called magic. This was the real thing: the raw, wild power.

"Keith Doyle, you were right," Holl said out loud, "and I'm sorry you're not here for me to tell you so." He clutched Keith's camera at his side. Whatever was on the film would tell him a lot about what he was dealing with. Holl slipped out of the garden and went to have a look.

Michaels emerged from the bushes, and surveyed the ground next to the stone. That was a pretty trick. Must have been something to do with the light. One minute O'Day and his contact were on the top of the hill in plain sight. A bright flash, and suddenly they were nowhere to be seen. Good optics, and good timing with it. He hadn't had even so much as a glance at the face of the contact. The chief wouldn't be pleased about that. The office still had no clue as to whom O'Day's client was. Michaels had missed his brief chance to make an identification.

"Hey, presto, and they're gone." O'Day and his contact had eluded him, their minder, and gone off somewhere to have their private chat. Obviously, they hadn't let the boy in on the secret of the vanishing act; from what Michaels could see of the lad running to and fro on the hilltop. He seemed genuinely worried. Well, better to have one than neither. He would get what he could out of the boy. Certainly neither of them could have seen Michaels. The agent prided himself that he had been completely discreet in tailing them, even down to watching them at their third, interminable archaeological dig. Here was a perfect opportunity to approach the young one and take him into custody. No fuss, no fight. He could get the older one when he turned up again.

• Chapter 17 •

Holl left the farm by the road and trotted downhill until he found a break in the fence that would let him in under the bottom of the garden. Stones and chunks of peat lay tumbled in a heap against a sheer face at the top of the field. Evidently, one of the hidden air bubbles in the uneven gneiss had given way in the same explosion that had exposed the Leodhas Cairns. It had crumbled away the edge of the bluff on which Mrs. Mackenzie's garden rested, leaving a dangerous patch that could cause any unwary walker to tumble over. Easy to see why she thought Keith had simply fallen.

No footsteps, no signs were here at all to suggest that anyone had been here in the past week, let alone the last hour, but that also could be a trick of camouflage played by the *bodach*. Holl started poking through the tumbled rocks, hoping to find the way into the earth. The shifting mass was too heavy for him to deal with on his own. He didn't feel any natural openings in the stone wall behind it.

He stood up, unsatisfied. For all appearances, the *bodach* must have opened up the ground and gone straight through it with Keith Doyle in tow. That smacked of true experience, familiarity with the terrain, and great power. Holl's heart sank. He didn't have enough of what Keith called "oomph" to open the way for himself, even if he knew where to start. Once he had rested and calmed down, he *might* be able to trace where Keith had gone by listening for him, and try to figure out what to do from there. Holl felt very small and alone. The situation was too much for him to handle by himself; that he knew.

Resigned, he left the field and made his way down to the telephone booth at the bottom of the hill. He would have to call home. It griped at his very sense of independence, but there he was. There was no good reason to put off the inevitable, humbling as it would be. He had plenty of change in his pocket. He calculated it was no more than mid-evening at home. He didn't want to alarm the other Folk unduly, even if it was an emergency. The only person who could be hurt by a delay was Keith Doyle. It wouldn't serve the Big Person at all for Holl to be proud and stiffnecked. He owed Keith that, at least.

His heart was beating like a bronze gong in his chest as he dialed the international number, and waited for the distant phone to ring. It didn't bode well for his hope of future responsibilities to have to cry for help, but he knew he was too much a stranger in the outside world.

One of the children answered the ringing. Holl cleared his throat.

"Good evening, Borget. It's Holl." He spoke in the Folks'

own language, in case there was anyone near to overhear him. "It is late; shouldn't you be asleep?...Ah, how is Keith Doyle?" Holl grimaced, and quickly devised a phrase that wasn't a falsehood. The Folk never lied to children, it was counterproductive to their development. "Well, he is much as you would expect he is." *In trouble, as usual,* he thought. "Can you fetch the Master and tell him that I would like to speak with him? Thank you."

The Master came on the line, and Holl explained the situation to him, keeping his voice under tight control. "I've done all that I can, except continue to search and hope I am lucky," he concluded. "I could go on until I stick my foot in it, but if the *bodach* takes me, too, then there's two of us lost, instead of just one, and no one will be left to look. I'm unequal to the problem, which is well out of my ken. I would welcome any help or suggestions you can offer."

There was a long silence on the other end of the line. Holl shifted uneasily, waiting.

When at last he answered, the Master sounded curiously distant. "I vill see to it that help vill reach you vithin a day."

Holl felt a wash of relief. "Thank you, Master."

He hung up, buoyed up by lighter spirits than he'd felt in hours. Who would come? Probably Aylmer, or Dennet, Holl's father, two who were good at hunting and tracking. Possibly Enoch, the Master's own son, who had been giving Keith lessons, and with whom the Big Person might have a traceable bond. In the meanwhile, Holl had best keep trying to pick up a trail. There was no sympathy to be had for one of the Folk who met a situation without having all the facts at hand. He decided to go back and examine the fallen rock again.

In thirty paces, it hit him again that he had abrogated his responsibility for finishing his task on his own. Someone older and wiser was coming to take over. He felt suddenly that he had failed in his mission by calling for help, showing that he was really in tow to his Big Person protector, and not out on his own. He kicked a stone, which skipped noisily over the road and into the nettles at the side. Well, he couldn't just abandon Keith Doyle, no matter whether his pride was whole or in tatters.

A few minutes more careful examination of the field convinced Holl that there was nothing more to be learned from the scree or the garden. The *bodach* had hidden his path well. The whole hill was imbued and riddled with old magic, the product of thousands of years. Holl needed to catch the precise end of the latest thread to have it lead him back to Keith Doyle. That would take time. He stood up, wiping his hands forlornly on his trouser legs and directing a sensing around for clues. He wondered where to start, for there was a lot of geography to cover. "Thank heavens you didn't vanish in Asia, Keith Doyle. I'm fortunate this is only an island."

"Hallo?" A man's head appeared through the break in the hedge. "Lost something, my lad?" The man stepped over the fallen bracken and approached him. He was a kindly-faced, middle-aged, middle-sized Big Person with a droopy moustache and spectacles. He was wearing a rumpled tweed suit and carrying a walking stick.

"My cousin, sir," Holl answered. He combed his hair down with his fingers and concentrated on keeping the man from looking at his ears.

"What, down here?" The man surveyed the scene with an eye of concern, and poked at the tumble of rocks with his stick.

"I don't know!" Holl lost control of his voice, and the reply sounded like a wail.

"Now, now," the man said soothingly, hooking the cane over his wrist and patting Holl on the back. "None of that. We'll soon turn him up. You come with me, and we'll find him. What's your cousin's name?"

"Keith Doyle. He's an American." Meekly, Holl accompanied the man down the edge of the field. Big People certainly could be kind. It was very fortunate that this man had turned up when he had. There was sure to be a procedure for finding missing persons, though he didn't know how much good it would do if the person had been kidnapped by a mythical being.

Together, they searched the farm and the area around it, calling in low voices for Keith. It turned out that the landscape lent itself amazingly well to concealing things. There were places among the boulders and shallow ravines where an entire house could be hidden, invisible from all eyes except for those of birds. It promised to be a long job on foot.

Michaels was still convinced that O'Day must have disappeared to make a rendezvous with a contact, but the boy was genuinely upset by his companion's disappearance. It began to occur to him that perhaps O'Day had been abducted by someone who didn't bid high enough for his services. On the other hand, it might be that the meeting with the mysterious contact was still going on. That wasn't uncommon in these illicit matters. Where there was little trust, negotiations could take hours, or more. Michaels himself had sat surveillance on days-long "stake-outs," as the Americans liked to call them. Or perhaps he had just gotten lost. This island had fewer signs and directions than anyplace he'd ever been, and that included London. Michaels could understand him being lost.

Delicate questioning of his young associate revealed that the boy didn't seem to know that he'd been under scrutiny. In fact, he seemed grateful for Michaels's assistance in helping him to look for O'Day. He was refreshingly naive. It was almost as if he didn't realize that there was any reason to hide their presence in the island. Michaels was struck by a horrific thought: could O'Day have brought this innocent with him, and not revealed the mission to him? The boy would be in genuine danger, with a prison sentence at one end, or death at the other, never knowing he was a target. That was monstrous! Indecent! He wanted to find O'Day now to give him a piece of his mind.

"Of a' the scunnersome, junting fuils to interrupt a ca'm evening with a nasty licht like tha'," the mocking voice, as brown-black as mascara, echoed in Keith's head, as the skinny figure wrestled with him. "A curse on ye, then. A curse!" The creature was amazingly strong, and hard to get a grip on. His hands always seemed to miss the hold he aimed for.

Keith had already dropped the camera somewhere in the grass. A tiny, unoccupied part of his mind hoped it was all right. The rest of him was involved actively in wishing he could get away from this angry thing, but it was a lot stronger than he was.

Both of them had been surprised when the mysterious figure popped right out of the ground next to the stone and reached for the milk. Keith was amazed that anyone had really come for the offering, but the *bodach,* if that's what it was, appeared completely thunderstruck that anything should be there waiting for him.

When the thing first appeared, Keith had unwound like a spring, bounding astonished to his feet. He realized he should have been expecting an entrance like that. You could hardly expect a mystical household guardian to use a gate. The reality stunned him. By comparison, discovering the Little Folk in the bottom of Gillington Library was ordinary. *They* used doors. The Little Folk were a heck of a lot more friendly to strangers than this creature was. It sure didn't look like the illustration in his guide book. There was nothing benign or playful about this creature. He wondered what they would call it. The being's coloration seemed to blend with the landscape, so Keith couldn't get a very clear idea of what it actually looked like. It didn't resemble the picture in the book, or the old man that some of the fairy tales referred to. It was creepy looking, and wasn't at all pleased to see him. Their eyes met in the shadowy light, the stranger's round and dark, with hidden lights like obsidian. Before it could move again, possibly disappearing through the ground again, Keith had raised his waiting camera, and snapped its picture. The figure was flooded with the hot, white light. It threw up a limb, a skinny arm, in front of its eyes, and then lunged for Keith, shouting. Keith tried to hold the being off at arm's length, but it let him have it with all four limbs, kicking and scratching with long nails like talons. He pushed it away, but it sprang back to him like a yo-yo. They grappled all around the end of the garden, then something hit Keith solidly on the side of the head.

He cried out. The landscape around him, the house, the garden, the sea and the stone, faded away into darkness. As he felt himself losing consciousness, the angry voice muttered in his ears. "No speech ye shall have ever in your life of three of the pleasures: women, wine, nor gold. I curse yer tongue as so ye've cursed my een!" The voice grew into a wail, and died away.

Keith was lying on his side in a shallow puddle of water when he came to. His head felt like he'd spent the night drinking rotgut, or maybe cider, but he couldn't remember a day in the last month when he'd had more than a beer, two at the most. He pried his eyes open. That was no help. It was just as dark outside as it was under his eyelids. The summer sun hadn't left any part of Scotland in absolute darkness for the last month. So where was he? Or was he blind? He held up a hand in front of his nose. Nothing. Not even a shadow. Groaning, he started to sit up.

Suddenly, his invisible whiskers broadcast an alert to his brain: Don't move any further to the right! Keith raised a tentative hand toward his right shoulder. A quarter inch beyond it was a rough stone wall, damp and slimy. Ech. Keith's fingers recoiled. So he was inside something, he thought. *Well, that's progress. Nothing's wrong with my eyes. Where is this place? And what?*

Using hands and whiskers, he explored his new environment. The invisible wiry hairs, spread forward as well as to the side, kept him from smashing his nose into the stone walls. It was a tiny chamber, roughly round like a flattened sphere, almost four feet high, and about five feet in diameter, too small for him either to stand up or lie down in any comfort. The slimy stuff smelled fresh and green, like moss, so he stopped flinching from its touch. Two feet up in the middle of one side was an irregular hole as wide as his shoulders and approximately the shape of an inverted triangle. Apart from several smaller holes on the opposite side of the floor, it was the only thing which suggested an exit from the bubble of rock. He was alone, but that, he reflected, depended on whom you're alone from. Holl was nowhere nearby, which was bad, but then neither was the *bodach*, which was good.

"Oh, well, I had no idea the little guy would get so mad. I must be right under the hill," he reasoned, turning his head upward to gaze blindly into the darkness. He wondered how long he had been down there. A good, deep yawn summoned up no sensation of fatigue, suggesting that he had slept at least a few hours. It was probably near dawn outside. He felt for his watch. It was gone. For a wild moment, he considered pounding on the ceiling of his chamber and shouting for help. "Nope, I'm probably halfway to Australia. No one would hear a thing. I've got to get out of here on my own."

It was cool in the chamber, but not oppressively so. Keith had read somewhere that the constant temperature underground was 57° Fahrenheit. The scientists who had discovered that never accounted for the subjective reaction to damp, which made it feel more chilly. Keith was glad of his tweed jacket and woolly hat, but suspected that those garments were going to make it difficult for him to wriggle through the passageway. If only he knew how far the passage extended, or what it looked like. It could be a long narrow tube, or it might drop off suddenly if this was a small bubble on the side of a larger cavern. He wished he hadn't dropped the flashlight. It would be so comforting right now to see.

What he needed was some alternate form of illumination. He wondered if Enoch's lessons in magic extended to providing light in slimy, moss-covered underground caverns. Keith stuck his head through the opening, and felt a tiny breeze of cool air. There was no source of light anywhere nearby, but he wasn't imagining it: the air was moving. He raised two fingers to feel its strength and source of direction. "Great!" he said out loud. "This opens out into the upper air someplace. I'll just follow it. Ow!"

Keith pulled his head back, clutching his jaw. It felt like something had just socked him on both sides of his face. One of his teeth had just suffered a stabbing pain in the cold air. It hurt abominably. He probed it with his tongue. The top surface of the tooth felt rough, and his tongue dipped into a depression that hadn't been there earlier. "I think my filling fell out when I hit my head," Keith moaned. "Great. here I am being Darby O'Gill, or maybe Rip Van Winkle in the depths of the Scottish mountains, and I've got dental repair problems." On further investigation, he discovered that every one of his silver fillings were gone. They couldn't all have fallen out. There had to be another reason, maybe a magical one. Keith grimaced. The *bodach*, teaching him another lesson. That was probably where his watch had gone, too. Well, fixing his mouth would have to wait until he got the mouth, and the rest of his body, out of this cavern and back in civilization.

"No offense!" he said hopefully to the air, wondering if the *bodach* was listening. "Sorry I spooked you! I was just being curious." No answer. He sighed. It was probably long gone, sulking in a hole somewhere. He wished Holl or Enoch was with him. He thought of Diane, too, and wondered if he'd ever see her again. Well, there was no use being morbid. Either he would get himself out of here, or he wouldn't. It wasn't hopeless, he told his twisting stomach. He had a lot of resources he hadn't even used yet. So with that firm resolution, why did he feel like he wanted to cry? Light, that's what he needed. It would lift his mood if he could see. He let out a yowl of frustration.

Together, Michaels and the boy explored the fields around the Mackenzie farm. They scrambled over huge hillocks of peat, calling Keith's name among herds of huge, somnolent sheep. Holl skidded to a halt and clung to a wet clump of heather when a voice that sounded like Keith's answered their call.

"Do you hear that? I think that's him!"

"Yes, I do. Which way is he?"

The cry came again, sounding more distressed. Holl clambered almost on all fours over the next rise, and dropped flat on his belly. On the other side, there was a pit six or eight feet deep. In the bottom stood a half-grown lamb. As Holl appeared, the lamb started calling again, in a consonantless cry that sounded just like the one they had been following. "Eeeehhhhhhh-hhhhh!"

The ewe was on the lip of the pit, peering through the heather fronds at her offspring, wondering how he got down there.

"That's . . . my cousin, without a doubt," Holl said disappointed, slumping partway down into a sitting position. "The lost lamb." He slid down the slope, and dropped cautiously into the pit. With a heave, he boosted the young sheep out. Both it and its mother ran away while Michaels gave Holl a hand up. "But no Keith, anywhere around here."

"You'd very likely need a helicopter to survey the place properly," the man said resignedly. "If you broke a leg, no one might find you for weeks."

Holl thought about spending weeks searching the island, and his heart sank.

"By now, he'd have wandered farther afield," Michaels speculated. "We can describe a greater radius tomorrow. I'll lay on a car. You'd best get some rest now, lad." There was no fear that he'd run away overnight, the agent told himself, or wonder where Michaels had come from. The boy's concern was genuine.

Holl was too exhausted by the end of the day to do more than thank his newfound friend and stagger back into the Mackenzie home. Disorientingly, the light was no different than it had been early that morning when he had begun his search. He had the hopeless feeling that no time had passed at all, and that all his efforts were in vain.

Keith tried to apply scientific detachment to his situation. To make light in the depths of the cave, he needed something that had natural tendencies toward giving off light. Crystals of some kinds did, when you crushed them. Unfortunately, if the rock around him was of the same type as the stuff on the surface, and he had no reason to believe it wasn't, the matrix was too flimsy to have very productive crystals for magic-making, and besides, he had nothing with which he could crush it. It ought to be granite or quartz, not shale. So what else was there with him?

He shifted to get out of the puddle, which was getting deeper—probably because he was sitting on one of its drainage holes—and moved closer to one of the moss-covered walls. There was a soft gurgle as the water ran out. Keith sat idly playing with the clumps of moss. Didn't decaying vegetation have light-emitting qualities? Unless this chamber flooded completely at times, washing away all the dead stuff, there should be plenty here to make a light.

Nervously, he stroked a bit of moss and thought about how to construct the magical process around it. This was the first time he had tried to do anything serious without supervision. On the outer surface, the moss was like damp fur, but it got more fibrous inside where it hung on to the rock face. Keith tried to think of the dead fibers as bulb filaments. Reaching down deep inside himself, he worked at *knowing* that it was right for moss to glow in the dark, that it did all the time, and shaped his energies to fit that thought.

He opened his eyes. It was still dark. He sank back, feeling defeated. Doing magic took a lot out of him. Well, there was no point in waiting for the crosstown bus. He'd have to make his way out in the dark. Keith started to feel his way toward the opening, then realized that he could just see it, as a blacker darkness at the other side of the bubble. There was the faintest, spooky glimmer everywhere in the chamber, just on the edge of vision, like fluorescent lines in a haunted house. It wasn't a dramatic difference, but it was good enough. He had light! Now, to get out of here.

Once he could distinguish the shape of the triangular passage, it occurred to him how uncomfortable it would be to crawl through. He'd have to keep one knee on each of the sloping faces, and hope he didn't get stuck anywhere. His own weight would press him into the trench like peanut butter in a celery stalk. It was a wonder to him how the *bodach* had gotten him in there. Never mind; he was leaving.

An absurd litany sang itself in his head, "You'd better go before you go." Feeling a little foolish, he relieved himself over one of the drainage holes. The simple, natural action took part of the urgency off his need to get moving, and gave him one less concern to think about.

"Okay, here goes." Expelling a deep breath, Keith crawled into the passage and, with an effort of will, dragged the spell in after him. The faint glow touched the walls of the narrow tunnel wherever there was moss. It extended the full length of his body behind, but only a couple of feet in front of him. He convinced the glow to move further forward, illuminating more of the passage ahead. His legs and back could take care of themselves. There was so little room he could hardly turn his head to look back over his shoulder.

He found as he went along that he could see better as he became accustomed to the fairy light of the moss. The light didn't extend far enough to give him much view ahead, so Keith let his whiskers guide him through the zig-zagging tube. His hands and knees shifted and slipped on the slick stone. Several times his supports shot out from under him, dropping him painfully onto his stomach in the narrow crevice between the rocks. Below him in the angle of the slabs, a trickle of water flowed back toward the way he had come. "At least I can tell I'm going uphill," he reasoned.

Sometimes the tunnel was so tight that his nose was only an inch from the streaks of mosslight. The layers of rock were neither smooth nor evenly laid. The upthrust which had exposed this interstice through which he was crawling had also splintered pieces which shifted suddenly under his hands. More than once, Keith had to catch himself to keep from sliding back toward the round chamber. He edged forward, concentrating on keeping the fairy light in sight. Suddenly, he found a place where the glow was interrupted, and resumed a few feet further along the tunnel.

He lowered himself and crept up to the dark spot on his belly, and peered over the edge. Perhaps it was just a dip in the path, and he could drop into it on his feet, and hoist himself up on the other side. There was no light beneath him. He felt the stone with his fingers, and discovered that the slab he was on ended. His fingers walked downward until his whole arm was extended into the abyss. Nothing at all lay within reach. He called down into it, but no echo came back. With his thumb, he loosened a pebble and dropped it into the gap. A long, long interval went by before he heard the faint *plop* as it struck, but it was so far away he couldn't tell if it had hit water or more stone. That was *deep*. He squinted up at the mosslight on the other side of the gap. It would take almost a running start to get over it, and he was already traveling uphill. Once committed to crossing, he would be unable to pull himself back again.

Keith rose to his knees. He was thankful that he couldn't see the sheer drop into the pit. It would only frighten him to know that what he was about to do was impossible. He pushed back half a pace, and then with all his strength, flung himself across.

He landed on the other side, and hastily scrabbled up onto the new slab, bracing his knees against the side to keep from falling backwards. His legs slipped partway into the gap, and he flailed his arms for anything to grab onto.

A long splinter of stone protruding from the right side of the tunnel met his grasp. He battened onto it like a sea urchin clinging for dear life to its ship. Just as he slipped past his waist into the pit, he got his arms around the stone, and hauled himself upward. The stone wrenched partway out of its socket, but by then Keith was sitting on the far side of the gap.

He sat on the edge of the pit panting. His heart was beating so loudly it was pounding in his ears. He had to go on.

Crawling over one of the gigantic splinters, he found that the passage had leveled out. The stream issued from beneath a new slab in a different direction, which had only a handspan's clearance. He could no longer follow the flow of the water.

"Last oasis for twenty miles," he told himself. This junction was the largest opening in which he had been, with just enough room to stretch. He wiggled his shoulders, feeling the cramp relax slightly. Twisting and maneuvering in the narrow tunnel with difficulty, he reversed his position so his head was hanging over the edge of the slab just above the source of the stream. With a cupped hand, he scooped up water. It was cold, and except for being mineral heavy, tasted pure. It was probably rainwater, precipitating down through the porous construction of the rock.

He became conscious of a panting, gasping noise echoing around him, and felt hot sweat break out on his forehead in fear. Was there something following him? Was the *bodach* right behind him? Keith felt a wash of terror break over him. He held his breath to listen, and the sound ceased. Keith expelled air in a gasp that turned into relieved, nearly hysterical laughter, and heard the gasping start again, "It's me."

It was his own breathing, magnified by the enveloping walls.

The *bodach* was certainly seeing to it that he was sufficiently punished for disturbing it. He had nearly scared himself to death.

At the top of the next slab, he came to a dead end. Keith was forced to snake his way downhill slightly and to the right, where he had seen the blackness of a new passageway. His sodden jacket caught on a projection. Keith stopped to pull it loose. It didn't want to come. He yanked. The fabric came free suddenly, sending him sliding quickly down the tube on the mass of wet wool as if he had been greased.

"Help!"

Keith tried to stop his fall by sticking out his hands and feet into the tunnel's narrow sides, but that only got them bruised. At last, with an effort, he rose to his knees. bracing his back against the top of the sloping tunnel. He knelt there panting for a moment, before cautiously beginning the climb back to his turnoff. He was getting tired, and, he hated to admit, hungry. He had been too excited to eat much dinner. How long ago was that? A few hours or a few days?

The passage to the right led him to a perfectly level T-junction. Keith waited for a moment, feeling for the air currents before he decided which way to go. The only clue he had for leaving this labyrinth was the wind from the outside world. He put his chin down on his folded arms to rest.

• Chapter 18 •

Mrs. Mackenzie caught up with Holl as he was making his way back to his room. She was taken aback by his ragged and dirty appearance, but more concerned by the worried look on his face that made him look many times his years.

"Lad, where have you been? Your Miss Anderson's been here seeking after ye. Where's your cousin Keith?"

"I'm not sure," Holl croaked. His voice was worn out from calling Keith's name. "I hope he's all right."

The landlady looked him up and down with a calculating

eye. "Ah, he's just gotten himself lost. Possibly a thump on the heid, and he's mooching about. You've had nothing to eat all day, I'll gi'e odds. Hmm?" Holl nodded. Suddenly he was hungry. The delicious aroma of the family dinner was still in the air. "Well, there's a bacon sandwich or so that needs a home. I'll bring you a plate in the sitting room, with some tea. Go and sit down, and warm yourself."

"Mrs. Mackenzie, would you have another sleeping room?" Holl asked, hopefully, trying to hold himself upright though exhaustion was tugging at his muscles. "I think there's going to be another one of us here by tomorrow."

"Of course I do," the woman asserted heartily. "And happy to have him. Now, you go and sit down, and eat, and then you sleep a good sleep. You must think of nowt more to worry you. All will be well in the morning."

"That's what I'm hoping," Holl said, wearily.

Michaels picked up Holl the next morning in a small car requisitioned from the local authorities. There was only time for a quick circuit of the area before the boy directed Michaels to drive to the Stornoway airport.

"Some of our relatives have heard that Keith has gone missing. They're concerned. I think one of our cousins is coming to see if he can help," the youth explained enigmatically.

Michaels shrugged. It was a transparent story. Without a doubt, this was the original contact coming to verify O'Day's disappearance for himself before the youth would be let off the hook. Best to stay on guard, or he'd likely be missing this lad, too. At the youth's request, Michaels stopped at a chemist's to let him drop off a roll of film. It was Keith's, the boy explained. Michaels began to think that the next time that film manufacturer declared a stock dividend, they could attribute it solely to Danny O'Day.

The airport was small, and not set up for international travel, so Michaels was stunned when the passenger turned out to be two, not one, and both had foreign accents. The caper had begun to take on more and more of an international flavor.

"Holl!" a girl cried. She was a pretty thing, slim and fairly tall, with blue-green eyes and long, blond hair unimproved by nature, so far as Michaels could tell, and quite young. She and the boy met halfway in a warm embrace that all but swept the lad off his feet. An American. "Oh, Holl, what happened to Keith?"

"Wait until I tell you. So they've sent you?" Holl asked, eagerly, inadvertantly ignoring his escort, who stayed close by, listening.

"Not exactly sent," the girl said, glancing sideways at Michaels. "I came along with him." She gestured by tilting her head at the gate door through which a short man was entering.

The second passenger had red hair and a silky, red beard. Michaels was taken aback by the cool, summing glance that the small man gave him through a pair of gold-rimmed spectacles. Those cold, blue eyes had considerable intelligence and determination behind them. This must be the spymaster.

"Diane, this is my friend," Holl said, fluttering a hand toward Michaels, then realizing he didn't know the man's name.

"Michaels," the agent supplied, extending a hand to the man and girl in turn. "How do you do?"

"Well, this is my. . . uncle Friedrich," Diane said. There was something about this man she didn't like, even if Holl did seem to trust him. "My name's Diane Londen. I'm, I'm Holl's sister."

"A pleasure, Miss Londen. I'm no more than a Good Samaritan, encountered upon the road. I'm helping the lad here to find his cousin." Michaels realized that he really towered over the red-haired man. He started to say something, but Diane interrupted him, and dragged him to one side.

"He's very sensitive about his height, you know. Please don't mention it."

"I wouldn't think of it," Michaels promised her. "Is he, er, Keith's father? I couldn't help but notice the, er, similarity of coloring."

Diane raised her eyebrows at him curiously, but smiled winningly. "No, he's our uncle. Cousin Keith takes after his mother. She's *really* tall." Diane sketched a ridiculous distance above the ground with one hand.

"Friedrich Alfheim. How do you do?" the small man demanded in a Teutonic accent, shaking Michaels's hand.

"Alfheim?" Michaels asked, appealing to Diane. "I thought you said he was a Doyle, too?"

"He writes books, you know," Diane whispered, thinking

fast. "This is his pen name. Shh. We don't want his fans to know he's here."

"How did you come so soon?" Holl demanded, taking Diane's bag. Michaels relieved the older man of his suitcase, and led the way out to the car park.

"We came standby," Diane explained. "We just caught the jet; they held it for us while we ran for the gate. It didn't make us very popular, but we made it. If your call had been ten minutes later, we would have missed it completely. As it is, we've been on four planes in the last twenty-four hours, and I'm pooped. What exactly happened?"

"I'm not sure." Reluctant to mention anything to do with magic in front of a stranger, Holl gave them a bowdlerized version of Keith's disappearance. "He vanished last night under the moonlight. My landlady thinks he fell over the edge of her garden where there's been a lot of subsidence. You know Keith. I think he might have wandered off when I wasn't looking, and got lost in the dark. He might have fallen into a pit or over a precipice and hurt himself. This island is made up of geological odds and ends. As we discovered in our searches yesterday, there are thousands of places where things may be concealed."

Once again, Michaels was impressed by the midget playing the part of Holland Doyle, and wondered if he had been wrong thinking that he was a kid. He sounded too intelligent to be a youngster, but you never know with young ones these days. He was concerned—what could have happened to Danny O'Day? Left the boy here to hold the bag while he headed for greener pastures? But this older one, now he was something to watch. A formidable old bastard. He reminded Michaels of his fifth form master.

Keith stirred as he felt something light brush his skin. It was only the faintest hint, but the breeze felt stronger against his left cheek and whiskers than his right. In a moment, he picked himself up and rubbed his palms together. They were raw and hurt, and he knew that if he could see them, they'd be as red as hamburger meat. He thought about taking his socks off his feet and putting them on his hands.

"So long as I'm walking on them, that is. I'm not up to crawling like this any more," Keith admitted to himself. "It's just not a habit that stays with you once you graduate to walking." He decided against it only because he needed the sensitivity of his fingers to help guide him through this labyrinth. Somehow, he'd make it up to his shredded palms later.

There seemed to be more moss wedged into the crevices of the stones. Some of it dangled in his way like ghostly spider webs. The glow had increased to where Keith could distinguish the outline of his own hands and arms. Realizing that he couldn't go on indefinitely without food, he decided to try and alter the spell. If the spelled light could follow him so easily, maybe a ring of the glow could go up toward the sunshine outside, and come back toward him, over and over again, like a neon sign arrow in reverse. He could follow that out. Of course, there were dangers in an idea like that, if the end of the line terminated in a hole too small for him to crawl through, or over a sheer cliff face. Or maybe he was so far underground it would take forever for the light to get back to him. But if the idea worked, Keith felt it was worth the risk. He concentrated, and the glow diminished around him to total darkness.

He waited. Nothing happened for a long time, and Keith felt his hopeful mood start to ebb. "I didn't know when I was well off," he groaned, and started to reverse the spell.

A tiny light appeared just out of the edge of vision, and crept toward him. It was no more than a bit of spidery tracing on the floor, but Keith stared at it with growing joy. "It worked!" he crowed. He crawled energetically along it, as it faded out beneath his hands.

Periodically, his neon sign would disappear completely. Keith took these opportunities to stop and rest until the sun-line renewed itself again. He was making progress steadily upward. Without a regular source of light, he had to rely more heavily than before on his whiskers. He blessed Holl for giving them to him as last year's Christmas gift. At the time, they had been a kind of running family joke. Now, they were saving him.

"I wish Holl was here. No, that's rotten. I wish I was with Holl. He's probably drinking tea and playing with Mrs. Mackenzie's cats." The discomfort in his hands and knees was increasing, but he ignored it. He had to.

As Keith had feared, the next turnoff ended in a T-junction at a solid stone wall with a handsized hole in it. The light, instead of following either of the available paths, came through the wall. In dismay, Keith slapped at the rock. His palm stung, and he winced.

"Now what? Hey, spell, this doesn't help!"

The mosslight continued to glow dispassionately through the hole in the wall. Apparently, this was all the aid his spell could muster. Keith put his eye to the opening and squinted through.

There seemed to be a passageway on the other side, because the light followed the thickness of the wall, then dropped off. He could see a thinner line reappear some distance away, but that was all. Flipping a mental coin, he chose to turn right. The fine yellow glow died away again as he crept away from the T-junction, leaving him in the dark.

This path turned unexpectedly again and again, growing smaller all the while. Keith had to pay close attention to his whiskers to avoid bashing his head on the irregular ceiling. The tunnel had narrowed to barely a foot in diameter. In the end, he was reduced to creeping forward on his belly like a snake. He had to crawl with one arm extended forward to keep from getting his shoulders wedged in.

"I feel like I'm being swallowed by the mountain," he thought. He put his head down and scrabbled his way out of the tight spot. Without the light breeze playing constantly on his face, he knew he would go out of his mind with fear. He had to keep from thinking about the tons of rock, poised above him only by a fluke of nature. If they did anymore blasting nearby, the strata could come down on him and squash him flat, and no one would ever know.

The passage led him steadily around in a loop that went in the general direction of his mosslight. Any minute, he expected to see the burning yellow-white line. That hope was almost all that kept him pushing forward through the stone tube.

Keith crept over a slight bump in the passage floor, and down again. As soon as his hands touched down, he realized he had found the stream once more. There was two inches of water pooling in the worn floor of the tunnel, only this time, it was flowing in the direction he was going. Miserably, he plowed through it, feeling the water soak in through his clothes to his chafed and chilled skin.

He came to a Y-shaped intersection. The left-hand side of the Y leveled off, and its ceiling rose to nearly three feet in height. Keith measured it with a tentative hand following the wall in the darkness. It was a much more inviting tunnel than the right turning. Keith blinked. There was a tiny spark of light down toward the left. That was the way back to his mosslight!

Happily, he rose to his hands and knees, and crawled as fast as he could toward the light.

The golden glow grew much faster than he thought it would. *I must be a lot closer to the way out,* Keith thought, cheerfully. Hot bath and food soon! He was able to urge greater efforts from his hands and knees by promising them that their ordeal would be over very shortly. Head bent to take the strain off his back, Keith made his way along the tunnel. Strangely, the air was heavy and damp here, instead of fresh, as it had been all along the way the mosslight took before.

A sudden roar shook the passage under Keith's knees, like the sound of thunder. His eyes flew up in horror. There was a golden glow only a few feet before him, but it wasn't his little line of spelled moss. It was two points of light like eyes, and the rest of the fearsome face was coalescing around them as he watched. There was a brief suggestion of fangs, then horns, then a loose, stringy mane. He had blundered into something's lair. What was it? The creature roared again, right in his face.

Keith let out a yell and turned almost double on himself to get away from the wide open maw. He backpedaled in the tunnel, flipped over like a cat in a box, and fled back up the passage. The apparition pursued him, its roar causing the whole mountain to vibrate. Pebbles worked loose from the ceiling and fell on him as he scrabbled toward the lower tunnel.

Maybe it's too big to follow me, he prayed. He couldn't make any speed in the low tunnel, not on his elbows and toes, not in the water. All too soon, his whiskers signaled that there was an obstruction in his way. He ducked, and squirmed into the low passage, huddling his body into the smallest knot he could.

The bellowing face was almost on top of him now, bearing down on him like an approaching express train. Keith had nowhere to retreat. The yellow fangs clashed against one another like a boar's tusks, and the hot strings of the mane whipped like summer lightning in the utter blackness of the tunnel, leaving burning after-images. Terrified, Keith threw his arms over his head and waited for the inevitable. He was going to die.

In his ears, the roaring grew and grew, buffeting his ears with sound. Keith imagined the fangs lowering toward his back. His skin grew taut waiting for the first points to tear through the cloth, then his flesh.

Nothing touched him. His whiskers didn't so much as twitch. The beast's noise died away suddenly, leaving silence in its wake. Keith looked up. The beast was nowhere in sight. It had vanished.

If something that big was heading straight at him, and it didn't pass him, and it didn't have room to turn around, a) it must have been an illusion, or b) it went right into one of the stone sides of the tunnel without using a door. Keith was pulling for option A with all his might. In any case, he recognized it as a warning. He'd have to follow the right fork, water, low ceiling, and all. The next time, those fangs probably wouldn't be illusionary.

He wondered briefly if other magical things affected each other. Could passing through another magic field possibly have taken off the spell that the *bodach* laid on him? It was worth an experiment. He felt in his mouth for his fillings. Nothing. His teeth were still hollow and aching in the cold. He tried bucking the terms of the curse. "Say, mister, can you give me change for a d-,d-,doh-." He attempted heroically to force the word "dollar" out of his mouth, and his teeth still ached horribly whenever the cold air hit the open cavities. "No way," he said unhappily. "I need expert help."

The right passage bore a striking resemblance to household plumbing. Keith found himself snaking through smoother tunnels than before, though they were low and narrow. His jacket and trousers were no longer catching on the stone.

Something clicked as he put his hand down on it in the water. It felt like a flat stick. It was too knobbly to ease his way over, so he elected to push it along in front of him in the extended hand. As he crept downhill, the flow of the water started to become stronger. Little trickles joined the main tunnel from small cataracts that rained down on Keith as he passed. Now there was a genuine stream gurgling around him.

Keith's whiskers broadcast an emergency message as soon as his hands touched a ring of rock ahead of him. This was going to be a really tight fit. Gently, Keith eased forward, trying to ignore the water building up behind him. First one shoulder passed through, then the other. He pushed all the air out of his ribcage, and got his chest through next. Everything was going fine until he tried to get his hips into the hole, and remembered too late about his Pocket Scots Dictionary. It stuck up like a deadbolt in his rear jeans pocket, holding him pinned head down under the lip of the rock. Keith's heart started pounding. He bit his tongue. His legs were now awash in stream water. He kicked.

Bracing his elbows on the other side of the ring, Keith took a deep breath and shoved *down*. There was a rip as his jeans pocket tore loose. He was free! With nothing left to hold him in place, Keith tumbled over the lip of the rock and down, followed by a cataract of water.

He landed with a splash in a fast-flowing pond several feet deep, which swirled him around, then dragged him into a broader stream leading further into the bowels of the mountain. Keith banged into rocks and projections sticking out into the water. Gasping, he fought to stay at the surface, but not too high, fearing there might be a low ceiling above him.

His mind started composing epitaphs for an empty tomb in his family cemetery back in Illinois: "Keith Doyle, Died Aged 21. He Rediscovered the Little Folk." "Keith Doyle, Died Aged 21. He Duked it out with a Bogey and Lost." "Keith Doyle, Died Aged 21, Drowned. . . ."

Boy, am I morbid, he thought. At that moment, the stream turned, and deposited him, along with a lot of other debris, in a small hollow. Gratefully, he crawled onto the small bank and held tightly to an outcropping of coarse rock as a shower of small pebbles cascaded down on him from higher up. Every square inch of his body felt as if it had been bruised. I wonder if I should be talking about muchnesses or something, like Alice in Wonderland down the rabbit hole. He coughed up stream water and gasped, tossing his wet hair out of his eyes.

He remembered the voice of the *bodach*, writhing in fury, as it threw the curse on him. The moment played itself over and over again in his memory: the skinny creature with its claws reaching for his face, calling him a mouthful of Scottish maledicta, then pronouncing his doom. "*No speech ye shall have ever in your life of three of the pleasures: women, wine, nor gold. I curse yer tongue as so ye've cursed my een!*" The dark claws raked at him, then the terrible feeling of falling, falling through solid rock. Keith tried to reach out, to run away, but his feet were stuck as if he was standing in wet cement. The ground slipped upward, swallowing him. He saw the outline of the *bodach* seeming to grow taller until the earth and stone covered Keith's eyes and shut off all light. Keith tried to scream, but his mouth didn't seem to be connected to his ears any longer. Something solid connected with the side of his head. The darkness went on and on, deepening the nightmare, until the first tiny glow of mosslight started to dispel the fear. Being drowned in darkness was worse than any curse, although this particular one was going to be *incredibly* inconvenient.

I can live with it, Keith vowed, shuddering. All he could think of were longing visions of food, warmth, and not being wet any more. *Maybe Holl can find a way to take the curse off before I have to deal with it in public*.

He realized that he could think about the future again. Though he was still lost, he was safe for the moment. Even exhausted, that thought gave him some hope. So long as the *bodach* didn't pop out of nowhere again and put him back in the round cave.

• Chapter 19 •

"Now, vhere exactly did you lose him?" the Master asked, pausing at the gate to the Mackenzie garden.

"This way," Holl said, leading the others down to the holed stone. Though he still resented giving up authority, he had to admire how quickly the Master could sum up the facts of a situation. It was possible for him to walk in cold and instantly take over in a crisis. Holl was still a schoolboy in comparison. The Master studied the holed stone with interest, then focused on the whiskey bottle, as Holl had done, as a clue to the way the *bodach* worked. He stood rubbing a fragment of glass between his fingers, thinking.

Holl could sense the directions his thoughts took. He had some finding process he wanted to try, and he didn't want the strange but helpful Mr. Michaels to watch him. That meant Holl had to remove the stranger. Fine and good. With two parties searching, the chances of finding Keith Doyle were raised significantly. He cleared his throat and spoke up. "We'll continue looking in Mr. Michaels's car. It was his suggestion the other day that Keith may have become lost and strayed further. I'll let Mrs. Mackenzie know you're here."

"Gut," the Master said, seeming to come back from very far away. "You go that vay, and ve vill start to familiarize ourselves vith this area. Ve can meet later and share our impressions." He pottered around the garden, and looked over the edge of the field.

"Dismissed, are we?" the Big Person asked, feeling left a little behind by the conversation. "Come on, then. I've got a topo map of this part of the island." He led the way back toward the house. He wasn't sure what the other two actually had to do with his case, but so long as he could keep his quarry under his eye, he was happy.

Diane stood under the apple trees, swaying slightly with fatigue. She had had little sleep in the last twenty-four hours, but she was too worried to go lie down and let the Little Folk alone. The Master noticed as she tried to stifle a yawn, and smiled.

"Mees Londen, I vould be grateful for your assistance, but it is not necessary." As Diane tried to protest, he interrupted her. "I know vhat promises the others extracted from you to look after my vell-being, but I assure you, I vill be fine."

Diane forced her brain to clear, shoving down the sleep toxins like coffee under a plunger. "No, I can't do that. A promise is a promise. Your son Enoch would slice me into little bits and build lanterns out of me if I didn't make sure you were all right. I don't know why they asked, because you'll probably end up looking after me. Besides, I have *got* to know what's happened to Keith. Is he alive?" she asked plaintively.

"Yes, I belief he is, but he is a long vay from here. Let us go into the house and find our starting point."

When he felt like making the effort, the small teacher could be charming. In Diane's opinion, the Master positively buttered up Mrs. Mackenzie while she was showing them the house in general and their rooms in specific.

"Qvite a lofely place," the Master insisted. "A hafen uf calm and beauty against the backdrop uf the vild sea outside."

"I wasna expecting two, since the lad only asked for one extra room," the landlady said, much flattered by the little man with the thick German accent. "It's good fortune I've just seen off one of my other guests. Pity about the young man, is it not?

The village constable is having a wee look around for him. He's likely gathering his wits. So easy to take a wrong turning when you don't know the way. The road dips away when you're no more than a few paces doun it."

"Funny he couldn't see those creepy stones on the top of the hill," Diane mused.

"Ah, weel, they're not visible from every side," Mrs. Mackenzie explained.

"Thank you," the Master said. "Ve vill endeafor not to be in your vay."

The landlady left them alone in the room shared by Keith and Holl. It was an airy, pleasant chamber, the twin beds covered by yellow and white. With the small suitcases zipped closed, it looked as if both occupants had just stepped out for a moment. Diane flopped woefully on one of the beds and folded her arms.

"Now what do we do?"

The Master, who was rooting through Keith's belongings, didn't answer her. At last he rose, brandishing a gray wool sock. "This vill do."

"What for?" Diane asked, casting a skeptical eye on his discovery. Above the ankle, the sock featured a grimy brown ring that matched the dark soil outside.

"It is for the finding," the Master explained, beckoning to her to follow him out the door.

In the garden, he brushed away the broken glass from the place in the grass nearest the low stone plinth. While Diane watched curiously, the Master knelt and placed the sock on the grass, and held his hands over it, as if he were warming them.

She stared at the sock when he moved his hands away. It looked no different than it had before. In a moment, it began to twitch. Diane checked for a breeze, but the air was fairly still. In any case, it couldn't have made the sock do what it did next.

As if it had been pulled by a magnet, the sock started to slide along the ground, very slowly and jerkily at first, then with increasing speed.

"Ah, I vas not expecting such a strong response," the Master said, rising swiftly to his feet and trotting after the sock. "This is fery gut. Keep an eye on it." It disappeared around the corner of the garden and under the bushes toward the road. They ran after it.

"I've heard of laundry walking by itself, but this is the first time I've ever seen it," Diane admitted.

The Master, who was rather fond of Diane but did not show emotions easily, grunted a bit at her witticism. The matter was too serious to admit humor. The gray sock, moving as fast as a snake, had gained the road, and was already yards ahead of them when they emerged from the garden. Diane, with her longer legs, paced the sock as it took a sharp right at the bottom of the road and slid across to the left side.

"Where's it going?" she shouted back to the Master, who was huffing to catch up. The wind, now coming in off the sea, whisked away his words. "What?"

"Follow it!" the Master called. "Don't lose it! It is taking us to Meester Doyle!"

Holl felt in much better spirits this morning. Perhaps it was just the arrival of the Master which gave him confidence, but he had an indefinable feeling that Keith Doyle was alive, well, and not too far away. Mr. Michaels had driven him inland several miles, and they had explored the narrow tracks which led off the main road. Keith was nowhere in sight, and no one they met had seen anyone answering to his description. Michaels seemed concerned for him. Holl, preoccupied with organizing his thoughts, put off his attempts at cheerful conversation.

Instinctively, Holl knew that they were going the wrong way. As soon as they had circled back through Garynahine and were once again approaching Callanish from the south, the fragmented senses he had thought too scrambled to do him any good suddenly pulled together. They were now going the right way. He could almost imagine he heard the American student's mind somewhere ahead.

"I think we'll find him in this direction," Holl suggested.

"How the blazes do you know that?" Michaels demanded, slewing his gaze left at the vivid young face next to him.

"Only a feeling," Holl answered absently. He could sense the Master's strong personality nearby. It was on a vector to intersect with the way they were driving. Fairly soon, he and Michaels would pass by him. "Triangulation," was what they called this process, and it seemed to be working. "I think he's near the sea. I think he'd head for the water."

They drove back into Callanish by the lower road, which took them past the public telephone booth, and the intersection that led to the farm. Before too long, he noticed a fall of blond hair deep in the field to the left.

"Stop! That's Diane," Holl said. Michaels pulled to the side of the road, and the Little Person jumped out. Once he stood up, he could see the Master. They were climbing over a hillock of peat. Another moment and they would have been out of sight on the other side. He pushed through the wires of the fence and ran to them.

"What news?" Holl shouted.

They looked up at the sound of his voice. Michaels had parked the car, and was climbing over the fence to join them. Quickly, Diane picked up the topographical map she was carrying, and pretended to sight down it over the edge of the sharp fall of the land to her right.

"Keith Doyle is here," the Master announced.

Holl leaned under the lip of rock and shouted into the dark tunnel entrance he found there. "Keith Doyle! This way. Come out, Keith Doyle."

Keith clambered up further into the fall of pebbles, and drew his legs out of the stream's flow. With blind hands, he patted the mossy wall over his head, seeking an escape from the underground river bed. He knelt suddenly in a trickle of water traveling across his shelf. There had to be a way back to the source, perhaps big enough for him to fit through. Hopefully, he followed the flow upstream. About five feet from where he had washed up was a large opening. The sides were rough, but it was more than adequate in size. He leaned through it, prepared to crawl onward.

"Yahoo!" He let out a shout of delight, which echoed in the cavern. On the other side of the opening he could see the golden lines of mosslight, banking the narrow cataract of water. The magic was gleaming more brightly than ever. He was never more glad to see anything in his life. It seemed the stream had not dragged him out of his way. He had probably been going parallel with the airway all along.

Hands and knees straddling the cataract, he scuttled along the floor of the cavern. Every muscle protested.

"Boy, after this, a marathon actually standing up would be a piece of cake!"

The passage twisted and wound upward in a more sinuous, smoother fashion and at a more gentle angle than had any of the tunnels he had been in yet. Keith had a hopeful suspicion, but was trying to keep from believing in it, in case it was another disappointment. In a few more turns, there was a glimmer of light ahead of him, not the gold of mosslight, but the genuine, white glow of sunlight. Excitement spurred him the rest of the way. His hands and knees slipped painfully into the stream bed once and again, but he splashed his way out and kept going.

What if the bright light was a decoy? he thought suddenly, stopping in midcrawl. What if the *bodach* had decided to keep him running around in circles for the rest of his life, which wouldn't be long, stuck underground as he was. Confused and exhausted, he collapsed down full length on the wet stone.

Holl's voice intruded itself into his consciousness, almost like a sound heard in a dream. "Come out, Keith Doyle." It had to be an illusion, but he was willing to grasp at straws. With one more effort, he pushed himself forward.

He emerged into the brilliant day. The moss under his hands changed suddenly to cress, then to warm grass. The sky seemed blinding white at first, but resolved through a squint into blue. Keith drew a huge breath. He was out! Grateful and exhausted, he threw his hands out in front of him and flopped onto the grass. The wind sang hallelujahs in his ears. In a moment he would get up, he promised himself.

Something smooth under his hand moved. He thought it was a stone, but stones usually didn't move by themselves. Nervously, he raised his head to look. In front of him was a shoe. A woman's casual shoe. There was a woman's leg in it, and another one with a matching foot and leg beside it. He raised his head further. At the top of a much foreshortened body surrounded by a corona of tossing, white light was a face he knew. It was Diane. There were tears in her eyes as she stooped down to him.

Surprised, he stuttered out a greeting. "H-hi, there." His voice sounded rusty in his own ears.

"Hello, sailor," she returned, relieved to find him safe, but quick enough to throw him a line. "Buy a girl a drink?"

Snappy reports having to do with money, women, and liquor swirled through his mind, but because of the creature's mocking curse, none of them would go anywhere near his mouth. In the effort to say something, *anything*, in reply, Keith passed out.

* * *

Michaels joined the others in jubilation as they gathered up their lost lad, patting him on the cheeks to bring him back to consciousness. The young man's clothes were torn and wet, and the red waves of his hair lay plastered to his head. There were streaks of moss on his clothes and skin, but he was alive. Michaels found he was as relieved as the rest to find that Danny O'Day was all right. The youth had been abducted, all right, by one of his scummy compatriots, then pushed out into one of these littoral caves. *Can't trust 'em even when you have to work with 'em,* he thought. Good thing they'd been there waiting when the youth crawled out of his hidey hole. Sunblinded as he was, he'd have fallen smack over the precipice only a few feet beyond the cavern mouth.

"Meester Doyle," Mr. Alfheim said patiently, as they raised the youth to his feet, "I see I find you as I have always found you, prostrate and half in, half out of trouble."

Michaels chuckled. "Come on," he said. "It's only a few hundred yards back to your B&B. I'll give you a lift."

The young man seemed astonished. "D'you mean after all that I'm *walking distance* from the garden?" he croaked.

As he helped hand the young man into the car, Michaels gave him a quick patdown. Nothing on him. In fact, his clothes had been half torn off him, leaving no way to tell if there had been a drop or not. There was no money on the lad, not a coin—literally empty handed except for a broken stick. Time to report back to the chief. So long as O'Day had been recovered alive, he had to remove himself and go back to observation. His well-being was no longer Michaels's concern. He'd already jeopardized his cover enough.

In a daze, Keith wiped his shoes carefully on the mat, kept upright by Diane on one side and Holl on the other.

"They're just about hopeless," Diane said, looking at the worn shoes. The toes were nearly worn away, and something had ripped off the metal buckles. She squeezed Keith's arm. His hands were still half-balled up, probably a muscular spasm of some kind, and he was clutching a piece of an old stick. She was trying not to cry at the pitiful picture he made. "So are your clothes. You look half dead."

"I feel great," Keith insisted, smiling brilliantly at her. He made his way unsteadily into the house.

"Is that you, Keith dear?" Mrs. Mackenzie called from the sitting room.

Keith cleared his throat with difficulty. He remembered he hadn't had anything to drink for hours. "Yes, ma'am."

The door to the front room swung open. Instead of the patient face of Mrs. Mackenzie, Keith was confronted with the furious countenance of Miss Anderson. Professor Parker appeared under her arm, and studied Keith with sympathetic eyes. Keith goggled at them.

"Where have you been?" the teacher demanded. "I have had the Educatours main office calling every few hours wondering if you have been found! When you hadn't reported to the site for two days or been seen by any of the others, I came here. Mrs. Mackenzie told me that young Holl had been beside himself because you took it into your head to go wandering in the moonlight two days ago. Your irresponsibility has caused a great deal of inconvenience and worry for a lot of people. I've been concerned for you, too, but the contract you signed specified that you would behave with care because Educatours is responsible for your welfare while you are part of one of our groups!"

Keith tried to explain where he had been, with an occasional astounded glance back at the Elf Master, who was standing in the doorway, out of the line of fire. He still couldn't believe the little teacher was there with him. Miss Anderson let him get out half a sentence, then started her lecture off anew. Educatours couldn't be responsible for such inconsideration. If he had been seriously hurt or killed,the company was liable for damages to Keith's family.

He waited for her to run down, and tried to apologize when she paused for breath. "I got lost, Miss Anderson. I'm sorry. I don't know this area at all." He started to put down the bit of old stick in his hand. Holl reached out to take it from him, but Professor Parker beat him to it with a swift grab that surprised both of them.

"Miss Anderson!" the archaeologist yelped. "Look here!" With careful fingers, he brushed away the traces of mud caking the flat stick. A pattern of lines began to emerge. "Forgive me making a mess of your rug, Mrs. Mackenzie," Parker said, without looking up. "What a wonder! It's a comb! Horn, with sawn bone teeth inset. Dear, dear, dear, look at it! This is a very important find. It's contemporary to the Cairns, I'm certain of it, and in such fine shape. Yes, look at those markings. How fortunate it isn't broken. Where did it come from?''

Miss Anderson stopped her tirade, and looked down curiously at the object the professor was holding. ''Keith, where did you find this?''

''In a . . . a streambed,'' Keith said carefully, not wanting to explain how this adventure actually began. ''I guess I forgot I was holding it.''

''He found the underground tunnel system on the shores west of here,'' Holl explained, pointing out the location on his map for the two Big People. ''He must have become turned around down there after he found it.''

''That was very dangerous,'' Miss Anderson said sternly. She had been somewhat appeased by the find of the comb, but was still concerned for her company. ''Even if you are an expert spelunker you could have died down there.''

''I was fine, until one of the tunnels flooded behind me,'' Keith said truthfully, hoping he appeared to be more of a hero than he looked. His stained and torn clothes looked even more pitiful in daylight than he had feared. His jaw was aching in the cool air, and his eyes were going nuts trying to keep out the blinding light of midday.

''Off you go to bed, then,'' Miss Anderson ordered. ''I will tell everyone that you are back, Everyone has missed you greatly. I hope we can expect you back on the site in a day or so? Going into caverns without a helmet, hmp!''

She exited magnificently. Parker followed her out, chuckling and cooing over the comb, now cradled protectively in a handkerchief.

Stripping off his sodden, torn clothes, Keith staggered through a hot shower and collapsed into his bed. The softness of the mattress and pillow came up to meet his shoulders and head. He scrunched his fingers into the clean sheets, and grinned with pure pleasure.

''No moss,'' he said happily.

Holl sat on the edge of the other bed and watched his Big friend's face. ''Mrs. Mackenzie has bought the story that you went treasure hunting for the dig and lost yourself, my lad, and she's making you tea and a hot meal. Now, what really happened to you?''

With the help of a pad of paper and pencil, and a lot of humorous sallies at his expense from Holl, Keith managed to explain his problems while avoiding any references to the three conditions of the curse. He discovered he couldn't actually mention the curse either, but Holl guessed the problem from context.

"You've come to no real harm," Holl announced at last, very amused. "What a thing for a lad like you to be unable to speak of three of the pleasures in life. But a typical Gaelic curse. Those *bodach* have a sense of humor."

"I don't think that could have been a *bodach*. They're supposed to be beneficent, and this one sure wasn't," Keith said emphatically. "Ooch." He clutched his jaw.

" '*Bodach*' means not only 'old man,' but also 'specter or bugbear,' if you'd read up on the Gaelic, Keith Doyle. In any case, it was something that you Big Folk can't classify with ease. And why do you expect beneficence, surprising a millenia-old hermit entity with a flash camera in the middle of the night?" Holl was enormously relieved, but not above taking a little of his anxiety out on Keith to teach him a lesson. "He's probably never been so taken aback in his long life. By the way, you owe me a few pounds sterling, too. Your pictures came out. I've got them right here." He showed the two frames to the red-haired youth, whose eyes widened with excitement. They showed Keith's quarry turned captor, standing up from a crouch, then coming toward the camera with its skinny arms outstretched. Both were perfectly in focus. Keith was jubilant.

"Thanks, Holl! Those pictures are worth a mi—a mi—," Keith stammered. The word "million" was stuck in the top of his mouth like peanut butter, and his tongue couldn't dislodge it.

Holl grinned. "Yer welcome, widdy." He got up to go.

"And Holl? It's nice to see you back in one piece again." Keith tugged the lobe of his own ear significantly, and smiled. Holl returned his smile, and closed the door behind him.

· Chapter 20 ·

Diane and the Master looked up as Holl joined them in the sitting room. The fire was turned on, warming the room pleasantly. Holl spread out his chilled hands before its glow. Two of the cats got up to salute the knees of his trousers with their cheeks.

"He's tucked in and resting," Holl announced. "He won't need anything but a quick trip to the dentist. All his fillings are gone, but there's nothing wrong with him that a meal and a sleep can't fix." He explained the details of the *bodach's* curse.

"So," said the Master. "Ve must now study how best to dispose of the curse. I observe that it comprises the classic forms of three prohibitions. . . ."

"Wait!" Diane interrupted him, outraged. "How can you sit and analyze it so coldly when it's Keith's welfare we're talking about?"

The Master eyed her over the tops of his spectacles. "Analysis vill help us to determine the structure, and perhaps suggest the means of ridding him of it. It appears to be no more than a geas, a prohibitive statement, vhich exacts a penalty for violations. In any case, this vun is not harmful. Fery Gilbertian, this *bodach*. The punishment seems to haf done no more than fit the crime."

"Thank God," Diane sighed, then sat up straight. "Say, Holl, I never thought of him until now; where's your friend Mr. Michaels? He didn't come in with us."

Holl looked surprised. "You're right!" He ran to the window, and glanced up and down the road for the car. "He just went off. I never had a chance to give him my thanks for his help."

"Where did he come from?" Diane pressed. Holl frowned thoughtfully at her.

"I . . . I don't know. He came up to help me when I needed transportation. I never questioned where he came from. Should I have?"

"No, he seems to have been a nice man," Diane said, hoping she wouldn't have to eat her words later. "He seemed to know a lot about looking for missing persons." It all seemed a little too convenient. Diane couldn't get over wondering how Michaels had known what Keith looked like, without ever having met him. Was Keith in some kind of trouble? She wondered if Michaels wasn't some sort of official, but she kept her misgivings from the Little Folk.

Holl turned to the Master, who was sitting complacently on Mrs. Mackenzie's couch, drinking tea. "I'd like to thank you for coming to help me, sir," he said politely.

Without a word, Diane got up from her armchair and went to the window to look out. With her back to them, she could pretend she wasn't listening. Holl was grateful for her discretion. It wasn't pleasant to be called on the carpet, and to suffer before witnesses only made the ordeal worse.

"You do understand that the process vith vhich I located Meester Doyle vas vun you yourself know?" the Master asked.

Holl studied a spot on the wall. "Yes. But I wasn't sure I had enough energy or experience to overcome the local interference."

"Are you certain that your concerns vere not simply the product of letting your emotions run away vith you? You spent two days running around physically, not to achieve the purpose vhich took, by my estimate, under two hours vhen properly performed."

That stung. "No. I've thought about that. In time, I might have realized the truth of that, but by then Keith Doyle might have fallen over a cliff." Holl tried to keep his voice from sounding defensive, but the matter did disturb him. He had foolishly run his feet off searching, when all one had to do was employ the Law of Contagion, and call like to like. He deserved to look a fool by comparison with his teacher. "It's true, you know. I tried seeking him earlier, sensing for his thoughts, but I was too upset to make my mind work clearly. It seems also that Keith Doyle did his own spell, to make light. He would probably have come out by himself in time, under his own power."

The Master stared at him with half-lidded eyes. "It vould be the mark of an immature ego to try and achief the impossible all alone,'' he said calmly, ''instead of svallowing vun's pride and admitting the situvation is too much for vun. I consider that you haf used good judgment in calling for aid.''

''Thank you, sir,'' Holl said, gratified. He had thought he was behaving like a helpless babe, but he was being praised for it! The situation put him one more down to the Master, which galled him, but he was so grateful to have Keith Doyle back again in one piece that he didn't care. ''Would you like to see the photographs Keith Doyle took?'' He displayed the small envelope he had picked up from the developer.

''No. It is his honor, as he took the risks to obtain them. I vill vait until he may offer,'' the Master stated, and poured more tea.

Parry and riposte, Holl thought. Bested again. He studied his feet, feeling ten years old all over again.

''But thank you,'' the Master said, his blue eyes glinting through his gold-rimmed spectacles.

Diane escaped from the sitting room, and went in to see Keith. She couldn't pretend to be invisible any longer, and she wanted to make certain for herself that Keith was all right.

''Do you want visitors?'' she asked, leaning halfway into the room.

''This feels like deja vu,'' Keith said. ''I was just visiting Holl in the hospital about two weeks ago.''

''It was longer ago than that,'' Diane corrected him. ''You probably don't realize how long you've been away.''

''I've missed you,'' Keith said, looking up at her fondly. ''How are you doing?''

Diane leaned over to give him a kiss. ''There. Better. Other than suffering from oxygen deprivation and partial deafness from the flight, not to mention worrying half to death about you all the way here, I'm fine.''

Keith gave an apologetic and sympathetic grimace. ''Well, time is having fun when you're flying,'' he quipped. ''What's it like traveling with the Master?''

''Not bad. You know he's never been on a plane in his life, but he was so cool about the whole thing, you'd think he does it twice a day. Everybody in the village volunteered to come when they found out you were in trouble, but he said he would be the one to go. We had lots of time to talk, just sitting there," Diane explained. "I like him. You know, he seems to think Holl has done something really great."

"What, by attempting to find the old folks? He hasn't found them yet. Unless you count my *bodach*," Keith shuddered.

"Nope, I mean by making the *attempt*."

"Whether or not he succeeds?"

"I think so," Diane answered, thoughtfully. "You know how they feel about going anywhere out of sight of the house, let alone halfway around the world. And then there's the small matter of his having saved you."

Keith looked amused. "That's the way it's been reported, huh?"

"That's the way it is," Diane snapped back, impatiently.

He smiled ruefully. "I know. I can take the lumps, if it'll help him look like a hero."

Diane relented. "Whether Holl will feel the same way, I don't know."

"I doubt it myself," Keith told her what Holl had heard from the village about Maura and Gerol. "He doesn't talk about it, but it's been on his mind a lot. He went away to sort of achieve the adulthood quest, and someone steals his g-, g-, girl behind his back."

Diane whistled through her teeth. "That's something Holl is going to have to work out for himself. I think the Master feels sorry for him, but he's not going to lift a finger to help him with his own daughter."

Keith sat up to protest. "That's not fair! No, wait, that's probably the best thing. There I go, being knee-jerk protective again, and Holl's twice my age. He's a lot more sensible than I am."

"Practically everybody is. What was it like, being underground?" Diane asked curiously.

He shivered, remembering the lion-headed apparition that charged him, the crowding of the damp stone walls, and the tunnel full of water where he tore his trousers. "Wet. Cramped. If Mrs. Mackenzie had been leaving a dry towel outside along with the bowl of milk every month, he'd be so grateful she'd probably be raising tropical fruit in her garden right now."

"Holl's got your pictures. I want to see your bogey man when you're out of bed," Diane said.

"Sure. Now, how did you get here? I mean, where. . . ." The prohibition on talking about money hit him and turned the rest of his question into numbtongued gibberish. Diane listened carefully for a moment, trying not to giggle, then held up a hand to stop him.

"I'm being mean. Holl told us what happened to you—all of it. Never mind, I get what you're asking," she assured him. "I think you paid for it. The Master said something about winning a lottery?"

On top of the contests they had entered in his name to send Holl with him? The IRS was going to love that. Keith groaned and threw an arm over his eyes. Idly, Diane turned over the sorry heap of clothes that Keith had been wearing in the underground tunnels. "All this stuff needs to be washed yesterday." She picked up Keith's wool jacket, which though filthy, was virtually unscathed by its ordeal. "Look at this. Is it made of iron or something? Your jeans are ruined, and this just needs cleaning. Are you really doing magic? Holl said you did a kind of spell, or something. I want to hear all about that. Is this part of it?"

"Oh!" Keith remembered. "It's not magic, it's Harris tweed. You know, local handcrafts. Did you get any of my postcards?"

"Yes, I did. So this is Harris tweed," Diane said, interested. She examined the jacket speculatively, humming as she turned it over in her hands.

"Do you want this one?" Keith asked generously. "You can have it if you want. I was going to buy some fabric for your gift, maybe enough for a skirt?"

She nodded approval absently, holding the garment before her in the mirror, though careful not to let the muddy cloth touch her blouse. "I might borrow this once in a while. You were going to choose my gift?" Keith nodded earnestly. "You chose that jacket yourself, huh? No help from Holl?" Diane demanded.

"Yup."

"Okay, I guess you have good taste. You can come with me and pay for my choice."

"Fine," Keith said. The curse limited him considerably in his responses. He hoped he didn't sound too abrupt. Besides, his teeth hurt when he tried to talk.

"So what's my limit?" Diane asked, careful not to mention money.

"The sky," Keith gestured gallantly. "Anything for my rescuer."

Diane shook a finger in his face and dropped the coat on the chair. "That's Holl, and don't you forget it."

"I won't. I never will," Keith assured her seriously. "But right now, there's nothing he needs that I can give him."

"I'm going to go and see if someone can get you to the dentist," Diane said, briskly gathering up the pile of clothes and rolling it together. "And then I am going to take a nap. I don't think I've slept in two days now. And it's all your fault." Keith lowered his eyes meekly and tried to look abashed.

"Well, now, laddie," Mrs. Mackenzie said as she bustled into the room with a steaming tray. "Did you see your little man, then, out in the garden? After all this, I'd near forgotten why you were out there."

"Um, not exactly," Keith stammered. Diane grinned over the landlady's shoulder as she settled the tray over Keith's knees.

"Ah, well, it was a braw try of yours. You've had an adventure, from all accounts. Have a sup of this, and then a long sleep. The best medicine in the world for wear and tear."

"I'd better go," Diane said. "Remember, except for now, I'm not letting you out of my sight for a minute. You can't be trusted out by yourself. I mean it."

"Hey," Keith whispered as she started to slip out of the door. Diane looked back at him. He smiled up into her eyes. "Welcome to Scotland."

Lacking other transportation, Keith had to wait until the evening coach trip into Stornoway to see the emergency dentist. His friends clustered around him, demanding to hear his adventures in full before they would let him go up to the small medical office.

"You won't believe a word of it," Keith warned them. "I mean, it's full of mystical things and fairy folk. You know, what you've been razzing me about for three weeks!"

"Oh, get away," Max said, disbelievingly.

"We've been working our fingers off shifting peat, and you've had a soft adventure," Martin chided him. "You must be chuffed, finding a rare artifact like that comb. The professor was all over the place about it. Locating that must have been exciting."

"Well . . ."

"Pay the bard, pay the bard," Edwin shushed them all.

"We'll wait until you've seen the dentist. We'll buy the drinks, and you can tell us all about it, eh?"

"That sounds fair," Keith acknowledged, happy to have some windfalls descend from his mishap. The fewer times he had to mention money, the less of a fool he would look in the pub.

"I'd like to hear all about it myself," said Holl, teasingly joining the clamor for Keith's story. "Make it a good one, Uncle Keith. Full of ghosties and ghoulies. . . ."

"Later, later," Keith promised.

Miss Anderson said nothing to him, but she was no longer looking as stormy as she had. Keith took that as a good sign. The Master had decided to stay behind in Callanish and get some sleep. The redhaired teacher hadn't confronted him yet. Keith had some time to compose an apology and a speech of thanks before actually having to face the formidable Master. He was glad he only had to deal with Miss Anderson that night.

Mr. McGill, the emergency dentist, was amused by Keith's predicament. In a soft Scottish burr, he told his assistant to mix up a large quantity of amalgam. "Yer fillings seem to hae evaporated. There's not a sign that they were dug out, and the traces of tooth sealant are still there. What have ye been doing to your teeth?"

Keith rearranged the suction hose in the corner of his mouth. "Would you believe the fairies took them?"

The dentist laughed. When the assistant returned with a small white bowl, he cleaned and refilled all of the rough holes, and smoothed them with a scraping tool. "There's been no decay since they've gone; you're lucky. I'm using porcelain amalgam here, to match with your enamel. No more temptation there for the selkies, eh, son?"

"I hope not," Keith agreed, giving him one of his best village idiot smiles, and unhooking the paper bib from around his neck. He tried his bite, grinding his molars together. It seemed to fit okay.

"Give it an hour before you eat or drink," Mr. McGill said. "And don't annoy the Little Folk any mair, eh?" The dentist laughed until he closed the door of the office behind Keith. Still chuckling, he stripped off his thin rubber gloves and went into his private office.

Michaels stood up from the chair in which he'd been waiting. "What do you make of it?"

The dentist was distrustful of the man in the tweed suit, even though he'd seen the important-looking identification card in his pocket, and knew he was bound by the law to help him. "I've never seen such a case in all my life. There was no digging, and not a fragment of metal left clinging to the enamel. It was as if they had never been put in."

"Curious," Michaels mused aloud.

McGill spoke up indignantly. "I demand to know if there's a new secret weapon that caused the boy's fillings to vanish like that. I don't approve of nee-uclear teechnology."

"That'd be classified information, Mr. McGill," Michaels said, patiently, his voice devoid of inflection. He had a lot to report back to the chief.

"Oh, aye, so you'd say, until we're all dead in our beds," the dentist raged. "Then what do you do? You blame the Americans or the French, don't you? Good day to you, Mr. Michaels." He stood by the door until the agent took his leave.

"It might be a taunt to us, chief," the agent said quietly into the telephone. "They might know we're shadowing him. He didn't have a thing on him except a ratty old comb. His pockets were stripped, his clothing was tattered. No microfilms, no packages."

"Sounds like he was double-crossed by his contact. Say he made a pickup of a formula, but there's no proof. There can be no arrests without proof."

"Unless you'd call this process for dissolving metal and leaving tissue intact behind it proof, sir," the agent reasoned.

"That would be handy. Defense would love us for it, wouldn't they. Upstairs doesn't want this lad getting away, Michaels."

"If proof is there to find, sir, I'll find it."

The tour bus took only a small party around the island for what Keith dubbed the "tweed tour" that Saturday. The other young men, though relieved to see Keith back and in one piece, would not be persuaded to join a sightseeing and shopping tour under any circumstances. As one, they elected to stay in town for the day. They teased Keith mercilessly over having a girlfriend who was so devoted that she would fly halfway around the world to see to his welfare.

"Throwing money around again," Edwin chided him, but

the teasing was affectionate now, "and all for your sake. As if you were worth more than ten pence. You didn't tell us she was such a knockout."

"There's some secrets I can keep," Keith returned, waggling his eyebrows. "I didn't want to make you poor dopes jealous."

Mrs. Green expressed herself interested in joining the bus tour to look at scenery but not at dry goods. She was coming along for the ride. Mrs. Turner, by contrast, was a keen craftmaker, and was eager to see what the locals had to offer. Narit and Diane had hit it off right away, and settled down in the back of the bus to talk.

Keith loaded up his pocket with three new rolls of film, and took over the seat behind Holl and the Elf Master, camera at the ready.

Though the day was fine, the sea wind made it "windcheater" weather again. Keith had on his old jacket with a sweater tucked underneath, leaving the new one behind at the laundry with his other sodden clothing.

The range of geography throughout the few miles of land comprising the Isles amazed the tourists. Only a short distance from the rocky hills lay long valleys of marsh grasses and wildflowers, a temperate environment attached at odd angles to the tundra-like terrain of the peat bog.

"This is nothing at all like the land we've been seeing," said Mrs. Green enthusiastically. She and Keith stopped to take photographs as they rolled along the narrow roads. "How lovely it all is."

"That bird you hear is a shore lark," Miss Anderson said, looking pleased, when they stopped to listen in the middle of a huge, flat plain completely full of tiny daisies. "They are extremely rare. Look, there he goes! The little, brown bird. See him!"

"That's one for my bird book," Mrs. Green said, breathlessly. "A shore lark!"

"Too quick for my camera," Keith announced regretfully. "But I did see him, anyway."

Further south, quiet sandy streams flowed down the hills and spread out across astonishingly white sand beaches. The brilliant aquamarines and blues of the water made the inlets look like they belonged in the tropics, instead of less than a thousand miles from the Arctic Circle.

"We ought to go for a paddle," Mrs. Green suggested. "That water looks marvelously refreshing."

"I don't know whether I'd advise that," Miss Anderson clucked. "The water might be bone-numbingly cold."

"The climate here is moderated by the current of the Gulf Stream," the Elf Master intoned austerely. "It is far varmer here than in the similar latitude on the vestern side of the Atlahntic. Certainly vhere it is so shallow vill be varmed by the sun as vell."

Keith snickered at the preponderance of 'v's' in the Elf Master's little speech. Miss Anderson stopped and looked at the small, redhaired man, the surprised expression on her face showing that she knew the Master was absolutely right. "Well, that's true. If any of you would like to try, we can wait here."

"No, thank you," Mrs. Green bubbled, snapping a picture of the sea. "It was only an impulse. But it does look so nice."

• Chapter 21 •

The first handpainted sign advertising Harris tweed appeared on their left. At the top of the long, unpaved drive was an ordinary house, but next to it was a smaller building with the door open, and colorful swags of cloth hanging in the window. Everyone, including Mrs. Green, came in to see what the first weaver's shop was like. Thereafter, the Englishwoman stayed outside to take photographs and chat with the coach driver.

The displays in most of them were like those in the tea shop. In only a few was the weaver actually at work. Most seemed to have their looms in a different building than they kept the goods for sale. Shelves and tables were set up to show off the cloth to its best advantage. Some of the weavers had readymade garments for sale, and a few offered colorful sweaters knit out of the same wool.

Holl and Diane were the keenest customers at the various stops. Holl's fascination with crafts intrigued Diane, and she watched as he made endless sketches of looms and spinning wheels. Together, they examined the various weaves made on the complicated mechanisms. They watched for the signs that directed them to the next weaver's place. The coach driver, amused, stopped looking out, and let his self-appointed navigators direct him.

Narit admired the colors, but said the wool was too scratchy for her. "It's warm. My skin gets hot with it just resting on my hand." She shivered in horror. "I would hate to feel that next to my skin."

"Lining, dear, that's the secret," one of the weavers told her patiently, patting her arm.

Diane hadn't yet made her choice, so Keith followed meekly along in her wake as she plowed through the shops. There was only the faintest idea in her mind of what she wanted to have made of the cloth, so she kept changing her mind as she looked. One fabric would make a beautiful coat, another was perfect for suitings, and still others suggested skirts and waistcoats, blazers, and heavy manlike trousers. She was looking after Holl, too, who seemed tentative and indecisive, unable to make a definite choice.

"This color would be nice on Maura," Holl said, shyly, "but I have no idea if I should bring it home or not." He blushed, and looked helplessly at Keith.

"Oh, buy it," Diane urged him. "*I'll* take it later if you don't have any use for it. It would look so good on her with that gorgeous auburn hair," she added soothingly, "but don't keep beating yourself up. You'll kick yourself later if you miss out getting something here that you want. How often are you coming all the way to Scotland?"

"I bow to your judgment," Holl said, happy to have the decision made for him.

Leaving Holl on his own, Diane walked away to have the weaver cut off skirt lengths of cloth as gifts to her sisters and mother. In a very short time, she nudged Keith. Holl had started showing some initiative, and even seemed to be having a good time. He was actually making a purchase. Keith squeezed Diane's hand for joy, and leaned over to give her a kiss.

Once they were back on the coach, Holl approached the Master with a paper-wrapped package on his outstretched hands. "This is for Orchadia," he said.

The Master tilted his head curiously, his spectacles glinting, but put out his hands for the parcel. "Thank you, on behalf of my vife," he accepted, with a ceremonious nod. "I shall not mention this to my daughter."

"Don't," said Holl, evenly. "I hadn't so much as considered the possibility that you would." The truth of that showed in his face, and the Master was inwardly pleased. "I don't want it to affect Maura's judgment. But the Illinois winters are cold. I believe that Orchadia will find this a useful gift."

The Master peeked under an edge of the paper at the folded cloth. It was a good choice, both in color and weight. He nodded again at Holl. "So she vould. My thanks. But let me gif this back to you, so you may present it yourself. She vould be pleased to know this thoughtfulness came directly from you."

With no one supervising the driver, he found the next sign on his own. The bus took a turn onto a narrow, unevenly paved piece of road, which dipped up and down toward a sunlit sound. On either side of the tarmacadam were pools of standing water of peat brown, with the dark blue sky reflected in them. When the little drama in the middle seats came to an end, his passengers were once again watching the view, but he was already slowing down for the stop.

The coach pulled up a steep, graveled drive, and rumbled to a halt in front of a cluster of older wooden buildings. The weaver, a tall man with grizzled salt-and-pepper hair, came out to meet them, and show them into his workshop.

The building was an old barn that had had a concrete floor poured in. It was kept spotlessly clean, except for hanks and shreds and bales of wool stored anywhere there was space to rest them. In the center of a wall was a huge, mechanical loom, set so that the light from the window poured over the weaver's shoulder. He had been working when they arrived, and the roll of red, blue, and dark green cloth gathering on a spool underneath the loom was already a handspan thick.

"Hands back," the weaver commanded, taking his seat. He started the loom. Six shuttles, set around on a wheel like rows of corn on a cob, flew crashing back and forth in turn.

They watched the weaver work, asking a question now and again, with their eyes fixed on his hands and the web of cloth growing between them. By this time, Holl was sketching out the structure of the loom, and making small observations about technique. The village would have its own weaving equipment by winter, or he'd know why not. The Master caught his eye and raised one carrot-red brow with an approving nod.

"Do you dye all the wool yourself?" Narit asked, keeping a wary distance from the clashing machine.

The man paused and the din died away. "Ah, no, that's all doon on the mainland now."

"Europe?" Keith asked, puzzled.

"Scotland," the man replied curtly, as if that should have been obvious to anyone but an idiot. Keith shrugged, with an apologetic grin. "The fleeces here are sheared off the sheep's back and takkin' awa'. We see them next in clean hanks of color."

"Doesn't anyone do it the old way anymore, making the dyes themself?" Keith asked, disappointed. He had been picturing huge, bubbling cauldrons of thick, brightly hued glop.

"Aye," the weaver said, offhandedly. "That's Annie MacLeod you want. She's kept all the old ways gaeng. Boils her own dyes from natural plants, and so on the like."

"Mrs. MacLeod. That's who the ladies in the shop said to look for," Keith affirmed to Holl.

"Good," Holl said. "I want to get all the information I can to bring home."

"You pay her a visit," the weaver encouraged them, dictating directions to Holl. "But dinna believe oot she tells ye, especially nor when she says she's seventy-nine. She's been sayin' that for ten years and maur." Since he never cracked a smile, Keith couldn't tell if the weaver was kidding them. They thanked him for the tour, and left. He grunted a farewell without looking up. Behind them, the hammering noise of the loom began again.

At his most persuasive, Keith convinced the weary coach driver to take the next precarious turnoff to one final destination before going on to town and his tea. Diane hadn't made her choice yet, and Holl was still keen on fact-gathering. The others, too, were tired. Only Mrs. Green accompanied the four travelers off the coach into the low, black house.

Keith could feel something different about Mrs. MacLeod's place the moment he set foot inside. There was a sensation just hanging in the air he couldn't identify, one that made his whiskers twitch. He could see that Holl felt it, too, by the catch in the young elf's step as he crossed the threshold. Nothing ever fazed the Master, at least not openly, but the teacher approached the small woman seated behind the great wooden loom with open respect. They made a strangely mismatched couple, but Keith sensed an inexplicable kinship between them. Their eyes were the same penetrating blue, but he felt the similarity went deeper than that. Physically, they couldn't have been more unalike. The Master was small, potbellied, upright, while the woman behind the loom had been tall, but had allowed the years to bend her spine at the shoulders. Her hands were huge and strong; the fingerpads were flattened into broad, spatulate disks.

Around the walls of the croft room hung floating hanks of unspun wool, dyed in dozens of colors: browns, reds, greens, golds, and one mass of electric blue, which Keith suspected wasn't entirely made of natural dyes, but had to admit he liked. Rolled bolts of fabric were stacked neatly on deep, low shelves built against the walls. The frame of the loom came within inches of the high, beamed ceiling.

This machine was simpler than the others they had seen. It appeared to be made almost entirely of wood, something Keith could see interested Holl closely. The blond elf had flipped over to a new page in his notebook, and was drawing with concentrated speed. Keith took a quick picture of the loom for his own records.

"This loom is more than a hundred years old," Mrs. MacLeod said, without preamble. Her voice was very clear and low. "My father built it. Over years, the worn bits and pieces have been replaced. It works in this way." The old woman reached up to a group of cords hanging over her head, and pulled one after another in a pattern her hands knew so well she didn't have to watch them. The loom responded, shooting the polished shuttles back and forth across the web.

"That's marvelous," exclaimed Mrs. Green. "Did you make all this cloth yourself?"

"Ach, of course," Mrs. MacLeod smiled, her eyes crinkling. "When I'm going well, I can make two pieces a week."

"That doesn't sound like a lot." Keith frowned, looking at the piles of fabric. "It must take you ages to make this much cloth."

"A piece is seventy to eighty yards, lad," the weaver said, eyeing him humorously.

Keith's eyes went wide. "Oh. Wow. Excuse me and my big mouth."

"Do you blend all of your yarn yourself?" Mrs. Green asked, sorting busily through the selection. The old woman nodded. "Wonderful! You have a lovely sense of color, Mrs. MacLeod. How much do you charge per yard?" The Englishwoman turned over one bolt after another, holding a fold of cloth up to the light to see it better. Diane joined her, exclaiming over the variety of weaves and hues. Keith decided not to enter the fray. At a safe distance, he took a picture of the ladies, then turned to photograph the rest of the inside of the croft. To his surprise, when he stopped to take a picture of the loom from a different angle, he noticed that the weaver was no longer in her place behind it. The old woman had instead appeared at his elbow. He raised the lens to snap off a closeup of her, but something in her expression stopped him. Keith waited while she studied his face.

"Ye've been fairy-nagged, lad," she said suddenly.

Keith's jaw fell open. "How did you know?"

"I see the marks on you. Weavers are some of the makers on Earth. We see the strands which go into the life around us. Yours have been tangled a bit."

"Like elf-knots?" Keith wanted to know.

"Aye. That's one of the ways. Been poking yer lang neb in where it oughn't to go?"

"I suppose so," Keith admitted, humbly. The memory of the bogey's voice rang in his ears, and he shivered.

"What did it do to ye? Never mind," the woman forestalled his attempt to explain with a toss of her head. "I suppose ye canna say."

Keith sighed, relieved, saved from trying to figure out how he could explain the thing's curse without stuttering like a jackhammer. The old woman gave him a searching look and wrapped one broad hand in the fabric of his jacket. She pulled him over to her worktable, and, one handed, rummaged through the scattered bits of fleece and spun yarn, talking all the while.

"Well, it might wear off in time. You ought to walk a straight path until then. But if you're fixed on doing things like twisting the tiger's tail, you need a bit more protection that you have in yerself. I'm likely locking the barn door after the horse is gone, but you never know. I see you have an aptness for wandering into such places."

She released him and selected three colors of unspun wool. Holding the ends together between her ring fingers, she braided and twisted the mass into a nearly solid knot of complicated design, and tied it off. "I'll gi' ye a wee bit of yarn to wear it about your neck, but ye should find a sma' poke of yer ain to keep it in."

"Will any kind of little bag do?" Keith asked, clutching the little mass of wool in his fist.

"Aye. Any will do. One more thing," the woman said, sounding a little hurt as he started to turn away. He faced her again, puzzled. "Dinna you not want to take my picture?"

Keith brightened immediately, and cranked the film forward in his camera. "You bet I do. I wasn't sure if you'd let me. Say cheese!"

"Wensleydale," the old woman said dourly, but her eyes twinkled in their network of lines. "You're like a monkey. I've seen plenty like you in my seventy-nine years. Go with good luck." She shook hands with him. Her broad, strong fingers closed on Keith's like a bear trap, and he concentrated on not wincing. "Dinna disturb the fair ones' nests again," she warned him in a low voice, pitching it so that Mrs. Green, only feet away, couldn't hear her. "That'll save ye only from glamours, not foolishness."

Keith fingered the wool charm, now safely tucked in his pocket. "I promise."

"That's good enough," said Mrs. MacLeod. "Now, ladies, what have ye found?"

"Keith," Diane bubbled, grabbing his arm with excitement, and pushing a mass of bittersweet, oatmeal, and blue-colored tweed under his nose. "This is it. This is perfect. I mean, picture a suit made of this stuff. My sisters will just die of jealousy!"

Keith snickered, taking out his wallet. "So long as they don't kill me, too."

As soon as the purchases were counted, and the yardage cut and folded, Mrs. MacLeod sat down again behind her loom and reached for the cords above her head. The shuttles began their rhythmic pattern. Keith tried to form some suitable words of thanks, but Diane grabbed his arm and yanked him out of the croft.

· Chapter 22 ·

On the last night of the tour, Educatours liked to host a special dinner as a farewell party for each group. The coach delivered the tourists, Professor Parker's team, and Diane and the Master, dressed in their finest, to a hotel in Stornoway they hadn't passed by or seen before. Holl and the Master were suitably hatted for the trip into town. Keith recognized the fedora the redhaired teacher sported as one he had once worn back home.

They were directed to a long table along one side of the elegant, high-ceilinged restaurant. Candles burned in crystal chimneys in the center of the table, their light glinting off silver and crystal. Keith seated Diane courteously, and settled down in the chair next to hers. The menus were passed among them, and everyone fell silent, comtemplating their choices. The lights were turned fashionably low, making it a little difficult to read. "What's good, Miss Anderson?"

"Everything is good," the tall woman said. "This hotel has a superb reputation. I have had it highly recommended by several people."

The food was excellent, and there was a small room in the center of the dining room which was used as a self-serve dessert bar. There was a good deal of toasting one another over the meal.

At last, the group moved somewhat unsteadily to the lounge bar to finish off the evening in greater comfort. The party commandeered several tables, and pulled all the chairs around them.

"So what are your plans from here?" Matthew asked Keith, across the table, where he was sitting between the Master and Diane.

"We're going on to Ireland for a week," Keith explained. "I'm going to do some work on my family genealogy, then I'm going to look for the secret home of the leprechauns."

The others laughed, but Keith tipped Holl and Diane a sly wink. Keith exchanged addresses with everyone, writing them in a brand new book purchased especially for the occasion. Because of the *bodach*'s curse, he was forced to stick closely to mineral water or a half-soda, half-orange juice combination the bartender recommended. Holl, who had long been relegated to ordering non-alcoholic beverages he altered himself, met Keith's eye with a sympathetic and humorous expression.

"And what are your orders, gentlemen?" the waiter asked, leaning over them with a pad.

"S—s—cider." Keith found to his pleasure and amazement that he could still ask for the hard drink, by concentrating on the non-alcoholic variety. The word had actually emerged with relative coherence. Take that, *bodach*, he thought.

"I'm sorry, sir. We haven't got any," the waiter apologized.

Keith's face fell. He thought longingly of bitter ale, which he could see on tap behind the bar. It was meaty and rich and almost like a food, and he could just about taste it. "How about a b—,b—, birale, no, I mean a btitaler, um—" He turned red, seeing everyone staring at him. He must have sounded as if he was having a seizure.

The waiter glanced at him sadly. "Ye've had too many, laddie. How about a nice coop o'coffee?"

"Um," said Keith decisively, peering into the wooden shelves beneath the hanging decanters. "Is there another Orange 50 back there? Make it a double."

"Cooming right oop," said the barman, relieved.

"What's the matter," Edwin asked. "Taken the pledge?"

"I can't keep up with you guys," Keith answered evasively. "I've given up trying."

"Keith," Miss Anderson began. "Normally I wouldn't think of passing anyone who missed as much class time as you had, but under the circumstances, if you would care to sit an oral examination—and pass it—I think I can guarantee you a suitably acceptable grade. In light of your accident, I am willing to take your past performance and your remarkable find into consideration." As Keith tried to protest his gratitude, she held up a hand to stop him. "No, don't thank me. I promise you the test will be a difficult one. Come and see me tomorrow morning."

"My father is going to be very displeased with me," Matthew announced, suddenly. "I'm not going into finance after him, I've been in touch with Dr. Crutchley on the phone, and he's agreed to take me on as a pupil if I transfer down to London University. I'll be going out with his team when he's on a dig."

"Most commendable, young man," Dr. Parker said. "You're a hard worker. I'm sure you're bound for great things. I wish I had a dozen like you myself. If you choose not to work with Dr. Crutchley, I'd be happy if you would join our little band. I'll give you a written recommendation, and look forward to seeing you at our meetings and conventions in the future."

"Your health," Martin said, raising his glass to his friend. Matthew made a half bow.

"Hear, hear," called Miss Anderson, applauding him.

Martin grinned, before touching his glass to his lips. "And believe me, you'll need it when your dad finds out you've chucked it all for some dry bones and old pots."

Everyone chuckled, but they raised their glasses to Matthew.

"Dr. Alfheim," Parker began, turning to the Master, "I am curious to have your impression of the find made by young Mr. Doyle. Perhaps I swept it away too quickly the other day, but I am really so delighted that such a piece has come to light. You'll have to forgive an enthusiast."

"I qvite understand," the Master agreed. "I vould appreciate a chance to examine the artifact. Such jewels look like vorthless discards to the untrained eye. I am not surprised you recognized its quality."

"Mr dear sir, how kind." Parker was warming up to his favorite topic. Keith had noticed when they were loading on the coach to come to the restaurant that the Master was a couple of inches taller than Parker. They still looked like different species to Keith's educated eye, but Parker helped hide the reality that the Master was much smaller than a normal man. The other lads didn't seem to have looked twice at him.

"What's he do for a living?" Alistair asked, nudging Keith and gesturing subtly at the Master.

"He's a teacher," Keith said, trying to decide which of the many subjects he's studied in the underground classroom to mention, and decided to let the statement stand as it was.

Alistair eyed the small, red-haired figure. Keith caught a glint of blue behind the Master's gold-rimmed glasses as he looked their way. The little teacher had a clairaudient's knack for knowing when he was being discussed. "Looks a tough old bird, too."

"The toughest. But you really learn from him. He's the best."

"That's the important thing," Alistair acknowledged. "Miss Anderson's like that during Term time. I'd rather have one I curse every day of term than one I curse later on for not drumming the facts into my head."

Keith winced at the word "curse," but he nodded. "I couldn't agree with you more."

At the other end of the table, Matthew turned his glass in his hands, pensively watching the liquid slosh in the bottom. "You don't think I'm wasting my time, do you, lad, budging into archaeology instead of banking?"

Holl looked up, and realized Matthew was talking to him. He was puzzled why Matthew addressed him so seriously, when he was supposed to be only a half-grown Big One, but he remembered he had been one of the ones to praise Matthew for his hard work on the site. He stopped to consider the question. "If you find merit in that course, pursue it. I think my own father would be proud that I was finding my own way in the world instead of following him blindly into a path on which I'd be unhappy."

"Very profound, small boy," Matthew said, blinking reddened eyes at him. "I raise your hat to you."

Before Holl could grab his hand, Matthew lifted the Cubs hat off his head. The points of his ears promptly poked through the waves of damp, blond hair. Holl said nothing, but he could feel his cheeks burning. Fortunately, it was fairly dark in the lounge, and no one else was paying attention. Matthew stared, and looked him carefully up and down.

"Well, wrap me in brown paper and ship me by Datapost," he murmured, impressed into a hushed whisper, "My, what big ears you have, granny."

Worried inside whether Matthew was drunk enough to make an outburst, Holl smiled sweetly at him, and spoke in a quiet voice."There are fairies at the bottom of the garden."

"I never saw them, myself," Matthew said, eyes misted with drink. "No wonder Doyle is so keen. Where'd he find you, then? Under a toadstool?"

Holl groaned. *I will not leave a string of Patrick Morgans behind me!* he thought in exasperation. Keith's college roommate had discovered what he was, too, but he was unlikely to talk. *I can't let it become a precedent, leaving people behind who have seen me and have a fair idea what it is they're looking at.* "Under a building, if you want to know the truth. I live in the sub-basement of his school library." Surreptitiously, he inched a hand forward and wrapped it around Matthew's pint glass. "Keith Doyle's been helping us keep our noses hidden. It's not so easy to get along with all you Big Folk chopping and changing everything." He let a "forget" seep into the amber liquid in the glass, hoping that it wasn't so strong it made the youth mislay his own name, but not so weak he'd remember boys with pointed ears.

"Here, drink up, my friend," he suggested. "The waters of Lethe are good for you. The next round will be on me." Digging into his pocket for a few pounds, he signaled to the bartender. "A St. Clement's here, and another pint of whatever it is he's drinking."

The man looked from Matthew to Holl to the money in Holl's hand. "I shouldn't do it," he warned them. "I could lose my licensing privileges for selling to a minor."

"Go on, he's older than he looks, he's a short eighteen," Matthew said, playfully, winking. He held up the half empty glass, toasting the bartender and Holl. "Your very good health." He drank the whole thing in a few well-practiced gulps and put down the empty glass. With a resigned air, the bartender took it and Holl's money, leaving them with the fresh drinks. Holl held his breath as Matthew studied his ears closely and handed him back his cap. He snapped his fingers. "I have it. Star-Trekker, right?"

"Right you are," Holl agreed, with a gusty sigh. "Pity there aren't many Vulcans in the new television series."

"Aye?" Matthew inquired, taking the fresh pint of ale and sipping through the foam. "I haven't seen it yet, myself. Do you watch *Dallas*?"

"Forgive me," Dr. Parker stopped himself in midstream and studied his new guest. "I've been er, hogging the floor, as they say. Please, er, Alfheim, tell me, where do you come from? You seem to be well up on the latest finds and techniques. I don't remember hearing of you or meeting you at any of our conclaves. I, er, would remember anyone who comes close to meeting me at my level, if you will excuse the pun."

"I am at an American University, Midvestern," the Master said with perfect honesty. "Allow me, though, to gif you my home address. I should be fery interested in continuing our confersation by mail, if you would like."

Parker's long face shone. "So should I. My, my, I am sure we've been boring our companions, talking shop at table." Stafford and the others nearby shook their heads. "You are too kind. This object most likely came from a similar burial to the one we are excavating. I wish we had time for you to see our work."

The Master seemed full of regret, too, handling the comb with careful fingers. "I am so sorry, since ve must leaf early tomorrow, vith the others."

"I wonder if there were more of these here once, before the waters rose," Parker said, getting a dreamy look on his face. "Combs were rare, and considered to be valuable. They were considered heirlooms among our Neolithic ancestors. Probably the last owner was not the original maker. He may have been given it or traded for it. Did you know, some were considered to have magical qualities."

"Yes, so I understand," said the Master. Keith looked up at the teacher's tone.

"Oh, really?" Holl said curiously, and reached out. "May I see it?" He had a close look at the comb and nodded significantly at the redhaired student.

Keith nearly went wild waiting while Holl passed nondescript conversation with Parker, and handed back the comb. He tried to catch Holl's eye, but the Little Person ignored him. Distractedly, Keith answered a question from Alastair, and got drawn into a conversation to which he gave only half of his attention.

"What's going on?" he demanded in a whisper of Holl when the party broke up for the evening.

"Congratulations, you widdy," Holl said, calmly. "You've hit the jackpot. That comb does have a charmed aura about it. That's why it's still intact after so long."

"One of the Little Folk made it?"

Overhearing them, the Master came up. "I vould estimate that that is correct."

Keith was shocked for a moment, wondering if he'd been talking too loudly. "Boy, I forgot how far away you people can hear. Was that made by some of *your* folk in particular?"

The Master was noncommittal. "It is possible. The carvings are not unfamiliar."

"But he's going to put it in a museum," Keith yelped, and clapped his hand over his mouth. He looked around to see hastily if anyone had heard him that time. No one was paying much attention to the antics of the odd Keith Doyle. "A magic comb, right out there in front of everyone."

"Who vill know?" the Master asked mildly, turning up his hands.

"Well, *I* will," said Keith, concerned.

"And who vould you tell?"

"No one, I guess," Keith said, after a moment's thought. He grinned impishly. "Well, they say three can keep a secret . . . if two of them are Little Folk."

"And I would like to thank all you ladies for producing my coat, which kept me warm through the middle of summer. I know my friends feel the same as I do, but are too shy to present their thanks in person. Ladies, I salute you."

Keith's audience set up stentorian bleating of what he hoped was appreciation. He bowed to the field of sheep, and prepared to declaim further, when he was interrupted by a shrill whistle.

"That's enough, you widdy!" Holl called from the window of the coach. "Come on, we're all waiting for you."

"That is all," Keith said to the sheep. "Carry on. I know you'll make me proud."

Chapter 23

"Sir, I'm speaking to you from Northern Ireland," Michaels said, and then held the receiver away from his ear, wincing. "No sir. I didn't have a chance to call before. They just vanished from Stornoway, and I had to check every passenger list leaving the islands before I found them. They knew where they were going, I assume. This blighter is bouncing from place to place like a bloody Phileas Fogg. No, he left the bloody comb in the hands of the archaeologist. It's a real item, a coup for the old man. You'll be seeing writeups on it in the journals.

"Once I got here, it wasn't hard to track them. O'Day isn't going to a lot of trouble to be inconspicuous. No, sir. I've got a positive identification on his passport photo. Apparently, he bent down and kissed the ground upon arrival." Michaels chuckled, echoing his employer's amusement. "Yes, sir. There were several witnesses."

Michaels looked up at the departures board on the terminal wall. "Oh, chief, must run now. The train for the south is about to pull out. It looks like he must have achieved his purpose in Scotland, doesn't it? We thought it was a drop at first, but I'm assuming a pickup, or else why is he going into the Republic? For payment? Aye, I'll look for the best opportunity, and apprehend him and the other three. There'll probably be a scuff-up about extradition, but what's new about that? Report back soon. Bye."

"People do look a little different here than they do at home," Diane said, surreptitiously people-watching from behind her magazine on the train. "Only, they look a lot like each other, too."

"I noticed that," Keith agreed, looking away from the window. He had been studying scenery, admiring the Irish countryside. He was out of film, and felt disappointed at missing photographing the first sunrise he'd seen in a month—not that he hadn't been up early every day. They had bundled aboard the train from the ferry at about six o'clock. It was not quite seven. Most of their fellow passengers were lounging listlessly in their seats. "I guess your basic gene pool is limited to whatever conquerors zoomed through here over the centuries."

"Yes, but *you* fit right in. I could lose you on a crowded street corner."

"Many have tried, my sweet," said Keith blithely, "but I've always found my way home again. Um," he said, seeing the worried look resurface on Diane's face. "I didn't mean to bring that up." He truly hadn't intended to refer to his misadventure. He was still having nightmares about being blind in a knee-high tunnel with hideous laughter echoing around him.

"See how you like being walked on a leash after this," Diane shot back, her eyes suddenly filling with tears. "Darn you, being lost and almost *killed* didn't even dent your sense of humor."

"Best armor plating in the world," Keith quipped. He poked around in his jacket pocket and came up with a handkerchief, which he offered to her. She shook her head.

"I'm okay. Come on," Diane said, suddenly, blinking her eyes fast. "Let's see some of this magic you're supposed to be able to do."

"Well, if you want," Keith said. He looked around. "Ah." There was a trash container behind their seat. From the top, he fished out a beer can and shook it. "Still a few drops left. Good."

He spilled the beer on the table in front of them. "Hey!" Diane protested. "Yuck!"

"No, really, this is how it works," Keith said. "You have to have something to work from. I do best with liquids so far."

"Well, all right." Diane was dubious. Keith winked at her, then put his cupped hands over the small puddle of beer. With his eyes closed, he concentrated on the principles Enoch had taught him.

"Okay," he said, dropping his hands back into his lap. There, on the table, in the place where the golden beer had been, was a coiled bracelet. It was made from a rich, deep gold, and it sparkled with rubies and emeralds. The clasp was only partially hooked.

"Ooh," Diane breathed, reaching for it to try it on. As soon as her finger touched the chain, the whole thing popped, and dissolved again into featureless beer. "Very funny!" She shook her dripping fingers.

"It's only an illusion," Keith said, apologetically. "That's all I know how to do so far."

"But that's wonderful." Diane gestured at the pooling liquid, now starting to run toward the edge of the table. Keith fished out his handkerchief and mopped it up. "The clasp was a nice touch. I couldn't resist it."

"Thank you, my dear," Keith replied, wiggling his eyebrows lasciviously. "We aim to be irresistible. Wait until I start working with solids."

"I know where *you're* going on this trip," Diane murmured softly. "But where are *they* going?" She tilted her head toward Holl and the Elf Master, who were sitting in the seat across from theirs. The two Little Folk were looking out of opposite windows, not talking, and appearing not to be aware that Keith and Diane were discussing them.

"I'm not sure," Keith replied. "Come on, let's get some sandwiches or something. Everyone else is going by with bacon and eggs, and I'm getting ravenous." They rose to their feet in the swaying aisle. Holl looked up at the movement. "I'm getting food. Want some?"

Listlessly, Holl lifted his shoulders and let them drop. "If you please."

"Okay," Keith said, cheerfully. "Breakfast for everyone."

On the way toward the buffet car, he explained what he knew of Holl's quest to Diane. "Do you know exactly what's going on here?"

"Not so's you'd notice," Diane said, pushing through the sliding doors between the cars. "Something to do with Maura, I thought."

"Sort of." Keith explained what Holl was looking for, and why. "He's been hounded to prove himself worthy of being the next headman, the village leader, not that the Master looks like he's stepping down any time soon. It's been like a charm said over his cradle, that it would be lucky to have him as leader because he was the first one born in the new place."

"Well, that's not a bad destiny," Diane replied. "All things considered."

"If that wasn't enough, on top of it, he's got to have one great deed under his belt to claim the leadership. Talk about performance pressure."

"How did the Master claim it, then?" she asked.

"I suppose because he brought the Little Folk to Midwestern, where they had a safe place to live. He's never said how or why, but I can guess that that was the big accomplishment."

"Isn't that enough?"

"It would be, in my book," Keith said, arriving at the end of a long queue of people waiting their turns at the buffet counter. "Here we are. A full breakfast for me, please?" He passed Diane his wallet, and gave her a beseeching look.

"All right. I'll take care of the money," Diane said, grinning wickedly, taking bills out of the leather fold and handing it back to Keith. "Do you think you should ask Holl to make part of his quest getting you back to normal?"

"I don't know," Keith said. "I think he might find it an

advantage to have me permanently silent on at least three subjects.''

''I've always wanted to go to Ireland,'' Diane said, sighing happily as the train passed over a river. She put down her tea cup and pushed the empty tray to one side of the table. The sun was higher, and there were more signs of life in the countryside surrounding the tracks. ''I love it here.''

After the remoteness of the Hebrides, Ireland was almost unbearably noisy and crowded. Backed by the smooth hills, which were clad in a brighter green than those of Scotland, children in school uniforms raced their bicycles alongside the train, shouting happily to each other. Dogs, running through yards facing the railway cut, barked as they rumbled past. Dozens of slender-hocked horses, nearly absent in northwest Scotland, grazed calmly in their paddocks. Men in flat, woven caps chatted on the street corners, and women in skirts and knitted sweaters went about their business among the shops or hung up washing on the lines in their gardens.

''Sort of the national uniform,'' Keith observed. ''But it's nice and homey.''

Just outside of Dublin, Diane poked his arm and cried, ''Look!''

High on the side of the railway cut was a billboard. In bright letters two feet high it advertised Doyle Hotels. Within a hundred yards, they could see signs on shopfronts for Doyle's Estate Agency, The Doyle Bookstore, and Doyle's Grocery.

''Enterprising family I've got,'' Keith said proudly. ''Wouldn't you say we're in the right place?''

In Dublin's Connolly Station, they left the train, and checked their bags in the left-luggage drop. Keith had unearthed pages of notes on his family tree from his suitcase, and was eager to get started on his research. ''I'm going down to the Genealogical Office. I've got all the facts my grandparents could remember from their parents, and some other stuff that's been handed down. Would anyone like to come with me?'' he asked the others.

''Not a chance!'' Diane said. ''I didn't expect to be coming over, but as long as I'm here, I'm going to go do tourist things for a while. There might be a tour leaving from one of the hotels.''

Keith looked hopefully at the other two.

"Not I, Keith Doyle," Holl said. "I want to walk in the sunshine. I'm not taking a Roman holiday with dusty books and tomes. I live in a library."

"He puts it vell," agreed the Elf Master, amused.

"Whatever," Keith said, somewhat crestfallen because no one wanted to join him. "Look, we'll meet for lunch at noon." They agreed on a meeting point, and Keith mounted the steps into the building.

The Genealogical Office offered help to people looking for their family lines on a per-hour basis with one of their researchers. Keith was assigned to a slender, fair-haired man named Mr. Dukes, who looked at Keith's records, and made some notes on a yellow pad.

"You've got more than some and less than others," Dukes said. "Pity you couldn't have thought of bringing the family Bible."

"My dad has it," Keith admitted, "but he didn't want me to take it with me. If anything happened to it, he'd be furious. I wrote out everything it said, though, all the births, deaths, and marriages."

"Good, good," said Dukes. "Let's see, now."

"The father of my ancestor who came to America was a landowner. We have a couple of his letters," Keith said, showing the fragile slips of paper to Mr. Dukes, "and it sounds like he never got over being upset that his eldest son left the country, keeping his skills as a doctor away from where his own people could benefit from them."

"Well, let's see what can be done with what is here." Dukes twisted his chair to face a computer terminal, and glancing at Keith's notes and sometimes at his own, brought up reference numbers, which he jotted down. "Some of this you'll have to look up at the Archives, but I think we may have a lot of what you need right here."

Typing expertly on the keyboard, Dukes requested cross-references to the data Keith had provided. He turned back to chat with Keith while the computer was digesting the information.

"So, are you enjoying Ireland?" he asked.

"For the few hours we've been here, yeah," Keith said, cheerfully. "It's beautiful. We took the train down from Larne."

"Well, that's only the north you've seen," Mr. Dukes chided him, deprecatingly. "You'll like the south that much more. Wait, here we are." The printer next to the workstation began to clatter, and ejected several sheets of paper. Mr. Dukes tore them off and separated them. He ran down the data with a pencil. "Good, this is what you'll want. We've got a match on several of your entries. Don't go away. I'll be right back with you. There's coffee over the way." The researcher left through a door at the other end of the room.

Keith waited at the desk, idly pushing his notes around, and reading the other papers upside down that lay on Mr. Dukes's desk. Soon, the researcher returned, pushing a library cart on which were stacked gigantic leatherbound books.

"The parish records for those entries we have," Dukes explained. "All the births, baptisms, deaths, and marriages recorded there, up to the present records, which are still in the parishes. We get them when they're through."

"How old are these?" Keith asked, touching one of the big books reverently.

Mr. Dukes turned to a page, and passed his finger down it carefully. "Some of these go back to 1800. These are the original documents, you understand. I can't let you take them out of the building, but I will give you copies of the entries, or you may write them down." He stopped at one line. "These are all in Latin, but this is the marriage record of a Fionn O'Doyle who married a woman named Emer O'Murphy on the fourteenth of June, 1818."

Several pages further on, he came across a baptism record for her firstborn, a boy named Emerson, born in 1820. Keith scribbled down the dates and names.

"Gee, that's creative," he observed. "Emer, Emerson. Wait! Aha, it's a family name. And I thought it was all rock and roll. I saw it in the family Bible, and it never dawned on me."

"A good match?"

"One I didn't expect," Keith said, pointing. "That's my middle name. This has to be the right family."

Mr. Dukes marked it with a tacky-backed tab for copying. "There's no death registered with that same name, so it looks like Emerson O'Doyle was the one who left."

"That's right. Grandpa said that he was a doctor," Keith added, referring to his notes.

"Possibly, but the birth register won't say so," the man said impishly, "and it's all we have to go on."

"You mean they didn't know at birth?" Keith innocently

carried on the joke. "I thought second sight was run of the mill here."

The man ran through the file once more. "It seems he married a Miss Butler. Yes, this entry does note him as a Dr. O'Doyle. Well done. Now we can trace back through to see the rest of your lines. The Butlers and the O'Doyles are both from just north of Arklow near the coast, but more O'Doyles and the O'Murphys come from the north end of County Wexford above Gorey."

Keith soon had a pile of photocopies with a list of addresses of the parish churches. Mr. Dukes directed him to a nearby Ordnance Survey bookstore for maps of the area south of Dublin. "I hope you find what you're looking for. The best of luck to you," said Dukes, shaking his hand. "If you've any questions, come back again."

"Top of the morning to you," Keith said cheerfully, gathering his papers under one arm. "And thanks a lot."

Keith emerged from the Genealogical Office and found his way to the rendezvous point where the others were waiting. Diane steered them to a place that was serving lunch. As soon as they had given their orders to the waiter, Diane pointed at the pile of photocopies under Keith's elbow.

"Is all that from the Genealogy Office?" Diane asked.

"Yup. I have a few starting places," Keith said, patting the sheaf of paper. "I've got a list of parish churches and an abbey which might have records of my ancestors that can fill in holes in the stuff we've already found. The rest of this is copies of the birth and death registers for a lot of my multiple-great-grandparents and their children. If we take the train south from here to Bray or Arklow, we can start out looking around there locally."

"It's still the season for wildflowers," Holl said meaningfully. "If there's no trouble involved, I'd like to keep a close watch out for the bellflowers. It is the reason I came here, after all."

"Of course," Keith assured him. "I think it'll have to be on bicycles, though, and that will take a lot of time, not to mention muscle power. I'm too young to rent a car over here. They want you to be twenty-five."

"Ah," said the Master. "I can solf that problem."

"You'll really be the first couple married in Illinois?" Diane asked Holl, sentimentally.

"Yes, indeed, as well as the first ones to be born there.

Because we're beginning a new page in our history, it's important to us to have a touch of the old ways about it. Maura and I have had a bond between us all our lives, and I want it to be a permanent one. I love her," he ended fiercely, looking off out of the restaurant window. *No interloper will have her,* he promised himself. *I will win her back.*

The Elf Master took off his spectacles and polished them with a pocket handkerchief. For the first time Keith had ever seen him so, the Master looked distressed.

"What's the matter, sir?" he asked.

"Ach, nothing. Both of my children are thinking of marriage. They grow so qvickly. I hardly think ve haf had enough time to enjoy them."

"Enoch is talking about getting married, too?" Keith asked, astonished. "Is he still dating Marcy?" Marcy Collier was a Big Person. She had been the object of Keith's affections for most of a school year. He had stopped chasing her when she revealed a preference for one of the Little Folk. Keith knew about her and Enoch, and applauded it, but the idea of matrimony between them amazed him somewhat.

"Yes, he is," the Master confirmed.

"You're just going through empty-nest syndrome," Keith said, thinking out loud. "Maybe you should have some more kids."

The Master glanced at him, looking for evidence of flippancy, and found none.

"You're younger than Holl's folks, and they have a three-year-old," Keith pressed.

The Master shrugged. "Perhaps ve vill consider it. But I do not think that is the answer, vith so much vork left to be done on our new home."

Keith thought then that it would be politic to change the subject. Holl was still staring off into space. He tried to catch the Little Person's eye, and decided to let him come back to Earth at his own pace. "So, what did you see in Dublin?"

"Trinity College is walking distance from here. I had a look around. That's where they keep the Book of Kells. It's kind of a pity," Diane complained. "The book is shut up in a glass case in a fairly dark library. You only get to see whatever page the curator decided to show off on a day. I mean, I didn't expect to get to handle it, but it would have been nice if they had someone up there who could answer questions. I think he was having his tea."

"It is a mastervork," the Elf Master put in. "This vas a splendid opportunity for me. There were other illuminated manuscripts on display, vhich I examined closely. I haf purchased a complete reproduction of the Book of Kells itself for class study on medieval art."

"I thought you might say that," Holl groaned. "So that is what made you put in an Interlibrary Loan request for works by the Master of Sarum."

"That is true," the Master said complacently. "I alvays seek new subjects to explore. Research is the backbone of knowledge."

Leaving the restaurant, the Master took the lead. He guided them along the street, into the next block, and over the threshold of a glass-fronted showroom on the corner. The sign over their heads read Ath Cliatha Auto Rentals. Keith caught his arm.

"Where are you going?" he yelped. "The train station is the other way."

"Solfing the problem of transportation. You can drive vun of these autos?" the Master asked calmly.

"I think so," Keith said, involuntarily glancing at the traffic. "It's on the wrong side of the road, but it looks pretty straightforward."

"Gut. Then come vith me and choose. I am certainly old enough to sign the contract."

Thunderstruck, Keith followed the small teacher into the agency. Holl and Diane tagged along behind. A slim woman with dark, brown hair and dusty, green eyes stood up as they entered.

"Back again, Professor?" the woman greeted him cheerfully, putting out a hand for his. The Master clasped it. "We have two four-passenger vehicles on the lot now." She named two manufacturers. The Master looked back at Keith.

"Uh, either one, I guess," he said, then watched as the young woman filled out the contract.

"May I have your driving license, please?" she asked the Master. Without murmur or hesitation, he duly produced a small card with a photograph in one corner. She turned to Keith. "If you're driving as well, I'll need to take your details, too." Keith handed his wallet card to her, and waited while she copied down his name and address.

He said nothing until the woman went for the keys to the car, then leaned over the Master's head. "I'm going to tell the Department of Transportation on you."

The Master glanced up at him with a conspiratorial wink. Keith was delighted.

"Here you are," the young woman said, leading them outside to a small, blue two-door compact. She put the keys in Keith's hand and opened the door for him. Keith slipped into the driver's seat and looked for the rearview mirror. It was on the wrong side. So was the leftview mirror. It was on the right. Panicking, he looked up at the young woman for help. She smiled, crinkled lines gathering at the corners of her eyes.

"Let me go over the controls with you. There's a full tank of petrol. The rest is fairly easy to understand. . . ."

• Chapter 24 •

Keith's first few miles driving the car were as tentative as the first flight of any baby bird from a nest surrounded by asphalt and wild birds zooming by at top speed within inches of his wings. Cautiously he made his way into the lane of traffic to the tune of racing engines and screeching brakes. The Dublin drivers didn't give an inch, and the roads seemed unaccountably narrow from his point of view on the wrong side of the car. Diane, navigating in the front passenger seat, was huddled as close to the center of the vehicle as she could be without obstructing the rear view mirror. As Keith began to relax, his driving improved, but his passengers took some time to lose the white around their eyes.

"Who says the Irish don't believe in magic?" Keith demanded, once they were out of the city and onto the smaller southbound roads. "Look at that. This road is almost as narrow as my bed. They paint a yellow stripe down the middle, and presto! Two lanes."

He glanced in the rear view mirror. His back seat passengers were not impressed by his levity. His jaw set, Holl was clutching the rubber loop hanging from the ceiling, and the Master simply sat looking pale. "Do you want me to stop and pick up some four leaf clovers?"

"No," the Master said. "Drive more slowly."

"Okay," said Keith, imperturbably, without turning his head. "So where do we go?"

Diane handed the map into the back seat, and the Master opened it up. "I do not know," he admitted, after examining it closely. "It has been a long time, and the names have changed somewhat. Mere lines on paper mean nothing to me. I think I may haf to see landmarks to be certain."

"You didn't see anything familiar on the train south into Dublin, did you?"

"Of that I am certain, no. I do remember Dublin, and it vas most definitely to the north of vhere ve lived."

"That's okay," Keith assured him, following a fork in the road to the left. "I'll just head toward where I'm going, and if you have a place you want to stop on the way, tell me, and we'll check it out."

With Diane directing him from the map, Keith drove through County Wicklow. The land changed gradually as they left Dublin. On the west side of the road, low mountains began to appear over the tops of the trees. They were not the dramatic black and gold peaks of Scotland, but rather more gently rounded, with bright, green grass and darker green trees covering their expanse. A high, nearly conical mountain passed by to their right, casting a long shadow across the road. At times they emerged into flattened valleys where the road was edged with trees, or wound along through small villages with signs written half in English and half in Gaelic. The iron mailboxes, which in Scotland had been red, were painted bright green.

"This is where you leave the Arklow road," Diane said, reading from the map, as they came to a sharp intersection to the right. Cutting across the right lane swiftly while there was no traffic, Keith turned inland, and started looking for the way to the first parish church on his list.

The road narrowed immediately to an unstriped lane between high hedges. Cautiously, Keith hugged the shrubbery on the left side. Though the road was frighteningly straitened, there always seemed to be enough room for two vehicles to pass one another. After one panicked moment when he had to dive into a blackberry thicket to avoid a farm vehicle and an old woman on a bicycle, their progress was much more calm.

"Hey, I'm getting the hang of this," he said happily, then glanced at his passengers, who were hanging on in silence. "Hey, don't you all applaud at once."

Through the brush bounding the road, they could see farm houses and manor houses, and well-trimmed fields with sheep or cows placidly grazing. A cluster of small cottages emerged among a stand of trees. "Look, Holl, it's your house," Keith said, cocking his head toward the roadside. A tiny white cottage with a high peaked roof of red slates lay nestled amid a wreath of rosebushes. Ivy climbed one wall and twined around the base of the chimney. A sheepdog lying in the middle of the drive regarded them with professional disinterest.

"It's amazingly similar," Holl said, staring as they passed the cottage.

"But old," Diane commented. "Really old."

"Vhere function does not change significantly, form rarely alters," the Master said, enigmatically.

"We're getting close to your village, aren't we?" Keith asked, excitedly.

"I am not certain," the Master said, without inflection. "I have seen nothing yet vhich awakens memory in me."

At last, a churchyard appeared on their right. The church, a fairly small building made of time-darkened stone, raised a square tower surmounted with a cross over the peak of the roof. The headstones, tilted this way and that in the tall grass around the building, were mostly flat and white, with sharp edges that made them look as if they had been cut out of a cake of wax. Beyond it was a residence, much newer than the church, but with the air of age. "This is it," Diane announced. "St. Michael's of the Downs."

"This is where I make sure that the Butler who I think married the grandfather who came to America actually left the area," Keith said, trying to avoid mentioning his female ancestor, but still get his meaning across. This curse was getting to be a pain.

"If I may understand your circumlocutions," Holl said, "you wish to find that the great-grandmother was not buried here, so that you have a match against the name of the one who left for America."

"Right," Keith said, relieved that someone understood his

problem. "If the parish clerk is in, he or she might be able to give me some help finding the name."

"I'll help you," Diane said.

"I'm staying here," Holl declared. "I don't feel much like being exorcised today."

"Oh," said Keith, curiously. "Well, okay. I'll leave the key in the ignition in case you want to listen to the radio." He and Diane disappeared through the creaking wrought iron gate.

As soon as they were out of sight, Holl threw an aversion around the body of the car to drive off the gazes of idle passersby.

"To vhat purpose do you do this?" the Master asked curiously, observing Holl's handiwork. "You know ve haf nothing to fear from their priests."

"I know," Holl said, and steeled himself. "But I wanted a chance to speak with you privately. It is important that we come to an understanding. I have thought long and deeply on the subject, and I am determined to follow the old ways—where they are good ones. Though I don't see why a bunch of simple flowers should be enough to prevent marriage among our people, I will follow the tradition set down. I am grateful that you came to help me when Keith Doyle was lost, but I feel that you have taken over the entire direction of this journey. All the decisions that have been made since you arrived have been yours. What about my task? How can I complete it if you take control?"

"I?" the Master asked, looking puzzled. "I shall do nothing to abrogate your task from you. Vunce ve are in the correct location, I intend that you shall complete your task on your own. My only concern is similar to that of Meester Doyle's. I vish to find our old home, and ensure that our folk still live. Vhether or not you haf a use for the flowers yourself vhen you return home, you have undertaken a responsibility on behalf of the others. I expect you to fulfill it."

Holl was mollified, but only just. He nodded.

"After all, unless you finish vhat you set out to do, you cannot reap the rewards of that action," the Master continued. "And it has alvays been my intention that you should do so."

Holl tried to find something to say in reply, but he found himself gaping at his teacher. So the Master was in favor of his match after all. He quickly turned away and went back to looking out of the window. Behind him, the Master chuckled softly.

A loud creak of protest from the churchyard gate heralded the return of the two Big Folk.

"Whew!" Keith said, swinging into the driver's seat, after he had unlocked the passenger door for Diane. "There was no one in the church, so we had to go over the tombstones one by one by ourselves. That was like taking attendance in a study hall. I counted 157 names."

"Were any of them the one you were seeking?" Holl asked.

"Nope," Keith replied, happily. "In this case, no news is good news."

"Well, it's getting pretty late. We'd better find a place to stay for the night," Keith said. "I have a booklet of B&Bs and guest houses from the Ordinance Survey office. We'll see if any of the ones nearby have room."

They pulled over beside the nearest green and yellow telephone box, and Keith started phoning down the list in the book. The first two had no room, and the third didn't answer. Keith grimaced apologetically to his passengers while waiting for the fourth to answer. There was a click, and a voice.

"Hello, Mrs. Keane? My name is Keith Doyle. I got your name from a tourist booklet. Do you have room for four people for about five nights? A twin room and two singles or a triple and a single is what we need. You can? That's terrific!" He scrawled down directions on the back of the book. "Right, see you soon." Keith returned to the car. "Voila. It's not far away, either. We're staying right in the middle of the clan area."

Under Diane's direction, Keith descended from the mountain valley and into the plain looking up into the heart of the range between the foothills. They followed the roads into a small town and out again, looking for the unmarked turnoff. Once they found it, they drove for a mile alongside a stretch of croplands interrupted only by telephone poles and odd lines of trees. They came to a gravel drive between white-painted gateposts, and drove through.

The house in the center of the grounds was a large manor in the Georgian style, with pillars around the entrance way. Keith parked next to a few other cars and stood up to stretch his legs.

"This is the place," he announced.

"Yes," said the Elf Master, getting out of the car and

looking around him with evident satisfaction. ''This *is* the place.''

Keith eyed him. ''Is there any more significance to that phrase than simply 'we are here'?''

The Master gestured with his chin toward the horizon. ''Those mountains are to the north of us, are they not?''

Keith glanced to his left, then back at the Master. ''Unless the sun has started setting somewhere else, yes.''

''Then this is the correct area. The village lies to the south of the mountains you see before you, and not far avay. The angle is correct.''

''Yahoo!'' Keith said, eagerly. ''Are you sure? Right here in the middle of Doyle country? Terrific! We'll get an early start tomorrow, and find your old home. I knew it, we're neighbors.'' Holl groaned.

Together, they climbed the broad stairs between the pillars and into the front hall. ''Hello?'' Keith called softly, hearing his voice echo in the high, ornate ceilings above.

Suddenly, there was the sound of activity deep inside the house. One of the heavy, wooden doors burst open, and a woman bore down on them, beaming. She was a handsome woman in her middle forties, roughly cylindrical in shape, with dark hair piled high on her head and milk-white skin. The woman glanced at Holl and Diane, stared curiously at the Master for a short moment, then her dark blue eyes fixed on Keith. She shook hands with him.

''Mr. Doyle, is it? How do you do. I'm Amanda Keane. Let me show you to your rooms.''

The family occupied only the ground floor of the grand house, leaving the upper floors available for numerous guests. Keith and the others had a small wing almost to themselves. Diane was installed in a corner room at one end of a corridor. Keith and Holl were to share a twin room a couple of doors down, next to the bathroom. The Master was given the other corner room. Each was furnished with antiques and handmade rugs. Diane was breathless with admiration.

''There's tea-making facilities in each room,'' Mrs. Keane explained. ''The bath is here. You should have it to yourselves, at least for tonight.'' She held out the keys to Keith.

''They're terrific, Mrs. Keane,'' Keith began, reaching for them, ''but I guess I forgot to ask how muh—, how muh—''

Holl swiftly stepped in to rescue him. "He was asking what the tariff is? We forgot to inquire."

"So that's what the young lad here was asking," Mrs. Keane laughed, patting him on the back. Keith shot a pleading look at Holl, who opened the tourist booklet and showed a page to the guest house owner.

"By the way, I notice that here in the book you have a weekly rate, which is less than we would pay for five nights' stay. May we pay that instead?"

"Done and done," Mrs. Keane agreed, shaking his hand solemnly, and putting the keys into his outstretched hand. "Breakfast at eight, if you please."

"Thank you," Holl said. "And now, can you tell us a good place near by where we can get a meal?"

"Well, you might try the White Wolf. Their food is good, and it's only just up the road," Mrs. Keane instructed him, watching as he wrote down the directions. "But there's no sign on the road, and it doesn't say White Wolf. It says 'Gibson's,' and only on the glass. You have to watch for it."

Holl thanked her and accepted the keys. She bid them good night and went down the stairs. He watched her go. How good it was to be treated as an adult again! Perhaps Keith Doyle was correct, and the people around here *did* know the look of his folk. Then he heard her say to someone below stairs in a highly amused voice, "such a *serious* child, you can't think!" He smiled to himself. And then again, perhaps not.

"Well, that's all too complicated for me," Diane yawned. "I still have jet lag. I'm going to bed."

The others went off in high energy to find the White Wolf and discuss their search for the village. Diane took the opportunity when the house was quiet to have a long, hot bath and wash her hair. While she was toweling her hair dry, there was a tap at one of the doors down the hall.

"Mr. Doyle?" Mrs. Keane's voice asked.

Diane opened the door and leaned out. "They've gone to dinner, Mrs. Keane."

"Ah, well, there's a man on the telephone for him," the landlady said.

Diane shook her head. "It's got to be a mistake. No one knows we're staying here yet. I haven't even called my folks."

"It's likely a wrong number, then," Mrs. Keane said,

reasonably. "Certainly our telephone system is none of the best, but I am sure he asked for a Mr. Doyle."

"Well, it's not like it's an uncommon name around here," Diane smiled. She closed the door and went back to drying her hair.

Michaels had got no joy from Genealogy Office. It seemed that O'Day had embarked on what would be a legitimate ancestor search. He must be planning to keep the Keith Doyle persona for a long time. Michaels was reassured then that O'Day and the others were unaware that they were being followed, or he would have discarded the pretended identity like a used tissue.

The Ordnance Survey Bookshop in Dublin had been much more forthcoming. The clerk remembered the red-haired American. O'Day had purchased a list of guest houses in the area south of Dublin, and if he was staying with his assumed identity, would be putting up in one of them. All Michaels had had to do was call down the list of numbers until he found them.

Chapter 25

The four travelers spent the next few days searching the countryside for anything which sounded a chord in the Master's memory. Keith worked out a system of triangulation by which they circled an area, covering all the small roads within it. They made progress, but it was slow. Keith knew the Master was looking for particular landmarks, some of them small. One for which he kept his eyes peeled was a rockfall. There were plenty in this part of the country. The Master looked at each one Keith stopped to examine, but he rejected one after another. They were hampered by their unfamiliarity with the area, and the incessant warm summer rain.

Keith had to keep the defogger running constantly to keep the windows clear, so the passengers had to shout over the noise of the fan. "It could be ground up into pebbles by now," Keith said, shouting over the roar. "It might not be here any more."

"They von't haf moved it," the Master assured him. "But I am not sure I remember vhy."

Diane checked off another small section as they turned off one of the narrow roads marked on the map, and noticed an interesting entry. "Well, that's that for this part. Say, did you know that those mountains out there are supposed to contain gold mines?"

"Yes, of course," the Master replied absently. "It vas a valuable resource to us. Though the mines were not safe after a time, and they began to yield less. They kept out the Big Folk, but of course ve did not ask their permission."

"Uh huh," Keith said. "And that's where you got your pots of gold, eh?"

"Keith Doyle!" Holl exclaimed, outraged, quickly deducing where that line of logic was leading. "In your own research, leprechauns are reputed to be hand high."

"Depends on how high you hold your hand," Keith replied, blithely.

"Stop the car," the Master ordered suddenly. Keith coasted to a halt, and the Master got out. Among a crowd of smaller trees down the slope from the roadside, two huge oak trees stood, seemingly sprouted from the same root. Keith followed him partway, to make sure nothing happened to him. Ignoring the rain, he watched the Master hurry toward them, almost sliding down the hillside, which was ankle-deep in last year's leaves. The teacher examined the trees, walking around them, and reaching as high into the fork as he could. Then the little man's shoulders slumped, all the starch gone out of them. He turned and walked back, not looking up at the car. By the time he ascended the slope, Keith was sitting behind the wheel, waiting politely.

"Shall we go on? I think you wanted us to try this way next."

From then on, Keith kept an eye out for twin oak trees. As they drove higher, trees became fewer. He took the next road which sloped downward. Ahead of him, he could see the brilliant green of leaves once more. The road twisted and rose higher, but this hill was copiously forested and prevented them from seeing more than fifty yards ahead. Keith felt hope stir when he saw the Master's face out of the corner of his eye. The little teacher wanted to smile, but he didn't dare. Keith felt his heart start beating faster. This time, it was the real thing. They must be close.

They passed several huge trees to which had been tied red and yellow signs. Keith couldn't read them through the rain, but they appeared to be protesting something to do with the Council.

"Take the next turning toward the hilltop," the Master ordered. "Tvin oak trees. Ah! Those are the vuns. They vere smaller vhen I vas last here." Holl gazed at the trees, as if their being remembered by the Master somehow ennobled them above all other oaks.

Keith pointed. "Is that your rockfall?" he asked. Across the valley to their left, half a hillside had collapsed, leaving a heap of gigantic boulders. A rare angle of perspective through the rain and clear air made the monument seem to be much smaller, and immediately beside them. "So that's why you were so sure no one would move it, over the years. It's a mountain! Here we are!"

Keith steered the car into a small turning, slick with mud, and stopped.

"Vhat's this?" the Master demanded. Before them was no village of cottages, but a small street of newly built houses, surrounded by churned-up earth.

"This is the hilltop," Keith said, looking around him in confusion.

"This vas not here before. Vhat is it?" the Master asked in an agitated voice.

"It's a housing project," Keith replied, reading a yellow sign tied to a tree at the entrance to the site. "Really recent. There's still mud all over the streets, and no grass yet. And I guess it's not a very popular project. Look at that."

Holl read the notice. "It asks the local folk to rally against the council and the developers. They wish others to boycott the project, and not buy the houses or prevent others from taking residence, 'because only Peeping Toms would live here.'" Several other signs had been tied up all over the street. They were visible on the young trees planted in front of every house, and tied to almost every doorknob.

Behind them, an engine raced, and a voice shouted at them through the rain. Keith glanced into the mirror, and hastily moved the car aside. A lorry thundered past them into the development, carrying a gang of skinny trees.

"Where are your folk?" Keith asked the Master.

"Gone." The Master climbed out of the car and walked blindly along the muddy street. Keith and the others followed him. The new houses watched them with blank glass eyes like rows of mannequins.

"Gone," the Master repeated forlornly. "All has been destroyed. Are they all dead?"

"It was a nice place," Keith offered, following the little teacher and trying to be soothing. "There's a great view."

The Master stopped and looked away, reminiscently. "And the river vas only a hundred paces away. The vells vere sweet. The air is as I remember it. There is as yet only the faintest stink of cifilization here yet."

"It looks like this place isn't happy," Keith said, wondering what made him think that.

The Master turned a penetrating gaze on him. "It is not. You can sense it. Imagine vhat anger *ve* can sense. The Big Folk down there think that it is bad because these new buildings overlook them. That is incorrect. It is because a magical place that has been here from the beginning has been uprooted. They shall have no joy of it. But it is too late." He raised his hands helplessly to encompass the muddy streets. "Too late. It is ruined. They do not know what they haf done, but the earth vill tell them."

Keith remembered being swallowed up by the earth on the hilltop in Callanish, and stopped the small teacher with a hand on his arm. "Is there, um, something sentient underneath here? Like a monster?"

The Master smiled sadly. "Ah, no, merely the Earth. Only Nature. But ve treated it vith respect, and they have not. Vill not," he added.

"Should we warn them?" Keith asked, with concern.

"Vhat good vould it do? Can you varn the developers in your own country that what they are disturbing is vengeful?"

"No," Keith admitted, honestly. "But what about the tenants? It's not their fault they're going to be living over a magic volcano."

"They'd call you a nut if you told them that," Diane said firmly. "Nobody is moving in here against their will. They'd think you owned one of the houses down there." She pointed to the offended neighborhood.

Together, they walked the perimeter of the entire housing estate, looking for anything which had been left undisturbed. The area around the streets had been piled high with the earth excavated from the building sites. Mature trees had been pushed down and left in scattered heaps like jackstraws.

"They must haf left directions to where they had gone," the leader said sadly, "if there vere any vho could leaf them. But it is all destroyed, beyond vhere they beliefed it might be, by the bigfooted fools. Are ve the only vuns left?"

"Maybe they're still close by," Keith suggested, hopefully, unwilling to declare the Master's folk dead. He threshed his way out into the nearest large field and called out a halloo with his hands cupped around his mouth. "Yo! Little People!"

"Oh, stop that," Diane said impatiently, running out after him and bringing him back. "This field is full of nettles. Let's get out of here. You're soaked, and so am I. So are they." She nodded back at the Master, who was standing in the growing downpour looking lost. "This place is too creepy to stay in."

There was silence in the little car for a long while. Keith turned the heater on full blast to try and dry them, but succeeded only in making them feel sticky and uncomfortable. He rolled down the window a crack, and let the coolness of tiny drops of rain come in.

"Do you think they stayed close by?" Keith asked the Master, who was sitting deep in thought, stroking his beard. "I mean, you guys are not too big on travel."

"I haf no idea. There is no vay to tell vhen the village was abandoned." The Master stared sadly into space.

The rain began to break up. Brave spears of sunlight poked between the clouds and lit up that much of a hill or this much of a valley, striking up the golds and greens in the landscape, and dropping curious shadows down the valleys. The photographer in Keith refused to be contained any longer.

He pulled the car over near a likely field, where the hedge was low, and climbed up. Beneath him lay a broad and handsome valley like a sampler, dotted with sheep or stitched with growing crops. Clusters of woods lay at the right intersection of the perfectly straight lines of trees and brush which separated fields.

"Yoo-hoo! Little Folk!" he called down, waving his arms. "Hey, Holl, how do you say 'where are you' in your language?"

"I don't," the Little Person shot back. "Don't waste your time. Take your picture and come down."

"All right, spoilsport," Keith said. "I'm only trying to help."

Michaels huddled over the wheel of his car and wished again for the omnidirectional microphones of the American secret service. O'Day was signaling to someone, with an air of expectancy. He feared that it was quite likely to be the connection that would make this entire investigation worthwhile, and his elderly listening mechanism couldn't pick up a sound. The small, blue car rolled again, and Michaels followed, careful to keep his distance. An unexpected turn could throw him into line-of-sight, or lose O'Day in the distance. Something was sure to happen imminently.

At any likely point when he wanted to take a picture, Keith repeated his antics on the hedge, and called out to any of the Little Folk who might be listening. Holl had given up trying to stop him, and sat in the car patiently with Diane, waiting for Keith to run out of film.

They stopped on a ridge of land overlooking two points in the great valley, both satisfyingly picturesque. Happily, Keith got out, and leaned over the gorse-covered wall on one side to take a picture. The hedge on the other side was too high and too flimsy to climb. Eyeing the nettles and gorse cautiously, Keith walked back to the car. Bracing one foot on the car bumper and the other among the heather, he hoisted himself up far enough to see over the wall.

Below was a broad sward of green populated by a herd of cows, who stood or lay on the flattened, wet grass, ignoring the waving and shouting of a figure like a demented scarecrow.

"Hello there," a voice called back from behind him. Keith twisted his spine around and glanced back. There was a tan car parked about fifty feet behind him. A man had climbed out of it, and was walking toward them. He was of middle height, and had wavy, red hair.

Keith jumped down with his hands on the car roof for balance. "Hi!" he called back. "What can I do for you?"

"Nothing for me," the man said, cheerfully, coming up close to him. "Having a bit of car trouble? I saw you waving. I thought you might be signaling for help."

Keith laughed. "Oh, no. Everything's fine. We're just taking pictures. Beautiful day for it."

The man looked up and down at his sodden clothes, and grinned at him. His eyes were hazel-green. "It is now. Goodbye, then."

"Thanks anyway," Keith called. The man threw him a salute and drove off.

"Didn't he look like the map of Ireland?" Keith commented. "As my grandmother would say."

"I would say he looked just like you, plus ten years or so," Holl called through the window in amusement.

"I noticed," Keith said, winding the film forward in his camera. "My uncle Rob and he could almost be twins."

"But what I found more interesting is that the sticker on the back window of his car said 'Doyle's Garage,'" Holl pointed out. "He did offer to help you fix your car. I wonder if he owns the place, or merely rents from them."

"What?" Keith leaped into the driver's seat. "He was a Doyle? Why didn't you say something?"

"I thought you could read that for yourself," Holl protested.

The others braced themselves as the little blue car leaped forward. It raced down the road in pursuit of the sedan. Keith thought he saw the tan car ahead of him.

"We'll catch him at the next turning," he said.

The next intersection was a blind angle to a crossroads. Each of the other three branches was empty. "We lost him," Keith said sadly.

"Never mind," Diane said. "If you had any doubts before if we were in the right place, you better have lost them now."

"Oh, well," Keith said, pulling over to the side of the road. It was narrow, so the left wheels were wedged up among the nettles and gorse. A quick glance in the mirror showed the Master's crestfallen face. He was still hurting after finding the old homestead abandoned. Keith needed a distraction, any distraction. He looked up at the wayposts at the crossroads. "Look, that way is Killargreany. Isn't the next place on my list there?"

Diane found the sheet of paper in the map compartment and read it. "That's right. Boy, that must have been right up the road from your family. Married, born, married, died, born, born, born, married, born . . ." she ticked off the highlighted entries in the sheaf of parish records. Keith took off the parking gear and headed toward Killargreany.

The Killargreany church was larger and more elaborately decorated than the small parish church of St. Michael's had been. Set in a valley embraced on two sides by the glowing golden-green mountains, it had a serene solidity that made the travelers stop simply to look at it. The stone walls had long ago gone green with lichen. The shrubbery around the churchyard side had been allowed to grow wild, but it had done so artistically. Birds sang from the great yew trees clustered within the low stone walls.

Numberless generations of local men and women had attended this church and had been buried here with its rites. Large tombs, some new, some old, and some decrepit, jostled elbows with every description of memorial stone, some of which stood at drunken angles in the ground. Keith took one look at the extensive churchyard, and made straight for the church door. "I've got to have expert help on this one. I wonder if anyone's here."

The huge wooden door opened quietly on its hinges. Inside, the church was cool and dim. Diane shivered once, violently, and felt all right after that. They stood for a moment to allow their eyes to become accustomed to the light.

Above them, the high, vaulted ceiling began to emerge from the gloom. It was held up by heavy beams of blackened wood. The door through which they had entered was at the rear of the right side of the building. At the front of the church, to their right, a window of jewel-colored stained glass glowed with warm blues and red.

"How beautiful," Diane breathed.

The altar was covered with an embroidered cloth and bedizened with colored dashes and dots from the window above. In the middle of the tabletop stood a gold cross with a circle set at the juncture of the crosspiece and upright.

Rows of carved wooden pews marched back toward them along the aisle. Keith stepped forward to caress the smooth polish with the palm of his hand and wondered what Holl would think of them, and why he wouldn't enter churches. That was something which would warrant investigation when he had the time to think about it.

A table stood at their side of the church, behind the last row of pews. On it were arranged stacks of small pamphlets. One showed a line drawing of the church, and said in two languages. "The History of Our Church." There was a box with a slot in the top nearby, which read "Pay Here Please" in black letters.

"Honor system," Keith noted, digging in his pocket for change.

The large coins falling into the box sounded like chains clanking, echoing in the quiet building. Keith was reading one of the flyers by the light from the door when he heard bustling near the altar place. A door opened, and an elderly priest in long, black vestments emerged, straightening his glasses on his nose.

"Visitors, by the look of you?" the old man said, a question and a statement in one phrase. "Welcome. Ah, it's getting late, and I'm behind in my duties. It's no excuse, but it's a sleepy summer day. The lights should be on by now. I'm Father Griffith." He smiled at their surprise. "One Welsh ancestor, and it's followed me for eight generations."

Keith introduced himself and Diane, and explained his reason for visiting. "I'm hunting down my family line. I think that this is the area where my folks came from. The Genealogy Office told me this would be the first place I should look, then branch out into the smaller parishes around here."

The priest shook their hands. "I'm pleased to meet you both. Do you know, we get many visitors over the year, most of them from America. And where is it you might be coming from?"

"I live outside Chicago. Diane is from Michigan."

The priest nodded expansively. "Ah, Chicago. A great place. I've never been there myself, you understand, but so I've been told, and the films that are made there! Shocking, some of it."

"They're all true," Diane said, impishly.

"Doyle, Doyle," Griffith mused, studying Keith's face. "There's enough of those, to be sure. What's the names you're looking for, then?" He took Keith's hand-drawn family tree and began to peruse it, steadying his thin-rimmed glasses with one hand. "Ah, well, you'll not find this one here," he pointed, then read the notation underneath. "I see you know that already. Good. I'm a great historian, if I am going to have to say it for myself. I'm always browsing among the stones out there, getting to know my parishioners, even the ones who are not precisely with us any more, if you understand me."

"It looks like my three-times-great grandfather, Emerson O'Doyle, was the one who moved away from here. He was born in this parish, and married here, too, I think. It looks like he went to open a practice in Arklow, and left from there to go to America," Keith explained, pointing out the names in the family tree.

"You don't know why they left, then?" Griffith asked, looking at him over the tops of his glasses.

"No," Keith said. "We've only got a few letters and things that were saved. None of them say why."

"You can make up great stories and all, but it's usually a fundamental thing which drives a family to leave the land of their birth. I think I know the reason for this one. The name stuck in my mind, which is why I remember it. It's this way." Griffith beckoned them around to the aisle and along the wall. He stopped before a white, engraved stone only a few inches square.

"Pray for the soul of Padraig Thomas O'Doyle, Died April 5, 1855, aged sixty-three days," Keith read. "Beloved son of Emerson and h..." His voice stopped on the reference to the dead child's mother.

Diane finished for him. "... His wife Grainhe Butler O'Doyle."

"How sad, to have survived the Famine, and lose his first little son like that," Father Griffith said, sympathetically. He nodded when Keith held up his camera, giving silent permission to take a picture of the cenotaph. "If it's a happier note you'd be wanting, I can show you where his uncle is buried: Eamon. He lived to be seventy-eight."

In spite of himself, Keith laughed. "I'd be happier if you could tell me where to find the living half of the family, Eamon's children—or great-great grandchildren now. My folks would like to get to know them. Do you know many Doyles?"

"Ah, yes, I know everyone. In a small place like this, we all know the ins and outs of each other's business. I've got to look up me records. It occurs to me that I might know someone who's come down from the family of Eamon O'Doyle, second son of Fionn," Griffith recalled suddenly, one finger in the air to mark a mental place. "And you might think of putting up a notice on the board with your name and address. That may stir memories I lack."

He guided Keith back to the pamphlet table, and gave him a sheet of paper, then disappeared into the rear of the church.

While Keith was printing his message, the priest arrived with an armload of big, leatherbound books. "These are the current birth and baptismal records, along with the marriage and death registers for this parish. The old ones go to the Central Archives when they're written to the last page. My clerk will as likely have my ears for pulling them out of her office, but as you've come all this way I'm not wanting to stand on ceremony."

"Thank you, Father!" Keith began to thumb through the pages. Here and there he spotted the name Doyle. Furiously, he jotted down names and dates and the names of babies' parents. "I should have given myself a lot more than one week for this job."

"Well, you'll be wanting to come back, then," the priest said hospitably, and dropped a fingertip on Keith's notice. "Just scratch down there the place you're staying while you're in Ireland. You'll excuse me now, as it's nearly time for evening prayers. You might think of staying yourself, if you have the time. And good afternoon, Mrs. Murphy. How are you this fine day? Not a drop of rain or a wisp of cloud." The priest moved away to place a hand on the arm of a very old woman walking slowly up the aisle of the church. Squinting through filmy blue eyes, she smiled up at the black-coated clergyman, who helped her to a pew. After he tacked up his notice, Keith waved a silent farewell to the priest. Father Griffith nodded companionably to him, never breaking off his conversation with the old woman.

"That's a great piece of luck," Diane said, as they wandered around the churchyard. "There were their names, right there, together, even carved in stone. Hmm!" She stretched out her arms in the sunshine and turned up her face to be warmed. "What a nice place to be buried, if you have to be dead. It's really lovely here."

• Chapter 26 •

They walked back to the car. Keith was jubilantly buoyant with the success of his visit. Holl listened to the narrative intently.

"So what will you do with the birth records you copied down?"

"Mr. Dukes suggested that I look in the phone books, and send letters explaining what I'm doing. A lot of the people might consider a phone call to be intruding, so I should just approach them politely from a distance."

"That sounds sensible," Holl agreed.

The Master, now seated in his old place in the back seat, said nothing. He seemed to have retreated inside himself to think. As they headed back to the Keane home, Keith tried several times to start cheerful conversations. After the Master ignored his questions and remarks, he decided wisely to leave the leader alone with his thoughts.

"I'm still soggy," Keith said. "We're not far away from the guesthouse, but why don't we stop and have a drink or something, and warm up? Then we can go back and change for dinner." On the backdrop of the still-gray sky, Keith had noticed a glow of white light over the treetops which might mean a pub or a farmhouse in the distance. He was hoping for a pub.

Following the glow, Keith wound upward through the two-lane roads, and arrived in front of a white-walled building that announced itself proudly as The Skylark, The Highest Pub in Ireland.

Keith coaxed the reluctant Master into the pub's lounge.

"There are many of your folk in this place," the Master said. "Are you not concerned that they vill see us?"

The American peered around the corner. "It's pretty dark in there. Look, there's a fireplace with no other lights around it. We'll go and dry out a little, and then if you think it's safe, we can have a drink. If not, we'll just go before there's any trouble."

"That sounds prudent," Holl said. He pushed the door open and stood by as the others passed inside.

"Ach," said the Master. "You are behaving like vun of the Big Folk. Too bold!"

Rather than being oppressed by the dimness of its lights, the Skylark was made cozy and inviting. A coal and peat fire glowed red in the ornamental iron firebox and touched lights in the complicated patterns of the enameled tiles with which the hearth and wall were lined. Overstuffed chairs and sofas sat under the curtained windows, which were shut tight against the cool evening wind. There were knick-knacks on the walls, some of them unidentifiable even in full light. With Keith between them and the customers at the rectangular bar, the Little Folk made their way toward the old-fashioned settees near the fireplace.

"Oh, that's better," Diane said, shaking out the legs of her jeans. "I wish I could wring out my shoes. They'll squish for a week."

Keith watched the bartender inside the bar moving back and forth between customers in the light of the single orange lamp behind the bottles. He was a burly young man with curly, dark hair and a beak of a nose between straight, dark brows. He set down glasses, and exchanged quiet jokes as he cleared away empties. Conversations between the locals, though animated, were in low tones.

"How about it?" Keith suggested.

He walked over and casually took a seat at the darkest corner of the bar, far removed from the next customer. Diane sat down next to him, and gave him a conspiratorial wink. In a moment, Holl joined them, sitting on Keith's other side. He was followed by a reluctant Elf Master, who wedged himself between a post and the wall.

"You are unreasonably bold," he told Holl sternly.

"They think I'm a child, Master," Holl replied reasonably. "They'll give me a fruit soda."

"Welcome," the server said, coming over and giving the bar in front of them a wipe with his towel.

"Hi," Keith said. "It's a wet night."

"Oh, I don't mind," the man said. Keith could see that he was quite young, not too far from his own age. "I was planning to swim home tonight. I brought me water wings." Diane laughed, and the young man smiled at her. "Americans, are you?"

"That's right."

"Over here for the holidays?"

"Sort of," Keith said, wondering where to begin. "Well, I'm researching my family tree. I was here for a combination tour and college course for credit. We both go to Midwestern University in Illinois."

"Do you?" the young man said, pausing in his polishing. "I'm at Trinity College in Dublin. I'm happy to meet fellow students."

"We were there," Diane said. "I went to look at the Book of Kells."

"What are you studying?" Keith asked him.

"I'm reading history," the young man said, with a wide grin on his face, "but I'm learning Mandarin Chinese on the side."

"Go on," Diane said, sensing a joke, "drop the other shoe. Why?"

"Well, me mam's expecting her fourth, you see," he told them seriously, "and they say that one out of every four babies born in the world is Chinese. I want to be able to understand him when he starts to talk."

"So why don't you move next door to a Chinese family?" Keith asked, joining in the game. "That way, if they get one of the other three, you can just swap babies with them."

"That's a grand idea," agreed the young man, just keeping a straight face while the others laughed. "The truth is that I'm learning Chinese to be a translator. It'd be a grand job. I have three other languages as well."

"That's great," Keith said. "I know a little Spanish, but that's all."

"And what's her name?" the lad asked with a wink, and presented Diane with a guileless mien. "Just in fun, miss."

Diane gave him her best image of outrage, then cracked up helplessly into laughter at the youth's wide-eyed innocence. "I know."

"What may I bring you?"

"Two pints," Diane ordered for herself and Keith. "Is it still called a pint here?"

"More than ever," the young man said. "You ought to have a Guinness. It's good for you."

"Sure," Diane said, looking at Keith for his approval. He nodded, eyes shining. "Hmm. Must be good stuff."

"Oh, it is, it is, miss," the bartender assured her. He reached for two pint mugs and set them under the pumps.

Diane gestured toward the two Little Folk. The young man glanced at them and back at her. "And I think they'll have . . ."

The bartender stopped her short, and turned to Holl and the Master. "I beg your pardon, miss," he said deferentially. "Gentlemen, what is your pleasure?"

The two Little Folk looked at each other. Some thought seemed to pass between them, and the Master nodded. As one, they removed their hats and set them on the bar. "A Guinness,"

Holl said, tousling his hair furiously with both hands and fluffing it out. ''Thank the powers, maybe now it'll dry.''

''The same, please,'' the Master said, watching the young man curiously. The bartender gave them a wink and stepped over to the pumps. Carefully, he drew half a glass of Guinness into each pint mug and put them on the back of the bar to settle. The mocha froth slowly began to separate into chocolate-colored beer below and cream foam above. The Master nodded approvingly.

''It takes time to pour one properly,'' said the young man. ''But it's worth it for the taste.'' Holl pushed a few pound notes across to him, but he pushed it back, with a shake of his head. ''Oh, no, it'd be unlucky to take your money from you. My compliments to you, sir. It's on the house.''

''Thank you kindly,'' Holl said, in surprise.

Keith watched this performance with a kind of outraged concern. He looked hastily around the bar to see if anyone had observed them. It was impossible now to disguise the fact that two of the customers in the Skylark had ears almost five inches long that ended in points on the top. Strangely, the Little Folk didn't seem to be worried. Keith wished that he could feel the same way. He was so used to protecting his small friends and drawing the attention of others away from them, to keep them from being carried off to be used for strange experiments or museum exhibits. He had no idea that it might be all right to expose the truth in some places, but apparently, they did. No one at all had turned their way. Maybe it was more of the aversion spell that Holl had used in the airport, and, now that Keith looked back, in the town around Midwestern University. Their own sort of protective coloration, he acknowledged.

The Guinness was topped off, and in a few minutes, set before them. Keith picked his up and offered a silent toast to his friends. He tasted it, and let out a sigh of satisfaction. It was rich and tasty, with a sort of astringency that in a poorer drink would be bitterness. Diane handed the young man a banknote, and picked up her mug.

''This is better than we got in Scotland,'' Keith said, sipping carefully through the foam. Diane tasted hers, with an expression of pleased concentration on her face. She nodded.

''Ah, it doesn't travel well,'' the server said. ''You have to come to Ireland to have real Guinness. The brewery is not far from here, just down the road a bit. They say that it's the best when you can see the smoke from the chimneys from where you're drinking it."

"Can you see it from here?" Keith asked. The young man nodded, his eyes twinkling. "Have one yourself."

"Not at present, but my thanks to you," the server said, taking the banknote and turning to the cash drawer. "I have to give it all my attention when I drink—in appreciation, you understand—and that's bad for business."

Keith was relieved to be just sitting still for a moment, and not staring at anything through fog. With one hand on the handle of his glass, he watched the goings-on in the pub. A giggling couple came in at the door and made for the fireplace. The girl unwound a scarf from her hair while the man came up to the rail to order from the bartender. He returned to her, sipping the top off an overfull glass, and disappeared into the red-tinged shadows next to the hearth. Other customers looked at their watches, and flicked money onto the bar top, calling farewells. The server picked up the change and bade them return soon.

A bandylegged figure in a leather coat and woolly scarf emerged from a darkened corner on the other side of the lounge and waddled silently toward the door. Lit only by the fireplace and the orange lamp, the bearded face under the flat cap bore a slight resemblance to the Elf Master. Of course, half the men over forty in this part of the world did. That didn't make him any different from most of the other gaffers in the bar. What made Keith take notice was when the bearded man opened the door to leave. He seemed to be no more than eyelevel to the doorknob. Keith blinked. It was probably a trick of the light. Keith caught a glimpse of bright blue eyes glancing his way, lit by the swinging lanterns outside. He turned back to the bar, shaking his head.

"I think we just saw one of your relatives," he said in a voice pitched only for Holl and the Master to hear.

"This is no time for one of your jokes, Keith Doyle," Holl said in a frosty voice.

"I mean it," Keith persisted. "I'm not betting my Uncle Arthur's hotel towel collection on it, but I really think so."

Holl lowered his glass, with eyes narrowed. "I thought you said your family broke no laws."

Keith assumed an expression of wounded innocence. "I did. He's in the textile business. He gets one of each as samples."

Holl looked over his shoulder. "Then where is the man you saw?"

"He's gone now," Keith said, glancing back, too. The outer door had swung shut. "Really, he could have been your cousin."

The Master said nothing, and drank his Guinness gloomily. Frivolous references to his loss thickened the shell around the small leader. He ignored Keith and Holl stolidly.

"We ought to think about finding a place where we might be able to have dinner," Diane said, and did a double take. "God, I'm starting to talk like the locals, with the eightfold sentences. I'm getting hungry."

"Me, too," Keith said, referring to his watch. "It's just about the time they start serving. We're dry now. I think I could face the car seats again. Come on." Diane smiled at the bartender, and the four of them stood up.

Amid merry calls of farewell, Keith assured the publican they would stop by again soon. "We'll get back here at least once before we go home," he promised. The door swung shut behind them. The moon overhead was not far from full, and Keith felt alive and full of good spirits, both figurative and literal.

He jingled his car keys, and started across the car park to the blue compact, followed by Diane and the two Little Folk. It was full dark, and the sky overhead was clear and spangled with stars. As they passed under the shadow of the brick arch, a voice issued from the darkness, smooth and warm like melted caramel. It asked a question in an unintelligible lingo. The Master's head went up. He stopped, and replied tentatively in the same language. A small figure darted from behind the wall and waylaid the Master, pulling him to one side. Keith jumped forward to defend his teacher, but the Master held up a hand.

It was the small man in the cap. He slapped out a barrage of words, his nose within inches of the Master's, who replied to him slowly in the same tongue, without a trace of the Deutsch accent with which he spoke English. Keith hovered nearby, getting more and more excited.

"Listen!" he hissed to Diane. "Listen!"

"I think they know each other," she murmured. "Is that your little man?"

"Yup."

The small man turned his head to glance at the Master's

companions. The two Big Folk he dismissed immediately, and ignored thereafter, but Holl he studied. He asked another question, a short one, and Holl, clearly fascinated, approached more closely to answer. The stranger clasped his forearm and drew him forward, looking him carefully up and down. Keith was burning with curiosity.

The stranger made a final exclamation, and guided the two Little Folk under the archway toward the road. Keith, with Diane holding on to his arm, started to follow them. Holl heard the crunch of gravel behind him and looked over his shoulder.

"Go home," he ordered. "Don't follow us."

"But, Holl, I want to know who he is, and where. . . ."

"Go home, Keith Doyle," Holl repeated, seriously. "This is not Gillington Library. You might wind up with your teeth pulled, not only your fillings. We will be safe, and we'll find our own way back."

Keith's hand flew protectively over his mouth. Diane tugged him back into the car park.

"Come on," she said. "He's right. Let's go have dinner." Keith stayed next to the car until the three small figures disappeared into the darkness. Glumly, he unlocked the door and climbed in.

After changing out of their sodden jeans and running shoes at the guest house, Diane asked the proprietress for recommendations of good places to eat. Mrs. Keane had flyers from a number of restaurants, but she pointed out two as being the best of the lot. They chose the one that was the easiest to find, a small restaurant named The Abbot's Table a few miles to the north.

The daily specials and their prices were chalked on a black slate over the hearth in the small dining room. The candlelit tables, about twelve in number, were crowded fairly close together, but there was still some elbow room left over. They slid into their seats, and read the menus in silence. Diane ordered their meals for them, and chatted for a few minutes with the waitress. Keith sat looking glumly out of the window at the darkness, wondering what Holl and the Master were doing. Who was the little man? A relative or a friend? Did he know they were going to be in that pub that day, or was it chance?

"Come on," Diane said, breaking into his thoughts. "You're obsessed. Let's just have a nice time, and you can interrogate

Holl tomorrow morning. Let's talk about something else other than them."

"Sorry," Keith said, apologetically. "I'm only half human, you know. The rest is pure curiosity. I won't be rotten company any more, I promise." Keith roused himself, determined to be entertaining. Over the excellent dinner, they talked about the countryside they'd seen, and travel in general. He was fine so long as he avoided any of the *bodach*'s prohibited subjects.

"My dad always wanted to come here to Ireland. I think with all the stuff I've found for him, he'll be even more rarin' to come over and pick up where I left off," Keith said. "There's a list of Doyles in the phone book a mile long. Dad will be thrilled. I found two Eamon Doyles. You know, given names sometimes run in cycles, skipping generations, so one of these guys might be a direct descendant of my multi-great-granduncle."

"It's fun to watch you working on your family tree," Diane confessed, after they had ordered dessert. "I don't have the energy, or maybe not the interest, to do my own. Part of the problem is that I don't speak Swedish or Danish, or any of the other parts of my family's background. I could do the maternal line, I suppose. Some of my mother's family is English."

"Shh!" Keith silenced her playfully, looking suspiciously around the restaurant in case they were overheard. "Don't talk about that here!"

"Oh, knock it off," she retorted, shaking her head at him affectionately.

"Excuse me," said the older woman seated at the table next to them.

"See," Keith told Diane. "Now you've done it."

"Oh, shut up. Yes, ma'am?"

"You're Americans, aren't you?" They nodded. "I thought so," she said to her husband. "How are you enjoying Ireland?"

"Oh, tremendously," Diane enthused. "It's gorgeous."

"I just had to ask, watching the two of you. You're so happy together. Are you on your honeymoon?"

"Um, no," Keith said, hurriedly, shocked all the way down to his new shoes. "I mean, no. We're here for research, and some sightseeing. We're not married."

"Well, then, you could hardly choose so lovely a young lady as this one when you come to be settling down, now could you?" the old man said, nodding charmingly to Diane. "So, when are you going to declare yourself?"

Keith looked helplessly at Diane, but she gave him an expectant blank stare. On that particular subject, she wasn't giving him any assistance. Anything he wanted to say about that was going to have to come out of his own mouth, however garbled. Mustering his words carefully, Keith tried to make some nondescript compliments to Diane without falling headlong over his own tongue. The *bodach*'s curse seemed to see them coming, and stuck out a foot. What Keith sputtered out sounded like gibberish.

The old man and his wife exchanged knowing glances. This young man's tongue-tiedness must mean that he had honorable intentions sometime in the future. He was certainly in love.

"Your very good health, young man, young lady," they said, toasting them with glasses of wine.

"Um, the same to you," Keith said, raising his own glass. He looked back at Diane, who was still watching him. He did a little pantomime, spreading out helpless palms toward the older couple, and pointing at his mouth. She shut her eyes and shook her head, longsufferingly.

The waitress returned with their desserts and refilled their glasses, rescuing Keith from his efforts to explain himself. He let out a relieved sigh. Diane relented, and gave him a warm smile.

"That's all right. It would be nice to know where I stand. But I'll wait until you can tell me what you're thinking yourself," she said.

"Thanks," Keith offered humbly. He wished he could tell her how lovely she looked in the candlelight, or how much he cared for her, but he knew none of those phrases would ever make it out of his mouth alive. "To you," he said at last, raising the full glass to his lady. There was no stammer or stumble over the two simple words. Ha, ha, bogey, he thought. I'm showing *you*.

• Chapter 27 •

"A pity you had to struggle to find us," said their new companion, whose name was Fergus. "We'd never have left our home, as well you know, only the honest country folk were moving out, and the fast-moving ones coming in their places. It was only a matter of time before they'd want to intrude upon us, so we made tracks first."

Fergus led the two Little Folk down the road and through a break in the hedge. There was a small pathway that led downward.

"Watch your footing, if you please. It slips a bit."

The moon disappeared as they passed under a canopy of boughs. Fergus went first, indicating that the other two should stay as far to the left of the pathway as they could.

"It's a wee bit wet," he explained, enigmatically.

It was wet where they walked, too. The water in the sopping grass soaked through Holl's sneakers. He wished he had Wellington boots, like their guide's. They had covered nearly half a mile when Holl felt some sort of compulsion to turn back which grew stronger as he struggled forward, then suddenly, he pierced through a nearly tangible, fearsome curtain of sensation, emerging into clear air once more. Panting, he looked around to find that he was at the top of a street overlooking a country village. It was like the Big Folks' ones they had been passing through for days, but scaled down to size, his size. The humped shapes of ordinary farm animals, pigs and sheep and geese that rested in paddocks and folds between and behind the houses, were almost comically huge in comparison. Holl could hear ponies snorting in the darkness beyond. Torches and lanterns burned at the doors of most of the cottages. Along the lane which ran between them, lanterns on standards lit the way for pedestrians. Cats slunk across the path on business of their own. There were no dogs that Holl could hear. Nothing in this place made a noise that could be heard at a distance to attract attention, but still, the village was of a fairly good size. In fact, it was a lot like the one in which he grew up, but there were differences.

"Aren't you afraid the Big Folks will find you here?" Holl asked.

"Oh, sometimes they can see the vale from the road, but you can't get to it on foot, there's nowhere to land by hellycopter, and somehow you and your poor little computer forget all about the coordinates when you want to find it later."

"It vorked for years on the hilltop in this vay," the Master put in.

"I'll take you to see the Niall, then," Fergus told them.

"The Niall?" asked Holl.

"Aye. We like to think of him as the last king in Ireland, but his title is merely the Chief of Chiefs, which he considers is quite important enough. But you should know all that, laddie."

Holl shook his head. Fergus shot a puzzled look at the Master, but dropped the topic.

"He'll be curious to see *you*, and how you grew up! Eh, you were such a wild one. But I'm glad to see you back and all, and so will he be."

"A wild one?" Holl whispered to the Master, whose face had twisted into an expression of disapproval. He waved Holl away.

"How many live here?" Holl asked, looking around in awe, trying to count the houses as they walked among them. No one was outside in the lane, but in the windows he could see shadows of figures thrown up on the curtains by firelight within.

"As many as there are," Fergus answered vaguely. "Eh, you're only a child, to ask so many questions. Have a look about, if you please, but it'd be better in daylight. Why not wait until then?"

"I haf not been here either," the Master reminded Fergus.

"Ah, that's right, then. You went off long before we moved here." Fergus moved ahead of them, chuckling.

"Vhen vas that?"

"Oh, a wee while ago," Fergus replied.

The path continued on down a gentle slope. They came to a fork, where Fergus turned right and continued on past more of the little cottages to a grander, more elaborate residence on the edge of the settlement, two storys in height. Lanterns burned at the corners of the house, and inside, behind the window curtains.

"Well, himself is at home, for a wonder," Fergus said. "Come along inside."

Inside the house, a woman sat spinning at a treadle-driven wheel next to a carved and ornamented fireplace in a large, airy room. Her knee-length dress was of a supple, woven material that flowed around her like water, rippling when she moved her foot. The movement echoed the sway of her long hair, bound back in a ribbon to keep it out of the wheel's spokes. The interior walls of the house were plain except where flowering vines grew and entwined, making a handsome living mural. The woman glanced up when the three of them entered, and her eyes rounded with surprise. The thread between her hands, which had been smooth and thin, suddenly knotted, but she ignored it. She rose from her seat in a single graceful movement and flew to embrace the Master.

"I don't believe it!" she exclaimed, standing back to gaze at him at arm's length. "Niall! Niall!"

"Women are like birds," said a musical voice from the next room. "They're beautiful, ornamental, and they should be kept in yards or cages, so they should. For what are you screaming, my love?" The speaker entered. He was Holl's height, but thinner. His fair hair was of a lint white, something like Holl's grand-nephew Tay's. Holl tried to gauge how old he was, but the face with its sharp nose and chin and equally sharp eyes had only enough skin stretched across it to cover the fine bones. His eyes crossed their faces impassively, until they came to the Master. In a moment, the Niall had recognized him, and his jaw dropped.

Holl saw that the Master had braced himself for a cold reception. When the Niall advanced on him and wrung his hand, the Master relaxed, and returned the following embrace heartily.

"I never thought on this side of life that I would ever see you again!" the Niall exclaimed, thumping him soundly on the back.

"Nor I you," said the Master. He extended a hand toward Holl. "I present to you this young man, whose name is Holland,"

"Holl," Holl corrected.

The deepset, dark blue eyes turned to study Holl. "He's not yours, to be sure. This'll be one of Curran's get, will it not?"

"That's right," Holl said. "My parents are Dennet and Calla."

"Ah, of course. And he can speak for himself. I remember your sister, and a sharp-tongued young wench she was. Very good! So, my dears, sit down." Niall gestured them toward the cluster of low, wooden-backed chairs at the side of the fireplace across from the spinning wheel. Fergus, forgotten on the threshold, cleared his throat significantly. "Sit down, Fergus, do. You're welcome, as always. Ah, here are the others. I thought word might spread like a grassfire. Come in, friends." Five or six other men and women had come in from the outside, and greeted the Master warmly. Holl was introduced in a flurry of kisses, pats on the back, and handshakes to the other Clan Chiefs. "Ketlin, will you kindly get us something to drink?"

"Certainly I will. And you hold the talk until I'm back, hear me?" Ketlin insisted.

"Ah, women." Niall saw to it that everyone was made comfortable. "Now, then, the question that's knocking at every lip begging to get out is *why*? Why have you come back to us? Do you need sanctuary? Are you the only ones left alive, then?" the Chief asked, anxiously.

"Not at all," said the Master. "The village is thriving. We haf doubled our numbers. There are many children, and all are healthy."

There were quiet exclamations of "Ah!" around the circle, and a spate of whispering.

One of the women spoke up. "We hoped for word or glance of you, but you went straight out of our ken. Who dreamed you could go so far away that no one could touch you? You were all given up for dead. Many's the curse called down on your head for leading away some of our children and loved ones to die."

"None died in the traveling," the Master promised solemnly. "Ve lived in many places before arriving in the one we now occupy, but that vill be a home and a haven now forever. The land is good. Ve haf plenty of food, and there is wood for building. Only one house stands on the property at this time, but it is a Big Folk house, vith plenty of room. Others are planned."

"Ah, I feel the truth of your words," the Chief of Chiefs

said, with one hand on his heart. "But I'd be content if I could look into the faces of our lost ones."

"In a way, you can," Holl spoke up. The old ones had been ignoring him, treating him as a nestling barely out of the egg, and he found it annoying. He wanted to defend the Master, who was so obviously on trial before them. "Keith Doyle has several rolls of photographs of our folk, taken at the going away party."

Memory dawned on the Master's face. "That is true. I had forgotten his posing and prancing. Ve haf the faces preserved. All of them, or I do not know Keith Doyle."

"May we see these preserved pictures?" the Chief asked.

"With Keith's photographs comes Keith," Holl warned the Master.

"That is true," the Master acknowledged. "His curiosity must be past the bursting point already. May he come?" he asked the Niall.

"Big Folk among us in our fastness? Never! We'll have no peace from them thereafter." There was protest among the elders. Holl waited them out. Their curiosity was aroused. They would eventually capitulate.

The fire was replenished many times during the course of the night. None of the chiefs seemed to become bored with having the Master repeat the details of his journey to America. Clan by clan, he ticked off the children that had been born, who their parents were, and what capabilities the children seemed to be showing as they grew up.

"And who has married whom?" asked Aine, another of the female chiefs.

"None in my lifetime," Holl said.

"None yet in the new place," the Master replied.

"None yet?" Aine echoed, disbelievingly. "In all that time? Heavens above, why not?"

Holl thought it would be appropriate to bring up the point of his quest. "By our custom, or so I've been taught," he began, with a seated bow toward the Master, "none of us can marry unless there are white bellflowers in hand to bless the union. We have none."

"The last seeds appear to haf been lost in one of the transits to our present home," the Master affirmed.

"Ah, well, it's impossible then, isn't it?" the Niall said, nodding.

Holl noted the serious expressions on the faces of those seated around him. He had been inclined to dismiss the flowers as a fillip; a gesture, no more; but clearly they were not.

"I know of none at present," the Chief continued. "Fiona, have you seen any weddingbells in the fields?"

"There have been no weddings or engagements planned for the year, so none sought them," one of the female chiefs answered. "It's nearly the end of the season. It may be past their time. I'll have the children go out and seek them in the morning."

Holl felt panic rising in his belly. What if there were none?

"There'll have to be the gathering ceremony," one of the very old chieftains said. The Master turned to him with an expression of annoyance barely concealed. The old man missed none of it. "Ah, don't look at me that way. You've forgotten, have ye? It's been a long time since you married my daughter. Hah! Do you not know about the weddingbells? To take them off the sacred places requires respect to be shown. Never do we hasten the blooming of the bells, never! Three blessings those flowers give. Are you willing to show the proper respect, young one, to receive the benefits?"

"Yes," Holl replied, returning to the present and wondering exactly what was going on between the Master and this man. It must be an old feud. So this was Orchadia's father. Enoch resembled him somewhat. Grandfather and grandson seemed to have identical tempers, at any rate.

"Perhaps if you wait a wee while we can put you on the way to finding some weddingbells," Fiona said, interceding, and turned the conversation to other matters.

Holl understood that there was no point in trying to hurry them. If none were found before the date he was expecting to leave, he would change his plane ticket to a later date. It was that simple. There must be some way to break the news to Keith Doyle.

"I'd be remiss if I didn't ask again on behalf of my Big friend if he may visit your home. He can be well behaved, and it would be a joy to him if he could meet you."

"Certainly not," the old man stated firmly.

Most of the chiefs still protested against it, but one or two held their tongues. They were becoming interested.

"I, too, must speak on Keith Doyle's behalf," the Master

said, unexpectedly. "He is, if not the author, then the director of our present prosperity. Ve owe him much."

"And at present, he's got a tongue-tying curse on him," Holl reminded the Master, who nodded.

"Laid by one of the two of you?" Fiona asked, humorously.

"No, by a being of the earth in the Scottish Islands. He has a photograph."

"Ah, well, we can't touch that, but the weddingbells could take care of it," she insisted. "They cure many ills, you may know."

"Tell us about the haven," one of the other clan chiefs demanded, interrupting them. A rooster, immediately underneath the window, interjected at that moment to announce dawn. Holl looked up. Orange and pink streaks were reaching up from the east to color the sky. They had stayed up all night talking, and at this rate, would be here all day.

The Master gave them every detail that concerned Hollow Tree Farm: how many acres it comprised, how many of each kind of tree, what condition of farmland and how many lengths. They pressed him to know how the Folk lived on the farm, and what that life was like.

"Ve are not yet self-sufficient. There's more to be made, and time needed in vhich to make it. Ve could not do all ve vanted in the Big Folks' building, but now ve haf land of our own."

"I would like to introduce weaving and spinning to the farm," Holl put in. "We have never had textile capability of our own, and now that we have room to graze them, we should have sheep. I observed the weaving in the Scottish Islands. There's nothing they do that we can't. In fact, quite a lot of the wool fabric here looks a lot like the cloth that the Hebrideans make."

"We use an old style loom, with several shuttles," Ketlin said. She brought Holl back to examine the one in her workroom, behind the Niall's study. "It's old, but it does its work well."

"It's just like Mrs. MacLeod's." Holl showed off the sketch he made of the Big Person's loom. His notebook, which had been in his back pocket all day and all night, was creased, and some of the drawings were smudged, but that one had been spared.

"So it is," Ketlin said, studying the sketch. "You've got a skilled hand, lad."

"I'm planning to have the others help me to make some of these looms so we can make our own wool cloth, and some finer ones for cotton percale and so on. The United States is great for growing fiber plants."

"You should talk to Tiron," the Niall said when they returned to the front room. "And now it seems we should think of having breakfast. Go back, all of you, and tell your folk we have a couple of honored guests this day. We can breakfast together on the common. I think it will be fair this morning."

"Meet Tiron, who is the child of Ardigh and Gerome," the Niall said, introducing them formally over breakfast. "Holl, son of Dennet and Calla. Holl is interested in the making of looms, my lad."

"Ah, good!" Tiron said. He had brilliant green eyes, and a cap of curling, dark hair under a peaked cap with a buckled band around the crown. He wore a short, sleeveless coat over a long-sleeved shirt, unlike many of his seniors, who wore coats and woolly vests, like the Big Folk in the nearby towns. "And I'm pleased to meet you. Well, there's nothing I can't tell you. I made all the looms in this village. My design is better than the one they were using while I was growing up. It took a little persuasion to force out the bad ways," Tiron wiggled a hand sideways to show the direction his machinations took, "but it's been worth it, they say. A wee bit of tinkering was all a loom needed to run more smoothly, with less chance of the web wrinkling or the thread snapping. What's more, I know all there is to know in caring for them. Nearly all the clothing you see here is from cloth woven on one of my looms," Tiron bragged. "I can make one in a fortnight, by myself."

Holl looked around at the others for someone to give Tiron's statement the lie, but no one did. They were all nodding at the young craftsman. "All of it! I am impressed," Holl acceded. "It must be sound work indeed."

"So they tell me. You're from America, are you?" Tiron went on, with interest. "I've wanted to go there all my life. You ought to take me back with you."

"I don't know how that would be possible," Holl said, cautiously. He was by no means eager to take this cocky fellow back to the farm with him, even if he could figure out how.

"If you did, Holl vould haf to fall back on leadership," the Master said teasingly. "He is our finest woodworker and ornamenter.'' Holl displayed the small box he had been working on in idle moments.

''He *is*?'' said Tiron, affecting surprise. ''Let's see what you've got there.'' He twitched Holl's work out of his hands and inspected it closely. The featureless stick Holl had begun with in Inverness had become a cylindrical box three inches high covered solidly with his favorite ivy pattern. He watched Tiron examine it with a gimlet eye. ''Well, now, what a pretty pattern,'' the other said, somewhat patronizingly, ''but you've forgotten to give the poor little leaves any backbones. Here, now.''

He whipped out his own knife, a tool with a simple bronze blade. Holl eyed it. With the knife held an inch from the point with his fingers, Tiron bent over the box. ''There,'' he said after a moment. ''If you'd take the trouble to look at that, I'd be most pleased.''

Holl accepted the box back. Tiron had carved minute spines and veins on the ivy in the pattern in the lid, swiftly and without error. The leaves suddenly looked real, a monochrome illumination for a calligraphed manuscript, and made the rest of the little carving look clumsy. Holl turned red.

''There's still a few things for you to learn, my boy,'' Tiron winked at him in a friendly manner. ''No hard feelings, I hope.''

''None,'' said Holl, humbly, inspecting the work more closely once the fierce blush of embarrassment had subsided. ''It's so easy to enlarge upon the detail, now I've seen what you do, and I never thought of it, never felt to add it.''

''You have the look of someone who's done it by rote, from a design or drawing, not the real thing,'' Tiron said, summing him up with a critical but not unfriendly eye. ''You've all the ways and skills to be good. Come and see real ivy.'' He clapped a hand on Holl's back and led him toward a low stone wall that ran around the rear of one row of the small cottages. ''Ah, pity. I could teach you so much, but we have so little time. Come and talk!''

The Master and the Chief of Chiefs looked after them. ''You've chosen well, if that's your choice,'' the Niall said. ''You don't mind that he isn't your own son?''

''My son is not interested in leadership. He is a fine craftsman,'' the Master said proudly.

''In Holl I'd say our continued future is well assured.''

"Ve knew it almost from his birth," the Master said, with equal satisfaction.

"And so we knew with you, my boy. And so we knew. But we expected you to stay *here* and lead."

The Master clicked his tongue. "There could not be two of us, could there? You had the same promise. Vhy should you not be permitted to use your talents? And I could not stay. I did not vant to stay. There vere too many of us, and not enough room. The rules vere not stringent, they vere silly. I could not lead, vith the old men crying for dusty precedent in efery unimportant case."

"You were right to go," the Chief said at last. "When the Hunger came, careful as we'd been to bank our harvests, so many died. If you and the others had stayed, we'd have had too many mouths to feed. I think some would have followed your trail then if they could have. And I promise you," Niall said slyly, "I've had my own confrontations with those dusty old ones. You might be pleased at some of the progress I've made. Come back again soon—today—and bring along your tame Big Folk. We'll give them greeting."

• Chapter 28 •

Keith and Diane waited anxiously for the Master and Holl at the guesthouse until almost noon. At that time Mrs. Keane had made it clear that she wanted the rooms vacated so she could clean them. She began to vacuum the hall outside Diane's room aggressively about eleven-thirty. Keith was so keyed up he leaped in the air when the vacuum started.

"My nerves are shot, too, waiting around. Why don't we go back to the Skylark?" Diane suggested. "They're just as likely to turn up there as here. We can have lunch while we wait. The sign said they have seafood. I wouldn't mind some of that."

"That's a good idea," Keith agreed. He shouldered his camera bag.

"And what's that for?" Diane asked, raising her eyebrows.

"Well . . . just in case," Keith said. "I'm the eternal optimist."

"I know," Diane said, looking heavenward for patience. "I know. Come on."

The young bartender greeted them as they came into the Skylark and sat down at the bar. "Back again, so soon? You're very welcome. What may I bring you? Lunch? We've a prawn salad on special today."

Diane pulled over the cardboard lunch menu, and ordered for the two of them. "And Guinness. Only make mine half the size of the one I had last night."

The bartender put in the lunch order and came over to talk to them while he pulled the beer. As it was still early, there were only a few people in the pub. "Since we're going to be friends, my name is Peter," the young man said. "Pleased to know you."

Diane and Keith introduced themselves. "There's something I've been meaning to ask," Keith said. "It hit me after we left last night. You didn't seem too surprised when my two friends came in the other day." He sketched a tall ear on the side of his head with a finger.

Peter looked over his shoulder, then shook his head. "Ah, no, they're in here all the time. You learn not to talk about it. It doesn't do to offend the Fair Folk, as my granda always said. They'll wish you bad luck. Did you say now that those two came in with you?"

"Yeah. They're good friends of ours. They live near our university."

Peter was astonished. "In America? Well, fancy that. I thought the only ones in the wide world were here."

"Well, a whole lot of them moved to America. How long have these, er, Fair Folk been coming in here? I mean, into the Skylark."

"Oh, years now," Peter said, trying to count backward. "My da talked about them when I was just a wee one, and my granda before him. It wasn't until I was almost grown that I knew my da wasn't just telling stories."

"How many of them are there?" Keith asked curiously.

"I've only seen a handful, myself. That's enough for me. Some say they're a bad omen, coming in here, though truth to tell, not many notice them."

"I think you should take it as a good omen. My bunch make

their own beer. If they like yours enough to come out for it, you should feel complimented."

"That's good to know," Peter said, smiling. "I'll tell my da." He fetched their drinks, and left them alone on their side of the bar.

"Where *are* they?" Keith said to Diane, looking at his watch. "They've been gone all night."

"They're all right," Diane assured him. "They're adults, remember? Older than you?"

"Yeah, I know. I wonder if the others will let me visit them. I'd hate to have come all this way, and never see where they live."

"Trust Holl. If anyone can get you an invitation, he can." Diane patted his hand. "You are not to sit there feeling sorry for yourself. Do something. Call Doyles from the phone book."

"Nope, I've got a better idea. Hey, Peter?" The young bartender came over to them, hands busy with a glass and a towel. "You know a bunch of languages. Do you speak Gaelic?"

"Of course I do. It's me mother tongue," Peter said in an exaggerated brogue.

"Can you teach me how to say something? To greet someone important?"

"Ah," said Peter knowingly. "In case you meet the king of the fairies, is that it? I'd be glad to. It's *'Dia dhuit.'* Can you say that?"

"No," said Keith, trying to separate Peter's phrases into manageable syllables. "Say it again, slower."

Patiently, Peter helped Keith rehearse the greeting over and over again. He wrote it out on a paper napkin in Gaelic with the translation in English below, and left him alone to try it out for himself.

"This doesn't look like what I'm saying," Keith said to Diane. "There's way too many letters." Keith tried to pronounce the sentence.

"That sounded more like it. Try again."

"I thought we'd find you here," Holl said, interrupting the language lesson. He slapped Keith soundly on the back.

"Where've you been?" Keith demanded, rounding on him. "Are you all right? Who was that other one? Can I go and see the new village?"

"The answers are, we've been visiting relatives," Holl said, "as well you know. We are fine, though I've not slept all night; his name is Fergus; and yes."

"Yee-hah!" Keith cheered, throwing his napkin in the air.

"That is, they're willing to trust you with their secret, if you can behave yourself," Holl said sternly.

"Oh, I will. I promise." Keith retrieved the little piece of paper. "Let's go!" He caught Peter's eye and showed him he was leaving money on the bar. Peter nodded, and waved farewell.

Fergus and the Master were waiting behind the pub on the side opposite the car park.

"Boy, am I glad to see you—sir," Keith finished, stifling his enthusiasm under the Master's quelling gaze. "I was worried about you."

"Ve vere neffer in any danger," the Master assured him calmly.

Fergus shook hands solemnly with Diane and Keith. "He says you're friendly and worthy of trust," the Little Person said, dubiously, as Holl made formal introductions. "I suppose I must believe him. A Doyle, are you? There are many of that name who live near here."

"I know," said Keith. "I'm descended from some of them."

"Are you now?" Fergus snapped his fingers. "I thought your face looked familiar. The man I knew must have been one of your grandfathers. Ah, but that was a wee while ago."

"It sure was," Keith exclaimed. "At least a hundred and forty years! You sure don't look it."

"Thank you for the kind words," Fergus grimaced, though he was clearly pleased. "A fine man. You're shorter though. That's what threw me off. Come along, then."

With Keith and Diane in tow, the Little Folk turned off the road and down into the little path broken through the growth at the side. Fergus paused to let the big Folk catch up, and traced its outline with his hands. "The Big Ones think badgers made this, and sheep use it, so we let them think so."

"It's so close to the pub. I'd never dreamed that you'd live so near to hum—I mean, Big Folk habitation."

"Our neighbors don't bother us," Fergus assured him. "We have privacy in plenty."

They made their way down the path until it was interrupted by a tiny stream with a concrete block over it. The block had a semicircular hole in the lower half to let the stream through. Keith helped Diane over it, and then climbed over himself.

The bushes were lower beyond the barrier than they had been on the sheep track. "I can't stand up in here," Keith complained.

"Aye, well, if we knew you were coming to visit us," Fergus said, looking up at him regretfully, "but there! This is our way backward and forward, always."

"Not alvays," the Master said, dreamily.

"Well, now it is. The farmers leave the trees and bushes over the river to themselves, so as not to run their machinery straight into the water. We like that quite well, for they've left us a covered pathway. We don't have to skulk," Fergus explained, "for no one comes this way but us and a few other natural creatures. There's passages like this all over Ireland. Some join with the Big People's paths, like the *Sli' Cualann Nua*. But mostly they're alone."

"Great!" Keith said, ducking to miss a raspberry cane. He walked half stooped over, watching the three Little Folk make steady progress along the stream path ahead of him. Inwardly, he was thrilled. To think that he was going to visit the Elf Master's old home, and meet the rest of the clans! "That was lucky, finding a river close to where you wanted to set up a home."

"Luck? What luck? We needed water, so by water we must be."

They walked past a low thicket, whose floor was carpeted by wildflowers, most of them white. Keith recognized lily-of-the-valley and a few other summer flowers, but the tall, stalky flowers caught his attention next. He recognized the shape in an instant.

"Holl, look!" Keith exclaimed. "White bellflowers! Just like the pink ones in Scotland."

"Ah, no," Fergus corrected him. "That's just white fox-glove. It's one of the fairy flowers, but nothing as fine as the bellflowers."

"There are fairies around here, too?" Keith asked, eagerly.

"At the bottom of every garden," the elf assured him solemnly. "But to be serious, you might see a dancing light on the fields of an evening."

"I thought those were fireflies," Keith struggled to understand.

"Ah, well, sometimes they are."

Holl turned to watch as first Diane, then Keith, passed through the protective spell surrounding the village environs. Diane was terrified, and started to retreat back into Keith's arms. Holl and the Master hastened back to take her hands and lead her through it. In a moment, she was all right. Keith eyed her, then took a deep breath. He plunged into the thickest part of the spell, and burst through it, letting his breath out on the other side. He stood with his hands braced on his knees, supporting his back, shaking his head as if to clear it.

"Are you all right?" Holl asked.

"If that's what I have to do to boldly go where no Big Folk has gone before, I can take it," Keith said, stolidly, making a face. "It felt like I rammed my head into a stone wall. I think I broke something. What *was* that?"

"A charm of great strength," Fergus said. "If someone should make his way this far seeking us, we need it to be strong enough to erode even that determination."

"It didn't feel solid to me," Diane said. "It felt like getting smothered in a quilt. Horrible!"

"At the risk of getting my knuckles rapped," Keith asked, "are we there yet?"

"We're there," Fergus said.

Most of the village was waiting for them on the other side of the trees. Murmuring broke out when the two Big Folk appeared. Keith surveyed the faces of the crowd of Little Folk staring up at him. He had a definite feeling of deja vu, experiencing all over again the delight and wonder he felt at discovering the Midwestern village of the Little Folk. He walked among them, feeling as if he must be dreaming, but it was a dream in infinite detail. This hamlet had more of an established air about it than the Gillington Library village did, and the roofs, which were recreated in loving detail in the basement of the library, existed for real here, and kept off real rain and wind. "Holl, we are definitely not in Kansas any more."

"Illinois," Holl corrected him, with a puzzled glance.

"Whatever."

Keith looked, taking in all that he could with a feeling that he had never been so happy. There were flower gardens here, something that looked odd next to the houses he had never seen anywhere but on a plain dirt and concrete floor. There were animals, too: sheared sheep grazing quietly in a field at the end of the lane, ponies snorting quietly over their food, and geese and chickens wandering everywhere as if they owned the place. It was more alive than the Gillington complex, and a lot more noisy. There were children laughing out loud, and the sounds of music playing. He realized now that the hidden village was a copy done from memory of this place. He became vaguely aware that Holl was pulling him down the lane by one arm.

"This is the Chief of Chiefs," Holl said, presenting him to the Niall, who was seated on a chair under an oak tree in the middle of the village green. "Keith Doyle."

"*Dia dhuit*," said Keith, bowing low from the waist.

The Chief looked surprised, but he replied in the same way. "*Tá failte romhat*, Keith Doyle."

"Sorry, that's all I know," Keith said, with a sheepish grin. "I'm going to have to go on from here in English."

"But that's grand," the Niall told him, his eyes dancing. "We expected it." He rose before Diane, took her hand in both of his, and said something to her with a very formal bow. She looked embarrassed and glanced at Keith for help.

"This is the Chief of Chiefs," Keith said to her.

"Pleased to meet you," Diane told Niall, unable to think of anything better.

"The pleasure is mine." The Chief affected introductions all around. First, he brought forward the clan chiefs, including one sour-faced squirt who shot a surly look at the Master. Keith found he couldn't keep up with the torrent of names, but he smiled and shook hands with everyone.

"This is Tiron," Holl said, introducing him to one young fellow with a wispy, little beard on his chin.

"How do?" Keith asked.

"As well as I can," Tiron replied. Tiron reminded Keith of a young Hollywood actor from the Golden Age, maybe one of the Dead End kids who had worked hard all his life from age ten, self-possessed and tough. Not that he looked much older than ten. Like all of the Little Folk, he had the face of a child.

"So we hear you had a wee bit of a malediction read over you," the Niall said. "We'll see if we can't do something to help you. In the meanwhile, my people would like to get to know you."

"I'd like to get to know them," Keith said eagerly. "Can I take pictures?"

Niall waved a hand grandly. Without waiting to ask twice,

Keith started making the rounds of the village, with a whole herd of children in attendance, spouting questions. They wanted to know everything about him, and about where he lived and what he did. As an American, he was a genuine curiosity. He learned that he was the first contact many of them had had with the Big People. "So I'm the good will ambassador after all, huh?"

"More than that," Holl informed him. "You're the representative of your entire race. Keep that in mind."

In the context of the Irish relations, as Keith called them to himself, Holl seemed more than ever to be really an adult. And the Master, the immutable Elf Master, bane of his classroom existence? He seemed younger, and a bit embarrassed. "I vas qvite a child vhen I departed. I think my folk here see me the same vay still. Some treat me as vun. They vanted to meet you, because of the great task I undertook in my youth, to lead my people avay and find them prosperity elsevhere. It vas not actually completed until you provided assistance, Meester Doyle. And for that, I thank you."

"Really?" Keith said, very flattered. "What did the other folk say when you told them you were leaving, all those years ago?"

"They vere shocked because I vas taking away half the population vith me. It vas a hard decision, but to survive we needed to divide. I am pleased to say that it vorked. The anger they felt is gone now. This is the first time that they knew that ve survived, and they are glad."

"Wow. How *did* you get to America?" Keith asked.

"On a ship vith sails," the Master explained.

"When was that?" Keith asked, but the Master ignored the question. Keith felt frustrated. He was getting to know more about his mysterious friends than ever before, but he realized that there were some things that he wouldn't find out. Their explanations tended to be a little bare of detail.

"How old were you when you led your half of the Folk away from here?" Keith asked him impulsively, trying another tack.

"I vas very young; only a boy, perhaps twenty, twenty-two."

"Mmm." Keith knew that the Master was at least twenty-five years older than his son Enoch, who was born in America. Enoch was forty-seven. That made the Master seventy at a minimum. But then, they came to the U.S. in a sailing ship. There were no sailing ships crossing the Atlantic during the twentieth century. Unless they built their own? No, that was unlikely. There were hardly any trees to speak of in the countryside. A whole boat's worth would be missed. "So you're about seventy-two, sir?" Keith asked hopefully, hoping the teacher would fill in a number. The Master smiled slightly, ignoring the pry. Holl nudged Keith with an elbow and steered him in another direction.

"Well, how can I learn if I don't ask questions?" Keith said innocently.

"You wouldn't just happen to have your pictures with you?" Holl asked. "The Niall would like to see the rolls of the folk at Hollow Tree Farm."

Keith smiled brilliantly. "I had a hunch I'd need the whole kit," he said cheerfully, swinging the camera bag around. "Here." He dug out the envelopes and handed them to Holl. Immediately, a crowd gathered around to look at the photographs. Holl looked helplessly at the Niall, who waved a resigned hand.

"I can wait. Bring them along to my home when you can wrench them away, and your tall friend, too."

• Chapter 29 •

Keith and Diane dined with their new friends, who guided them out of the vale and back to their car by moonlight. There had been dancing and games on the green until it was too dark to see. They were both quite exhausted by the party.

"I think I danced with everyone in town," Diane said, limping up the bank. "But it was fun!"

"The Niall's compliments," Fergus said as he bade them goodbye at the head of the path, "and he'd be pleased if you'd all come back along in the morning."

"You bet," Keith said, enthusiastically. "I'll be there with bells on."

"Er, there's no need," Fergus said deprecatingly. "They make too much noise. Come as you are."

Holl started laughing. "They'll need a lexicon to understand you, Keith Doyle."

The next morning was overcast and showed threatening signs of rain. With Peter's permission, Keith left his car in the lane behind the pub. He stood in the stone courtyard and looked out over the fields below. There was the village, nestled among trees like an egg in the nest. A few rooftops were actually just visible from there, which made Keith fear for its vulnerability. Holl assured him that no one could reach it.

The only place where the two Big Folk could fit comfortably out of the weather was sitting on the floor in the Chief's front room, so that was where they spent the morning. The furniture looked comfortable, but it was too small for them to sit in. The Niall's wife, Ketlin, piled wool rugs and sheepskins for them to recline upon. What Keith took at first to be bouquets of purple and blue flowers with attendant greens turned out to be living blossoms growing right there inside the house. So was the vine design on the walls and ceiling. A bee actually flew out of one of the trumpet flowers as they watched.

The Niall and his wife had as many questions for them as the children had the day before. Other Little Folk wandered in and out of the great house at will to pass a few moments with their odd guests. Keith discussed the problem of visibility with the Niall.

"It's been no worry so far," the Chief told Keith. "Yet there will come a day when long-held belief will no longer stay the curious, or strangers will stumble on our secret and reveal it to the world of Big Folk. Then we may have to move on."

Keith, keenly aware that he was one of those stumbling Big Folk, assured the Chief that he'd keep their secret. "I mean, except for my father, I don't know who I'd tell, but Dad understands. He knows Holl."

"That's good. We need friends. There was a time when the Big Folk and the Little had a war to divide up all the land in the world. The Big had many more people, and took the best, leaving us what little they did not care to own. In the ripeness of time, and with good health and many children, we came to be at elbow's point," the Niall said.

"The hilltop. We were there," Keith said. "And that was when the Master left."

"Aye, that's a fair summation."

"You know, I don't see a lot of difference between the way you folk live here and the way they do at home, barring differences of surrounding culture, to quote my unlamented sociology professor. Um, how long ago was that they left?"

"Oh, a wee while ago," the Niall said, disinterestedly. Keith was disappointed again. The way people talked around here, that could have been a year or an eon. Tiron poked his head in.

"Good morning to you all, though I'm disinclined to believe the good. Will it rain or not?" the green-eyed lad asked. "Holl, come and see. I've made you a set of plans for the loom."

Holl rose from the chair next to the fireplace. "With your permission, Niall?"

The leader waved a hand blithely. "Be free as you will."

"Ah, a chair left for me next the fire," said Fiona, arriving as Holl and Tiron departed. "There's kindness itself." She seated herself and spread her skirts around her.

"Fiona is the one of us who seems best to understand the language of plants," Niall explained. "You see a bit of her handwork on the walls here."

"They're wonderful. Um, has Holl mentioned what he's here looking for?" Keith asked diplomatically.

"The weddingbells?" Fiona asked. "Oh, yes. We're trying to find some for him, to be sure. Though we only use them when we find them, I can see that tradition will have to change when you have to come four thousand miles to look for clumps."

"I saw white foxglove on the way here, but they said that those aren't the ones, is that right?"

"Here, now," the herbwoman said, showing him one of the living nosegays. Keith was amused to find clover of the ordinary three-leafed variety growing there. It ought to have been four-leafed. "This is the bellflower wearing its everyday clothes." Fiona bent a stem toward him. Keith saw a cluster of purple-blue flowers. "It's just an ordinary blossom which closely resembles the weddingbells. They call it 'cuckoo's shoe' here," she said with a grin, "but some know it as 'thimble of the goblin.'"

"Appropriate, I guess," Keith chuckled, then started. "Wait, I saw some of this in Scotland, just before Holl got sick. Actual white ones, a whole clump of them. We overlooked it for the foxglove. It was right there on the fairy mound." He bashed himself in the forehead with disgust. "Well, it's too late to go back now. What a dope I am! I was expecting something a lot more—you know, large or impressive. It looks so tiny and insignificant."

"But it is, except as one of Nature's works. Sometimes the smallest or most unimportant seeming things have the most virtue to them," the Niall said. "We let the Big Folk know the white foxglove is a fairy flower, so they'll let our other resources be. This one has no magic. Only the white variety does."

"How do you know?" Diane asked.

"By the feel," Niall said simply.

"Well, what does magic feel like?" Keith asked.

"Well, we've time for a lesson, haven't we, then? Hold up your hands, palms in front of you." Keith raised them obediently. "If you don't look straight at them, you can hardly see a sort of field around them like a glowing glove, can't you?"

Taking "hardly" to mean "barely," Keith looked off into the distance, but glanced at his hands in his peripheral vision.

Diane tried it. "I don't see a thing." She dropped her hands in her lap in disappointment.

"There is sort of a glow there. I think," Keith said slowly, seeing a faint halo surrounding his hand. "It could be an illusion, or just my eyesight."

"It's not an illusion. It's part of your body, though you can't see it, feel it, or cut it off," Niall explained. "Now, it's in this glove that lie the senses for feeling magic, and doing some types. There are some charms worked in which the hand of the body never touches the physical form of the subject. The work is all done in the aura, which affects the subject's reality. Good magic feels good to you, like velvet or joy. Evil magic has a nasty prickle, like nettles."

"Then why do people do black magic on purpose?" Keith said.

The Niall clicked his tongue. "I can't imagine why, for all of me. There's a lot of power in black magic, and nothing with the senses to feel it will blunder into its sway, so you have less to expend doing it. The workings of all are very subtle, and it changes the character of the worker over time to something twisted and warped."

Keith gulped. "Can you do it by accident?" He was beginning to go crosseyed trying not to look directly at his hand but to keep his aura in view.

"No. There must always be intent."

"A good-intentioned repulsion spell will keep things out without being evil," Fiona said. "There's a born necessity around the lettuce patch, we've so many rabbits."

"But strong magic," Niall continued, smiling at Keith's expression of concentration, "that feels powerful like a white-hot fire or a wall or a terrible fall, whether it was designed by good or evil intentions or by nature. It can do as much harm as boon if a charm is too strong."

"So there's everyday magic, like magic lanterns," Keith said, thinking of the Hollow Tree crafts. "And then there's the serious stuff."

"Well put," Niall laughed. "If you're willing, we'll teach you to feel it first with strongly imbued articles, working downward in concentration as you become accustomed to it, to the most subtle, featherlight touch."

"The exact opposite of Szechuan food, huh?" Keith reasoned, giving up the struggle to watch the aura, and rubbed his eyes. "There you start with mild, and end up flat on your back."

They practiced for a while, letting Keith try out his newly trained sensitivity on a variety of objects. The other Little Folk seemed to be impressed that the Niall was taking so much interest in a Big Person, but Keith was so interested and so respectful, they soon got over their resentment. In time, the whole room was coaching him, calling out suggestions as he tried his new skill with varying results. Diane sat back and watched, interested, but not interested enough to try for herself.

"How about this," Ketlin said, holding up a lantern by the ring.

"We have those at home," Keith said. He took it and looked at it, trying to see an aura. "On a scale of one to ten, I'd say this was a two. I can feel it, too."

"Good!" she said. "And this?"

Keith stared at the carved needlecase she laid in his palm. "Barely a tickle. Right?"

"Right. Good lad!"

"How about this?" the sourfaced elder said, passing him a bronze key.

Keith felt it and looked at it. Nothing. By the expression on the old man's face, he was expecting something. Keith felt sweat starting on his forehead, and they were all looking at him. "Not a thing," he admitted at last.

"Well, you're honest, at any rate," the old man said, grudgingly. "It's only an ordinary key."

"Not too bad for the first day's attempt," Niall said, praising Keith. "You've a bit of aptitude. If I had twenty years of the teaching of you, you'd be one of us in no time."

A youth running up the path to the house skittered to a halt in the doorway. "Fiona, Niall," he panted, "we've found a wee spot where the flowers are growing."

The Chief of Chiefs led a grand procession through the stream path, up over the road, and down into the next meadow. Everyone wanted to be present when Holl plucked the weddingbells. On either side at eye level, the fields were full of crops. Because of the leafy outcroppings overhead, they couldn't see more until they clambered up out of the trench beyond the next crosspoint.

This little piece of land had been left to grow wild by the Big Folk owner. It was too steep to make good farmland. Bushes and wildflowers sprang through the sparse, knee-high grass over most of the rocky ground, but on the far side, under a lush carpet of green, there was the unmistakable shape of a fairy mound. Faint lights floated in the air around the hillock like fireflies, though it was just barely evening.

"There's a lot of flowers growing there," Keith said, squinting across the field, "but nothing special."

The Niall clapped him on the back. "With your new eyes, see!"

Obediently, Keith concentrated. It was hard to let his eyes go unfocused and still look at an object eighty feet away. Suddenly, there was a white glimmer, like a candle flame, in the midst of the flowers covering the hillock.

"Hey!" Keith exclaimed.

"Ah, you see it now, do you. And there they are. Not easy to locate, are they?"

"You remember what to do," Fiona instructed Holl seriously. She handed him a small sickle with a crescent-shaped blade. "Concentrate on your purpose. You cannot take them if you are married or promised already. The flowers will stand no nonsense."

Repeating to himself the strictures, Holl walked across the open land. He stopped at the perimeter of the fairy mound, and spoke quietly. "I am Holl. I mean no harm. I crave permission to walk upon this hill. I want to gather these flowers."

A tiny voice like the jangling of silver bells answered him, not in his ears, but in his mind. "Walk and be welcome."

Holl stepped onto the smooth grass. The tiny clump of bellflowers beckoned him. The clustered blossoms were white and shining and more alive than anything he had ever seen in his life. They positively radiated power. Holl understood why no one picked these without a good purpose. He knelt beside them, and glanced up at the waiting crowd one more time. Across the field, Keith Doyle threw him a thumbs-up. He smiled, and grasped the stems with one hand.

Hot power coursed into him like an electric shock and threw him backward across the mound and halfway down the other side. Holl struggled to his hands and knees, and sat up again. Dumbfounded, he stared at the flowers, and down at his hand, which was red and felt burned. Why did they do that? Were they refusing to be harvested? Had he come all this way to fail at the last minute? He moved toward them again, but the flowers emitted an angry noise, like static, as soon as he placed his hand near them. He drew away.

"What's the matter?" Keith called.

"I don't know!" Holl shouted back.

"Tch, tch," Fiona said. "You've gone and promised yourself to your lass before this, lad. It'll never work."

"Do you mean I can't do it myself?" Holl asked, panic-stricken. "After all this, I can't finish my own task?" He looked helplessly at his own hands.

"Holl! A good leader knows when to delegate responsibility," Keith called out suddenly. "Order someone else to do it!"

Light dawned on the young elf's face as Keith's meaning sank in. "Ah. Keith Doyle, if you're willing, would you undertake this task for me, under my direction?"

"I could do it," Keith agreed. "I'm not promised yet. I mean, with the you-know, I can't even say anything."

There was a momentary discussion among the elders. "All right," Fiona said at last. "But be careful. You must wear no silver nor gold, nor carry any iron."

Keith laughed shortly. "The *bodach* took care of my fillings. I can empty my pockets." He handed his camera to Diane, and put all his change and the car keys into her purse.

"I think the lacings in your shoes are steel," Diane said, pointing at his sneakers. He doffed them, too.

In his stocking feet, Keith strode out into the field to where Holl was nursing his palm. "Once again you write yourself into our history, Keith Doyle. But thank you."

"What do I do first?" Keith asked.

"Ask permission to climb the hill."

Keith repeated the phrases Holl had had to learn. "Holl, did something just say to you 'walk and be welcome'?"

Holl raised an eyebrow. "You heard it, then. Go ahead."

The youth stepped up onto the grassy side of the hillock, and started to bring the other foot up behind him. He found himself tumbling backward in a somersault across the field. "Stone wall," he said, shaking his head and feeling his nose to make certain it was still straight. Holl watched him with bewilderment. "I'll try again."

He threw himself against the invisible barricade. Again and again, it repelled him, rebounding him backward like a springboard. He was bouncing off of the fairy defenses like a cartoon character. "Hey, I thought you said I could walk here," he complained to the invisible silver voices. His bones felt as though they had been jarred askew.

"What could you possibly hold that would keep you from entering?" Holl asked.

"I don't know," Keith said. "Pants zipper? I think it's brass." He patted himself down from shoulders to socks. "Wait!" He fished under his shirt and came up with a small bag on a cord. "Mrs. MacLeod gave me this to protect me."

"Well, it is. It's protecting you from picking flowers," Holl said wryly. With a grin, Keith pulled the cord up over his head and dropped the charm on the grass. Now there was no barrier to climbing the fairy mound. He stepped up and joined Holl. The grass felt pleasant and springy under his stockinged feet.

"Hey, Diane, can you take some pictures?" Keith called out. "This could be interesting!"

"You're out of film," Diane shouted back, after checking the indicator on the back of the camera. "I'll go and get some out of the car. Wait a minute."

Michaels had managed to get a positive identification from the bartender in the Skylark. O'Day had picked his place well. No one who hadn't business in the immediate area would ever find this godforsaken hole in the wall. O'Day and the boy were not here, and hadn't been in to the pub that day. The landlady hadn't seen them either. They must be out waiting for the contact to arrive.

Suddenly, the blond girl appeared out of a break in the hedge across the road from the pub. If she was here, O'Day couldn't be far away. Here was an opportunity to divide the party and conquer.

Diane walked toward the car park, jingling the keys in her hand. She was paying no attention to him. He walked up and quietly put his hand through her arm and leaned against her side.

"What?" she demanded, in surprise, and tried to pull away. She recognized him in a second. "You!" She raised her other hand with nails bared to tear out his eyes. Michaels grabbed her hand and pinned it.

"Please, miss, don't try to attack me. The martial arts I'm trained in aren't the slap-the-mat-and-get-up kind. I'm sorry, but that's the way it is."

"You've been following us!" Diane realized. "Why? Hey, I knew there was something fishy about you, Mr. Good Samaritan. Let me go!"

"I thought I must have made some slip up," Michaels affirmed. He palmed his ID out of his pocket and showed it to her. "British Intelligence. Your boyfriend down there is a smuggler. Tell me, what's he here to get?"

"Keith?" Diane asked, astonished. "Not a chance. He's too honest to cheat on his income tax. You must be mistaken."

"Acting on information received, miss. How long have you known him?"

"About a year, as if it's any of your business." The girl was impressed by the identification card, and very frightened.

Michaels counted back in his mind. The last big delivery carried off by O'Day was about fifteen months back. It had been nothing but small stuff since then. "I think it's quite possible you don't know about it. But I can't risk having you tip him off. This way, please." Diane started to fight free of him. He twisted her arm behind her, and frog-marched her to his car, parked on the side of the road. "I'm sorry, but I can't allow you to interfere and tip him off. I've got my job to do."

"Let me go!" she screamed. "I'm an American citizen!"

Out of his overcoat pocket, he pulled a pair of handcuffs. He locked one loop around Diane's wrist, and held onto the chain while he opened the left rear door of the sedan. When Diane protested and dug in her heels, he put one hand firmly on the top of her head and pushed down, propelling her into the car. Swiftly, he passed the loose end of the handcuffs over the rubber handle over the car window, and locked up her other wrist.

Outraged, Diane started yelling for help and banging on the door with her elbows. He shut the door on her, and locked it. Her hands were too high up even to roll down a window. Down the road a short distance, he couldn't hear her at all. O'Day wouldn't even know where she had gone. I'll nab the others when they come out.

• Chapter 30 •

Keith watched the river path for Diane, and was disappointed at how long it was taking her to get back. Holl jogged his elbow impatiently.

"We can wait no longer. Please," he urged.

Keith sighed. "Okay, but we're missing a great photo opportunity." He accepted the small golden sickle and hunkered down next to the flowers. "These are really pretty. Hi, guys. Look at me, I'm a druid!" He brandished the curved blade.

"More respect, Keith Doyle," Holl chided him.

"Okay," Keith said. "Ready."

"Concentrate on the purpose for which you are taking the flowers," Holl said, staying at arm's distance but watching anxiously.

Keith squeezed his eyes shut and mentally told the flowers that they were being picked to help Holl win his ladylove, and to make him a great leader. He opened his eyes again, and took hold of the stalks, bundling them tightly together in his fist. They didn't kick him backward. He took a breath. "Here goes."

The golden sickle cut through the flower stems as effortlessly and frictionlessly as if it had passed through air. Keith, expecting some kind of resistance, found himself sitting back on his rump, holding the bunch aloft. He started to say "A piece of cake," to Holl, but something exploded suddenly in the middle of his body, and he lost all sensation in a brilliant, white light. The hot light raced through him, reached his extremities and shot off in every direction like a laser hitting a broken mirror.

He could hear Holl shouting at him. "Concentrate! Take control!"

With all the willpower he had, Keith pulled in his thoughts and focused only on Holl and Maura as he had last seen them. While Keith waited in his car for Holl, they had kissed goodbye at the door of the farmhouse. That was a beautiful thing, an event that should last forever. It was meant to be.

In a moment, the fire in his body died away, so suddenly that he shivered. The hot, white light concentrated once again in the shining blossoms in his hand. Keith waved them at the others, who swarmed across the field toward the mound. They gathered around him to cheer him and Holl. Keith stood up, and with a flourish, presented the bouquet to his friend. Holl took them gingerly, treating the blossoms with the greatest respect.

"I'm embarrassed to say I thought these were only a gesture," Holl said. "How wrong I was."

"Merely a gesture," Keith squawked. "They're magic flowers! *Boy,* are they magic." He shook his hand up and down. "I don't think I'll ever be the same."

"Normal for us," Holl said. "But these are of a caliber that even I handle with respect."

"You don't know eferything yet," the Master reminded him, but there was no reproof in his voice.

"I know that well enough," Holl said humbly. "This trip has shown me enough to prove it if I did not."

"The first blessing is yours, then," the sour-faced elder told Keith. "Don't waste it."

"What's he talking about?" Keith asked Holl.

"I don't know, but I am certain you'll find out."

From his vantage point on the road above, Michaels spotted the two Doyles sitting on the grass through his field glasses. He saw a glint of yellow metal pass between them. Michaels smiled to himself. "Being paid in solid gold, eh?" This was the payoff. Good, that's easy to find with a metal detector.

"Once we have all four in custody, I'll have no trouble taking them in."

A crowd, hidden before behind the high hedging, rushed forward. These must be O'Day's local contacts, and they seemed awfully cheery about something. He ought to get some pictures. O'Day was a hero, and here were his employers.

Suddenly, the redhaired man stood up. He was head, shoulders, and chest above the crowd. Michaels reminded himself that the young man had been sitting on a hill. But then O'Day started to walk with them toward the river path, and the bunch of flowers in his hand were glowing. He looked more closely at the crowd through his glasses. Children? More midgets? There was something unusual about their profiles. They looked like ordinary people—except for the big, pointy ears.

Flowers that glow? Little people with sharp, pointed ears? That was impossible. It must be a trick of the twilight. Michaels lowered the glasses in disbelief. *It's the perspective,* he told himself. No, it wasn't. Everything looked exactly the same with the naked eye. He peered through the binoculars and had a good stare. "Up the airy mountain, down the rushy glen. We daren't go a-hunting for fear of little men," he recited to himself. "I don't bloody believe it. I wish I had never been assigned to this case."

A thumping sound on glass reminded him that he had a prisoner to release. He walked back to his car. Diane had worked one shoe off her foot, and had her leg hooked over the front seat, reaching for the horn with her toes. Her determination and resourcefulness were to be admired. She'd probably make a fine agent. He opened the front door, grabbed her foot, and tossed her leg back over. While she sputtered and swore at him, he leaned in and unlocked the gyves.

"You can go now, miss," Michaels said, handing her the discarded shoe.

"Why?" she demanded, tauntingly. "What made you change your mind? I thought you were going to arrest the big smugglers."

Michaels started to tell her what he had seen, then decided not to say it out loud. *If I'm mad, I'm mad,* he said to himself. No need for two of us to know it. "Go on, miss. It's a mistake. On behalf of the British government, I tender you my sincerest apologies, and I request that you do not take any action against me."

"Oh, I get it," Diane said, fuming, putting her shoe back

on. Hanging up in the metal bracelets had hurt her wrists, but anger and the pain kept her from feeling scared. "The secretary will disavow any knowledge of your actions."

"That's about the size of it, miss."

"I suppose you helped rescue Keith in Scotland just so you could keep an eye on him."

The agent regarded her mournfully. "You won't believe me, but I was helping the little lad. He was worried sick, and I hated to see that." Michaels made an impatient gesture. "Look, miss, I can take you in, if you like, and you can spend a lot of time assisting me with my inquiries, which is a code term for wasting a lot of time, when we both know there's nothing to find. Wouldn't you rather spend it shopping in Dublin instead of in a nasty room with a draft?"

Sullenly, Diane said, "I suppose so."

"Good. Then if I hear nothing more from you, you'll hear nothing more from me."

"Promise?" Diane sneered.

"Yes, miss, I promise you," Michaels sighed. "You won't believe me, but I do mean what I say."

As soon as Michaels unlocked the handcuffs, he stood away, his hands held out from his sides to show he wasn't holding a weapon. With her eyes on him Diane backed off until she was far enough away she was certain he couldn't reach her if he jumped. Then she ran down the road and into the stream path, crying out to the others.

"What's the matter?" Keith said, gathering her into his arms. "Did something happen to you? To the car?" Diane kept shaking her head.

"It was that man," she told them, her words coming out in a rush. "Holl's friend—he followed us from Scotland. He thinks Keith is a smuggler. He's an agent of some kind. I knew there was something weird about him. How he knew what you looked like when he had never met you."

"Ah," Holl said, light dawning. "I remember him saying something about Keith's red hair. I was too worried even to think about what that might mean. You were right not to trust him."

"He's up there," Diane pointed toward the road.

"Well, I want to find out why he's here," Keith said. "What can he do, shoot me?"

"You'll probably want this, Keith Doyle." One of the others

handed Keith the discarded wool bag containing Mrs. MacLeod's charm. Another one held up his sneakers.

The Little Folk mustered protectively around Diane as they followed Keith along the path. When they emerged onto the roadway, Michaels's car was gone. Diane looked around vainly for it. "He's gone. He saw all of you through binoculars. I watched him."

"Oh, don't worry about him," the Niall said. "If he goes for a drink anywhere hereabout, we'll drop a forget in his beer. That's a good idea of yours," he said, ruffling Holl's hair. "We'll recall that when strangers see us in the pub or down in town. If I know my Big Folk, he'll probably want a cool sip to clear his throat soon."

"Likely to be the Skylark," Fergus suggested.

"There's a telephone in the Skylark," Keith pointed out. "If you want to keep in touch with us, I'm sure that Peter and his father will make sure you can have some privacy. You can bless their beer or something in return." He jotted down the dialing code for the United States, his telephone number, the number at the farm, and at Diane's request, the one for her apartment. "There. Now you can call any of us, or write to us, too. I've added all the addresses. Um, international calling's kind of expensive. Do you need me to leave you some money?" he asked delicately.

"Ach, money, we've got a muckle of that," the elders said.

"And isn't there a gold mine close by here which we can walk in and out of?" said the Chief of Chiefs. "Do you need some? We have plenty to give."

"It's occupation we lack," Tiron added. "And curiosity, forbye, to see the rest of the world, and to come back again. But it's these passport things and the like preventing us.'

"Well, once you're in the States, no one ever asks you for identification," Keith explained. "Unless you try to pay for something by check."

The Little Folk looked at each other, then back at Keith. "Tell us more," they said.

"Now, I'll only remove this curse," the Niall said sternly, "if you give me your word to employ a wee bit of good sense in future when making your inquiries. We're all the better that you decided to take a hand in our welfare, but not all would feel the same to have their privacy invaded. If your *bodach* was something bigger and nastier, it might have eaten you alive for punishment, and then where would you be?"

Keith tried to follow his chain of thought to its logical conclusion. "I don't know. Or I don't want to. I promise. I already promised Mrs. MacLeod."

"Good enough." The Niall signaled for Holl to come and stand by him. "The natural magic can often blunt the wild magic. Now, silence for the ensorcellment." He touched the glowing blossoms of the weddingbells with one hand, and put his other forefinger to the middle of Keith's forehead. Keith closed his eyes.

With a wink to Holl and Diane, the Niall tapped Keith smartly on the head, mouth, and throat in succession, and made a wrenching gesture before Keith's Adams's apple with his fist. "That'll do it. Let that be a lesson to you, my Big friend."

Keith worked his jaw and rubbed his neck with one hand.

"How do you feel?" Diane asked.

"You're beautiful," Keith said, and his eyes lit up as he realized his voice wasn't going to betray him. "By the way, to answer a question you asked me a while back, I'd buy you a drink any time."

"Congratulations," Diane said. "I'll take you up on that."

"I regret that you are leaving us tomorrow," the Niall said sadly. "If you will come back to us in the morning, we have some gifts of friendship we wish to give you."

"I've got something for you, now," Keith said, taking an envelope out of his pocket and presenting it to the Niall. "I've got the negatives, so you can keep the pictures I took of Holl's people. I promise to send you copies of the ones of you in care of the Skylark, as soon as I get home. You can work out the details with Peter."

"May I keep them?" Fiona asked, glancing avidly over the Chief's shoulder. "I've a handsome book they can go into, that I use for pressing flowers. They'll smell sweetly."

"I think not," Fergus said with some asperity. "I brought the Big Folk in, so I will keep them. I'm an old friend of his grandfather." He pointed at Keith. Others spoke up to protest and stake their claims.

"None of you will," the Niall said, raising his voice over all. "The photographic pictures will stay in my house, and any who wish to come and see them may do so at any time. That is enough bickering between you. I have spoken."

"I am ready to go home," the Master said. "This is precisely vhy I left in the first place."

Michaels sat mournfully at the bar in the Skylark, nursing a pint. He was tired of getting the mickey teased out of him by his co-workers for following will-o-the-wisps and Loch Ness Monsters. If he told a soul what he had just seen take place, with fairies and leprechauns, he'd never hear the end of it. They might even send him for psychiatric counseling. He'd be genuinely glad to see the back of his quarries, whatever the chief might say.

He rang through to his office on the pay telephone in the rear of the pub and asked for his superior. "Chief, you know the old story of the lad on the bicycle, who the customs and excise men would stop peddling furiously south over the border, with a heavy bag on the back? Always full of peat. No one could figure out why he was always smuggling peat. It's worthless. There's plenty of peat in the south, there for the taking."

"So?" the chief asked, impatiently. "What has this to do with your investigation? Have you apprehended them? Was there a pickup?"

"Turned out that he was smuggling bicycles, chief," Michaels went on doggedly. "Remember?"

"What's your point?" the voice in his ear roared.

Holl and the others came into the pub at that moment, and the four sat down at the bar. Michaels eyed Holl suspiciously. The blond boy still wore his Cubs hat. Michaels had rather liked the lad, but now he was convinced there was something strange about Holl he didn't want to know. Better to write the whole thing off as a bad dream and take his lumps in the office. "Well, we've been looking at the peat instead of the bicycles, sir. It's got all the form we were looking for, but none of the reality. This one's not our man. He's not a smuggler at all. I'm convinced that our pigeon's name here really is Keith Doyle. Trust me on this one."

"What about his kissing the ground and all that rot?" the chief growled.

"The silly things he does are just because he's a Yank, sir," Michaels said, with conviction. "Danny O'Day is still back in the states, if I don't miss my guess. He must be hanging back waiting for something else. If I were you I'd step up the alert in the airports again. Can I come back home now, please, sir?"

* * *

Keith opened the door of the Keane house with a flourish, and gestured the others through before him. Mrs. Keane looked up in surprise, and her brows wrinkled apologetically. "Mr. Doyle, there's been a telephone call for you. I'm so sorry. He just rang off. I don't know where my mind has been these last few days. He called on the Wednesday, and yesterday, too, though he didn't give me the number."

"Who's that, Mrs. Keane?"

"Well, his name is Doyle, too, fancy that. It must have been he who called the first night, too. Here you are." The landlady rummaged through the papers on her telephone table and came up with a slip which she handed to Keith. "Do go right ahead and call, if you please."

Curiously, Keith dialed the number on the slip. The phone on the other end rang twice, then there was a click. A plummy voice said, "Hello?"

"Hi, there. My name is Keith Doyle. Someone called and left your number here. I'm returning the call," Keith said, uncertainly.

"Ah, well!" the voice said, pleased. "Greetings, then, cousin. I'm Patrick Doyle. The family dropped the O' about the same time your great-great grandfather left for America. I've been trying to get through to you for a few days now."

"What? Oh, no."

"Yes, indeed. I got word from my sister-in-law's family that there was a notice up in the old church, looking for details of us. So you've come all the way from America to look for us, have you?"

Keith became animated, and began pacing up and down in the hallway, twisting the phone cord nervously between his fingertips. He'd been so involved with the Little Folk, he'd forgotten entirely about hunting down his own family tree. It sounded like a root had sprung right underneath his feet, and he had nearly missed it. "That's right. You're Eamon O'Doyle's great-grandson, or great-great?"

"I am that. Great-great, if you will call it that."

"Can we meet?" Keith asked. "I've got to go home tomorrow morning, but I've got a car. I can drive anywhere."

Patrick Doyle was full of regret. "Ah, well, I'm just out the door for France this very minute. I do a job in public relations, and I was hoping you'd have called me back sooner than this, but no harm done."

"I guess not," Keith replied, dejectedly.

"You'll only just have to come back again, and meet your cousins then."

The idea immediately perked Keith up. "Yeah! I've just about promised to come back anyway."

"Good on ya. Let's keep in touch, now, shall we? Here's my address."

Seizing a pencil, Keith scrawled down the information. "That's great. My father will be thrilled."

"Must go now. It takes a long hour and some to get to the airport. It's good that you called. I'm pleased to have been hearing from you, Keith. Give my best to your folks, and come again soon!" Patrick rang off.

Keith set down the receiver and looked at the others, who had been watching him curiously. "Well, how do you like that?" He waved the paper at them. "Said he's tried to call a few times, but we were always out."

Holl bowed his head, abashed. "My apologies, Keith Doyle. You've missed your own opportunities by assisting us, once again."

"Oh, it's all right," Keith said, dismissively. "I couldn't have concentrated on what he was saying anyway, not with all the things going on with you and your kin. I'll meet him eventually. It's not like he was going to disappear into the mists," he said playfully. "He's only going to France."

Chapter 31

Holl hummed happily to himself as they rode the shuttle bus to the Dublin airport. He had a packet of white bellflower seeds in his pocket, a gift from Fiona, who had worked hard and at some little risk to cull them overnight. That and the bunch of cut flowers tucked into the hastily sewn inside pocket of his jacket gave him a contented feeling of accomplishment. Diane was twirling a featherlight woolen shawl, woven by Ketlin's own hands, and talking of accessories. Keith was more thoughtful. The Niall had taken him aside and presented him with a pair of golden rings. "You'll know when best to make use of these," the Chief had said, "if you'll allow an old man like me to meddle in your private life."

"Why not?" Keith agreed, lightly. "I meddle in everybody else's."

The Niall smiled. "I agree it's a little soon yet, but one day it won't be."

Keith had accepted them with thanks, and put them away carefully in an inside pocket. He hadn't mentioned the rings to the others. Niall had also presented him with a flat, woolen cap like most of the elders wore. He showed that instead.

No one knew what the Master had been given. He had hardly spoken a word since breakfast.

Diane folded her shawl away at last. "Well, now we know where they come from," she told Keith, glancing backward significantly toward the direction of the vale. "And the mystery is solved."

"Maybe for you," Keith said, "but for me it's deeper now than it was before."

"What? Why?"

"Well, I learned the Gaelic greeting from Peter, right?"

"Right. You said it perfectly. And Niall repeated it back to you, or something a lot like it."

"But it's not the same thing he said to you when *you* arrived. It's not Irish they're speaking. It sounds like it, with the lilt and all, but it isn't. Probably some Irish words have drifted into it over the years, like 'newspaper' has into our Little Folks' dialect. But they don't belong there."

"You mean it isn't their native land?" Diane asked, puzzled.

"Probably not the same way it is for the Irish. This means their culture comes from some place else, and they've managed to keep it up, inviolate, over the years they've been there."

"So where *do* they come from?"

"I don't know, but I'm going to find out."

"I don't doubt that for a minute," Diane said definitely.

"Unless," Keith offered, after a considering pause, "they've been there lots *longer* than the Big Folk. That would make sense. Wow. What a concept. I wonder if the Celtic people mentioned the presence of Little Folk before they settled in

Ireland—or if they found them when they got there—or if maybe they moved in at the same time.'' He made a note on the back of his ticket envelope. ''Maybe I should start learning Lapp after all.''

''Now I'm really confused,'' Diane complained.

''So am I,'' said Keith, thoughtfully chewing on his pen. ''I didn't ask nearly enough questions. I'll probably have to go back.''

''I'll come with you,'' said Diane.

''So what do you think of your relatives, after all this time,'' Keith asked, while they were waiting their turn in line to pass through airport security. The Master grunted.

Holl replied instead. ''Oh, I like them. They're not much different than the folks at home, only I think the Conservatives outnumber the Progressives here. Thank goodness the Niall is a strong man.''

''I suppose it's easier for the Conservatives, when they've held the home ground so much longer. What about that Tiron? Nice guy. You and he looked like you were getting to be as thick as thieves.''

''We became friends,'' Holl said, shortly. ''He knows a great deal about woodworking that I never dreamed of.''

''Sure seemed to know it all,'' Keith asserted. ''He'd be a great asset to Hollow Tree Industries. So, did you promise to keep in touch and everything?''

''Oh, yes,'' Holl said. ''We'll be very close in the future.''

''It seems like everyone's aspirations came true on this trip,'' Keith said happily. ''But I've got to tell you, I'm going to be glad to get home.''

''Put your bags on the belt,'' the customs agent instructed them. Keith hoisted his bag up and put it on the conveyor, and stepped toward the magnetic arch.

''Wait, Keith Doyle, your camera,'' Holl cried. He took it from Keith and handed it to the x-ray technician seated behind the luggage machine. ''Please don't put this through. It has film in it.''

The technician looked away from his screen and turned to one of the other guards, who put the camera carefully on a small plastic tray and carried it to the other side.

Keith retrieved his suitcase and demonstrated to the security guards how his camera worked. When they were satisfied that it contained only film, they waved the party away and directed them toward the departure gate.

"Anyone for the duty free shop?" Keith asked.

"Anything to declare?" the U.S. customs agent asked Keith, when he presented his passport at the glass-sided booth.

"Yep," Keith announced. His nerves were a little strung out. He had spent the whole flight anticipating this moment, knowing that Holl was carrying a packet of highly questionable flower seeds in his pocket. If they were searched, the Little Folk were through. He knew he was babbling, but he couldn't help it.

Holl, waiting behind the red line five feet behind him, was thrown into a panic. He wasn't sure whether to grab Keith's suitcase and bolt, or just brazen it out. Then Keith grinned foolishly at the agent. "I want to declare that it's terrific to be home."

"Geddada here." The agent had heard this type of declaration before. He stamped Keith's passport for the Green Channel and shooed him away, shaking his head sadly. "Next!"

"How was the trip?" Keith's father asked, peering in the rear view mirror. Holl sat in the front seat between Mr. Doyle and Diane.

"Great," Keith said, enthusiastically. "The tour of Scotland was terrific. I shot about twenty rolls of film. I've got tons of information from the Irish Genealogy Office, and from the priest of the parish where our folks were born, Father Griffith. And I talked to one of our cousins. His name's Patrick Doyle."

"That's wonderful," Mr. Doyle said, cheerfully. "One of Emerson's descendants?"

"No, one of Eamon's, his brother, so he's a cousin something removed. You'll have to see the family tree now. We missed each other a few times, but I've got his address and phone number. We met a lot of other terrific people, too."

"It was full of surprises," agreed Holl, glancing sideways at the suitcase. He watched out of the sideview mirror as the Doyle car turned onto the tollway and pulled into traffic. "We're well away from the airport now," he said loudly.

"Thank the powers," said a muffled voice from inside Keith's suitcase. "Now let me out of here. My spine's at a permanent angle."

Keith stared openmouthed at the suitcase at his feet, and fumbled with the locks. The top burst open, and Tiron sprang out of it, clutching his back with both hands. "Ooh, I don't think I could have waited another tick. Well, what are you staring at?" he demanded of the gawking Keith. "Have you never seen an economy class passenger before, then?"

"What am I running here, an underground railroad?" Keith asked, in mock outrage.

"More on the order of an underground airline," Holl offered, innocently. "Though that is physically impossible, it's the best description."

"You said I'd be an asset to your business. Well, here I am." Tiron stretched up his arms to Keith and the Master. "Help me up. I don't think I'll ever sit straight again, so I won't."

"What happened to my blue jeans?" Keith asked, surveying the ruin of his suitcase.

"Ach, with my folk. They'll keep them safe for you," Tiron assured him.

"Oh, thanks. How do I explain to my mother I left my other pants with the leprechauns?"

"And all your books," Tiron added.

"My books!" Keith protested. "Hey! I wasn't finished reading them!"

"You've already promised to go back, to meet your cousin at least," Holl said reasonably, "so they're not really lost."

"I don't see any difference," Keith grumbled.

"Well, you're a hero in my eyes," Tiron assured him, "giving up your luggage space just for me. I've wanted to visit this continent all my life. So, how far is it to the haven from here?"

"Haven?" Mr. Doyle asked, speaking up for the first time, peering back at his new passenger in the rearview mirror.

"Hollow Tree Farm, Dad," Keith explained, and did a double take toward the front seat. He had completely forgotten that it was his father driving the car. "Um, Dad, you don't have any, well, negative feelings about Tiron appearing like this. I mean, I carried him home in my suitcase. He's sort of an . . . illegal alien."

"So far as I know, son," the senior Doyle said mildly, "the U.S. government doesn't believe that he exists, so what negative feelings could possibly affect me? I've accepted the reality of your other friends without losing my marbles. In fact, I wish I'd been the one who discovered them. I grew up on *The Lord of the Rings*. Personally speaking, I'm delighted he's here. Tiron, eh? Pleased to meet you."

"And I to make your acquaintance, sir," Tiron replied, settling into the car seat.

"I want to hear more about your vacation. When you come back from the farm, that is," Mr. Doyle finished, politely. "I think these gentlemen want to get home as soon as possible. You all look beat."

"That is true," the Master affirmed, nodding to Mr. Doyle. "Ve should be very grateful for all speed. My thanks."

"Definitely the block you were chipped from," Diane crowed gleefully to Keith.

"But, Keith?" his father put in.

"Yes, Dad?"

"Please don't bring home any dragons."

"No, sir."

Keith turned his blue Mustang into the gravel drive under the trees. It was very late, but lights still burned in the windows. The headlamps dipped down into the slope of the drive and up again, illuminating the side of the old, white farmhouse. "Wake up, everyone! We're here!"

A head peered around the curtains inside the house, and a cluster of laughing children poured out of the door to greet them.

Holl looked up at the old farmhouse with a feeling of completeness. He had traveled far, and was in possession of the object of his quest, but oh, it was good to be home! With the trees in full leaf, the outside world was hidden from view. He had had enough of it for the time being. Only a little of the sky showed overhead. He couldn't help but feel apprehensive about seeing Maura again. He had played scenarios all the way across the Atlantic of her refusing his formal proposal, of meeting her and hearing her say that she had already chosen a new lifemate or worse—accusing him of abandoning her deliberately to break it off.

"So this is it," Tiron said, taking it all in. "A lovely place. Quiet, though. Are there any pubs nearabouts?"

Aylmer, a stocky, dark-haired elf, and his quiet wife, Rose, came out of the house to shake hands with the Master and Holl, followed by a handful of children. "We've missed you," Rose said, sincerely. "But who is this?"

"This is Tiron," Holl announced, presenting him. "He is without a doubt the finest woodworker in the world." The Master looked approvingly at Holl's statement, and nodded.

"Thank you for your compliments," Tiron said flippantly, sketching a bow. "I assure you they're no more than true."

"All has gone vell," Aylmer assured the Master. "It is in your hands vunce more."

"Thank you for taking charge in my absence. But all is vell now. I haf messages from the old ones, and many gifts."

"I've got lots of pictures," Keith said, patting his camera bag.

"Come in, come in," Rose urged them, slipping her hand around Diane's arm as far up as she could reach. "Marcy is here. There is coffee, there is cider, and fresh milk, too."

"Cider!" Keith exclaimed. "It's been weeks since I had some of that."

'We want to hear all about the old place," demanded Borget, a boy of seven years, tugging on Holl's sleeve.

"All these stories vill be told in the fullness of time," the Master assured him.

"Hi!" Another Big Person, a girl with black hair curling around her shoulders, walked into the room wiping paste off her hands. "Welcome back!"

"Well, if it isn't Snow White and the Eighty-Seven Dwarves," Keith said, mischievously, as the girl's cheeks reddened prettily. "Hi, yourself, Marcy."

"How was your trip?"

"Great! Have I got stories to tell you!"

"Wait for the others before you start telling them," Marcy pleaded. "Enoch is in the attic fixing the chimney. Some of the bricks fell down inside the fireplace."

"I'm not in a hurry, believe me. Where's Dola?" Keith asked, looking around the faces of his friends. "I brought her a tam o'shanter doll. That is, if it's still in my suitcase."

"Aye, that's there," Tiron assured him.

"She's coming," said Catra, the village archivist. "I called the others down from the sleeping rooms."

"I have gifts to present, too," Holl remembered, following the others into the common room. While his friends watched curiously, he unpacked his case. There were sighs and exclamations as each item appeared.

"Well, you might have brought some of this lovely cloth for all," Catra's sister, Candlepat, sniffed, upon learning all the pieces were spoken for. She fingered one hopefully until Holl picked it up again.

"I've brought something better," Holl stated. "We'll have lengths of our own making in a few weeks' time, with Tiron's help."

"That's right, fair colleen," Tiron said, looking at Candlepat with interest. "Though you must understand it will take time and skill to make any which will properly adorn your beauty." She preened herself and looked coyly at him under her long, blond lashes. Catra sighed heavily. Tiron made her a gallant bow, too, and she smiled at him.

"Excuse me," Holl said, not wanting to be in the middle of another battle between the rival sisters. Tiron could no doubt take care of himself. "I must find Orchadia."

He encountered the Master's wife as she was coming out of the kitchen, with her daughter behind her. He was so taken by surprise to see Maura, he all but shoved Orchadia into the sitting room and closed the door. Maura looked at him with hurt shock on her face, and he was sorry.

"I wanted to give you this," Holl said, handing her the tissue-wrapped bundle of cloth, "before I spoke to Maura—in case she isn't speaking to me, that is."

"Haven't you gone to her yet to find out?" Orchadia asked, taking the bundle and giving it only the most cursory glance. For a moment, the snapping eyes were like those of her son Enoch, or her imperious father. "Do you mean you shut the door in her face that abruptly? For shame! You're getting to have too many of the Big People's ways. Now it's all hurry up and wait, and tomfoolery. Get along with you!"

Maura must have run away as soon as the door closed. Holl ran through the house to find her. When he discovered her, she was standing by the window in one of the upstairs sleeping chambers, very still. As soon as he could see her, Holl knew she was on the edge of weeping, curtaining her face with her long, red-brown hair. "So you come to speak to me at last, do you?" Maura asked, standing with her hands folded at her waist.

"I have thought about you a lot while I was gone," Holl said, at last. "And I went away so that when I came back we could be together for all time. I was distressed to hear that you were spending a lot of private time with Gerol."

Maura's green eyes caught fire. "Oh, you heard that? Oh, Holl, what sense have you? Sometimes you're as silly as Keith Doyle. You went off, for all everyone knew, forever. You might not know since I didn't complain openly about it, but Ronard made a certain set at me as soon as you left. And Catra is not speaking to me because Ronard was courting her until you went away. Gerol stepped in to help me keep him off. I thought about you, dreamed about you, and who could I talk to about you? Candlepat? Certainly not. She's interested in you herself, as she is in all males. She'd cut me out without a thought. My mother? She's got no patience with mooncalfing. Marm? I know he's your good friend, but all he'd do is agree with me and say 'Yah.'" Maura made a face. "Gerol's a good friend. He listened to me."

Holl dropped his gaze to the ground at her feet, his face red as a rose. "I'm sorry for doubting. But I was so far away, I couldn't hear any of you. I didn't know what you were thinking."

Maura's face softened, and she touched his cheek with tender fingers. "The same thing I've thought all our lives. We were worried about you, too, off in the great distance. It was only the sound of your voice over the telephone which reassured us."

The flowers were none the worse for their long travel in the inside pocket of his coat. Holl drew out the bouquet, as amazed as before by the purity of the power radiating from the tiny, white bells. Even though they had been cut days earlier, and had been without water, the blooms were still fresh, clad in their astonishing glow.

"How lovely," Maura sighed. Holl took one of her hands, and proffered the flowers to the free hand. When she reached for them, it was as if an electrical circuit had been completed. The elders had been right. When the match was true, the flowers sealed the bond. This was the second blessing. The third would come when the flowers produced seeds, continuing the circle of life.

"Will you be mine, then?" Holl asked, tenderly.

"Of course," Maura said, teasingly, her cheeks becoming

pink. "I was never anything else." She turned up her face to kiss him.

Holl pulled her out into the main room, where everyone was exclaiming over Keith's rolls of snapshots. "Now, wait, I got double prints of everything. Let me separate them, and you can have the second set. They'll be yours to keep. Don't mix them up. There's about twenty rolls. Hey, watch the fingerprints, Borget."

Borget's mother pulled his hands away and washed them with a surreptitious cloth. Everyone looked up from the colored squares as Holl held up his free hand for attention.

"May I have the pleasure of announcing that Maura has just consented to be my lifemate."

"As long as life lasts," Maura affirmed, her eyes shining when she looked at Holl. Everyone clustered around them to give their congratulations. With eyes shining, Orchadia kissed her daughter. "Bless you, my loves. May you be happy."

Keith shook Holl's hand over the heads of most of the villagers, then stepped back out of the way to let the others close in.

"I love true romances," Diane said happily, watching the others embracing Holl and Maura and offering good wishes. She clutched Keith's arm. He reached up to twine his hand with hers and squeezed her fingers. "Doesn't that give you some idea of your own?"

Keith pointed to his throat and mimed laryngitis. He produced a thin, squeaky voice. "Sorry," he croaked. "It's the curse. I can't talk about wine, women, or money."

"Oh, you!" Diane exclaimed. "One day! . . ."

Marcy sighed sentimentally. "I'm so happy for them. I wonder if this might get Enoch thinking along the same lines, eventually. It'll probably take a few years, but if it's right, I'll wait."

Keith was surprised to learn that she was seriously considering settling down permanently with the Little Folk. But why not? She had known them longer than he had. And he knew something that she didn't: that Enoch had already broached the subject with his father. She'd probably be thrilled. There might be another declared romance right here and now. He opened his mouth to speak.

The Master caught his eye and stared him down sternly. Keith closed his mouth again without having made a sound. He understood that perhaps that was another secret he'd better keep.

"You vould be better off if you vere silent on some topics for all time," the Master said, warningly, in a low tone. "Vhat the *bodach* did, I can do, too."

"Curses," Keith said ruefully, seizing Diane's hand and retreating hastily from the living room. "Foiled again."